When Zane's lips came down on hers tonight, they weren't gentle or light or just a brush.

Oh, no. Tonight they were hungry, searching for desire to be fulfilled.

Jeannette's body reacted as if she'd been born to respond to Zane. She enfolded her arms around his neck, and he pulled her in tighter. His tongue slid into her mouth and her gasp of pleasure opened her up more completely to him. She felt as if a low-burning fire inside of her burst into flame.

She couldn't get enough of his mouth on hers, his tongue retreating, then urging her on. Pressed against him, she longed for a satisfaction she had long ago forgotten.

When he withdrew and pulled away, they were both breathing hard. She was still trying to catch her breath when he said, "That was Zane the man who kissed you, not Zane Gunther the country singer."

Dear Reader,

I love country music. Its deep emotion and sheer joy
touch me whenever I listen to it. It's storytelling at
its finest. I've always wanted to write about a hero
who is a country singer, and in this continuity series I
was offered that chance. I created Zane Gunther in a
previous MONTANA MAVERICKS book, falling in
love with him even then. Now, as a hero, he's entirely
captured my heart.

Sometimes we live our lives thinking we're on the right
track, just involved in the day-to-day process. Then a
tragedy strikes and we find out what we're really made
of. That's what happened to Zane. For a while, he's
uncertain what course to take and almost becomes a
hermit! But then a resilient single mom intrigues him
and he finds being alone can be downright lonely.
Jeannette and her son give Zane's life meaning he's
never found before. But can she accept his lifestyle?
Can he really consider becoming a husband and a dad?

I hope you fall under the spell of this romance the
same way you would a great country song! Visit me at
my website at www.karenrosesmith.com or follow me
on Facebook.

All my best,

Karen Rose Smith

HIS COUNTRY CINDERELLA

BY
KAREN ROSE SMITH

MILLS & BOON

First published in Great Britain 2013
by Mills & Boon, an imprint of Harlequin (UK) Limited,
Eton House, 18-24 Paradise Road, Richmond, Surrey TW9 1SR

© Harlequin Books S.A. 2011

Special thanks and acknowledgement are given to Karen Rose Smith for her contribution to the Montana Mavericks series.

ISBN: 978 0 263 90101 6
ebook ISBN: 978 1 472 00467 3

23-0413

Karen Rose Smith is an award-winning and bestselling author who writes about friends and family. Music has always played a huge part in her life, from her crush on the Beatles to her endeavor to write a script for the Monkees TV show with her cousin. Her love of country music developed after she began writing. She found listening to it enhanced her creativity when developing cowboys! Living in Pennsylvania with her husband and two cats, music enriches her life along with gardening and cooking. Readers can follow her on Facebook, visit with her on her website at www.karenrosesmith.com or write to her at PO Box 1545, Hanover, PA 17331, USA.

To my bff Suzanne, who shares my love of
country music and is always there to listen and support.

Chapter One

Jeannette Williams hurriedly pushed the vacuum cleaner into the closet and closed the door, then nervously tightened the band on her ponytail. She was frazzled. More frazzled than when she had to run after her four-and-a-half-year-old son. If she didn't finish her duties at this mountaintop log home by four o'clock, she could get fired.

In the kitchen she seemed to be all thumbs as she poured expensive ground coffee into a canister. Suddenly her fingers slipped on the glossy bag and the grounds spilled over the counter and onto the floor.

Jeannette was used to rolling with the punches and picking up the pieces. She'd had to do that after her fiancé died before Jonah was born. But today, knowing she still had an evening's worth of work in a restaurant she didn't like, she almost felt defeated. Still, defeat wasn't in her vocabulary. Jonah was her focus.

She hurried to the closet, found a dustpan and brush

and fell to her knees in the kitchen, cleaning up the ceramic-tiled floor.

When she heard a noise outside, she glanced up at the kitchen door the moment it opened. A tall man with a black Stetson stood in the doorway, looking as startled to see her as she was to see him. His jaw was covered with what looked like a week's worth of beard stubble. His cheeks were gaunt. His chambray shirt was tucked into blue jeans, but the sleeves were rolled up, revealing strong forearms. His brown boots were dusty. For an eternal moment she gazed into his green eyes. He looked so…sad. A second later she thought she must be mistaken because they were snapping with impatience and annoyance.

Her words came out in a rush. "I'm sorry I'm still here. I'll be gone in a few minutes. I was a little late getting here and I was just ready to leave when the coffee spilled—"

"Just leave," he said gruffly.

"Really," she insisted, "I'll just be a few minutes."

"Go on," he commanded. "I'll do it myself."

She knew from her instructions that he valued his privacy, that he was a solitary man who didn't want to be disturbed. Tears came to her eyes as she blinked fast to keep them from falling. Wouldn't that just be altogether humiliating? She didn't even cry at the lewd comments some of the customers made at LipSmackin' Ribs. But this man's sadness, demeanor and penetrating gaze shook her. Still…although he was obviously angry with her, there was something in his bearing, something underlying the gruffness in his voice, something in those green eyes that… appealed to her. She was going crazy, she knew she was. A tear did slip from her eye and rolled down her cheek.

Her mountain man, obviously seeing her distress, blew

out a breath, closed the door and came over to where she knelt. He was over six feet, so broad-shouldered, so...virile.

A little tremor ran through her and she wasn't exactly sure where it came from. He was studying her as if he was trying to figure out something.

Then he crouched down beside her. "I'll help you clean up the mess."

That she hadn't expected. But as she'd learned long ago, both the good things and the troubling things in life were usually unexpected. For a few moments, silence trembled between them as she used the brush, and he slid one very large hand with long, tapered fingers across the rust-colored tile, pushing coffee grounds into the dustpan.

She had to make another stab at saving her job. "I need this job. I have a son. I'll buy more coffee." In her effort to explain again, she peeked at his profile. It seemed a tad familiar, though it really couldn't be—

His hand brushed hers. She felt the tingle of contact to the tip of her ponytail.

Suddenly she was looking into those green eyes once more and falling...falling...falling. "Sorry," she murmured again, feeling like a total idiot. When was the last time she'd been this clumsy? This scattered? This...attracted to a man?

She shook her head as if to clear it, remembering Ed and the accident and all her fiancé had tried to do for them. Maybe trying to juggle two jobs was affecting her the same way it had affected him.

"I didn't pick up the tip you left." She swallowed hard. "I won't take it. If you have extra things you'd like me to do next time, just leave a list." She knew she sounded frantic and breathless, but she was. She wished he'd say something. Before she thought better of it, she clasped his forearm. "I really need this job."

His skin was tanned and hot and taut. And she could feel the brown hairs under her fingertips. Heavens, she was losing it!

She released his arm and just as she thought he was never going to speak to her, he finally said, "It's okay. Accidents happen. I should have checked the drive for your car when I got back from hiking, but you've always cleared out before I returned."

That's the way he wanted it. She could tell.

"This won't happen again," she promised.

With most of the coffee in the dustpan now, he took the brush and pan from her hands and stood with it. He strode to the closet, opened it and poured the coffee into the trash can inside.

Then he dusted off his hands and turned to face her. "We'll forget all this happened. It'll be our secret—under one condition."

Jeannette rose to her feet and had to tilt her chin up to meet his eyes. His one condition made her wary. Just what did he expect in return? As hunky as he was, she was not about to—

A half smile tilted the man's lips, as if he could read her mind. "Just don't tell anyone you saw me here."

Relief flooded Jeannette. Yet maybe there was just a little disappointment mixed in. In that moment he'd mentioned a condition, she'd imagined his strong arms around her! But checking his expression again, she could see he was serious.

"I won't tell anyone," she vowed.

Tilting his head, he held out a hand to her to seal the deal. She took it and was immediately affected by her proximity to him, the fall-air, man-smell of him, the skin contact that had already shaken her before. His grip was firm, though the press of his fingers was gentle. Her breath caught. Her heart raced. For propriety's sake, she pulled away.

Altogether flustered now, she gestured to the floor. "Are you sure you don't want me to wash it up?"

"I'm sure."

Although for a few minutes she'd felt a connection to him, now he wanted her gone. She could do "gone" if it meant holding on to her job. Quickly she snatched her keys and purse from the counter.

But the tall, well-built man's voice stopped her. "What's your name?"

"Jeannette. Jeannette Williams."

"You forgot something, Jeannette." He handed her the bill that had been tucked under the coffee canister.

"I don't deserve it."

"Sure, you do. A little spilled coffee doesn't wipe out all your cleaning sessions and grocery buying that have made my life easier."

She thought of Jonah and the apartment they'd moved into a few months ago. She thought of the bills stacked on her table, and she took the money from this enigmatic man's hand.

Then she fled his house, wondering if he ever used the silver SUV in his garage...wondering how he could stay on that mountain alone.

She considered her son again, and her job at Lip-Smackin' Ribs. She'd do whatever she had to do for Jonah, no matter how hard it was.

As she drove down the deserted, bumpy, unpaved road hoping she didn't get a flat tire, she remembered her mountain man's fleeting smile. Her heart beat faster all over again.

After Jeannette Williams left, Zane Gunther felt as if he'd just stepped into a whirlwind. Not only had she unsettled him and maybe blown his cover, but he was aroused!

Swiping off his Stetson, he plopped it on the hat rack

on the wall in the well-equipped country kitchen and ran his hand down over his face. He knew he was a changed man after what had happened in April. He couldn't write music anymore, let alone sing.

He went into the living room and stared up at the loft— the loft where his guitar was propped against a desk. He didn't even know why he'd brought it here.

How could he write songs when a thirteen-year-old had died after one of his concerts? How could he write songs when the tabloids and even the legitimate press were painting him as a celebrity who didn't care about ordinary people? When even his mother was being affected by the publicity? When everything around him seemed to be in shambles?

There was a rap at his front door and he swiveled toward it, wondering if his cleaning lady had forgotten something. She'd been pretty. That silky blond hair, those cornflower-blue eyes and a figure right out of a man's fantasies. Certainly she'd known who he was, hadn't she? Would she keep her promise?

He went to the living room and opened the door, not knowing whether to be disappointed or relieved when he stood aside to let his guest in. Up until today, Dillon Traub had been his only visitor.

"Who was that leaving?" Dillon asked, going straight to the kitchen and setting containers of Chinese food on the table.

"You passed her?"

"Her?" Dillon asked with a raised brow.

"She's my cleaning lady. When I came back from my hike, she was still here."

"Uh-oh."

"Yeah, well, we sort of made a deal. She said she won't tell anyone."

"And what are you giving her in return?" Dillon's voice was wary.

Dillon had moved to Thunder Canyon last year and was now happily married with an almost-three-year-old daughter. He and Zane went *way* back to grade school in Midland, Texas. They knew each other well, well enough that they didn't sugarcoat the truth.

"She was cleaning up a mess in my kitchen when I walked in, and she was afraid she'd lose her job. So I told her I wouldn't say anything to the cleaning service about the mess and her being late if she kept my secret. I think she's the type who might."

"How long did you talk to her?"

"About ten minutes, and we really didn't do much talking. Mostly just cleaned up coffee."

Dillon started opening the cardboard containers, but appeared even more suspicious than before. "So, what? You got a vibe off her or something? How old is she?"

"I'm not great with age, but I'd say probably late twenties. And yes, I did get a vibe."

Dillon met Zane's gaze and his lips quirked up. "Well!"

"Well, what?" Zane growled.

"Well, maybe you're coming back to life. Maybe you're seeing you can't live on this mountaintop forever. You've been here four months, Zane. You see no one but me and Erika. You don't even have a phone here so you can talk to your mom and your lawyer or your manager or band without going through me. By the way, your mom said you don't call enough."

Zane rolled his eyes to heaven. "You know I have my cell phone and I get a signal when I drive down the mountain. I call Mom once a week to check in. Are you getting tired of taking messages?"

Opening a drawer, Dillon found a serving spoon and

stuffed it into what looked like chicken lo mein. "No, that's not it, and you know it. Erika and I understand why you need time and silence. Why you have to live in secret because the paparazzi are chasing you. We get it. But at some point, you're going to have to jump back into the world and deal with all of it."

Zane glanced up at the loft again. "Not now." However, he was thinking, *Maybe not ever*.

Grabbing forks from another drawer, Dillon faced his friend. "So what color were her eyes?"

Jeannette emerged from Mops and Brooms Cleaning Services office the following morning, Jonah's little hand in hers. She stared almost uncomprehendingly at the traffic cruising up and down Oak Avenue. She'd just been fired! They'd given her a lame excuse, but she knew the truth.

Her son tugged on her hand as she focused on him. His brown hair always looked mussed, but his blue eyes, the same shade as hers, sparkled with a child's innocence and curiosity. "Are we gonna go to my open house now?"

Jeannette had worked out her schedule today so she could take Jonah to his preschool open house this morning, drop him off at Edna and Mel Lambert's—Ed's parents insisted they didn't mind babysitting while she worked—and arrive at LipSmackin' Ribs for Friday's eleven-to-four shift. She had to rotate with the other waitresses for those premium weekend night shifts, so she wouldn't be working tonight. Filling in cleaning assignments around her shifts had been fairly easy, but now she wouldn't have cleaning assignments. How was she going to pay for Jonah's tuition for preschool?

She swallowed hard as she gazed into Jonah's eyes. "Yes, we're going to your open house. Are you ready?"

He jumped up and down. "Let's go."

Jeannette couldn't believe her "mountain man" had complained about her. Not after the deal they'd made. She still remembered the feel of his strong fingers around hers, the outdoor, male scent of him, the soberness in his eyes.

She should have known better than to trust a stranger. Now she'd have to look for another job to fit with her schedule at LipSmackin' Ribs. That wouldn't be easy.

She was walking down Oak Avenue with Jonah when she spotted a silver SUV pull up to the curbside parking meter. That SUV looked just like the one that had been in the log house's garage—

She couldn't believe her eyes when the acerbic stranger himself climbed out of the vehicle! As he rounded his SUV, he was heading straight for the Mops and Brooms office.

His Stetson brim was pulled low and today he wore sunglasses. What was he doing here? Hadn't he done enough damage?

When he saw her, he stopped short. A trace of a smile turned up the corners of his lips. "Well, hello. I didn't expect to see *you* here."

"No, I suppose not," she returned frostily. She couldn't see his eyes today, just her own reflection in his mirrored sunglasses.

"A little cold out this morning," he joked and she could see he was obviously trying to lighten her mood. Why would he be doing that? Wouldn't he have known what had just happened to her?

"Is this your son?" he asked, even as his eyes dropped to her hand, checking for a wedding ring. He saw none there. She'd never had the chance to wear one.

"I'm Jonah," the little boy piped up, and Jeannette almost wanted to groan. He was too friendly. She'd talked to him about strangers more than once, but it obviously hadn't gotten through.

"Jonah's a great name. Where are you off to? That backpack looks new."

Proudly, Jonah swiveled around so the man could get a better view.

"SpongeBob. All right. I guess you're headed off to school."

"Open house," Jonah told him. "I'm gonna meet my teacher and other kids, too. Mommy says I have to sit still. I don't think I'm gonna like that. But she says we're gonna draw and make things and dance and jump around. So it might be okay."

The mountain man had to laugh at Jonah's unfettered enthusiasm. Jeannette wanted to bundle up her son and hurry him off to her car. But he really didn't see many people, other than her, Edna and Mel.

"If you're going to preschool, I'll bet you're about... four," the man guessed.

"I'm four-and-a-half," Jonah informed him. "My birthday's in Febwary. Mommy says I was her Val-en-tine's Day present."

Jeannette could see the man was finding it hard not to laugh again. She just wanted to be on their way, even though she still felt that darn tug of attraction toward him. How could she when he'd gotten her fired? And yet he was acting so natural.

"We've got to be going," she said stiffly.

But he didn't move to the side to let them pass. After a moment of studying her, he said, "I'm sorry about yesterday. I overreacted when I first came in. I should have never been so...gruff."

He was apologizing for acting rude when he'd gotten her fired? Somehow that didn't make sense.

Jonah wasn't getting the man's attention anymore and he didn't like that, so he tugged on his sleeve. "Mommy and I got up early this morning to come here. But she got *fired*." He looked up at Jeannette. "But we didn't have to call the firemen or anything."

The man in front of her suddenly went still. He flipped off his sunglasses and hung them on his shirt pocket. "So that's why you're acting like this," he mused. "You think I complained to the cleaning service."

She wasn't sure what was going on and her voice wasn't quite steady when she asked, "Didn't you?"

"No. I was coming here this morning to try to get you a raise—to compliment everything you'd done for me. I made a promise yesterday, remember?"

"Sometimes promises don't mean all that much." She remembered all the times Ed had told her they'd get married, but then he'd kept putting it off.

"I stand by my promises. What happened?"

"Well, if you didn't do it…" She paused. "The manager said business is slow and it was just a case of last hired, first fired. So I guess maybe that was true."

"I imagine not as many people are using cleaning services these days. It's still hard times for a lot of folks. If you'd like, maybe I can get you reinstated."

"How is that possible?"

His green eyes were probing as they assessed her, and she had no idea what he was looking for.

Out of the conversation now, Jonah was getting bored. "Can we go? You can come, too."

She crouched down to her son. "Oh, no, Jonah, I'm sure he can't."

"I hope you learn everything you need to know at your

open house," he said to her son, then his gaze fell on her again. "Would you like to go to lunch and talk about this some more?" He motioned to Mops and Brooms. "Your job?"

She stood. "Oh, I can't go to lunch. I start my other job at eleven, waiting tables at LipSmackin' Ribs."

The sexy stranger scowled and she wondered if he looked down on that kind of work. She'd been everything from a dog groomer to an assistant in a hair salon and said defensively, "It pays the bills."

"I always stick my foot in it with you, don't I?" He shook his head. "I'm a friend of Dillon Traub. His cousin, DJ, owns the Rib Shack. He's not pleased about the new competition, and I'm not all that impressed with the atmosphere at LipSmackin' Ribs. But that has nothing to do with you. Why don't I meet you when your shift ends?"

"I have to pick up Jonah at his babysitter's."

"Coffee break?" he teased.

When this man smiled, she felt something like hot butter running through her veins. She was amazed at his persistence. It had been about seven years since Ed had asked her on their first date. Since her fiancé's accident, she hadn't even thought about seeing another man.

But this one—

"You can even call Dillon for a reference if you need one." He took out his wallet, found a business card and handed it to her.

Jeannette glanced at it. Dr. Dillon Traub. She'd heard gossip in the restaurant about the doctor who was an heir to an oil fortune. There were two numbers. She was resisting this invitation because her good sense was telling her that she should. Besides, she didn't feel comfortable having to ask Ed's parents to watch Jonah so she could go on a date. Still… She'd heard Dr. Traub had opened a clinic in downtown Thunder Canyon. He was more than a reputable citizen, even though she wasn't sure about his brother Jackson. Other rumors that had made the rounds had said he'd caused a scene at his brother Corey's wedding in June.

"I don't even know your name," she said with another glance at Dillon's card.

When this stranger who wanted to date her didn't respond, she lifted her eyes to his. He canvassed her expression, then answered, "My name is Zane."

"Just Zane?" she asked.

Again he gave her a probing look. "Just Zane. For now."

One thing she usually wasn't was impulsive. How *could* she be with a son to think about? But right now, losing her job, not knowing what was on the horizon, she felt a little reckless. Not reckless enough to be alone with this man, though.

"Why don't you come for dinner tonight at my apartment? Jonah can be our chaperone." She thought that might put him off. She thought he might make an excuse, back out, run the other way. But she was sadly mistaken if she thought that's what he was going to do.

He considered her suggestion long enough to make her think he might refuse. Finally he said, "I don't want you to have to do the work, so I'll bring the food. Okay?"

What man brought food when he was invited over? And what had she just done?

Jonah started jumping up and down again, proving he'd been listening to the conversation. "You're gonna come to *our* place. Mom says my toys are everywhere."

Zane shook his head and suppressed a grin. "When I come over, you can show me some of those toys." His gaze fell on Jeannette then and she couldn't seem to look away.

This stranger was coming to dinner at her apartment. Was she crazy?

"Second thoughts?" he asked, seeming to read her mind as his grin faded. He took his cell phone from the holster on his belt and handed it to her. "Go ahead and call Dillon's cell. He doesn't start seeing patients until nine."

She studied Zane's phone, which was a pay-as-you-go model. She'd thought about purchasing one of those. Before she changed her mind, she jabbed in the number. Obviously Zane wanted her to do it herself to prove he wasn't scamming her.

Her call was answered on the second ring. "Hi, Zane. Did you—?"

"It's not Zane," she explained quickly. "My name is Jeannette Williams and Zane gave me your name as a reference. We're going to have dinner. I guess I want to know... Well, I have a son and—"

There was a short silence, then the doctor's voice telling her, "I'll definitely vouch for Zane. We've known each other since we were little. He's a good friend and always there when I need him. And he likes kids."

When she was silent, he asked, "Is there anything else you need to know?"

Everything, she thought. But then she said, "No, that's all for now."

"If you need to call again, you have my number."

Jeannette ended the call and turned to Zane. "Not as many second thoughts," she admitted with a smile. She gave him her address. "Is seven okay?"

"Seven is fine."

When she handed him his phone, their fingers brushed and she quickly pulled away, tingling from a current she didn't understand.

She had a date tonight with a stranger with no last name but good references.

What was she thinking?

Chapter Two

Zane found himself actually jittery as he stood in front of Jeannette Williams's apartment door. She lived on the second floor of a complex with a stairway leading up to her place. Unsure why it was so important for Jeannette to think well of him, Zane rang the bell.

She didn't know who he was so he had a clean slate. That meant so much right now. The press had taken the story of Ashley Tuller's fall, coma and death and run with it. Before coming to Montana, friends had invited Zane to have supper with them. They'd been trying to be supportive and he'd gone. But he'd left early because he just couldn't eat or make conversation. The tabloids, however, had snapped a photo of him leaving while his friends waved goodbye. The caption had read, COUNTRY SINGER PARTIES WHILE FAMILY MOURNS. They'd used other false headlines and older photos, too, until he'd had to escape all of it.

But now—

When Jeannette opened her door, Zane felt as if he'd been sucker punched. The first time he'd seen her she'd been wearing a yellow T-shirt and jeans, her hair in a ponytail. Earlier, she'd worn those same jeans and a crisp, white Oxford shirt. Tonight, however…she was wearing an above-the-knees khaki skirt with a silky red blouse. Her blond hair was long, loose and wavy. He felt an excited thump in his chest as his blood rushed faster. Whoa, he'd have to put a lid on that. After all, a four-and-a-half-year-old was going to be their chaperone.

"Hi," he said, knowing that wasn't a foray into great conversational territory.

Nevertheless, she smiled back. "Hi. Come on in."

He was carrying a bag of takeout from DJ's and he stepped into her small kitchen, setting it all on the table. Glancing around, he saw that the room was charming, with its yellow- and green-flowered café curtains, matching mixer cover and placemats. The appliances weren't new, but everything looked spotless, from the off-white countertop to the pale green tiled floor. "This is nice."

"It's small, but we like it."

They gazed at each other for a few seconds, a buzz of electricity shimmering back and forth between them. He motioned to the packages on the table. "I brought ribs from DJ's so you can taste the real deal."

"You want me to judge which is better?"

"I have no doubt which is better."

She laughed—a sweet sound that pleased his ears as much as music did.

Taking off his sunglasses, he hooked them in his shirt pocket, half expecting her to recognize him. But she turned away and went to the refrigerator, taking out a pitcher of iced tea.

Jonah ran into the kitchen and skidded to a stop beside him. "I put my toys away. Mommy said I had to."

"I didn't want you to trip over something," Jeannette explained with another one of those smiles that made him wonder if this *was* a good idea. Every time they looked at each other the room shook a little.

"Can we eat? Somethin' smells good," Jonah decided with a child's propensity for getting to the bottom line.

Zane laughed. "We've got barbecued ribs, mashed potatoes, a fine helping of green beans because you *do* need something healthy, corn bread and a fresh-baked apple pie."

"Wow!" Jonah said, impressed, his eyes big.

"Wow!" Jeannette agreed. "You really went all out."

"That's easy at DJ's." He'd seen the ads for LipSmackin' Ribs with the manager, Woody Paulson, pointing to their offerings. Zane didn't think they could compare to DJ's food.

Going to the cupboard, Jeannette pulled out a few serving dishes to go with the place settings already on the table. "Sweet tea okay? Or would you rather have a beer?"

"Tea," Zane said, knowing he needed to keep a clear head tonight.

Jonah headed for the arch leading to the living room. "I'm gonna wash my hands."

"Good boy," Jeannette complimented him.

Alone again, Zane asked, "So what did Dillon tell you about me when you called him? I mean, you gave me your address, so I must have passed the test."

She gave him a sly smile. "The verdict's still out."

He thought about the civil trial he was facing, and the verdict that might come in that could change lots of people's lives.

His expression must have gone all serious because

Jeannette assured him, "Hey, I'm kidding. Sort of. I'll make my own opinion about you."

He took a step closer to her. "That's the way it should be."

He was still wearing his hat. Jeannette seemed to be staring at his mouth. He'd thought about shaving, but had decided against it. Before the past few months, he'd always had a neat, clean-cut persona—short hair and no beard. But now he really was another person, and he was becoming more comfortable with that person each day.

He noticed the pulse in the hollow of Jeannette's neck was beating fast. It seemed to match the tempo of his. She picked up the pitcher to pour the tea. "Dr. Traub said he could vouch for your character, that he'd known you since you were both kids. He said you were still a good friend and always there when he needed you and that you liked children."

Zane had always been grateful for Dillon's friendship, never more so than now. "That's a lot to live up to."

"From the way it sounds, you already have. I know Dr. Traub is from Texas. I hear bits of conversation at the restaurant. You both have a Texas drawl."

"Dillon and I are from Midland."

"You're a long way from home."

"Yes, I am." He realized she wanted more, but he didn't know if he was ready to give it right now.

"What about you? Where did you grow up?"

"In Bozeman."

Bozeman was about a half hour east of Thunder Canyon. Truth be told, he was more interested in other things about her than where she grew up. "I don't know a tactful way to ask this, so I'm going to just ask. Is Jonah's father involved in his life?" His gaze dropped again to her hand that was devoid of a wedding ring.

"Jonah's father died before he was born."

"I'm sorry." Zane saw her swallow hard and take a breath. Obviously she'd loved the man a lot.

Before Zane could say anything else, Jonah scrambled back through the doorway and up onto a chair. "I'm ready," he announced.

"So are we," Jeannette singsonged back, recovering from whatever turmoil Zane's question had caused. Already he could tell she was a good mom. Whenever he'd dated before, he hadn't even thought of something like that. Of course he'd never dated anyone who had kids. And he wasn't dating Jeannette, either. He was just— Having a meal with her…and her son.

The small table hardly fit the three of them. Zane's long legs seemed to extend to the other side. As tall as he was, he couldn't move without his elbow brushing Jeannette's, or shift his legs without bumping Jonah's knees. The little boy laughed when it happened. Zane made a game of it and Jonah giggled every time he did. With barbecue sauce smeared all over his face, on his fingers and on the spoon he used to scoop mashed potatoes into his mouth, he looked like he was having a great experience.

Zane wiped his fingers on a napkin as Jeannette ate another forkful of her dinner. "So, what do you think about the ribs?"

She seemed to consider his question with the importance he wanted her to give it. But then she shrugged. "They're great, but the sauce tastes like the sauce we use at LipSmackin' Ribs. I do have to admit the corn bread is wonderful and not something I should consider eating on a daily basis or my clothes won't fit."

Zane let his gaze run over her and there was male appreciation in his voice when he commented, "You don't have to worry about a thing."

Her face turned a pretty color of pink and he wondered if she didn't get many compliments. She had a smudge of barbecue sauce on her upper lip and without thinking about it he leaned forward and wiped it away with his thumb. He hadn't realized this simple gesture could have such an impact.

They both stilled as his finger lingered on her skin. She didn't pull away, and he realized from the radar he'd perfected over the years that she was affected, too, by whatever this attraction was between them. It wasn't one-sided. That pleased him a great deal. Yet it was too soon for him to touch her, or kiss her or anything like that. Jeannette had a son. Zane's life was so chaotic no woman would ever want to set foot in it.

He pulled his hand away from her reluctantly, and then took his napkin and said to Jonah, "I think you're going to have a permanent barbecue mustache if I don't get some of this off." He wiped the barbecue sauce from around Jonah's mouth and set the napkin on the table. "Your fingers are going to need soap and water."

"Gran tells me to use *lots* of soap," Jonah informed Zane.

He glanced at Jeannette and she explained, "Jonah stays with his dad's parents while I work. Ed and I weren't married, but they've become like parents to me."

Zane considered Jeannette's expression. It was watchful as if being a mother and not married would elicit some kind of judgment from him. He wasn't in a position to judge *anyone*.

"I'm full," Jonah suddenly announced.

"No apple pie?" his mother asked.

"Not now," he said as he scooted off his chair. "Can Zane play a game with me?"

Jeannette glanced at Zane. "You'll have to check with him."

"Sure, we can play a game. But you'll have to teach me whatever it is."

"We could have pie and coffee after he goes to bed," Jeannette suggested.

"Sounds good."

Two hours later in Jonah's bedroom, Jeannette finished buttoning Jonah's pajama top, well aware Zane was seated in her living room, TV turned off, as he paged through a photo album with baby pictures of Jonah. Tall and muscled, he almost looked out of place on her mauve-and-green plaid sofa. She'd told him he could watch TV if he wanted to, but he'd just shrugged and said he'd rather page through the photo album.

"Mommy, can I give Zane a good-night hug?"

A lump came to her throat. "You'll have to ask him if it's okay."

"I will. I like Zane."

It was obvious that Jonah did. Zane had played with him as if they'd been buddies for a while. Mel and Edna were great with Jonah, and she appreciated everything they did for him. But they were overprotective at times. Mel didn't play with him in the yard, just watched Jonah as he played by himself. There weren't children in Edna and Mel's neighborhood, and that's one of the reasons Jeannette had wanted to enroll him in preschool. Zane, however, had played with Jonah as if he was used to being with kids, and Jonah had taken to him, lapping up the attention like a new puppy.

As Jonah ran down the hall into the living room—he never walked anywhere—Jeannette followed him. He went over to Zane and asked, "Can I give you a hug?"

Zane didn't hesitate. He enveloped her son in a bear hug and squeezed tight until Jonah giggled. "You sleep good tonight, cowboy."

"I will," Jonah said as he waved to Zane, then walked with Jeannette to his bedroom.

She tucked him in and kissed his forehead, seeing that his eyelids were already drooping with sleep. "I love you, Jonah. I'll see you in the morning."

When she kissed his cheek, he mumbled, "'Night, Mommy."

As she returned to the living room, she heard Zane in the kitchen and realized he was on the phone. She didn't mean to eavesdrop, really she didn't, but she heard her name mentioned, so she listened. "I understand why you fired her," he was saying. "But I'm telling you if you keep her on, I'll pay her salary."

She was thunderstruck. He would do *what*? She walked into the kitchen straight-backed and square-shouldered.

Zane didn't hide what he was doing. He didn't put down the phone. "Yes, I'm sure about it. I'll let you settle the details with her. I'm sure Jeannette will be speaking with you. You have a good night, too."

Jeannette didn't know what to say or how to say it, so she asked, "Why would you possibly do that? *How* could you possibly do that?"

"It's easy. I had looked up the owner's number on my laptop this afternoon. So I just made her an offer that was hard to refuse. You're reinstated. You have your job back."

"No, I don't. You will *not* pay my salary. I'll find a job and I'll get it on my own."

He stood very close to her, close enough to kiss. Where did *that* thought come from?

"Did anyone ever tell you that maybe you have too much pride?" he asked, almost rhetorically.

"Didn't a woman ever tell you she might want to live her life on her own terms?"

He seemed to wince at that, but then he shook his head. "I don't want to be bad karma for you. I don't want you to worry about how you're going to pay your bills."

"I've been worrying about that for years, but I've managed."

"Life is about more than managing...when it's good."

As he said those words, Jeannette saw pain in Zane's eyes. They hadn't gotten a chance tonight to talk about more than where he was from. She didn't know much more about him now than she had before dinner. Had he kept his life hidden on purpose? If so, why?

So she asked again. "All right, so now I know *why* you would do it. Let me ask you now *how* you would do it. I mean, my salary's not stupendous, but most people couldn't just add that into their budget as another bill."

"You really don't know who I am, do you?" he asked, studying her so probingly that she felt almost turned inside out.

"Who are you?" She heard the wobble in her voice because she was suddenly afraid to learn the answer. After all, Dillon Traub had indicated he was a stand-up guy.

"I'm Zane Gunther."

She must have still looked blank because he added, "The country singer."

The only music she listened to blared from the Disney Channel. She'd ignored country music over the years because it had always touched her too much—bringing back memories she'd rather forget. But as she studied the man before her, a man she hadn't recognized out of his stage-presence context, she remembered a poster she'd seen last year for Frontier Days—a community celebration to bring in tourists. She now remembered Zane Gunther's ruggedly handsome, clean-shaven face, his black Stetson, the much-shorter hair, his twinkling green eyes. Her lips opened in surprise and she was absolutely speechless. Zane Gunther—the singer—had brought ribs to her house for dinner?

Zane had picked up his Stetson from the counter and plopped it on his head. Then he leaned into her, kissed her parted lips for a soul-stirring moment and backed away.

By the time Jeannette recovered her wits, he'd stepped outside and closed the door.

Too stunned to go after him, too shaken by his kiss, she touched her fingers to her lips and wondered if she'd ever see the mega-star again.

Jeannette mounted the steps to the Thunder Canyon Library on Saturday afternoon, determined to find out everything she could about Zane Gunther. She'd heard the name bandied about on TV shows after the Country Music Awards and, of course, during last year's Frontier Days. But he looked so different! She didn't know his music. And she certainly didn't know why he'd be staying on top of a mountain near Thunder Canyon.

After five minutes at the library's computer, however, she knew exactly why. He was escaping the paparazzi furor, anyone who wanted to interview him, as well as what had happened. She didn't know which account to believe. Everyone spun a story the way they wanted it to be heard. She'd like to hear the truth from Zane himself. But which Zane? Mountain Man Zane? Or Zane Gunther, the country singer?

She might never have the chance to hear anything from him. He could be gone tomorrow!

Yet she remembered that kiss. Surely he hadn't been

as affected as she had. After all, he *was* Zane Gunther. Why had he even wanted to come to dinner at her place?

The woman at the computer next to her, obviously nosy, saw the content of what she'd been searching. "It's a shame, isn't it?" The curly redhead in jeans, who looked to be near sixty, around Edna's age, obviously wanted to strike up a conversation.

"I don't know much about him," Jeannette admitted. "That's why I was doing a search on him."

"I heard he was asked to perform at Frontier Days again, but he turned it down. Maybe he's afraid to show his face."

Jeannette mulled over everything she'd read. "Or maybe he's had enough of showing his face and everybody jumping on him."

"Have you seen him in concert?"

"No, I haven't. Have you?"

"Oh, I was there last year. He was wonderful! Makes you think he's a regular guy."

"Maybe he is."

"Not with all *that* money. I heard he's got a place in Nashville and one in Utah."

"I suppose he travels a lot."

"Especially when he's on tour. No wonder he doesn't have a family. Who *could* with that kind of schedule?"

Jeannette's heart took a nosedive. She supposed that was true. On the other hand, she knew there were singers who had successful relationships and children. Why did that matter to her?

She shut down the search engine and was about to get up when the woman next to her asked, "So why were you looking him up?"

Why, indeed? She almost said, *Because I met him and was curious.* But then she thought about the story she'd read, the pain in Zane's eyes, the way he'd looked at her. "Like you said, I heard a rumor he might perform at Frontier Days again this year. I was just curious."

"Never happen," the woman said with certainty. "We probably won't see his face again until he goes to trial. I bet that family will win."

Jeannette had no idea what would happen. But she did know one thing. From the change in Zane Gunther's appearance, from the way he was living on that mountain, she guessed his life had already changed irrevocably.

Jeannette's car was running rough as she pulled up in front of Edna and Mel's two-story colonial house in an older section of Thunder Canyon. Since before Jonah was born, this house had been her home. She'd moved in during her pregnancy and stayed until a few months ago. But she had to be on her own now. That was best for her and Jonah.

She rapped on the door to announce her arrival and went inside. Mel and Edna were sitting in matching recliners watching TV, while Jonah played with blocks over in the corner.

He ran to her and hugged her around the waist. "I missed you."

"I missed you, too, honey. Ready to go?"

"You look beat," Mel said matter-of-factly. He was usually cheery but always to the point.

"I should wear roller skates on Saturday nights," she joked. "LipSmackin' Ribs was hopping."

Edna frowned. "Do you think they'll have a winter uniform?"

Jeannette looked down at her royal blue short shorts, the skimpy white T-shirt that left part of her tummy showing, the logo on the front with its big red lips. "I'm pretty sure this is an all-year-round uniform. As fast as we move, we don't get cold."

She understood Edna wasn't worried about her getting cold. She disapproved of her showing off her body. When Jeannette worked at LipSmackin' Ribs with the other waitresses, she could make herself believe the uniform wasn't so bad. But outside of the restaurant, she found it hard to defend. What happened when values and the need for money smashed into each other?

She had to pay the bills. A few business classes taken at night didn't qualify her for a CEO position. Right out of high school she'd worked as a secretary for a textile company in Thunder Canyon. But it had closed its doors a few years later. After that, she'd worked for an insurance company in Bozeman as a receptionist. That's where she'd met Ed. But early in her pregnancy she'd had to quit that job because of severe morning sickness and then a near miscarriage. After Ed died, Edna and Mel had insisted she come live with them to make sure she could carry the baby to term. Once Jonah had been born, they hadn't wanted her to leave.

"Did you have something to eat?" Edna was a little plump, with silver wire-rimmed glasses and salt-and-pepper hair that curled around her face. She'd had a difficult time conceiving children. She'd had a couple of miscarriages and that's why she'd understood the care Jeannette had needed so well.

Jeannette smiled at this woman who had become a surrogate mother to her. "I'll get something when I get home. I used my break times to make calls."

"Calls?" Mel asked, turning away from the TV again.

Jeannette absolutely shouldn't have said anything. But now it was too late. She wasn't going to lie and they'd eventually find out from her work schedule that she didn't have her cleaning job anymore. She would *not* let Zane pay her way. "I was let go from Mops and Brooms. They claim they just don't have the business they once had. So I'm trying to find something else that will fit in with waitressing."

Mel and Edna exchanged a look and Edna became the couple's spokesperson. "If you need to move back here, you know you're welcome. Your main job should be raising Jonah, not scrambling from here to there to try to put pennies together."

Jeannette wished that was so, she really did. But reality was reality. "I appreciate your offer and everything you've done. I hope you know that. But Jonah and I will be okay. I have insurance for him at the restaurant and I'm sure I'll be able to pick up something else part-time. The next time I have a break, I'll go to the library and put together my résumé on the computer there." That's what she *should* have been doing this afternoon, instead of researching Zane Gunther.

After another disapproving look that told Jeannette Edna and Mel wanted her and Jonah back here under their watchful eye, Edna said, "I made chicken salad. You can take that along. I know you. You'll just eat a salad and yogurt at home."

Jeannette didn't know what was wrong with a salad and yogurt, but she held her tongue as Jonah put his blocks away and then slipped into his jacket.

Back at her apartment a short time later, Jeannette made herself a sandwich while Jonah got ready for bed. She'd just taken it to the living room with a glass of milk when he came running in, brown hair standing up all over, pajama top crooked. "Is this late night?"

When Jonah didn't have to go to school the next day,

she let him stay up a little longer. It gave them much-needed time together. "This is late night. What do you want to do?"

"Puzzles," he said without hesitation.

"Okay. Pick out two favorites and dump them on the coffee table."

Jeannette took a few bites of her sandwich and a sip of milk, planning to finish it while she played with Jonah. But there was a knock at the door and she stopped mid-bite. She and Jonah didn't get many visitors. They weren't here that much. She was on a waving basis with two of her neighbors. Maybe one of them needed something.

Going to the door, she looked through the peephole and froze. It was Zane Gunther!

So many thoughts ran through her head. Why was he here? Was he here because he wanted to see her again? Or was he here to sum things up before he left her life completely?

She looked down at her uniform and wished she could go change, even if it was to put a robe on top of it. But she didn't have time for that. Not if she didn't want him to leave.

When she opened the door, his eyes lingered on her face. Their gazes held for what seemed like a *very* long time. When he glanced at her snug but short T-shirt and the rest of her, she saw his mouth tighten and his jaw set.

Maybe he disapproved as much as Edna. Or maybe—

His eyes darkened under the glare of the outside apartment light. She'd seen that same change in him last night right before he'd kissed her.

She stepped aside and opened the door wider. "This is a surprise." Knowing who he was made her nervous, when she hadn't been jittery around him before.

After he closed the door behind him, he took off his

Stetson and held it in his hands. "I didn't know if you'd let me in now that you know who I am."

He was dressed in a black T-shirt, black jeans and black boots that weren't as worn as his brown ones. The air of masculinity emanating from him was as powerful now as it had been the first day she'd met him. Her fingers itched to touch his biceps, let alone the beard stubble on his face. No wonder women mobbed him in droves!

"I *don't* know you," she admitted. "Not really."

Tension pulled between them and vibrated. "I wanted to be an ordinary guy for a little while. I still do."

"But you're *not* an ordinary guy."

Jonah rushed into the kitchen then. "Zane! You can help with puzzles!"

Zane tore his eyes from hers and ruffled the boy's already-disheveled hair. "Life's one big puzzle, partner. But I guess I can try and help you figure one out, if your mom thinks that's okay."

He leveled a look at her that seemed to say, *This is your call.*

Common sense battled with the attraction she felt for him. She'd never let hormones sway her before. On the other hand, what could it hurt to find out more about him? About the man behind the guitar.

A wise voice inside her head whispered back, *It could hurt your heart a lot.*

She silenced that voice. "I'll make a pot of coffee. Why don't you two get started?"

Chapter Three

Jeannette watched Zane carefully as he picked up a puzzle piece and showed Jonah how to look for straight and crooked edges. He looked relaxed now, leaning over the coffee table with her son. She couldn't keep her gaze from skimming down his torso, over his slim hips and his long jean-clad legs.

Easily, she remembered everything she'd read about Zane for the last decade of his career—number one singles, Grammys, CMA awards for Best Male Vocalist, sellout concerts, a multimillion-dollar tour cut short. Curiously, she'd examined photos of him with glamorous women, climbing in and out of limos, even a helicopter flight to one of the concerts. She'd never even seen a helicopter live, let alone *been* in one. The same with a limo.

So why was he here in her living room, spending time with her and her son? And what was the truth about what had happened at the concert and how he'd reacted afterward? She had so many questions and she didn't know if she'd ever have the answers.

When Zane glanced her way, her outfit almost made her cringe. "I'm going to change out of my work clothes. I'll be right back."

Quickly, she mentally flashed through her wardrobe which wasn't that extensive, and in a few minutes came up with a pink scoop-necked sweater and jeans. After she slipped on an old pair of espadrilles, she took the band from her hair and brushed it. With a touch of lip gloss, she knew she was about as ready as she'd ever be—to face Zane, his private and public persona and anything he wanted to tell her.

As she reentered the living room, Zane nudged Jonah's shoulder. "Doesn't your mom look pretty?"

Jonah stared at her for a couple of seconds, then glanced back at Zane. "She looks like she *always* does."

Although she'd first been embarrassed, Jonah's remark helped her smile when Zane chuckled. "Kids say it like it is," Zane decided with a shrug. "You must be pretty all the time."

She was twenty-eight years old and shouldn't feel like a shy teenager, but she did, especially now that she knew who he was. Did glib remarks fly off his tongue easily? Was that honesty she saw in his eyes? Or practiced flirting? How would she ever know?

Once Jeannette was seated on the sofa beside Zane, she helped Jonah put together the last few pieces of the puzzle.

"You didn't eat." Zane motioned to her sandwich, half eaten, on the dish on the coffee table.

"I had enough."

His brows arched.

She felt she had to explain. "Sometimes I'm just too tired to eat when I get home. Or too busy."

"Jeannette, you have to—"

"I know what you're going to say. But I did sample a new recipe for wings at the restaurant, and a square of bread pudding, too.

"That's what you had to eat all day?"

"And breakfast. Jonah and I had scrambled eggs, toast and a little bit of fruit."

"Mom makes great eggs."

"I'll bet she does. Ready to start on that second puzzle?"

Jonah looked at Jeannette with one of those "little boy" looks that told her he wanted something. She waited.

Finally, he asked, "Can Zane read me a book?"

Zane seemed to know intuitively what to do. He gave her a little nod, showing her he was game.

"It's a book or a puzzle. Then you *do* have to go to bed."

"Oh, Mom. It's *late* night."

"Yes, I know, and it's already getting late. One or the other. You choose."

After a few seconds Jonah decided, "A book. In *my* room."

Jeannette knew if she let Zane into Jonah's room, she was letting him further into her life. Yet sitting beside him on the sofa, almost aware of every breath he took, definitely aware of his cologne and the restrained strength of him beside her, she felt as if she were fighting a losing battle. "Go pick out the book. Then we'll be in."

After Jonah was out of earshot, Zane asked, "Does he often back you into a corner like that?"

"More often than I'd like him to. For four-and-a-half he has great manipulative skills." She lifted her chin and studied Zane's face. "Why did you come tonight?" Could she get even one of her answers?

"Because I wanted to see you again...because I hoped you didn't believe everything you read."

She had to be honest with him. "I hadn't read much, not until this afternoon when I went to the library and searched your name on the computer."

"I see." His voice was tense and much more distant.

"No, I don't think you do."

"Mommy! Zane! I found a book."

Rising to her feet Jeannette said, "My guess is he picked the longest one he could find."

But when they reached Jonah's room, Jeannette found he had picked one of his favorite books rather than the longest. It was a funny book with silly pictures and lots of rhymes.

Sitting on the bed beside Jonah, Zane put expression into the words without half trying. Jonah laughed and so did Zane, and her heart ached with everything Jonah needed that she couldn't provide. A dad's love was different than a mom's. Her gaze fell on the photograph of Ed on Jonah's bedside table. He would have loved his son and done anything for him. He'd proven that when he'd taken two jobs and worked so many hours she'd hardly seen him. That had been her fault. If she hadn't missed so many days of work because of morning sickness, if she hadn't started spotting...if she hadn't gotten pregnant...

She had switched from birth control pills to patches and one week she'd simply forgotten to change it. When she discovered she was pregnant, she hadn't known how Ed would react. They'd been together for three years and he'd been dragging his feet about commitment. They'd been living together, but sometimes she still felt he could walk away at any time. Yet when she told him she was pregnant, he'd said they should get married. However, he kept putting it off, finally pushing the event until after the baby was born. She would have liked to have gotten married *before* Jonah was born. But she was just so glad Ed was finally ready that she hadn't questioned him and hadn't pushed, although a part of her had always wondered if he was doing it out of duty or out of love.

She still didn't know. She'd never know.

"All done," Jonah suddenly said, slapping the covers of the book together. "We could read it again."

"Or not," Jeannette said firmly. "Say good-night to Zane and I'll help you get ready for bed."

Jonah's good-night for Zane came accompanied with another hug. Her little boy was getting attached very quickly. Maybe if Zane were an ordinary man, she'd let it continue. But how could she when she knew who he was? When he didn't have a normal life? When his interlude in Thunder Canyon might not last very long? When he could be gone tomorrow?

Tonight when she finished Jonah's bedtime ritual and left his door open a crack, she found Zane pacing the living room. "What's wrong?" she asked, knowing something was.

"I have no business being here. If a journalist got wind of what I was doing and where I was, I'd be dragging you and Jonah into everything that's going on."

"You call that tripe written about you journalism?"

He grimaced. "Well, at least *you* could see it wasn't that. Some people can't see through it. They think an article in a publication that writes about alien abductions is the same as one in the *New York Times*."

She eyed him thoughtfully. "Would you like a beer?"

"Yes, I would."

"Did *you* have supper?"

"I ate one of those frozen dinners you stocked my freezer with."

"How about a Southwestern omelet? I bought salsa on sale at the grocery store and Woody, my manager, was going to throw away perfectly good containers of sour cream. The waitresses divided them up."

"That sounds great. But if you're too tired to cook, I don't need anything."

"This will take five minutes. And from your pictures six months ago and the way you look now, I'd say you need to eat a little more than *you're* eating, too."

"You sound like Dillon."

"With good reason. How much weight have you lost?"

"About fifteen pounds. But I often lose ten when I start a new tour."

"Really?"

"It happens. My hours aren't regular and I'm a perfectionist. I work in my bus, not only writing music, but staying on top of the business, promotion with my publicist, gigs with my manager, money flow with the accountant. I delegate, but I still oversee everything. I don't want any unhappy surprises when I least expect them."

Jeannette took eggs from the refrigerator and pulled out the jar of salsa. The frying pan, though clean, was sitting on the stove from that morning. "Is *any* part of your life normal?"

"Normal becomes what we make it, don't you think?"

"Is that an excuse for saying no?"

"You cut right through it, don't you?"

"I have to, Zane. I'm a single mom. I can't lie to myself and I can usually read evasive tactics in others. It's a gift," she added teasingly, trying to lighten the conversation a little.

Shaking his head, Zane took a spatula from a utensil

crock on the counter and handed it to her. "Do you need anything else from the refrigerator?"

"There's some grated cheese in there. If you could get that—"

In five minutes the omelet was finished and divided in two. Jeannette had popped bread into the toaster and grabbed the strawberry jelly from the fridge. "Edna made it. It's good."

Zane ate like a man who was enjoying his food. After he finished, he said, "That hit the spot. Maybe I just enjoy food more when I have someone to eat with." He motioned to *her* empty plate. "It might be the same for you."

"It might be. I eat more with Jonah, or when we have a Sunday dinner with Edna and Mel."

"Does that happen often?"

"Not lately. With this job at LipSmackin' Ribs, my hours are all over the place. I work weekends whenever I can." She didn't have to say because of the tips. He knew that already.

Zane picked up his fork and hers with both their plates and loaded it all into the small dishwasher.

"You don't have to—"

"Yes, I do. You cooked. I clean up. It's an unwritten contract."

"I think there are a lot of men in this world who are unaware of that contract."

Zane closed the door to the dishwasher. "Let's go sit on the sofa and talk. You deserve to know the truth about what happened at my last concert."

In the living room they settled on the sofa a few inches apart. Jeannette thought about sitting in the matching chair, but she wanted to be near Zane for a reason other than her attraction to him. Maybe he'd give off signals that would tell her if he was being glib or guarded or dishonest. She also had to admit she just wanted to be close to him. Because he was a star? Actually, no. It was because there was something about him that made her heart race and her skin tingle and her stomach flip-flop.

Zane glanced at her, then raked his hand through his thick brown hair. With the table lamp beside him, she realized there were burnished strands in it. He wore a Stetson so much of the time that she hadn't noticed them before.

"I began promoting my new CD last September when I performed at Frontier Days. I had written a lead song—'Movin' On'—and performed it for the first time here at the arena at the fairgrounds. When my CD was released last year, sales skyrocketed and the tour started off with a bang."

"How many concerts do you do a week?"

"That depends. I'd rather do several close together, and then give everybody a break for a week or two. That's easier on their family life. But spring through summer is our busiest time."

"You said you have a bus?"

He frowned. "Yep. I used to call it my home away from home. But now—"

"Tell me what happened," she requested, knowing the bus was involved.

He hesitated, obviously reluctant. After heaving a deep breath, he began, "It was early April. I'd done a bunch of media events in New York and L.A. We'd started a month-long series of concerts and did a few in the Southwest. Texas concerts are great because I can usually wiggle in time to see my mom and old friends who still live in Midland."

When he stopped, she could see the shadows in his eyes, the click of memories playing that he'd rather avoid. He shifted on the sofa, leaned forward, placed his hands on his knees. "We performed at a venue near Austin. It was an outdoor arena with stadiumlike seats under cover, others close to the stage, not covered. It was an evening show with all the lights and hoopla that can make a concert spectacular. The audience was great. They'd come to enjoy themselves, to sing along, clap, stomp, whatever it took to feel part of the music."

Jeannette could see Zane was reliving it, maybe feeling the rhythm under his feet, his guitar in his hands, the songs in his head.

"Because it was a night concert, I did the meet and greet beforehand," he explained. "I met with folks in the fan club, spoke with others who'd won tickets through radio contests, that sort of thing. But I also signed autographs for about an hour before the concert with the general audience. I wanted to get on the road and didn't want it to go too late afterward."

She could imagine the crowd, the concertgoers vying for his autograph on hands and T-shirts and CD covers. It had been a long, long time since she'd been at a concert, but she remembered the feel of it, the excitement, the bass vibrating in her chest.

Zane rubbed his palms on his jeans and stared straight ahead. "The audience got more revved up with each song, and we found ourselves doing more than we scheduled, just because we were enjoying it so much. I usually plan two encores, but I think I did five that night. I'll admit it's hard for me to leave the stage when the audience is that encouraging. Or at least it was."

From the tone in Zane's voice she could tell he felt differently about all of it now.

"Tell me what happened," she requested gently.

He turned to look at her for a moment, and then he closed his eyes and shook his head. "I'll never forget it, as long as I live." He paused. "I had a bodyguard who went with me everywhere. Roscoe handled my personal security team. They're supposed to keep me safe and they always did a terrific job of it. My promoter was in charge of the security force for the concert venue. They'd done a fine job with that large crowd. The concert had gone off without a hitch. The band had already left. Then..."

He stopped. "I'm not sure what happened. My tour bus was parked at the back of the stage. Often a crowd gathers there to catch a glimpse of me leaving. It happens everywhere we go and it's not unusual. There had never been a problem before. But that night the crowd around the bus suddenly got too large and too close. Roscoe and his team formed a line for me to get to the bus. I was on the first step when I heard and felt the surge, saw the fans break through the guard line. The next thing I knew, someone was down and there was screaming. The 9-1-1 call went out and I still wasn't sure what had happened. Roscoe shoved me into the bus and I was fighting him to get into the crowd. But he insisted they would tear me apart. I told him I wasn't leaving until I knew what had happened. We'd called the police to tell them we were circling the venue. As far as I was concerned, this was *my* concert, *my* responsibility. I made the calls myself to the chief of police and the nearest hospital, but nobody would tell me anything. During all that, my manager called a lawyer. I didn't want to talk to him. I wasn't worried about liability. I was worried about whoever got hurt."

Jeannette could hear the emotion in Zane's voice, the rough huskiness that stopped him from telling more.

Finally he shifted on the sofa. His knee grazed hers as he faced her. "I shouldn't be telling you any of this. My lawyer has instructed me not to talk about it to anybody, not to go near Ashley's family or talk to *them*."

Jeannette knew Ashley Tuller had been thirteen. This was breaking her heart, imagining what her parents felt... what Zane was feeling. "You don't know me very well, Zane," she admitted. "But I can tell you I won't go to a tabloid and I won't talk to a reporter. That doesn't mean you'll believe me. I think I already understand that Ashley's death was life-changing for you, so if you don't want to talk about it more, or can't, that's okay."

"I haven't talked to anyone about it except for my lawyer. I haven't even spoken to Dillon or the guys in my band about the details."

If he hadn't told his best friend, his closest friends, she doubted he'd tell her. She didn't know if she should, but she reached out and covered his hand with hers.

The nerve in his jaw jumped. "Ashley had a head injury, severe trauma. She was airlifted to a hospital in Dallas best equipped to deal with that. For three days she was in a coma—three days when her parents didn't know if she was going to live or die. From what I understand, her older sister was by her side twenty-four hours a day." He shook his head. "I can't even imagine their pain. Even if I could talk to them, what would I say? Dillon lost his son and I know what *he* went through. I just wish—"

"What do you wish?"

"I wish I could do something so I didn't feel so powerless. I wish they could know I didn't leave the scene like some of the tabloids reported. Since the family filed a civil suit, everyone around me is telling me to listen to my lawyer. I feel like he's tied my hands and feet and taped my mouth shut. This isn't me. I do something when I can. I don't wait around to see what happens next."

"You're waiting for the trial."

Zane nodded. "It will probably be sometime in December. We haven't gotten the official date yet."

"I guess your lawyer's trying to settle?"

Zane leaned back against the sofa cushions and shook his head. "This isn't about money. I know that. No amount of money will bring Ashley back. Her parents want someone to pay. And need somebody to blame. I understand. But I don't think a trial or settlement is going to be the answer."

Her hand was still covering his. She pulled hers away and put it back in her lap where it belonged. She knew Zane had arrived in May. She'd been cleaning his house and taking him supplies for that long. But she wasn't completely sure why he'd come. "You came to Thunder Canyon to escape the paparazzi?"

Again he studied her, maybe unsure he could trust her. She could probably earn a bank account full of money if she took his story to any number of magazines. After all, it seemed like former acquaintances of Zane and anyone who had been there that night was doing just that. But no one had the words from his mouth but her.

The thing was, Jeannette knew in her heart that she would never sell Zane's story to anyone or even talk about it.

Maybe he saw that.

"My lawyer suggested a leave of absence. But I couldn't have returned to the tour if I'd wanted to. The night this happened, I felt like I'd grown a stone in my chest. That feeling hasn't gone away. At first I couldn't think about anything else. All I could think about was Ashley, day and night, and what her family was feeling. Even when her parents started giving interviews, saying it was my fault, I couldn't be angry with them because I felt it *was* my fault, in spite of what my lawyer says, or my promoter or my manager or my band. They all have a lot to lose—their livelihood, but also their reputation, which really matters in this business. My bodyguard quit. He felt as guilty as hell. I've been with Roscoe since I won my first award. My mother is torn up because I'm torn up. That's the kind of relationship we've always had."

Jeannette remembered the one headline she'd read: RIFT BETWEEN ZANE GUNTHER AND HIS MOTHER.

"Has this caused problems between you and your mom?"

He gave a twisted smile. "You read the tabloid, huh?"

"No, I just saw the headline."

"No rift. I call her when I can, so she knows I'm okay. I can't do it from the mountain. I can't get a signal till I'm down on the road. I went home once since this happened and photojournalists—" he made quote marks with his fingers "—took advantage of it, so I thought it was better if I stayed away."

"You really are isolated."

Quickly, he straightened. "Hey, don't feel sorry for me. That isn't why I'm telling you this. I just wanted you to understand what happened, not what the press *says* happened. Not what the lawyers say happened. Heck, I couldn't believe you didn't know who I was. I was grateful and humbled. Maybe I need a little more humbling."

"Because?"

"Because before all this happened I could have had anything I wanted. I could go anyplace I wanted. I could do whatever I wanted. That's not how normal people live. I haven't had a normal life since my first CD took off." He blew out a breath. "Now I sound like I'm complaining about it. I'm not. I appreciate absolutely everything that's happened to me. But the truth is, since this happened, I have no music in my head, let alone in my heart. It used to be that a verse would just fly into my thoughts no matter what I was doing, and then the music to match it would play, or vice versa. Now there's nothing. Just silence. Even when there's noise all around me, there's silence *in* me."

"I haven't listened to your music yet," she admitted. "I borrowed CDs from the library. But if you had the gift of music, something that was with you all the time and followed you everywhere and you could just snatch it when you wanted to, and then suddenly it was gone, I'd want to live on a mountaintop, too. I understand what happens when fate deals a blow that no one expects." She thought about Ed and his accident and how that had turned her life upside down when she'd least expected it. One day she was planning for the birth of her baby and a wedding, and the next...

"That happened with Jonah's father?" Zane asked with real concern and interest.

"Yes, it did."

"But you don't want to go into that now?"

He had just shared so much with her, and she wanted to tell him about Ed, but—

"It's late and you're tired," he realized. "I probably shouldn't have come over tonight, but I didn't want to wait. Too much can happen when you wait."

Feeling shy and a little awkward, she smiled at him. "I'm glad you came over. I was wondering about so much."

He looked as if he were about to say something more, maybe ask her something. But he didn't. Instead, he pushed himself to his feet.

She was afraid this was it. Or maybe relieved this was it. They really had nothing in common. Their lifestyles were worlds apart.

Standing, she followed him to the door. She suddenly wanted to say, *Please don't go.* But she had a child, and she was a waitress and she had a life here. He could be gone in a flash, in a helicopter or a private plane or a limo.

At the open door, with his Stetson on now, he gazed down at her with an intense look in his eyes. "I like you, Jeannette. I like you a lot. But I have a complicated life right now and I don't want anybody else to be tainted by it."

How could they be? He had done nothing wrong. Yet the world was portraying him as selfish, as just another star who was out for the money and the glory and the fame without caring about his fans. But she could see that wasn't true at all.

"Do you work tomorrow?" he asked.

"I do. But Jonah and I will have time to go to church first. Edna and Mel like to make a big brunch afterward."

"Sounds nice."

She'd love to invite him along, but how crazy would that be? Edna and Mel would have a fit at the thought of any man taking their son's place in her life. Besides, Zane's cover would be blown. She could see he needed as much peace as he could get right now.

"You enjoy yourselves. Family is really all we have when the going gets rough."

He was supposed to be leaving and she was supposed to be saying goodbye. But the magnet of their attraction drew them together until they seemed mesmerized by each other.

When Zane slid his hand under her hair, she felt a cool breeze waft along her cheek. It emphasized the warmth of his hand, her own temperature seeming to rise at his touch. It had taken a few dates with Ed before she'd kissed him. This man she'd kissed before she'd even known him. But then, could last night's brief touching of lips even be considered a kiss?

"I want a taste of you," he said huskily as his lips descended closer to hers.

His words sent a rippling thrill through her body until she realized a need that had gone unsatisfied within her for years. When Zane's lips came down on hers tonight, they weren't gentle or light. Oh, no. Tonight they were hungry, searching for desire to be fulfilled, searching for a response that might or might not be there.

Her body reacted as if she'd been born to respond to Zane. She enfolded her arms around his neck, and he pulled her in tighter. His tongue slid into her mouth and her gasp of pleasure opened her up more completely to him. He explored with a possessive need that almost made her moan. She felt as if a low-burning fire inside of her burst into flames. She couldn't get enough of his mouth on hers, his tongue retreating, then urging her on. Pressed against him, she felt his arousal and a satisfaction she had long ago forgotten.

When he withdrew and pulled away, they were both breathing hard. She was still trying to catch her breath when he said, "That was Zane the man who kissed you, not Zane Gunther the country singer."

Then he let her go and walked away, his steps quick, his stride long. She heard him gallop down the stairs and then his bootfalls faded away.

She knew one thing for certain. If Zane Gunther could sing as well as he kissed, his music would come back to him. She was sure of it.

Chapter Four

"Are you ready?" Jeannette called to Jonah.

Today was Labor Day which was ironic because she'd spent the morning doing household chores. This afternoon she and Jonah were going to the park. This was a rare day off for her and she was going to spend the rest of the afternoon and evening with her son.

"Soon," Jonah called back from his room and she had to smile.

The phone on her kitchen counter rang just as she was about to find out what was keeping him. "Hello," she answered, not recognizing the number, hoping beyond hope it would be Zane. She'd listened to his CDs last night after Jonah had gone to bed and had been touched by Zane's voice as well as his heartfelt lyrics. His kiss had taken up most of her waking thoughts and had invaded her dreams. But she wasn't Cinderella, and she was silly if she believed anything could come of the two of them kissing.

"Hi. Is this Jeannette Williams?"

"Yes, it is," Jeannette answered warily, wondering if this was a sales call.

"This is Erika Traub, Dillon Traub's wife. We're friends of Zane."

Of course, Jeannette remembered Dillon.

"Is this a bad time?" Erika asked. "I know I'm calling on a holiday."

She couldn't imagine what Dr. Dillon Traub's wife could want with *her*. "No problem. My son and I were getting ready to go to the park. You just caught me."

"Good. Zane told me you were looking for a part-time position. He also said you're independent and wanted to get it on your own. But he knew I was looking for someone to help me."

"Help you? Do you need your house cleaned?"

Erika laughed. "No, I manage to do that myself, though sometimes I think the help would be nice. Zane told me you're a single mom trying to juggle two jobs and I know what that's like. I was a single mom for a while. He also said you're smart and seem organized. I need someone to help me with Frontier Days. Last year, Thunder Canyon Resort was the driving force for Frontier Days. This year, all the town's businesses are kicking in their fair share. I coordinated Frontier Days last year so the head of the town council asked me if I would do it again. Since I'm Dillon's office manager at the clinic, I decided to donate my services for Frontier Days but asked for a part-time helper in the budget for those few weeks before the celebration begins. Everyone on the fundraising and budget committee agreed. I just had to find the right person and I think you might be the one. It would include… It would include a variety of tasks—from having flyers printed to making schedules and contacting businesses downtown. Do you think you'd be interested?"

It sounded like a *wonderful* part-time job. "I work at LipSmackin' Ribs and my schedule varies from day to day. Would that be a problem?"

"No. You could fit in the work however you need to. Would you like to meet tomorrow and talk about it?"

"I'd love that. Jonah has preschool tomorrow morning. His sitter will pick him up afterward, so I'm free until the afternoon. What would be good for you?"

"Why don't you come over to our house after you drop off your son at school? I don't have to be at the clinic until ten. Let me give you my address."

As Erika rattled it off, Jeannette pictured the older section of town with restored row houses on many of the blocks. She was surprised Dr. Traub hadn't bought a place in a shiny new neighborhood. Maybe Zane's friends were ordinary people, like he seemed to be.

Only he wasn't.

"That would be great. Is there anything I should bring along?"

"You could write up a paragraph or so about your background. Nothing formal."

"Thank you for this opportunity. I really appreciate it."

"I'll be thanking you if you fit the bill. I'm already snowed under and Frontier Days is at the end of the month. I'll see you tomorrow. Have fun at the park."

"We will."

Jeannette put down the phone, thinking about what this job could mean. Granted, it was only temporary, but it would look great on her résumé. It might help her get a job doing something other than cleaning houses or serving ribs.

Too many dreams were floating around her head… all because of Zane Gunther.

Jeannette left the Traubs' house the next morning feeling as if she'd won the lottery. Erika liked her! She'd also liked the paragraph Jeannette had written about her work history, her patience with customers at LipSmackin' Ribs, her joy in being a mom.

As Jeannette climbed into her car, she looked back at the row house, its brick facing, blue trim, window boxes with purple mums. It was a charming house and Erika had told her she had refinished the floors herself after she'd bought it before she'd met Dillon. She explained Dillon wanted to move to someplace bigger, but her mom lived next door and they were very close.

Jeannette had thought about her relationship with Ed's parents. Although she'd lived in their home, sometimes she didn't know how close they were. Ever since Ed had died they'd been welcoming, but she felt some type of barrier between them. Maybe it was because Ed had been their connecting link. Now with him gone…

Sometimes Jeannette wondered if Mel and Edna didn't try to keep close to her simply because of Jonah. She hoped that wasn't so. She liked to think they cared about her as much as she cared about them. But then that had always been a problem she'd faced in relationships. After all, her dad had left and had never contacted her again. He'd never wanted kids. She'd overheard her mom arguing with him more than once about that and bills and responsibility. When Ed hadn't wanted to commit to getting married, Jeannette hadn't known whether to cut off the relationship or stick with it. But then she'd gotten pregnant, and the winds of fate had directed her life.

She wanted to direct her own life now. A good job

would come if she was determined and persistent enough. She was sure of it. Most of all, right now, she wanted to see Zane again. She had to thank him, didn't she? Edna would be picking up Jonah after preschool, so Jeannette pretty much had the day free until one-thirty.

She didn't only owe Zane her thanks, but she also owed him a pound of his favorite coffee. She could pick up the coffee and pastries at the Mountain Bluebell Bakery and drive up the mountain. Yes, she might surprise him, but he'd surprised her more than once. Maybe it was *her* turn.

During the ride to Zane's retreat, Jeannette was distracted, but not distracted enough that she didn't notice the beautiful scenery. Snowcapped peaks reached up to a more-than-blue sky. As she turned onto the rough lane that led to the log house, her car hit a few rocks that skittered into the brush. Although Zane's property wasn't as high in altitude as the peaks in the distance, there could be snow up here by mid-October. Did he want to get snowed in and continue shutting out the rest of the world? Would he consider her visit today an intrusion? She could be making a huge mistake. Still, she felt drawn to him in a way she'd never felt drawn to a man. Maybe that was just his charisma. Maybe that's why he was a star, and crowds cheered and stomped and wanted to get close to him any way they could. She didn't know, but she wanted to find out how he felt. Maybe she just wanted to show him he had a friend through a tough time in his life.

A friend? That's what you want to be?

She ignored the question.

After she parked in the gravel driveway in front of the garage, she studied the house under the porch. The blinds were always open because there were no neighbors. But even through the large picture window she couldn't see

Zane moving around inside. Maybe he'd gone into town for something. Maybe to make a call.

As soon as she slid out of her car clutching the coffee and pastries, she heard the thump of an ax on wood. She followed the sound around to the back where there was a huge brick patio and a shed. Zane was about ten yards from it with a stack of timber too large to use in a fireplace. A wide log slanted across a tree stump. Fascinated by Zane's tall, broad-shouldered stance, she watched the play of his muscles under his flannel shirt as he brought the ax up into position and slung it onto the log. The blade didn't quite split the wood and he swung it again, this time succeeding.

There was a lot of energy in that swing. Is this how he worked out his conflict? With pure physical labor? Was this the way he expressed emotion over what was happening to him?

Not wanting to come up behind him and startle him, she made a wide circle until she came within his line of vision. Then she smiled and held up the bag of pastries. "Muffins and danishes from the Mountain Bluebell Bakery. Are you interested?"

He stood expressionless for a moment, then broke into a grin. "Just passing through the neighborhood?" he teased.

"Do you mind?" she asked seriously. "If you don't want company, I can just leave the pastries on your kitchen table."

He whacked the ax into the tree stump, and she thought no man had ever looked more like he belonged out here.

"The right company is always welcome, especially when there's a bag of pastries in the offing. Breakfast was a long time ago." He came to join her.

"What time do you get up?" Once she'd asked the question she realized it was a personal one and pictures flashed in her head. Pictures of Zane in briefs, in boxers, in jogging shorts, in—

The sun was getting warmer but had nothing to do with the flush she felt heating her cheeks.

His green eyes twinkled as if he could read her thoughts. Well, almost twinkled. She wondered what he'd been like before all this had happened to him.

"I'm usually up before first light, at least here."

"And before?" He couldn't just swipe his past life away as if it wasn't there anymore.

He looked as if he wanted to, though. "It changed a lot. If I wasn't on tour, sometimes I'd stay up, writing all night. I have a music studio at my place in Nashville, so once I got into it, I'd forget about the time and just work. When I was on the road, I'd wind down for a couple of hours after the concert and then turn in."

"So you're a night owl *and* a morning person."

He motioned her around the house to the kitchen door. "I'd carry those for you, but I'm pretty dirty. I need to wash up."

When they reached the door, he put his hand on the doorknob and asked, "So what are *you?* Night owl or sunrise watcher?"

"I used to be a sunrise watcher. For the first couple of years, Jonah was up by six. But lately I'm turning into more of a night owl. After I get home from my shift, I find it hard to wind down."

While Zane went to the sink to wash up, she pulled two plates from the cupboard and set them on the table. It was odd being familiar with his house, but she'd been here so many times.

After Zane dried his hands, he nodded toward the coffee she'd brought. "Interested in a cup?"

"Sure. I've always put it away but I've never tasted it."

He filled the carafe with water and poured it into the back of the stainless steel unit. "So," he drawled, "if you weren't just in the neighborhood, you must have had a reason for driving up here."

"I came to thank you. Erika called me yesterday and we met this morning. She gave me the job as her assistant. Zane, I can't tell you what this means to me."

"You don't have to. I can see it on your face. I'm glad it worked out. Miss Independence that you are, I thought you might blow off Erika."

"I *never* would have done that. I mean, she's your friend. Even if she weren't, there's a big difference with getting a job on my own merit and having you pay the salary. Big, *big* difference."

While the coffee perked, Jeannette told him about the paragraph she'd written, the questions Erika had asked before she decided Jeannette had the position.

"Erika's a good judge of character. That's why she married my best friend." He smiled. "And that's why she hired you. I knew you were a slam dunk."

"Hardly. I wish I had more of an education."

"I know what you mean. I've always wanted to earn a degree."

"In what?"

Straight-faced, he responded, "Oceanography."

At her expression he laughed. "Music theory. I've never had any formal music training, and I'd like some. I might even like to learn how to play the sax."

"There's never enough time, is there?"

"I'm learning you have to make time for what's important."

The coffee spat and gurgled. The sun streamed in the kitchen window, illuminating the side of Zane's face. She *so* wanted to stroke his beard stubble. She *so* wanted to see laughter back in his eyes…a guitar in his hands.

He got that look she was coming to know that meant he wanted to kiss her. Then his jaw tightened and instead, he took a step back, plucked two mugs from the wooden tree on the counter and set them in front of the coffeepot. "Why don't you pull out whatever pastry you want first? I'm liable to eat the whole bag."

As she chose a cranberry-orange muffin and Zane began with a cheese danish, he asked about Jonah.

She related some of his antics in the park. "I'm still the kind of mom who doesn't want him climbing the jungle gym, but I know I can't prevent it. All I can do is show him how to do it safely."

"*You* climb the jungle gym?" Zane's amusement was obvious.

"I also slide down the sliding board. When you have kids, you find yourself doing a lot of things you never thought you'd do."

"Do you want more kids?"

She hadn't thought about that for the past few years. Having more kids hadn't seemed likely. "I think I would… with the right partner."

Neither of them could look away for a while, but finally Jeannette did. She was beginning to see those wispy dreams coalesce again, and that was just too dangerous. She popped up out of her chair, and like a waitress, picked up their plates and mugs and carried them to the sink. Zane stood, too, went over to the dishwasher and dropped their plates inside.

They were elbow to elbow, shoulder to shoulder, and Jeannette couldn't keep her heart from pounding much too fast. "Thank you again for convincing Erika to call me."

"It didn't take much convincing."

As they stood there, time seemed to stop. Jeannette said, "I didn't know if you'd want me here."

"Oh, I want you here." His voice was filled with something raw, something that excited her and scared her.

"But I don't know if we should be alone here," he added. "We're better off with Jonah around to keep us in line, to keep *me* in line."

"What if I don't want you to stay…in line?"

She hardly had time to take a breath until he mumbled, "Geez, Jeannette," and kissed her.

It had been years since a man had desired her. Zane's kisses took her to that special place all women wanted to go where passion became a real word rather than a fantasy in a novel. Zane's hands passed up and down her back, caressing her in a way that made her wish she was naked. She gripped his shoulders until he knew she was as excited as he was. They melted together as the kiss turned even more intense, more hungry, more full of what they both wanted. She wasn't thinking, only feeling. She wasn't searching for answers, just enjoying the moment.

But the moment had to end, and they both knew it. Maybe Zane knew it even better than she did. He broke away first and rubbed his jaw against her cheek as he held her. "Do you want to take a walk?"

She didn't want to leave the strength of his arms, but she knew she had to. Leaning back, she smiled. "A walk?"

His voice was still husky as he explained, "There's a trail out back that goes up the mountain a ways. Are you game?"

Oh, she was game. That was the problem.

A short time later, Zane maintained a slight distance between them as they walked side by side up the trail at the back of his property. Not touching her was damn hard. He felt as if he was coming alive after being in a numb state for the past few months. Was that why everything about her turned him on, from the swing of her hair to the cut of her jeans?

That kiss could have taken them to bed, *would* have taken them to bed if he hadn't stopped it. Or would Jeannette have stopped him?

He was back at the same old dilemma really. Now that she knew who he was, was she attracted to him as a man or was she attracted to Zane Gunther, with all the spangles and glitz that involved? He could either stop seeing her if he didn't want to risk anything else happening, or he could get to know her better.

The early September day was perfect for a hike. They didn't hurry, but rather stopped every once in a while to take in the view. The mountain vista was breathtaking, yet he found himself more enchanted by the woman beside him.

Reluctantly tearing his gaze from Jeannette's profile, Zane became more aware of his surroundings. Out of the corner of his eye he saw movement near a stand of scruffy pines. He capped Jeannette's shoulder and put his finger to his lips. She spied immediately what he pointed out—a mother elk and her calf.

She came closer to Zane and whispered near his ear, "Jonah would love this."

Her breath was an erotic tickle. He kept his arms at his sides so that he didn't enfold her in them and kiss her until the sun stopped shining. Her perfume or lotion or shampoo or whatever the hell it was held a hint of lavender. When he breathed it in, his stomach tightened and adrenaline rushed. They seemed to stand there, practically in each other's pockets, until the mama and baby lumbered off.

When Jeannette moved away, he felt as if he'd lost a

gigantic opportunity—to do *what* he didn't know. The feelings he was having were new and different and conflicted.

A few minutes later they came to a rise and they stopped. "Do you want to go on?" Jeannette asked.

Gesturing to an immense boulder, he said, "Why don't we sit for a couple of minutes?"

They settled side by side on the love seat-size boulder, looking down over the valley and the changing colors fall always delivered.

"Tell me about Jonah," Zane requested.

"You want to know about his father," Jeannette interpreted.

"I guess I do."

She pulled her knee up onto the rock and faced him more squarely. "I met him when I was working as a receptionist for an insurance company in Bozeman. He was one of the claims managers. At first we were just friends, but then our relationship became more serious." She sighed. "I wanted to get married, but Ed didn't. Maybe because both of my parents were gone then, I wanted to dig in roots and settle down, make a life, have a family. But I guess he didn't want to be tied down. He had been an only child and he'd told me more than once his parents had been overprotective and in some ways stifling when he wanted to try something new. The idea of marriage really seemed to spook him. Eventually I agreed to move in with him. I thought if I did, he'd see what marriage could be like."

"Did he change his mind?"

"No, not until…I got pregnant. He said we should plan the wedding. But he kept postponing a date until finally he insisted we wait until after the baby was born."

Zane's brows arched and he wondered what type of

man would propose *that* way. A scared one? "How did you feel about *that*?"

She took her arms from around her knee and met his gaze. He could see this was something she probably tried *not* to remember. "I felt he was giving himself an out, in case something happened."

"So your pregnancy was an accident?"

Jeannette hesitated and Zane wondered what that was about. "I've thought about this over and over again. I was always precise about birth control. I was using a patch that I changed once a week, and I faithfully did it on Sunday nights before the workweek started. I'm not exactly sure what happened. We went to Ed's parents for dinner one Sunday night. We stayed later than usual, and that week I just forgot. A few weeks later I couldn't keep any food down. If I hadn't had severe morning sickness and had to quit my job, Ed might still be alive."

So…she felt guilty and had regrets. Zane knew all about if-onlys and what-ifs. He wanted to put his arms around Jeannette now, but felt she was at another place, another time. "Tell me what happened," he said gently, curious about her in a way he'd never been curious about a woman.

Pushing her hair behind her ear, she looked out over the valley. "With only one salary coming in, we couldn't pay our bills. We'd gotten a bigger apartment when we'd moved in together and the rent was high. On top of that, Ed's hours were cut, so he took on a second job."

Zane could hear her voice shake a little and realized this was hard for her to tell. Because she felt her fiancé's death was her fault? Because getting pregnant might have been her fault? Because she couldn't control the morning sickness? He knew irrational ideas went through your head when tragedy struck.

"His second job," she went on, "was a six-to-midnight position at a convenience store that was open twenty-four hours. It was all he could find, and we desperately needed the money for the baby. I think he felt the job was beneath him. He hated it. I kept hoping I could get back to work soon and my symptoms were only temporary. But I was weak from not being able to keep any food down, and then I started spotting." She blushed a little as she revealed that detail as if it was too intimate to share. But it explained what came next. "My doctor threatened to hospitalize me. The insurance company didn't want me back if I was going to be out for a lot of sick days. They said I couldn't fulfill my duties, and I couldn't, the way I was."

"You were both trapped," Zane murmured.

"I guess we were. Then one night at two in the morning, I got a call from Mel, Ed's dad. Ed had been in an accident. He'd fallen asleep at the wheel and crashed into an abutment. He died on impact. I knew he was worn out and not getting enough sleep. The coroner told Mel and Edna he'd fallen asleep at the wheel and he wasn't wearing a seat belt. If only Ed had worn his seat belt."

She paused, obviously still bothered by the thought. Then she went on, "I was on bed rest so I didn't lose the baby and the doctor wouldn't even allow me to go to the funeral. I think he was afraid the stress of it, let alone being on my feet, would cause a miscarriage."

"Oh, Jeannette, I'm so sorry that you had to go through that."

She looked up at him, her eyes teary. "Edna and Mel were wonderful. In Bozeman I was depending on a friend who came in and got me lunch and made sure I was okay. After Ed died, Edna insisted I move in with her and Mel, so someone would be there twenty-four hours a day. She was great. They both were. I think it's their doing that Jonah was only a few weeks premature, that I didn't lose him. We lived with them until just a few months ago. But then I decided Jonah and I needed to be on our own. Ed's parents still aren't happy about it, but I feel I made the right decision."

They sat in silence for a good long time. Zane knew what he wanted to ask but wasn't sure he should ask it. Nothing ventured—

"You're not over it all yet, are you?"

She waited to answer and he didn't know if that was good or bad.

When she spoke, her voice was solemn. "I loved Ed. I was dreaming of a future with him. That was snatched away and I still feel guilty about my part in it. I'm with his parents often and that reminds me of everything that happened. But I have Jonah and his future to build, so I am trying to move on."

She gave him a quick sideways glance. "I haven't dated, though, because having a son makes me ten times more cautious and because…" After hesitating, she finished, "I just wasn't ready."

Zane knew that just because you put one foot in front of the other didn't mean you were really moving on. His notoriety, as well as his life as a singer, might be an obstacle between them. But her love of her fiancé and her guilt over his death could be a huge one, too.

Odds were, they didn't have a chance.

When Jeannette left Zane's, she didn't know what she felt—stirred up, emotional, in turmoil. After she'd told him about Ed, Zane had become quiet. The buzz was still there between them, but he wasn't acting on it. Neither was she. There seemed to be a wall between them.

Because he thought she was still in love with Ed? She was, wasn't she? Until she'd met Zane, that hadn't even been a question.

She and Zane weren't serious, so what did it matter? He would never get serious about her. After all, she was just a waitress at a rib joint, and not even a high-class rib joint. Wouldn't the tabloids have a field day with that? He was probably thinking the same thing.

She wished she knew exactly *what* he was thinking.

Her car felt a little odd when she started off, but she assumed that was because of the rough lane. However, before she'd gotten a quarter of the way down the mountain, her vehicle was listing to the right. Even though she'd never experienced it before, she knew she had a flat tire.

What was she going to do about a flat tire? She didn't know how to change it, and she didn't belong to the auto club. If she was late for her job at LipSmackin' Ribs, she could get fired. She crossed her arms over the steering wheel and put her head down for a moment. But then she lifted it and squared her shoulders, knowing what she had to do.

Deserting her car, she hiked up the lane to Zane's house, her purse swinging from her shoulder. Mel had told her that her tires were going bald. No wonder she'd gotten a flat. At Zane's door she hesitated and then knocked hard. He might have gone out back. He might be getting a shower. He might be glad she'd gone and didn't want to see her again.

When he opened his front door, surprise flickered in his eyes, but not much else.

She launched into an explanation. "I have a flat tire and I don't know how to change it. I can't be late for work because I need this job. I know you don't have a phone. Not that that would help me, because I don't belong to an auto club, but I thought maybe you'd know how to change a tire? I promise it's the last time I'll ask you for *anything*."

Suddenly he held up his hand. "Whoa! Slow down."

"I can't slow down or I'll be late."

He checked his watch. "What time do you have to be there?"

"One-thirty and it's already one." She stopped and took a deep breath. "But it'll take as long as it takes. I'm just hoping there will be somebody there to cover for me and Woody won't get too mad and fire me."

Zane was silent for a moment. Then he said, "Come with me." He opened the door wider so she could step inside.

"But my car…" She gestured down the mountain lane.

"Come on."

She followed him into the kitchen where he took something from a hook under a set of cupboards. Then he led her down the hall to the back of the house. They went through the laundry room to the garage.

He handed her the starter remote. "Take my SUV. After work, pick up Jonah and bring him back up here. I'll have your tire fixed and you'll be good to go." He eyed her thoughtfully. "Unless you and Jonah would like to stay for supper so I can use up some of that food you keep bringing me."

"I *can't* take your car!" She was astonished that he'd let her.

"Why not?"

"Do you trust me with it?"

"Dillon leased it for me. It's got so many bells and whistles it practically drives itself." He checked his watch. "It's either take my SUV or be late for work."

She knew Jonah would like to see Zane again. And he'd

love the backyard, with its grassy area, scrubby pines, woodshed and the possibility of sighting elk.

"I'll have to transfer Jonah's car seat to your SUV."

He shrugged, still dangling the starter remote.

"Thank you," she breathed gratefully as she took the key chain he offered. Then she stood on tiptoe and kissed his cheek. His beard stubble brushed against her lips and she liked the sensation. There was simmering desire in his eyes as she stepped back and went to the driver's door of his SUV.

He climbed in the passenger's side, pushed the button and his garage door opened. Moments later they were on their way. Glancing at his profile, her pulse raced. On her way to what, she didn't know.

But with Zane in the picture, whatever it was, it was going to be exciting.

Chapter Five

After work, Jeannette turned off the big vehicle—at least it was big to her—climbed out and ran up the steps to Mel and Edna's. Zane had transferred Jonah's car seat to the back of the SUV. She was eager to take Jonah to Zane's with her. Hopefully she could make a quick exit from here and they'd be on their way.

But the moment she stepped inside the house, she didn't know if "quick" was going to be possible. Mel had pushed the curtain aside and was looking out the window. "Did you buy a new car?"

She knew what he was thinking. There was no way she could afford one, especially not one like that. "No. I had a flat tire and a friend loaned me this."

"That must be some friend," Edna said, obviously having examined the vehicle, too. "It beeped when you were parking. It must have sensors on it."

"It *is* nice," Jeannette admitted, more impressed by

the fact that Zane had let her borrow it than by the type of vehicle it was.

"Am I gonna ride in it?" Jonah asked.

"You sure are. Your car seat's in the back."

Edna narrowed her eyes. "Is this a male friend who lent it to you? Jonah said something about a man coming over to the house and playing with him, putting puzzles together." She didn't sound pleased about that.

"Yes, it is a male friend, but I'm taking the SUV back tonight. He was going to put my spare tire on for me and I'm grateful for that. Maybe tomorrow I can have the old one fixed."

"The thing is," Mel said, "you shouldn't just buy *one* tire. You have to buy two or your alignment will be off."

Jeannette could hardly afford one tire, let alone two. That would really wreck her budget. Even though she'd gotten this job with Erika Traub, she had to be cautious and save as much as she could for when the job ended. Still, because babysitting Jonah would affect Mel and Edna, she really had to tell them about it. "I found another part-time job, but it's only going to last a month."

"That hardly seems worth taking it," Edna decided.

"Oh, I think it is. Erika Traub hired me to work with her on Frontier Days. It'll be good experience for my résumé."

"Well," Edna said, exchanging a look with Mel, "Erika Traub. She married that doctor whose brother just got married in June. I think his name is Corey Traub. And another brother Ethan opened an office here. Something about searching for oil in shale. That family has money from what I hear."

Jeannette didn't want to get pulled into gossip about the Traubs because there was plenty floating around. She'd heard in the restaurant today that Jackson Traub had returned to Thunder Canyon to work with Ethan. In the same conversation she'd heard their sister Rose's name mentioned. Apparently she'd moved to Thunder Canyon, too.

Jeannette looked to her son. "Are you ready? You can tell me all about school while we take the SUV back."

Jeannette helped Jonah with his jacket and, as he was saying goodbye to Mel, Edna asked in a low voice, "Where did you meet this man?"

Knowing she couldn't say too much, she answered, "He's renting one of the houses I cleaned."

"So this has been going on for a while?"

She was about to say there was nothing going on, but that certainly wasn't true, not after the kisses she'd shared with Zane. "No, it hasn't."

"You have to be careful," Edna warned her. "You have a child to think about."

Almost bristling, she short-circuited a curt reply. "I always put Jonah first. You know that." She knew Edna meant well.

After a long assessing look, Edna nodded.

With hugs all around, they were out the door, Jonah's backpack swaying on his shoulders.

The SUV was high, so she had to help him up into his car seat. After he was buckled in, he said, "I like this car."

"I do, too, but it's not ours. We're taking it back to Zane so we can pick up our car."

"We're going to *his* house?"

"Yes, we are."

Twenty minutes later, Jeannette pulled into Zane's driveway and helped her son out of the SUV. Zane came around from the back of the house, a broad smile on his face, a child-size version of his Stetson in his hand.

When Jonah saw him, he ran to him.

Zane caught him, plopped the hat on Jonah's head and lifted him high in the air. "Howdy, partner. How would you like to play some football?"

Jonah looked toward his mom. "I got a hat like his!" In the next breath, he asked, "Can I play football?"

Zane added, "I got a football that's also just his size so he won't get hurt. You can play, too, if you want to." Zane's arched brows said he'd like to play at more than one thing and Jeannette felt her cheeks heating in the cooler evening air.

"I've never played football."

"We won't hold that against her, will we, Jonah?"

Her son shook his head vigorously, the hat toppling sideways.

He straightened it and assured Zane, "She's good at catching."

"We'll see about that."

As they rounded the house, Zane said, "There wasn't a good reason to have your old tire fixed. I got you two new ones and a tune-up, too."

Jeannette couldn't keep from blurting out her worry. "I can't afford a tune-up right now. The tires—"

Zane took hold of her shoulder. "Slow down. It's not your fault you got a flat. My driveway needs work. And the tune-up is on me. I didn't want your car giving you trouble. It was running rough and you wouldn't want to get stranded. I would have changed the oil myself, but I didn't have the supplies I needed here."

Already Jeannette knew that Zane was the type of man who took other people's responsibility on *his* shoulders. But she couldn't let him feel responsible for her. "I'm going to pay you for the tires. It might take me a while, but I *will* pay you."

"I'm not going to be able to talk you out of doing that, am I?"

"No."

He gave her a look that wasn't agreement but was filled with respect. His arm around her shoulders, he said, "Let's play ball."

Jeannette didn't know much about catching a football, but she sure was catching something else. Zane Gunther fever? She felt hot whenever she was around him. She felt so much that surprised her, so much she wanted to run away from, so much she wanted to grab on to. It was all confusing and she didn't know the right tack to take. But tonight, if this was all about Jonah, she'd be safe.

At least she hoped so.

An hour later as the sun slipped in back of the mountains, Jeannette put her hands on her knees and tried to catch her breath. The football game had been rough-and-tumble and fun. Jonah's giggles had almost made her want to cry. She hadn't seen him this happy in a long time. Zane had tossed him the ball and tackled him and let Jonah tackle *him,* too. The roughhousing was just what a four-year-old needed. Zane had tackled her a couple of times, and those times with his arms around her, his body pressing down on hers, she'd almost wanted to forget she was a mother and make mad, passionate love right there in Zane's backyard.

But, thank goodness, she couldn't forget.

After they went back into the house, Jeannette took Jonah to the hall bathroom to clean up. After the football game, he'd plopped his newly acquired hat on his head again. He was still washing his hands when she smelled something good permeating the whole house. Jonah said he could finish up on his own and he'd wash his hands "real good," so she went to the kitchen to see if she could help with supper.

Zane was standing at the stove, flannel shirtsleeves rolled up. "I'm making my version of goulash. Think Jonah will like it? It's sautéed vegetables, thin sliced beef, lots of tomatoes and then we pour it over noodles."

"Tomatoes and noodles. He'll love it."

Zane grinned at her and they just stared at each other, trembling awareness between them. He broke eye contact first, went to the refrigerator and took out a beer. Unscrewing the top, he handed it to her. "Here. Go sit on the sofa and relax. You've been on your feet all afternoon, and just played a championship game of football."

"I want to help."

"No need. I bought one of those inside basketball games for Jonah. You can watch him toss the ball in or help him. Either way, you don't have to cook. I'll let you know when it's ready."

After a moment of really studying him, noticing every crinkle around his eyes, the tilt of his lips, the kindness in his expression, she asked, "Do you know you're a very nice man?"

He scowled at her. "Nice? I'll have to live that one down somehow. No self-respecting cowboy wants to be called *nice.*"

She laughed. "I could think of a few other words, too."

Again, she knew they were both remembering kisses and how their bodies felt pressed together.

"Like?" he prodded.

"Like all those words the tabloids call you—hot, sexy, hunky."

She was surprised when his cheeks seemed to turn a little ruddy. "I shouldn't have asked," he mumbled.

Taking a few steps closer to him, she stood on tiptoe

and kissed his cheek. "But you're nice, too, and that matters a lot to me."

"You know what I want to do right now, don't you?" he growled.

"I can guess," she said a little shakily. "But we have a pint-size chaperone here."

"Hey, Mom! Come see this."

"I think he found the basketball net."

And not a moment too soon, she thought.

Jeannette couldn't help remembering Ed while she sat on the sumptuous teal-colored leather sofa and stared at the fire in the floor-to-ceiling, native rock fireplace. Her feet sank into the plush area rug with a western motif. What kind of father would he have been? She hadn't seen him around children much. She'd known he hadn't wanted to think about them, even about settling down, for another few years. But that didn't mean he wouldn't have been a good father. That didn't mean he wouldn't have loved Jonah exactly the way a father should. She focused again on Jonah, tossing a Nerf ball into the child-size basketball net.

It wasn't too long before Zane called them into dinner. He had a salad ready to go along with the goulash and a loaf of crusty bread.

As Jonah dug in, Jeannette asked, "Who's bringing in your groceries now?"

"I went to that new grocery store in the mall on the same lot with the movie theaters. It's so busy the cashiers don't even look up when they check you out. With my hat and beard, no one takes a second look. It's amazing really, how blind people are when they think you're ordinary. They don't expect to see me, so they don't see me. Hiding in plain sight is sometimes the best way to go."

"I play hide-and-seek," Jonah said proudly, proving he was listening.

"There are lots of trees out back. Sometime you come up here, we might have to try hide-and-seek out there."

Jonah swiped the back of his hand across his mouth. "I'm done, Mom."

She checked his plate. "I guess you like Zane's cooking. You did a good job."

"If you're tired of playing basketball, there's a new box of crayons, paper and a coloring book on the TV stand, bottom shelf. You're welcome to them."

Jonah quickly slid off his chair and ran back to the living room, pulling the crayons, paper and book off the shelf and settling on the floor.

Jeannette knew Zane was a big star and probably had enough money to buy the moon. But whether she was attracted to him or not, she didn't want to feel beholden to him. She also didn't want him to think he had to buy Jonah presents to gain her son's affection.

She picked up her own dish, stood and went to the sink.

She heard the scrape of the legs of Zane's chair and the sound of his boot soles on the tile. She could practically feel his body heat as he stood behind her and asked, "What's wrong?"

If she said nothing, they could just go on enjoying the evening. Pretending what? That they were a family?

The fact she was even entertaining the idea made her go cold inside. This could never work. He was a star. She was a single mom struggling to make ends meet. She could see the headline now. IS THE WAITRESS A GOLD DIGGER? IS SHE AFTER ZANE GUNTHER'S MONEY? Sometimes she couldn't even figure out if she was in awe of Zane because he *was* a country singer who'd made it big, or simply because of the intense attraction between them. How could she ever know?

"Jeannette?" he asked.

"There's a lot on my mind."

"There's something *particular* on your mind."

She put down her dish and ran her hand across her forehead, ruffling her bangs. "I don't know how to say this because it will sound ungrateful."

He put his hands on her shoulders and nudged her around toward him. "Tell me."

"I appreciate the new tires and the tune-up. I really do. But they weren't in my budget for at least another six months."

"I told you, you don't have to pay me back."

"I *do* have to pay you back. I wouldn't accept something like that even if we were—"

"Dating?" he filled in.

She was getting in deeper and didn't know what to do about it. "I knew this was going to come out all wrong."

"Keep going. What else is clicking through your head?"

His steady green eyes wouldn't let her look away. "I can't just go out and buy Jonah toys or a hat on a whim. I wish I could, but I can't. We make do because we have to. Everything you bought him to play with here is wonderful, but I guess I want you to realize it's your ease with him that matters, the fact you want to play with him that matters. You don't have to buy anything to make him happy."

"I thought getting him something to do would be a good thing. And every cowboy needs a hat," he added with one of those irresistible smiles that could disarm an audience of twenty thousand.

"I appreciate all of it. But I don't want to feel—"

"Like what? It's not like I bought you diamonds."

She could see he was taking her concerns to heart and that touched her. She clasped his arm. "Playing football with Jonah was plenty to make him happy. Giving me a beer and telling me I could relax while you cooked dinner was plenty to make *me* happy. Can you see that?"

The way Zane was looking at her said he *could* see that, and maybe a whole lot more. He moved in a little closer and caressed her shoulder. "Jeannette."

She knew he would have kissed her. He would have made it quick and thorough and Jonah would have never known.

But suddenly, both of them were startled by a sound coming from the loft, the sound of guitar strings being plucked. Jeannette saw immediately that even those tentative notes affected Zane. Had he even picked up his guitar since he'd been here? He said he hadn't been able to hear lyrics or the music in his head. But did that mean that he hadn't played, either? Did the plucking of those strings remind him of his last concert?

Emotion passed over his face in an instant until a mask settled into place, a mask that said no one would know what he was feeling. Still, he moved quickly, and so did she, toward the stairs. He took the steps up to the loft ahead of her and she didn't know what was going to happen. But she did know who was making that sound. Jonah loved to explore and she should have checked on him. She should have made sure he was coloring.

What would Zane's reaction be? Would he be angry? Would her son be hurt from this evening that had gone so well up until now?

In the loft, Jeannette took a second to take it all in—Jonah sitting by the guitar on the floor, his fingers inquisitive on the strings. Zane's scowl was ferocious. Because her son had ventured into sacred territory? The sight of

Jonah at Zane's guitar must have reminded him of the tragedy that had happened, the career he was letting go of, the gift of music he was no longer capable of using. She was about to take a step forward between Zane and her son. But then she saw Zane's expression change. He took a deep breath and reached over Jonah, lifting the guitar out of his grasp.

Seeing her son's obvious disappointment, Zane laid the guitar on the desk and crouched down beside him. "The next time you come, maybe I'll have some blocks here for you to play with. Do you like blocks?"

"I like LEGOs," Jonah said with a little uncertainty.

Jeannette knew it was time to step in for lots of reasons. "Jonah, this loft is off-limits for you. This is Zane's private place. You know better than to get into someone else's things without permission."

Jonah looked at her and she nodded to Zane.

With a sigh, Jonah stared Zane right in the eye. "I'm sorry."

Zane's expression gentled even more as he straightened Jonah's hat. "It's okay. Everybody steps into territory they shouldn't once in a while."

Jeannette said to Jonah, "Go on downstairs and clean up those art supplies. We have to go. You have school tomorrow."

"Do we have to?" he whined.

"We have to. Go on now."

Jonah pushed up from his kneeling position on the floor, took a look at Zane and then at his mom and went down the stairs.

The awkwardness between her and Zane came from a lot of things, but she decided to tackle the most likely one. "It wasn't okay for him to touch your guitar."

"He's a kid and he was curious."

"Yes, he was. But he has to know boundaries. When we lived at Edna and Mel's, they would often let him do things that he shouldn't. Then it was that much harder for me to reinforce the rules."

"He seems to listen to you."

"He's had a lot of practice." She paused and added, "And the whole blocks thing, Zane. That's exactly what I was talking about. You can't turn around and buy him something else, especially when he's done something wrong."

"Geez, Jeannette, it's just blocks. They don't cost much and—"

"They would probably cost me a couple of hours' worth of tips. It's not much to *you,* but it is to *me.* We live in different worlds, Zane."

"And that bothers you?"

"Doesn't it bother *you?*" Of course, why should it? Kisses weren't commitment. Kisses didn't have to lead to anything more.

She shook her head. "I can guess you're used to uncomplicated and not getting involved in anything messy. My life is messy, Zane. I'm a single mom with a son, bills to pay and jobs to keep. I should have known better than to—"

"Bring me coffee and pastries?" he suggested wryly.

She avoided Zane's knowing gaze. "Yes." Then she glanced down the stairs. "I'd better get down there before he delves into something else. That's what four-and-a-half-year-olds do. They explore and they get attached and they can get hurt really easily. I can't let Jonah get hurt any more than he already has when he lost his father."

Before Zane could remind her that Jonah had never known his dad, before his probing gaze saw that she was afraid of getting hurt, too, before his powerful male presence convinced her to stay longer, she hurried down the stairs to her son, knowing leaving Zane's house was the best thing she could do for both of them.

On Friday, Jeannette felt as if she needed wheels on her sneakers. She'd worked an eight-hour shift yesterday to cover for someone who had gotten sick, and she had an eight-hour shift again today. This was her good tips night, she hoped. LipSmackin' Ribs had had a crowd all day. Tonight, however, she couldn't deliver food fast enough. Yet in the midst of all of it, the past few days she'd still thought about Zane and longed to see him again, although she knew it would be a waste of time. Then again she understood it wasn't time she was worried about wasting. Jonah had presented Zane with a crayon drawing before they'd left. She was worried about her feelings *and* Jonah's.

She hustled to a table of newcomers who sat under a huge poster of a rack of the restaurant's barbecued ribs. They didn't even want to study the menu. The two men leered at her, told her just to bring on the ribs and anything else she might want to deliver. One of the men, Bob Collins, who had a heavy red beard and a baseball cap turned backward, came in for lunch regularly. He always made sure to sit in her station and she dreaded waiting on him. She'd mentioned some of his remarks to her manager, but Woody hadn't been concerned. She tried to let Collins's comments fly over her head. She pretended not to hear them and was as professional as a waitress could be, even though she knew he stared at her belly when her shirt shifted, even though she could feel his gaze on her back, or lower, as she walked away.

As she headed for the kitchen with the orders, she heard

a whistle. Not like a wolf whistle, but more like a whistle to call a dog. When she turned, she saw Jasper Fowler motioning to her. He was the crotchety old owner of the Tattered Saddle, an antique shop in Thunder Canyon. He usually didn't say two words to her, just grumbled his order and snapped the menu shut as if he was angry at it. She'd delivered his order of ribs about ten minutes ago and as she approached him, she saw his meal was half-eaten.

"These ain't as good as usual," he said with a scowl. "I wanna talk to the manager."

Woody was usually busy supervising the kitchen. She was afraid if she interrupted him he'd be displeased with her, so she tried to appease the old man. "Is there anything I can help with? I could bring you another serving."

"No. I need to speak to Woody. *Now.*"

If she didn't do something, Mr. Fowler was going to make a scene. Woody would appreciate that even less than being interrupted. So she assured the antique shop owner, "I'll see if I can find him."

When she went to the kitchen, she found Woody studying the computer at a back corner. "Mr. Paulson."

Woody pressed a key and then looked up from his keyboard. "This better be good, Williams. I'm trying to close out the night."

"There's a customer who's unhappy with the food. He asked to see you. It's Jasper Fowler."

Woody's face changed from annoyance to…worry? When he didn't move for a few seconds or say anything, she explained, "I offered to get him another serving, but he insisted I call you."

Woody stood. "You did the right thing. Go back to your customers. I'll take care of Fowler."

Relieved, Jeannette hurried back to Fowler's table.

"He'll be right out," she told him. Then she rushed to the new customers the hostess had seated.

She was waiting for them to decide what they wanted to order when she noticed Woody at Fowler's table. The two of them seemed to be having an intense conversation. Very intense.

About the food?

She heard the name Swinton, then knew the two men weren't talking about ribs. Arthur Swinton had run for the office of mayor of Thunder Canyon against Bo Clifton. After Bo had won, the town found out that Swinton had been embezzling funds from the city. He'd gone to jail, but in July had suffered a heart attack and died. Why were Woody and Fowler talking about him?

Woody saw her glance their way and they lowered their voices. The clatter of dishes, the chatter of customers, the movement of diners coming and going muffled their conversation and she couldn't hear anything else. Not that she wanted to. Not that it was any of her business.

She took the orders at her table, glad her shift was almost ending, glad the day was practically over and she could go home with Jonah.

A half hour later she was getting the empty tables ready for the next day when Woody appeared by her side. "Can I talk to you for a minute?"

"Sure," she said, wanting to get home, yet needing to have her boss's approval, too.

"I appreciate the way you handled Fowler. You have good people skills."

"Thank you."

He studied her assessingly. "I know you have a kid. I know you're always willing to work an extra shift. Money's tight?"

"Most of the time," she admitted, seeing no reason to lie.

"How would you like to earn some extra money?"

Her radar went on high alert, but she attempted to be nonchalant. "By working more shifts?"

"Not exactly." He glanced around and saw no one else was in earshot. "I need somebody to apply for a job at the Rib Shack. I'd like to know whether or not waitresses might have access to DJ's recipes. I'd also like to know what new items he has planned for his menu, and when that new menu will go into effect. I'd pay you your salary here, cover your tips, plus add five hundred bucks to it. If you could get in at DJ's then you could report back to me. I'd only need you in there for a week or two, just until you got the lowdown on what was happening there."

Jeannette was absolutely appalled. Yes, she needed money, but she would *not* be a spy. The problem was, if she said no, she might lose her job. The only way to know was to ask Woody outright. "If I say 'No, I don't want to do that,' will I lose my job here?"

Woody contemplated her question, gave her the once-over and studied two other waitresses who were younger and scurrying to get home for the night. "You're a good waitress, Jeannette. You know how to handle people, you know how to work, you're dependable and my customers like you. So…if you keep your mouth shut about this, if you pretend I never asked you the question or made you the offer, I'll still consider you a valued employee." He waited a few beats and then asked, "Did this conversation ever happen?"

"What conversation?" she asked, completely serious.

Woody nodded. "Good. Now go ahead and get home to your son. If anybody wimps out next week, I'll make sure you get her shift."

Jeannette knew she should be grateful, yet she had a terribly unsettled feeling in her stomach. She felt sullied in some way. Yet for her sake and Jonah's, she had to keep silent.

Later that night, after Jonah was in bed, she thought about her conversation with Woody all over again. She shouldn't keep dwelling on it. She should put it out of her head. But still, that was hard to do.

She was slipping on her nightgown when her phone rang. It was after ten and she was afraid something might have happened with Mel or Edna. She snatched up the phone without checking the caller ID. But it wasn't Mel or Edna's voice she heard after she answered.

"Jeannette? It's Zane."

"I didn't expect to hear from you."

"No, I guess you didn't."

She heard voices in the background. "You're not at home?"

"No, I'm at Dillon's. I can't call you from my place. Remember?"

She remembered. She remembered everything about Zane from his thick brown lashes and beard-stubbled sexy jawline to the pain in his eyes from the tragedy he thought was his fault, to his smile when he was playing with Jonah.

Let's not forget his desire, a little voice reminded her, as if she needed to be reminded of that.

"I remember." She waited for him to tell her why he was calling.

"I thought about what you said—how in the past I probably didn't want a relationship that was messy or complicated. That was true."

"Was?" She could hardly breathe because her heart had started beating way too fast.

"Look, I'll be honest. I don't know where this is going. But I do know I want to see you again. I want to spend some time with you…and Jonah. Can you be open to that?"

Whatever she answered now could change the course of her life in so many ways. Was she open to a relationship with Zane? Could she forget about Ed and move on? Could she risk getting hurt?

Taking a deep breath and making a decision, she asked, "What do you have in mind?"

Chapter Six

"What did she say?" Dillon asked as he came into his living room from the kitchen.

Zane's hand was still on the cordless phone although he'd ended his call moments before. "She wasn't so sure at first. But she agreed to come up Monday evening and camp out overnight. Maybe she's willing because it's an experience she wants Jonah to have. I'm not sure."

"And what happens after Monday night?"

"Well, believe it or not, I'm going to babysit on Tuesday. Jonah doesn't have preschool and Jeannette has to work. She's helping Erika in the morning and then she's waitressing at LipSmackin' Ribs in the evening."

Erika came down the stairs then and looked from one man to the other. "What are you two plotting?"

At one time Zane would have responded with a chuckle and a joke. But now everything seemed different. Everything *was* different. Jeannette wasn't just a woman he wanted to get lucky with and then leave in the morning. Yes, he wanted to take her to bed. But he also wanted to spend time with her and Jonah as if they were a family. That was so strange to him. He'd never quite had these feelings before.

"Not plotting, *planning*," he protested. "I'm setting up a campout with Jeannette and Jonah. You could help me plan the menu. I'm hoping to make it through the grocery store another time without anyone recognizing me."

"No one has until now," Erika reminded him.

"I know. But if I start feeling too free, a tabloid journalist will turn up right under my nose."

"Thunder Canyon isn't your average town," Dillon assured him. "Folks here could rally around you."

Zane shook his head. "I don't have that kind of faith anymore, Dillon. All these years of signing autographs and talking to fans and having meals interrupted, I haven't minded one bit. They put me where I am. But now with Ashley's death, everything has turned ugly. This leave of absence my lawyer suggested is probably a good thing. If I was up on stage, I don't know if I'd remember the lyrics to my songs. But on the other hand, it's keeping me away from audiences, from music, from my band, from friends in the business. If my lawyer knew I'd told Jeannette everything that had happened—"

"How did she react?" Erika asked.

"She wanted to know my side."

"What more could you ask?" Dillon wondered.

Zane knew the answer to that. He wanted to take her to bed. He wanted to go out in public with her. He wanted to take Jonah to an amusement park and not have reporters hound them.

But most of all, he wanted Jeannette to be able to withstand the glaring spotlight of dating someone famous.

Maybe that was just too much to ask.

"It's a real tent, Mom!" Jonah said, obviously excited, as he looked inside and outside and all around it, the hat Zane gave him tilting to one side on his head.

"As opposed to a make-believe tent?" she teased.

Zane was showing her son how the flap attached with Velcro to the side.

Jonah darted inside again and yelled, "We even have sleeping bags. Mine has trains on it. Can I try it?"

"Go ahead," Jeannette called to him. Then she cast a probing look at Zane. "You told me you already had the tent."

"I did. Dillon and I used it a couple of times. When I first got here, the house seemed confining. We slept in the mountains for a few nights."

"And the sleeping bags?"

"I had two of them. I bought one for Jonah. With a kid-size one, he'll stay warmer."

She couldn't fault him for his caring.

She was standing a few feet from Zane where he'd set up lawn chairs on the patio around a fire pit. He crossed to her, took both her hands in his and squeezed them gently. Of course, she'd dated men before. Of course, men had touched her before, although Ed had been reserved in that regard and she'd just accepted that because there were so many other good things about their relationship. However, she could tell Zane was a man who liked to touch, who liked to show affection, who didn't deny his desire. As he held her hands now and gazed into her eyes, she felt like the most special woman on earth. That feeling scared her as well as bowled her over. Heat crept through her from his skin on hers.

"I have lots of money, Jeannette. Right now I don't care one whit about it. I understand your concern about toys and the like. I get that. You don't want me to buy Jonah's affection and you don't want Jonah to be spoiled, thinking a new toy will give him any sustaining happiness. I didn't spend a lot of money for this campout, but I did want Jonah to be comfortable. And I did want us to have an enjoyable night. So can you just enjoy this and not analyze it too much?"

He was also asking her not to analyze their relationship, not to analyze what was happening between them, but just to live in the moment. "It's hard for me to stop worrying and thinking and planning and just live for now. Usually I don't have the time to watch a sunset, or even to spend an evening like this."

"But you took the time tonight."

"Because I wanted to be with you," she admitted.

The look he gave her almost made her breath hitch in anticipation of another stolen kiss.

"I'm glad you're here," he said in a low, sexy drawl that made her wonder what he might whisper in her ear during a long, dark night.

He let go of her hand and slipped his arm around her. She leaned into him as they faced the sunset, purples and golds melting into the blue, stretching around the golden sun as it began its descent. It was beautiful. But she was even more aware of the man beside her. He'd worn a dark green T-shirt tonight with his jeans, and a heavy flannel shirt that he'd left unbuttoned. Even through her jacket, she could feel his body heat and liked his protective arm surrounding her.

Zane was taller than Ed had been, more broad-shouldered. There was a strength in him she'd never felt from Ed, an inner confidence that was as magnetic as the rest of him.

She felt guilty for making comparisons. She'd loved Jonah's father. She still felt connected to him in so many ways and always would be. Is that why she was resisting the absolute pull of Zane's personality? Of the sexual relationship they could have if she let down her walls, stopped asking questions and forgot about being responsible?

"You were thinking," Zane accused her with a twinkle of amusement in his eyes. "Stop that for tonight. That's an order."

She laughed. "Yes, sir. No thinking heavy thoughts tonight."

She suspected he would have kissed her then, but Jonah emerged from the tent, his smile infectious.

"Ready for hot dogs, veggies and dip and s'mores?" Zane asked, moving toward the shed to find wood for the fire pit.

Jonah watched in wonder as Zane laid the fire and lit it, warning him it was something children should never do. Jeannette smiled at his firm tone, his understanding that kids mimicked adults. He would make a wonderful father.

Don't think about that, she warned herself. *Don't think about his world tours or his lifestyle or the women he's dated in the past. No thinking!*

As they sat around the fire cooking hot dogs, the night was perfect with its dazzling stars, full moon and cold nip in the air. Zane told Jonah stories about growing up in Texas, about his friend Dillon riding the school bus with him. He talked about trading lunches, sitting in the kitchen with his mom eating macaroni and cheese and listening to her read to him about faraway places. Through

Zane's conversation with Jonah, Jeannette learned so much about him, and still she wanted to know more.

The s'mores were sticky and gooey and totally delicious. When had a chocolate bar smashed between toasted marshmallows and graham crackers tasted so good? More than once Zane ran his thumb over a smudge of marshmallow on her lip, a brush of chocolate on her chin. Inside, she felt as gooey as one of those marshmallows and knew if Jonah wasn't there, she and Zane would be prone in that tent, doing more than sleeping.

Jonah counted stars and Zane pointed out constellations until her son was yawning and could hardly keep his eyes open. She took him inside the house to wash up and get ready for bed, letting him wear his sweatshirt and jeans instead of pajamas. After all, that was part of the fun of camping out.

She'd settled Jonah in his sleeping bag with a battery powered lantern not far away when Zane peeked his head into the tent. "We'll be right outside, cowboy, in case you need us."

Jonah gave Zane a thumbs-up sign, and Zane chuckled. A few minutes later, after a good-night kiss and another hug, Jeannette sat by the fire with Zane, staring into it. She cast a sideways glance at Zane's profile and saw he was looking pensive.

"Jonah had a good time tonight. Thank you."

"He's a terrific kid."

"He loved your stories. I could tell."

"I needed somebody new to tell them to. He was a great audience."

Zane was saying all the right things, giving her all tactful responses. She wanted to probe a little deeper and didn't know if he'd let her do it, but she decided to try. "Only one thing was missing."

"What was that?" He looked at her now, studying her.

"Singing songs around the campfire."

Zane shook his head and gave her a don't-go-there look.

"Tell me how you began singing." That seemed safe enough. He'd left out all references to that in his childhood.

"You aren't going to give up, are you?" he growled.

"Give up? On what? I'm just making conversation."

He gave a sound halfway between a grunt and a snort. Then he gave in to her curiosity. "My mom worked long hours waitressing, just like you. Only she worked at a family diner that was more conventional than LipSmackin' Ribs."

Jeannette knew he didn't exactly approve of her job there, but she kept silent, waiting for him to go on.

"She *loved* country music. While she was getting a late supper for the two of us, I'd imitate country singers I'd heard. She got a kick out of that, but she told me I needed to develop my own style and write my own songs if I really wanted to be good. So I did. Whenever I could get near an instrument, I would play. I was pretty good at picking out a song by ear on the piano. There was one at school and I'd often stay late to use it. But then one Christmas, Dillon got me a guitar. Mom and I didn't have much, but Dillon's family did. He was thoughtful, even when we were kids. That guitar really opened up the world of music for me. I could play or write lyrics whenever I wanted."

"So you're completely self-taught?"

"Sure am."

The wind whistled in the pines and Jeannette shivered. She should have brought a heavier jacket.

"Are you cold?"

"Just a little. I'm fine."

"No, if you're cold, you're not fine. Hold on a minute.

I'll be right back." He was, a few minutes later, with a thick blanket. He moved his chair closer to hers and tossed the blanket over the two of them. "How's that?"

The warmth of their body heat combining under the blanket was utterly intimate. "That's good. I'll warm up fast."

When he cocked his head and gazed into her eyes, his expression became…intense. He took her hand and intertwined their fingers under the blanket.

They sat there that way for a little while, until she asked, "What motivated you to succeed?"

"Other than the fame or the money?" he joked.

"Yes. I don't think that was your motivation."

"You're wrong about that. I wanted to give my mom a better life. But there was something else, too."

"Some*one* else?" she asked perceptively.

"Dang, that woman's intuition. A man can't keep any secrets."

She gave his hand a squeeze. "Do you want to? Keep them, I mean."

Without removing his focus from the fire, he responded, "You've got to understand something, Jeannette. I think men have different defenses than women. Women like to talk, but men like to fix problems. If something went wrong in their past and they can't fix it, they don't like to talk about it."

She understood completely. Everybody had walls, men and women. But maybe a self-sufficient man who wanted to be the best at everything had a harder time than some in jumping over them. Again, she just waited. Either they got closer or they didn't. It was his choice as much as hers.

He must have realized that because he sighed, then said, "Her name was Beth Ann. She was my high school sweetheart and we thought we'd be in love forever. At least

I did. She wanted to get married out of high school, but I wanted to be able to support a family. To do that, I had to be able to get a singing gig at more than the downtown tavern. So she moved with me to Nashville."

"She was supportive?"

"I thought she was. We both had jobs during the day and then I had gigs at night, wherever I could find them. She came to every one of them. But looking back now, I think *that's* the life she wanted. I don't think she ever thought I'd make it. I'm not sure she wanted me to make it."

"Oh, Zane, how long did it take to find *that* out?"

"Years. After years of small gigs, a producer heard my demo. One night, he came to hear me sing. After that, life started moving fast. I made a CD. It did really well, and I won my first award from a cut on that album. I proposed to Beth Ann and she accepted, and I thought we were going to have the life we were always meant to have. But I was on the road while she was planning the wedding. She came to a couple of the concerts along the way, was backstage with me and even helped me outfit my first bus. But a couple of weeks before the wedding, she gave me my ring back. She said she couldn't sit home alone while I went on tour, that she wouldn't be a single mom with an absent dad. Her father had been a trucker and not home very much. She didn't want that for any kid of hers. On top of that, she said she couldn't stand to watch women look at me the way only *she* wanted to look at me."

"She was young."

"I guess. But you're not a whole lot older. And I've met women along the way who felt the same."

She never thought about or felt the age difference between her and Zane which was about eleven years. In researching him, she'd learned he was thirty-nine. "Have you had a serious relationship since?"

Slowly, he shook his head. "After Beth Ann called off our wedding, I had to make a choice. I could have given it all up. She might have married me then and maybe I didn't love her enough to sacrifice my dreams. I chose a career—a demanding one that, in the long run, didn't give me time to think about anything or anyone else."

Jeannette doubted that was the whole truth because he was the type of man who cared. But even if it was so... "But now you're giving it all up after you worked so hard and sacrificed so much."

"I don't know what I'm doing. The lyrics and music just aren't in my head anymore. More important, they're not in my heart."

Jeannette felt his pain and disillusionment and frustration with everything turning out the way it had. She leaned close to him, and he wrapped his arm around her. His hand caressed her shoulder and when she turned to look at him, his lips were a murmur away from hers.

"You're so damn tempting," he muttered. "You smell so good. And you understand too much. You have a son and I should be pushing you away instead of pulling you close."

"But?" she asked breathlessly.

"But I'm going to do this anyway."

His lips pressed into hers for only a few seconds before his tongue slid inside her mouth. She opened to him, wanting to let her walls down, too. What would it take to give in, to give up, to fall in love again?

She couldn't figure out the answers because she couldn't think when Zane kissed her. A heady intoxication tilted her world until the stars danced above, until the moon shone only for them, until the darkness folded them into its embrace. Being here with Zane was all that she wanted. Having his hands in her hair, his lips taking and giving desire filled her whole being until nothing else mattered.

Zane broke the kiss so they could both fill their lungs with some much-needed air. But then he whispered, "Let's do that again."

She was willing, and when she stroked his jaw, he knew it. Her heart pounded so hard she knew he could hear it. Her tongue glanced against his with a fervor she knew he could feel. Her fingers toyed with the hair at his collar. He groaned and ended the kiss by nibbling at the corner of her mouth, trailing his lips over her jaw and down her neck.

Leaning his forehead against hers, he whispered, "I don't want to stop. But we wouldn't want our chaperone to catch us."

What *would* Jonah think if he caught them kissing? What would she say? How would she explain?

She nodded and took several deep breaths. "I'd better check on him. Then I'll wrap up in my sleeping bag, too."

"I'll be in shortly. I'll clean up and make sure the fire is doused."

The problem was, Jeannette didn't believe they *could* douse the fire. At least not that easily.

Okay, she turns you on.

Zane stirred the fire, pouring water on the dying embers. What was it about Jeannette Williams that made him forget where he was…maybe even who he was? If he were an ordinary guy, that would be fine. But he wasn't, although these days he was thinking he would trade it all away for some peace and a regular life. If Ashley Tuller hadn't died, would he still feel this way?

It was a moot point. But he wondered if at thirty-nine he wasn't ready for a different kind of career and a different kind of life. Was Jeannette bringing out his restlessness, his need for a change? Or was she just a passing fancy, like so many women had been? He had to admit the last decade hadn't been about finding a woman of his dreams. Truth be told, he'd given that up as a song lyric that had run its course. His last CD hadn't been about love as much as a man's solitary life.

How could he be solitary with so many people buzzing around him all the time? Yet, many times he'd felt as if he was alone on an island of his own making. Maybe he just needed to spend some time in his studio in Nashville. The thing was, what would he do there? Wait for inspiration that might never return?

His career had caused the death of a beautiful young girl. How could he ever forget that *or* get past it?

With the lawn chairs folded and the fire out, Zane pushed aside the flap of the tent and stooped inside. Jonah seemed to be sound asleep, but Jeannette…

She was resting on her back, her hands propped under her head. She'd taken off her jacket and laid it on top of Jonah's. Her sneakers sat beside his, too. The sleeping bag skimmed the underside of her breasts. Although her cotton shirt was by no means formfitting, Zane could see their outline and his palms itched to touch them, to touch her.

As he pulled off his boots, he realized he should have bought a bigger tent instead of using this one. Their sleeping bags were practically edge-to-edge and even though they'd be sleeping in separate bedrolls, he would know she was right there.

"Does Jonah sleep soundly?" he asked in a low voice as he pulled back the top of his sleeping bag and slid inside. In spite of temperatures dropping at night, he knew he was going to be hot.

Jeannette turned her face toward his, although she didn't move her body. "Usually he does. He didn't even realize I came in, so I'm sure he's already in dreamland."

Dreamland. Zane knew what was going to fill *his* dreams tonight. Flat on his back, too, he stared up at the tent roof, concentrating on the shadows the lantern made. "Are you ready for me to turn out the light?"

"Whenever *you're* ready."

Ready for what? was the question. When he clicked off the lantern, the tent was practically in total darkness. His eyes adjusted and he suddenly understood something very important. "You had to trust me a lot to do this," he murmured.

"I had a character reference, remember?"

"Dillon. And Erika, too, I guess."

"They think the world of you."

Without comment he turned on his side to face her and changed the course of the conversation. "Do you ever talk to Jonah about his dad?"

He heard the rustle of her sleeping bag and realized she was turning to face him, too. This felt even more intimate than sitting outside under the blanket. He was aroused all over again, but glad she couldn't tell, glad she couldn't see his face. The darkness could cover his reactions to her, could act as a barrier as they slipped into territory where neither of them wanted to go.

"There's a picture of Ed in Jonah's room, one of the two of us in my room. I've told Jonah that's his father and of course he's seen pictures of Ed at Edna and Mel's, too. They talk about him a lot."

"Does Jonah understand?"

"He understands that he once had a dad. Now that he's

in school, he understands that other children still do. Edna talks to him about his dad watching over him and how proud Ed would be of him, but I think that all just soars over Jonah's head. When he starts asking questions and wants to know more, I'll bring out the photograph album. I want him to know who his father was and how much Ed would have loved him."

Zane could hear the emotion in Jeannette's voice and she sounded as if she still *did* love him. He knew how hard it had been to let go of what had happened between him and Beth Ann. How much harder it must be to realize the future you'd held in your hand had been cut short and that person no longer walked on this earth.

He didn't know what to say or what to ask that would change any of it for him or for her. She'd had a rough road and she'd been young when all of it had happened.

Her face was mere inches from his. "Why did you ask?"

"I was curious. I don't want to step where I shouldn't."

"We're getting to know each other, Zane. I don't have any secrets. You can ask whatever you want."

He didn't have any secrets, either, but there was still a lot they didn't know about each other. He was sure Jeannette didn't understand how brutal living in the public eye could be, especially when there was negative publicity.

"I want to kiss you again," he said bluntly. "But I know I can't because Jonah might wake up."

Instead of responding with words, she reached out and found his hand. His fingers closed over hers.

Minutes later, as their breathing became slower and deeper, he thought, *Holding hands like this was almost as good as a kiss.*

Chapter Seven

When Zane woke up, he knew it was almost daybreak. Gray shadows filled the tent instead of the black of night. Jeannette's chin touched his shoulder and her body slanted toward his, her knee lodged against his thigh. They were both inside their sleeping bags, but in their dreams they must have been drawn toward each other. Or maybe Jeannette had simply been cold. If he moved, he'd wake her. Yet he didn't know how long she needed to get ready for work. Some women took *hours* with their morning ritual.

Jeannette's hair drifted over her shoulder and lay against his arm. With his shirt on, he couldn't feel it, but it looked so silky and soft. It smelled a bit smoky, yet still like lavender, too. Jeannette was an intriguing combination of sexy woman, yet caring mom. She was alluring, yet absolutely natural. She could be a model with her face, hair and figure. Add a sequined dress or a designer gown and she'd be ready for the red carpet.

Why did he even care about that?

An echoing voice inside his head reminded him, *That used to be your life.*

Did he want it back even if he could have it?

He must have moved or something because Jeannette's eyes popped open. It took her only a moment to realize her sleeping bag was tucked against his.

An entrancing blush stained her cheeks as she murmured, "Sorry. I didn't mean to—"

He interrupted her apology by slipping his fingers under her hair and holding her still. "You're fine. Snuggling for warmth is a natural thing."

They gazed at each other in an interminable silence. But then uncertainty settled on her face. She summoned up a smile and then leaned away.

Glancing over her shoulder, she studied her son. "I have to get ready for work. I'm meeting Erika at eight o'clock. Do you want me to wake Jonah up and make him breakfast?"

"Don't be silly," Zane protested, his voice low. "Let him sleep. Once you're ready, then we'll see where we go from there."

She nodded, hiked herself up, unzipped her sleeping bag and silently left the tent.

Zane had to wonder what was going through her mind…because he knew a million things were going through his.

Forty-five minutes later Jeannette returned to his backyard and for him she was as much of a sight to see as morning breaking. For her meeting with Erika she wore a rust, casually tailored pantsuit with a silky cream blouse and brown flats. He knew she'd be changing again later into her LipSmackin' Ribs outfit. Even though the tight T-shirt and shorts were much more revealing, he preferred this outfit. It suited her. He knew if she got a foot up into a better job, she'd run with it.

She came over to him. He could smell the hint of a sweet, yet musky, perfume.

"Are you enjoying working with Erika?" he asked, his mouth suddenly going dry. He didn't want to be this hungry for a woman. It totally unnerved him.

"I am. Today we're going to go over the logistics for the pageant. The tent for the crowning ceremony is going to be at the fairgrounds near the concert hall."

"A full-blown pageant?" he asked.

"There's a talent competition as well as an evening gown judging. Miss Congeniality, too. Local business owners are the judges. There's a five-hundred-dollar prize to encourage single women to enter. So far ten have."

"You could enter."

"I don't think so. I have enough men judging me at LipSmackin' Ribs. But thanks for the compliment." She paused a moment, then said, "You played at the concert hall at the fairgrounds last year, didn't you?"

He didn't know where she was going with this but suspected he wouldn't like wherever her comment led. "Yes," he answered cautiously.

Instead of looking at the sunrise now, she was staring at him. "Erika explained she couldn't get anyone headline-worthy this year, so on Saturday local bands and singers will be playing all day into the night. I'm sure she'd make room on the schedule if you wanted to perform."

"Don't, Jeannette."

"You have a gift, Zane."

"Not anymore."

"I understand if you can't write music now, but you can still sing and play. Maybe if you did, you'd get your passion back for it."

He was already shaking his head. "Music is about heart and soul and laying it out on the table for everyone to see. My heart and soul isn't in it. And I'm too raw to lay anything out on the table."

They stood in silence until Jeannette said, "I'm sorry. I shouldn't have pushed." Then she gave him a little smile. "But I'm a new fan and I would be as excited as anyone else to hear you."

He wrapped his arms around her, then let his hands hang loosely at her back waist. "Maybe sometime I'll pick up the guitar for you. But right now I have something else on my mind."

"As if I didn't know what that might be."

"Jonah's not awake yet, so I think I'm going to take advantage of that."

He dipped his head, claimed her lips and got lost in her while the sunrise broke all around them. It was a satisfying kiss, long and breathtaking, and he knew he couldn't keep kissing her like this without taking her to bed.

So he broke it off, heart pounding, fiery heat rushing through him. When he opened his eyes, he expected to see that same satisfaction, as well as heady desire, in her eyes, too. But the same expression came over her face that he'd glimpsed this morning, and he knew something was coming.

"I have to ask you something," she murmured.

He could think of at least ten questions he wouldn't want to answer. He might as well find out what this one was. "What?"

"Have you ever slept with groupies?"

Damn, but that wasn't even on his list! And the idea that she could ask after a kiss like that irritated him, even made him angry. What kind of man did she think he was? "No, I haven't."

She obviously heard the edge in his voice, but she didn't back down. "You said you had affairs. Everybody knows about bands on the road."

"No, everybody doesn't know about bands on the road. We're not all alike. Sure, I'm an adrenaline junkie for the concert. But it ends there. I don't party till three. I don't ask my manager to bring me women. That's not me, Jeannette. Don't you know that yet?"

"We've known each other less than two weeks," she said reasonably.

He was so tempted to kiss her again, to let desire wipe away her doubts, to let it show her what they could have in bed. Then he remembered she'd said she hadn't dated since Jonah's father died. He'd been too touchy about her question and he didn't even know why.

Running his hand down over his face, he shook his head. "I shouldn't have minded your question. Of course, you'd believe the stories about groupies. Everyone does. There have been a few women I've slept with only once, but they weren't groupies. We were together because we were both alone, or because we both wanted companionship, or because we both didn't *know* what we wanted."

"I have to ask the questions, Zane, because I don't understand why you want to spend time with me."

Man, was she honest! She was making him look inward and maybe he didn't want to do that. He was *sure* he didn't want to do that. Not right now anyway. Still, he couldn't let her go on thinking she was like all the others.

"You keep asking the questions and I'll try to answer them if I can. I'm being as honest as I can, Jeannette. That's all I can give you."

He waited because he expected her to say that wasn't enough. But she didn't. Instead, she just looked troubled. "I'm going to give Jonah a hug goodbye. Are you sure you want to do this today? It's not too late. I could call Edna and Mel and tell them my other arrangements didn't work out."

Actually, she couldn't call. Not from here. "We'll be fine. I'll make breakfast, then maybe we'll toss around the football for a while or put puzzles together."

She studied him for a few moments to see if he meant what he said, if he really wanted to babysit her son. She must have been satisfied with what she saw because she went to the tent and ducked inside.

Zane had been around kids before. He and Dillon's little boy, Toby, had been buddies in a toddler/uncle sort of way. As Toby's godfather, Zane had bought the little boy presents, sung lullabies to him and even babysat on rare occasions when he was in town. Being supportive for Dillon when Toby was sick had been heartbreaking. But every minute he'd known Toby had given him a glimpse of what it would be like to be a dad.

After Jeannette left, Jonah was raring to go. He chattered through the making of pancakes, with blueberries for the eyes, nose and mouth. He brushed his teeth and washed up without complaint, and Zane knew part of the reason for that was because they were still trying to get to know each other and they were both on their best behavior. They tossed around the football in the crisp morning air, had hot chocolate for a snack and put puzzles together.

After the second one, Jonah looked up from his cross-legged position on the floor and asked Zane, "Mom said you have elk. Can I see one?"

Zane laughed. "I don't know if you can see one. That depends on if they come out of hiding for you to see. But we'd have to go for a walk. I don't often have them right in my backyard."

Jonah considered what Zane had said, then decided, "Let's walk."

The sun splayed over the golden brush as they walked along the path he and Jeannette had taken. When he and Jonah weren't talking, they listened to the call of birds. Zane pointed out a pair of blue jays. Jonah watched, transfixed by the birds' antics. He often stopped to pick up a rock and he put a few small ones in his pocket.

"Do *you* have a treasure box?" Zane asked him.

"What's that?"

"Well, it could be a shoe box or a box something came in in the mail, and you put all your favorite small things in there."

"Do you have a treasure box?"

"I used to. I collected rocks like you are. When I found pennies, I put them in there, too. Once, a friend gave me an arrowhead. I think I had three of my most special little cars in there. You put in whatever means a lot to you."

"Cool. Can I tell Mom?"

"Sure, if you want to."

As they climbed higher, rounded a bend and could see down into a stretch of pines, Jonah pointed and ran off the trail. "Look! Look! Is that elk?"

Jonah's quick darting ahead had surprised Zane. He ran to catch up, calling, "Jonah, don't go off the trail. Don't go too close—"

But before Zane could reach the little boy, Jonah had slipped on crumbling ground and fallen. Zane heard and saw Jonah hitting the ground. He scrambled to him and found Jonah lying facedown. His heart practically stopped. But then common sense and instinct kicked in.

First he placed his hand on Jonah's back and could feel him breathing. Then he heard Jonah start to cry.

"What hurts?" he asked, trying to remember every first aid course he'd ever taken.

Jonah was already scrambling to his knees in spite of Zane trying to keep him still. "Whoa, partner. Let me see if anything's hurt."

And then he spotted the blood.

He took Jonah onto his lap and saw that he'd cut his chin on a rock.

"It hurts," Jonah wailed.

"I know it does. Hold on a minute." Zane had a handkerchief in his pocket. He took it out, folded it and pressed it to Jonah's chin.

"That hurts more!"

"I know, but we have to stop the bleeding."

As Zane held the handkerchief to Jonah's chin, he asked, "Does anything else hurt?" Jonah's clothes had protected him from scrapes, although his sleeves and jeans were dirty from the fall.

The bleeding wasn't slowing down.

This was a child. This was an emergency. And he didn't have a damn phone at the house. His cell phone wouldn't be any good until they got down the mountain.

He swore.

Jonah looked up at him, wide-eyed, and Zane knew he wasn't making matters any better. The last thing he wanted to do was to scare Jonah further. But he knew that chin probably needed stitches, and there was only one way to get them.

He picked up the little boy into his arms and asked, "Can you be brave and hold that handkerchief on there until we get to the house?"

Jonah nodded and Zane climbed to his feet with him, starting back to the house and his SUV and medical treatment at the closest place he could find it.

Fifteen minutes later Zane was almost in a panic. The bleeding hadn't stopped. In fact, it hadn't even slowed. On top of that, he realized he didn't have a car seat. So he did the only thing he could. He grabbed pillows for Jonah to sit on as well as pillows to stuff in all around him in the backseat.

Attaching the seat belt, he told Jonah, "I'm going to drive fast but carefully. You just keep that towel on your chin and we'll be there before you know it."

"I want my mommy."

"I know you do. I'll call her as soon as we reach the bottom of the hill and tell her what a brave guy you're being. I'll ask her to meet us where we're going. Okay?"

Jonah nodded, his eyes filling with tears.

"It's okay to cry. I know it hurts."

Then he got into his SUV, mindful he was transporting the most precious cargo on earth.

He kept looking into the rearview mirror, meeting Jonah's eyes, smiling at him and giving him a thumbs-up. Why hadn't he had a phone put into that house? What did he think he was going to do in an emergency?

He hadn't expected an emergency. He hadn't expected to be babysitting a child.

Taking out his cell phone when he reached the foot of the mountain, he kept his foot on the accelerator and dialed Dillon's home number, hoping to heaven Jeannette was there. He knew she was going to blame him for this. So much for her trusting him. He blamed himself. He hadn't watched Jonah nearly close enough.

Speeding toward Thunder Canyon when Erika answered, Zane asked first, "Is Dillon at the clinic?"

Erika must have heard the strain in his voice. "Yes. Why?"

"I need him. Is Jeannette there? I have an emergency with Jonah."

Jeannette must have been sitting close by, because she sounded worried as she asked, "Zane?"

"Jonah took a fall. His chin is bleeding and I think he needs stitches. I'm taking him to Dillon's clinic. Can you meet me there?"

She didn't waste time asking questions. She just said, "I'll meet you."

Her voice had a trembling quality to it. Although Zane looked at his hands and they weren't shaking, he felt as if he were shaking inside. How had this happened? One instant the day was sunny and bright, and the next—

Checking the backseat again, Zane saw that Jonah was easing up on the pressure and the towel was falling away from his chin.

"Hold it on tight, cowboy. Just for a little longer, okay?"

Jonah did as Zane asked and Zane gave him a smile in the mirror. The last thing he felt like doing was smiling. He speed-dialed Dillon's cell phone number so his friend knew they were coming.

Dillon himself was in the reception area when Zane rushed in the sliding glass doors with Jonah.

"Is Jeannette here yet?" Zane asked, looking around.

"Not yet. Erika called me, too. She jotted down directions for Jeannette so she'd know exactly where to come."

Zane, who was now holding the towel to Jonah's chin himself, said to the little boy as nonchalantly as he could, "This is my best friend, Dillon. He's a doctor. He's going to make you feel a lot better. I promise." Then to distract Jonah, he told him, "Dillon knows all about my treasure box. He saw everything that was in it when we were kids."

Dillon pushed open the door to an exam room and Zane hurried inside, depositing Jonah on the table. Dillon came over to him and smiled. "It's good to meet you, Jonah. Zane's told me what a great little boy you are. Can I take a look at what happened here?"

Dillon was examining Jonah's chin when Jeannette rushed in with the nurse. She didn't meet Zane's eyes, but ran to her son. He started crying when he saw her and reached his little arms up to her.

For the next few minutes, Zane felt helpless. While Jeannette kept her arm around Jonah's shoulders, Dillon cleaned the wound. When Jonah cried, the sound broke Zane's heart.

But then Dillon explained to Jonah exactly what he was going to do. There would be a couple of pricks and they would be quick, and then he wouldn't feel anything.

Jonah suddenly sought Zane's gaze. He asked tentatively, "Can you hold my hand?"

Zane's throat clogged with emotion as he moved toward Jonah and stood beside Jeannette. She looked at him then, but he couldn't read her expression. She was being stoic for Jonah, keeping her hand on his head, on his back, anywhere that she thought would give him comfort.

Dillon spoke with Jonah as he put in four small stitches, making quick work of it. Afterward, the nurse brought over a plastic jar with dinosaur toys.

Jeannette asked Dillon, "Do you mind if Zane and I step outside for a minute?"

"No, go ahead. Jonah can tell me all the dinosaurs he knows about already and maybe I can add a couple to his list."

Zane followed Jeannette into the hall and swung the door closed almost the whole way. He jumped right in to explain in detail what had happened. "We were just taking a walk."

He knew his voice still held some surprise over what

had happened because it had occurred so quickly. "Jonah wanted to see elk, so we came around this bend and all of a sudden he ran ahead. I told him to stop, but by then he'd slipped on some crumbling ground and cut his chin on a sharp rock. I'm so sorry this happened, Jeannette. I know you put him in my care and I should have watched him more closely. I'm going to get a satellite phone. That way I'll be able to make calls. I know it's too late for that. I know you probably won't trust me with him—"

"Why did you bring Jonah to Dillon rather than the hospital? Was that to protect your identity?"

He expected to see recriminations in her eyes, but he didn't. He just saw questions and uncertainty.

He considered her question carefully because he knew why she was asking it. Did he put himself above Jonah? If he had taken him to the hospital, someone would surely have recognized him. He would have had to give his name and explain the situation.

But he could truthfully say he hadn't considered any of that. "No, that wasn't the reason. The clinic was closer and I thought Jonah's care might be quicker. That's all I thought about. That and getting down that mountain so I could call you."

Apparently she still had more questions. "I've heard of Dillon's clinic. Erika told me a little about it, too. I know a few days a week he runs free services for residents of Thunder Canyon who don't have insurance. I'm not a charity case, Zane. I have insurance for Jonah, and even though it might not be the best—"

Zane cut her off before she got too far into the analysis. She was thinking too much. But that's what Jeannette had to do to keep her life together. He wanted to pull her into his arms. He wanted to give her a hug. But he wasn't exactly sure where they stood.

So in a firm, clear voice he assured her, "That never crossed my mind."

As they studied each other in the quiet hallway, they could hear the sounds of Dillon's and Jonah's voices in a conversation about dinosaurs and where they lived. Just like that morning, Zane felt a hunger for Jeannette he couldn't understand, even in this situation. In some ways, being inside that room and caring about Jonah had seemed so natural. But he understood everything she was thinking and feeling.

He plunged into the conversation he wanted to have. "Is this the end of the road for us? You're not going to be able to trust me with Jonah again and rightly so. I messed up big time."

The doubts and uncertainty in her eyes transformed into something else…something that made his heart leap. In a gentle voice she assured him, "Not everything is your fault, Zane. I'm sorry I had questions, but I had to know what you were thinking and where Jonah fit into that."

She stepped closer to him. "Kids will be kids. Jonah's a rough-and-tumble boy. Even *I* can't catch him sometimes when he takes off and I'm used to his mad dashes. But if you plan to drive him anywhere else, we're going to have to get you a car seat."

He could tell she was thinking about Jonah's father and his accident. What she'd told him echoed in Zane's mind. *If only Ed had worn his seat belt.* He could see thinking about her fiancé filled her with sadness. He also understood she still felt guilty about it, even though none of it was her fault. They were a pair, they were.

Wrapping his arm around her, he brought her close for

a hug. He didn't let the embrace last because this wasn't the place for what he was feeling.

Leaning away from her, he asked, "Do you still want me to keep Jonah today?"

"The question is, do you want to? He's probably going to get cranky when his chin anesthetic wears off."

"I've dealt with cranky people before," Zane said with a smile.

"Would you mind watching him at my place? That way if he needs me I could get home quicker."

"Your place is fine. Jonah might feel better there."

She studied Zane again and stroked his beard-stubbled jaw. "This was not your fault, Zane. You can't control everything around you."

The tips of her fingers on his beard sent adrenaline coursing through his body. He wanted her, that was surely true. But her touch caused other sensations he'd been keeping under wraps. When he wrote songs, he went to this secret place inside of him, where memories and hurts and joys and unexpressed feelings resided. Somehow Jeannette was making her way to that place. And that unsettled him. It disturbed him. It worried him. He'd been alone for so long that he'd only accessed the depths of his heart when it was necessary to give meaning to lyrics, to find the melody that was eluding him.

He didn't know how Jeannette was making inroads into his soul, yet he knew he didn't like it. It made him feel vulnerable and that feeling was almost as bad as feeling powerless.

He stepped away and found a smile he often used when he was dealing with fans. "Let's see how Jonah feels about going back to your place with me."

Jeannette looked as if he'd just pushed her away. He

had. He needed time to mull over everything that was happening between them. Maybe while he cared for her son, he'd figure out what to do next.

Chapter Eight

"Did I do something bad?" Jonah looked up at Zane with questioning eyes that expected an answer.

They sat at the kitchen table in Jeannette's apartment, coloring a dinosaur in Jonah's coloring book. Jeannette had disappeared into the bedroom to change clothes for her waitressing shift.

Zane's answer was quick and decisive. "You didn't do *anything* wrong. I should have told you to stay by my side. I should have warned you you could get hurt if you ran off the path."

Tentatively, Jonah touched his chin. "Feels funny."

"It's going to and then it might hurt some."

With a frown, Jonah started coloring again. "Gran says if I stay in the house, I won't get hurt."

Not wanting to step on anyone's toes, yet knowing that overprotecting a child wasn't good parenting, either, Zane asked, "Do you like staying in the house?"

After a shake of his head, Jonah gave Zane a sly smile. "I like lookin' for elk."

"Even though you got hurt?"

Jonah nodded. "Can we look again?"

Zane suddenly became aware of Jeannette who was now standing in the doorway. He wondered if she'd overheard their conversation. "Maybe you should ask your mom."

Swiveling on his chair, Jonah faced her. "Can I, mom? I promise I won't fall again."

Jeannette cast a glance at Zane, then crouched down at her son's chair so she was at his eye level. "I think looking for elk is a fun thing to do. But I think you might have scared Zane when you got hurt. If you go with him again, you have to promise to listen and not go running off."

Jonah grinned at Zane. "I promise. Can we go?"

"After your stitches heal. Until then, we'll find something quieter to do."

Jonah thought about that, then slipped off the chair. "I'm gonna get another coloring book."

As soon as Jonah left the kitchen, Zane stood and focused his full attention on Jeannette. Her shorts gave him a spectacular view of her long legs. Her slim waist and flat belly were revealed by the short, tight T-shirt. Feeling like one of the jerks who eyed *her* instead of the ribs at LipSmackin', Zane lifted his gaze to her face. But that wasn't much better. He was as turned on by the curve of her mouth and her beautiful blue eyes as the rest of her.

"You'll let him go hiking with me again?" He was trying to concentrate on the conversation rather than the way she looked…and the way she made him feel. He'd shut down most of his feelings over the past few months and their reawakening was uncomfortable.

"I'm not like Edna," she said. "I know I can't keep

Jonah in the house. That would only make him afraid when he does go outside. Ed wasn't adventurous and I think his parents' attitude was the reason."

With Jonah returning any minute and Jeannette on her way to work, Zane didn't probe more about her deceased fiancé. But he wanted to. He wanted to know how attached she still was to him.

Yet right now, with her within arm's reach, alluring and sexy and with a look on her face as if she was hearing the same call of desire he was, he asked somewhat provocatively, "Are *you* adventurous?"

Sparkles of amusement danced in her eyes. "Are you asking if *I'd* like to go hiking again to spot elk?"

Overcome by a need to touch her that was too palpable to resist, he reached out and pushed her bangs to the side, teasing himself and her. "Spotting elk...snowboarding... skydiving."

"You jumped out of a plane?"

He gave her a grin and a half shrug. "A few years ago. It was a stunt to raise money for charity. Then I did it again a few months later, just for the heck of it."

"We are *so* different," she murmured. "I might try snowboarding but *never* skydiving."

"Even if you could skydive with a partner who promised to keep you safe?"

Although they were speaking hypothetically, both understood the subtext. "I'm a mom," she responded, serious now. "I'm not sure a promise would be enough."

What would be enough? he wondered. *A forever commitment that he'd take care of Jonah, too?*

He was sinking in way too deep...reading too much into a simple conversation. Still, he couldn't let it go. "How would you feel if I introduced Jonah to skateboarding, including, of course, the helmet, elbow and knee pads? Would you try it, too?"

"I might. You're determined to make me face the adventures he might want to have."

Actually, he was imagining the three of them experiencing life to its fullest. Yet he had only known this woman for two weeks. He must be certifiable. "I'm just imagining how cute you'd look in a snowboarding or skateboarding helmet."

"Cute? Not sexy?" she joked.

Didn't she know how sexy she was? How much he wanted her? His voice grew gruff as he let some of that wanting through to his voice into his words. "In that outfit, you're as sexy as I can ever imagine you'd be."

As she studied him, he wondered if he was giving too much away. "Zane," she said, her lips parting, her body leaning toward his.

"I wish you'd quit your job at the rib joint. I could have Dillon make a few calls. His brother Ethan opened an office in Thunder Canyon. Maybe he could use you."

With a sigh, Jeannette took a step away from him. "Do you think waitressing is beneath me?"

He wanted to shout, *Don't you?* Instead, he responded tersely, "I told you my mother was a waitress." As if that wasn't enough, he added, "But as I mentioned, she waitressed at a *family* diner. I don't think waitressing is beneath you, but I believe LipSmackin' Ribs *is*."

A conflicted look passed over Jeannette's face. Zane thought it stemmed from the fact that she felt trapped by circumstances. Averting her gaze from his, she glanced down the hall to her son's room.

Finally she admitted, "LipSmackin' Ribs isn't where I'd choose to work if I had other choices. But I don't want you making another call on my behalf. You did that with

Erika. I accepted you doing it because you felt responsible for me losing the cleaning position, which you *weren't*. And I really loved the idea of working on Frontier Days with her. But I don't want you to do it again. If I find out Ethan Traub has a position open, I'll apply. But any job I get, I want to win on my own merit."

"Miss Independence is raising her head again," he muttered.

This time Jeannette apparently couldn't keep from touching *him*. Her hand clasped his arm. Her fingers seemed to take slow pleasure in surrounding the muscles there. "I was on my own early…after my mom died. Then I met Ed and for the most part, we depended on each other. But then he had to take on the burden of me not working and of preparing for a family. During that time I felt as if I was letting him down."

"You weren't," Zane assured her swiftly. "When tough times happen, you have to let the person who loves you hold you up."

"Maybe," she gave in with a sigh. "But then I let Mel and Edna take over where Ed left off. The past few months, I've been able to stand on my own and take care of Jonah. My job at LipSmackin' Ribs enables me to do that. Knowing I can stand on my own gives me self-confidence and the feeling my world isn't out of control. Do you understand?"

"I understand," he answered grudgingly. "But I still don't have to like that rib joint." He found it hard to think at all when she was touching him.

He was almost relieved when Jonah scampered back into the kitchen, a coloring book waving in one hand. "I found it. We can color airplanes."

"So he's thinking about being a pilot someday?" Zane asked under his breath.

Jeannette released his arm, then gave him a poke there. "Don't even think it."

Crossing to the cupboard, she stood on tiptoe to reach the highest shelf. She took down a safety-capped bottle with grape-flavored liquid. "Dillon said to give Jonah one-and-a-half teaspoons every four hours if his chin hurts." She studied her son as he sat at the table and opened the coloring book. "He doesn't seem to be uncomfortable yet. Are you sure you'll be okay? He might not be able to get to sleep—"

"Stop worrying," Zane said firmly. "We'll be fine."

"For dinner—"

"I saw ground meat in the fridge. Jonah and I will experiment."

"Ex-pariment?" Jonah asked.

"Yep. You and I might come up with a new recipe. Maybe barbecued chili burgers. DJ might even put it on his menu."

When Jeannette frowned, he quickly added, "Or whatever Jonah likes. Call whenever you want to make sure we're good."

The frown slipped away, but Jeannette's gaze was troubled. Still, she gave her son a hug and a kiss, then went to the door. "Thank you," she said fervently.

As he waved and she left, Zane knew *he* was the one who should be thanking *her.* Without her and Jonah, he'd be at his log house, sunk into his troubled thoughts, eating alone.

That night Jeannette unlocked the door to her apartment and let herself in, hearing the television playing in the living room. The light in the stove hood glowed as well as the one next to the sofa in the living room. She liked the feel of someone already being there.

Today at the clinic when Jonah had asked for Zane to hold his hand, she'd almost lost it! She'd hated to see her son hurting. But the comfort he'd drawn from Zane had been inspiring. He needed a man like Zane in his life. The problem was, Thunder Canyon was merely a stopover for Zane.

To her surprise, when she entered the living room, she found Jonah slouched against Zane, his head tucked against Zane's chest. Her gaze found his. They both knew it was well past Jonah's bedtime.

Zane kept his voice low. "You look wiped out."

She was. Her feet hurt and she felt ready to collapse into bed. Yet seeing Zane in her living room seemed to give her a second wind.

"I didn't think my shift would ever end," she admitted. "How did Jonah do?"

"He was a trouper. After dinner he seemed more uncomfortable. I distracted him with games until I saw he was tiring. Then I read to him until he fell asleep. I thought he might wake up when you came home, but I think he's out for the night. Do you want me to carry him to his room?"

"You've done so much already—"

Zane gave her a look that silenced her and scooped up her son. "Are you hungry?"

"A little." She followed him to Jonah's bedroom. "I'll get something after I tuck him in."

While she arranged Jonah's spread and then covered him, she smelled food warming. She thought again how nice it was to come home to…

Not just to any man, but to Zane.

Jeannette stood looking down at Jonah for a long while, wondering what was best for him, wondering what was best for her.

She took a few minutes to slip out of her restaurant clothes, pulling on a pair of pink-and-black drawstring lounging pants and a pink T-shirt. She left her feet bare. Zane was waiting for her in the living room with a plate of warmed-up food on the coffee table and a tall glass of iced tea.

She sank down beside him on the sofa. "This looks great. I didn't think I was hungry, but now that I smell it—"

"Dig in. Jonah and I called it barbecued chili."

She smiled and took a bite. "You two will have to come up with recipes more often." As soon as she said it, she wished she hadn't. Cutting him a sideways glance, she saw he appeared to be unfazed.

"Did you expect me to protest?" he asked.

After another forkful of the barbecued chili, she wiped her mouth. "I didn't know if the day might have been trying for you. Some days Jonah has so many questions for me that I'm worried about a time when I won't be able to hand him the answers."

"That day will come, but not for a while. How was work?"

"Each shift is pretty much the same." She took a few sips of her iced tea. "Do you know Dillon's cousin DJ very well?"

"I haven't spent a lot of time with him, but he seems like an okay guy. Why?"

"I just wondered how approachable he is."

"Approachable? I don't get it. Are you thinking about asking him for a job?"

"Oh, no. No." She knew she was being a little too vehement. She wished she could tell Zane what Woody had wanted her to do. But Zane was the type of man who would want to do something about it and she just couldn't risk her job right now…or Jonah's insurance. So instead of answering the question in Zane's eyes, she looked toward the TV screen.

There was a twang of a guitar and it caught Zane's attention, too. Then the host of whatever show it was was saying, "Country music is still trying to recover from the death of a fan in April at a Zane Gunther concert. Earlier tonight we showed a clip of Max Landow interviewing the Tuller family. Ashley Tuller's parents are still setting the blame at the door of the country singer."

Jeannette said quickly, "Zane, we don't have to watch this." She went for the remote that was sitting in front of him on the coffee table.

But he stole it out of her hand. "Maybe I need a reality check," he muttered, turning up the volume, staring at the couple as well as Ashley's nineteen-year-old sister, Tania, who was pale and seemed subdued.

Tears were running down Mrs. Tuller's face. "Mr. Gunther just won't take responsibility for what happened to Ashley. It's *his* fault she was there. It's *his* fault all those kids weren't kept in line. And then he just drove off in that expensive bus as if what happened didn't matter!"

The host of the show came back on. "That about sums up the family's sentiment. As far as what the rest of the world thinks, all we have to do is check out the latest tabloid."

Zane switched off the TV. "I thought it all would have died down. But with the Country Music Awards coming up in November, and then the trial, I'd better prepare myself."

Jeannette moved closer to him until her arm was brushing his. "Her family is still wrong, Zane."

"I'm not blaming them. This *was* my fault. But I think we've handled it all wrong. Lawyers talking to lawyers, media interviewing my closest friends, my mother, anybody they can get their hands on. Everybody uses the cameras on their cell phone now or one of those little video cameras to try and catch you doing something wrong. The fishbowl celebrities live in somehow got magnified."

He studied the TV, the picture black now. "I have to figure out the right thing to do."

"You'll figure it out. I know you will. Sometimes you need more information. Sometimes you just need more time."

"Time is what you're giving me, Jeannette—time away from all of it. I can't tell you how much I appreciate that. Taking care of Jonah today wasn't a chore at all. I felt for the first time in a few months that I was actually doing something worthwhile."

She could see he was trying to put that interview out of his mind. He was trying to move on to different conversational territory.

Suddenly, he bent down, picked up her legs and swung them up onto his lap, her feet resting on his thighs. "Do you know what I think you need?"

"I'm afraid to ask," she answered shakily, his warm fingers sending tingles through her, the feel of his powerful thigh muscles under her feet arousing every womanly nerve in her body.

"Besides a good meal, which I've obviously given you, you need a foot rub."

One of his hands gently supported the underside of her foot while the other stroked across the top. His touch felt like heaven. Still, she managed to say, "We could talk about what you're thinking."

"Or we don't have to talk about what I'm thinking. Or we can move on to what I'm thinking next."

The simmering heat in his gaze was enough to make

her forget about whatever they had been talking about. He was so good, so practiced, she suddenly felt like a fool and would have swung her feet from his lap but he caught them. "Tonight I have special powers," he announced. "I can read minds."

She knew her expression became wary.

Placing one hand on top of each of her feet, he said seriously, "You're thinking I give all my dates foot rubs."

"Don't you?"

"I've never had a date who was a waitress before. So, no, I don't. You would be the first. This would be a virgin foot rub."

She laughed at the ridiculousness of it. Yet that was exactly what she'd been getting at. She plunged in, maybe taking their discussion farther than he wanted to go. "Was Beth Ann your first?"

He didn't seem to mind her asking. "My first, and I thought she'd be my only. How about you? Who was your first?"

Zane's question told her he wanted to delve deeper into her past, too. "His name was Drake and I liked him a lot. We were seniors on the same committee for the homecoming dance. He wanted to go to an Ivy League college and be a lawyer. I knew if I let myself fall in love with him, he'd leave and break my heart. I decided not to fall in love, but that didn't work too well, especially when he asked me to the homecoming dance…especially when Valentine's Day came and went with a giant flowery card. But then it was the end of senior year. We knew holding on to the feelings we had weren't enough to build a future on, so he left and I stayed."

"And he never looked back?"

"Nope. I guess it didn't seem so unusual to me. After all, that's what my father had done. My parents were never married. He moved out when I was six and we never heard from him again."

"Jeannette."

Zane's hands were cupping her feet now, his thumbs stroking her arches. When had a man done something so incredibly nice for her? Except, nice wasn't exactly nice. Nice was turning into *very* sensual. His fingers were slipping across her instep, making her sigh.

"Feel better?" he asked.

"It feels wonderful."

His thumbs inched up toward her ankles, brushed aside the hem of her slacks. Her breath began coming in short, shallow pants when she imagined where else he might touch.

"Why don't you swing around and let me massage your shoulders?" he asked. "They have to be tired after carrying those heavy trays."

They were. But she'd accepted the tiredness and the aches as part of the life she was trying to carve out for her and Jonah. She opened her eyes and when she looked at Zane, he was studying her, as if he was trying to figure out something. What he should do next? What *she* might do next?

The idea of having his hands on her shoulders sounded like heaven. She didn't hesitate, but rather scooted down the couch and shifted around until her back was facing him.

"Let's start with your neck." His fingers swung her hair to one side, then ruffled gently through it. He ran his thumbs along either side of her hairline and eased down her nape, applying some pressure. She felt her muscles relax and the knots melt under his hands.

"You could have a second career," she breathed.

He chuckled and as he massaged her upper arms, she

went completely still under his ministrations. She was lost in the pure comfort of his touch when she felt his lips against her nape. Comfort transformed into desire.

"Zane," she whispered.

He kissed her again. "I've wanted to do this since last night when you were sitting by the fire. Your profile was so perfectly beautiful. I imagined kissing your neck, having my arms around you, having you relax against me so we could enjoy more than our hurried embrace or a quick kiss."

"Jonah could still wake up."

"I know. But just for a little while I'd like to have you to myself."

She knew exactly what Zane meant.

He drew her onto his lap and held her, cradled against him. "I guess I want an old-fashioned make-out session."

She didn't know exactly how old-fashioned their make-out session might be, but as she ran the tips of her fingers through Zane's hair and drew his head down to hers, she knew she was going to enjoy it.

Zane's kiss flared with passion right from the start. His hunger wasn't a surprise, but her response to it was. She clasped his shoulders and revved up the kiss even wilder than it already was. Her fingers curled into his muscles and she remembered exactly how he'd looked while swinging the ax, while lifting Jonah, while throwing a football. Without his shirt he'd look even better.

He broke the kiss, trailed his lips to her earlobe, took it into his mouth. She felt the live-wire connection deeply and she couldn't ever remember wanting a man so badly before. While she drowned in all the sensations he was evoking, he slid his hand under her T-shirt. His fingers on her midriff were a temptation she didn't want to fight.

He unhooked the front clasp of her bra and pressed

his palm to her breast. She moved breathlessly, kissed his neck, started to unbutton his shirt when he whisked his thumb over one of her nipples. Laying her head against his chest, she reveled in the excruciating anticipation of desire. They kissed again, their foreplay intensifying. She told herself she wanted to feel *his* skin, too. She wanted to feel his chest hair against her cheek. But he was doing such wonderfully arousing things to her that she couldn't put thoughts into action until...

Until Zane pulled the drawstring open on her slacks. When he did that and rippled his fingers along her waistband, the imprint of his thumb erotically singeing just below her navel, their desire became so real that she couldn't pretend this was a fantasy. Worry and doubt invaded the room and suddenly she knew she couldn't take this further. She couldn't let Zane take this further.

She didn't have to pull away or say anything.

"What's wrong?" The question came out low and tense, as if he knew something would be.

"I didn't mean to be a tease," she murmured.

After he took a few deep breaths, he removed his hands from under her T-shirt. He still cradled her, still kept his arm around her, but his expression said he knew their make-out session had ended, not just for the moment, but for the night.

"You're no tease, Jeannette. I started this. But you stopped it. Can you tell me why?"

"I have to wonder—Is this the reason you took care of Jonah? Is this the reason you stayed?"

"Would I be sitting here if we wanted to discuss the weather? Probably. But I'd have something else on my mind. From the way you reacted when I kissed you, I think you had something else on *your* mind, too."

She couldn't deny needing him or wanting to lead him

to her bedroom. "I did. When I saw you, I forgot about work and how tired I was. And for a few minutes just now, I even forgot about Jonah being in the next room. That's what scares me. That's why I stopped. That's why I have to ask, am I an escape from everything you're trying to forget?"

She could see him asking himself the question. She could feel his defenses go up and sense his backing away. He was a man in turmoil and that's what prompted her to be exceptionally careful.

Seeing from his expression their intimacy was done, she awkwardly shifted off his lap to the sofa. She sat beside him, wanting more than anything for him to deny that she *was* an escape. But he wasn't doing that. Instead, he was already pushing to the edge of the cushion. He was already gathering himself together to leave.

Isn't that what men did? a little voice asked her. "I have to know why you're here with me, Zane. I don't want to just be a distraction."

Standing, he flicked his gaze toward the TV, as it reminded them both so harshly what was going on in the real world. Then without responding to her request, he said, "I'd better leave."

"Do you always walk away from discussions you don't want to have?" Ed had done the same thing over and over again, and she'd let him.

"I didn't take care of Jonah today hoping I'd get laid tonight. Is that what you want to hear?" he demanded gruffly.

Maybe that was *part* of what she wanted to hear.

"How long are you going to stay in Thunder Canyon?" she asked.

Her question was also met with silence.

Zane went into the kitchen and picked up his hat,

which was lying in front of her stack of cookbooks on the counter.

"I didn't want tonight to end like this." She knew he wouldn't appreciate her thanking him again.

"Neither did I."

Had he expected her to sleep with him? Would he have left before morning? What would Jonah think about the two of them being together?

But that was the crux of it. Would they be together? Or would they just have spent the night together?

He saw she still had questions, but he was in obvious conflict and couldn't give her answers.

"I'll be in touch," he said quietly. Then he left.

Jeannette crossed her arms over her chest as if she could hold herself together by doing that. Yet she knew if she spent much more time with this man, he'd break her heart in a much more elemental way than any man ever had.

The following night Zane picked up his new SAT phone that had been a courier delivery, not knowing whether it was a wonderful invention or a terrible one. Sometimes a man just wanted to be incommunicado. However, he'd learned how well *that* had turned out yesterday when Jonah had injured himself. For the past twenty-four hours he'd stewed about what had happened at Jeannette's last night. Part of him felt as if he'd taken advantage of her. Day by day he was getting in deeper with her. But he couldn't seem to stop. She was intelligent and challenging, and so pretty that her smile had the power to blind him. Maybe he liked her most because she stood up to him. One of the major drawbacks about being a celebrity, although not many would admit it, was having too many people saying what you wanted to hear, doing what you wanted them to do. Jeannette was her own person. She took him into consideration, but she wasn't buffaloed by him. His celebrity didn't impress her. That had irked his ego. That had humbled him.

Thank goodness something had.

Jeannette Williams confronted him and made him confront himself. That's why he'd walked away. Because he'd needed to find some answers for them both. Not that he had a whole lot of them now, but—

He'd written her work and home numbers on a piece of paper and attached it to his refrigerator door with a magnet in the shape of the state of Montana. He punched in the numbers, hoping she wouldn't hang up on him.

She answered on the second ring with a tentative, "Hello."

"It's Zane."

"I didn't recognize the number."

"I got a SAT phone, just in case I'd want to babysit again."

Silence met his attempt at levity.

He cleared his throat. "So, are you still speaking to me?"

After a moment she responded, "Of course. After all, *I'm* the one who wanted to talk."

He couldn't fault her for making *that* point. "Is Jonah asleep?"

"Yes."

An uncomfortable silence settled between them again and he knew *he* had to be the one to break it. "When's your next night off?"

"Tomorrow."

"Good. At least it's good if you and Jonah will spend it with me."

"What do you have in mind?"

"The movies—a family flick that should be just right for all of us."

"You're not concerned someone will recognize you?"

"Not the way we're going to do this. I'll give you a call tomorrow and tell you where I want you to meet me. You'll just have to trust me. Okay?"

There was only a slight hesitation. "Okay."

"What time do you work tomorrow?"

"I work the lunch shift. I should be finished around four."

"I'll have everything worked out by the time you're off work. I'll call you then."

"Should I tell Jonah about this? He'll be excited if I do."

"Sure, tell him. It's always good to have something to look forward to. One thing I'm sure of, Jeannette, I'm looking forward to tomorrow night."

"I am, too."

Although Zane didn't want to say goodbye, he did. Tomorrow night Jeannette would get just a small taste of how he lived his life. Maybe her reaction to it would tell him what he needed to know. Her reaction might tell him if he needed to end this now, or take a chance on what came next.

Chapter Nine

Jeannette wasn't sure what to make of Zane's instructions the following evening.

With Jonah's hand in hers, they stepped inside the lobby of the movie theater. Jonah's eyes went really wide as he saw all the people in line on the left side and customers stretched out across the food counter. He'd never been to the movies and this was going to be a big deal for him.

Zane had told Jeannette just to give her name at the cashier's counter. She had, and was handed two large red tickets with no printing on them. The cashier had told her to go to the movie theater on the *right* side of the food counter.

Self-consciously, Jeannette noticed there wasn't a line there, just a man standing at a cordoned-off area, wearing a red security vest. She supposed he was their next stop.

Still, she glanced around the lobby once more, wondering if Zane was in disguise. Scanning the crowd, she noticed Rose Traub, Dillon's sister. Rose had stopped in to see Erika one of the days Jeannette had been working with her. Jeannette recognized the man she was with, too—Dean Pritchett. They seemed to be talking amiably, standing close together, as if they were on a date.

Jonah suddenly tugged on her arm. "Are we gonna get somethin' to eat?"

"Not just yet. Let's find out what our surprise is first." She'd told Jonah that Zane had a surprise for them, but they had to follow directions to find out what it was.

"Let's take our tickets over here." She gestured to the security guard.

With curiosity all over his face, Jonah kept pace beside her until they reached the man and presented him with their tickets. He slipped the velvet cord from its mooring on the post, motioned them through and then attached it again behind them.

"This way," he said, directing them down the hall to a closed double door.

Jeannette knew the doors led into the second movie theater.

He told them, "Go on in. I have instructions to wait out here and make sure no one else goes in."

Jonah gazed expectantly at Jeannette. She gave a little shrug and opened the door. The two of them stepped inside.

They were standing in an empty movie theater. At least she thought it was empty until she heard footsteps, looked up at the stadium seating and saw Zane coming down the stairs toward them. He wore a huge grin. "Are you ready for a Disney flick?"

"What's a flick?" Jonah asked.

Zane laughed, stooped down and tipped her son's hat back. Jonah wore it whenever she let him. "It's a movie and one I think you'll like. Why don't you go pick out a seat?"

"Anywhere?" Jonah asked.

"Anywhere you want. The place is all yours."

Jonah ran to the first row. "I wanna sit here. Can I, Mom?"

"That's fine. But I think Zane and I will sit a few rows behind you. Okay?"

"Before you watch the movie, you have to sample some popcorn." Zane produced two huge containers of the treat from a seat on the row where they were standing. He handed one to Jonah. "Now don't eat it too fast. And if you get thirsty, I have drinks back here, too."

"Soda?" Jonah asked hopefully.

"If your mom says it's okay."

Jeannette told her son, "This is a treat tonight, so a little bit of soda will be okay."

The lights suddenly dimmed and a brilliantly bright introduction to the movie flared on the screen.

Hugging his popcorn, Jonah went to the first row and sat, waiting for all of it.

Jeannette wasn't exactly sure what this was all about, but she was sure Zane was going to tell her.

He offered her his arm. "Can I escort you to your seat?"

"You surely can. I wouldn't want to miss any of this."

They sat three rows behind Jonah. Her son glanced over his shoulder at them, grinned and ate a handful of popcorn.

"He's going to love this."

Zane's shoulder brushed hers. Neither of them moved away. They sat quietly, watching the beginning of the movie. Zane offered her popcorn.

"Maybe later," she whispered.

As the movie played, Jonah's laughter and squeals of delight made them both smile.

Taking off his Stetson, Zane laid it on the seat beside him, ran his hand through his hair and sat up a little straighter. He was wearing cologne tonight, a woodsy and musky scent that immediately brought to her mind the picture of him splitting wood. His arm was solid beside hers and as always, she felt strength emanating from him. Yet tonight she sensed something else, too, something not quite comfortable, something that was uncertain. Who they were when they were together? If they should even *be* together? Was this simply a giant gesture to please Jonah?

Tonight she kept silent instead of asking any of the questions. She knew innately that tonight required patience and she had to let it unfold however it would.

Finally Zane took something from his pocket and handed it to her. "That's my SAT phone number in case you need it." Then he leaned closer. "I thought about what you said the other night."

She whispered back, "Which part?"

"The part where you thought I was using you for an escape."

Her heart seemed to turn over. Was he admitting it?

"I do escape when I'm with you," he confessed in the same low voice. "I forget who I was, what happened before I came to Thunder Canyon and what I'm trying to leave behind. But that happens because of who you are and who I seem to become when I'm with you. So to answer your question, you *are* an escape for me right now, just like Thunder Canyon is, or that log house up on the hill. But I like you, Jeannette. I think you're beautiful and sexy and smart. And just being with you makes me feel happy."

Jeannette's face was close to his shoulder. She brought her lips to his ear. "If we slept together, what would happen afterward?"

This was the most intimate conversation she'd ever had in a public place. But in some ways it was a private place, too. Nothing Zane did would ever be ordinary.

He turned his head until his lips were almost against hers. "You want me to predict the future. I can't do that. Short-term scenario, we'd have an awful good time while I'm in Thunder Canyon. Long-term scenario… That's what I want you to think about tonight. That's one of the reasons I brought you here. Before all this happened, I didn't have an ordinary life. I doubt if I'll have one in the future."

"Tell me what bringing me here tonight was supposed to prove," she requested, needing to know what was in his head.

"I want you to think about a life where you're separated from the rest of the world. There's a reason why stars have huge estates with everything on them they might want or need. If they go into town, they could get mobbed. At the least, they get stopped by fans. In a public place it's hard to finish a meal without someone coming over to the table, not to mention what could happen on the street. I have a bodyguard for a reason, or at least I had one. It isn't because I like it, it's because he was a necessity. If you're with me anywhere, all this will affect you, too. You'll be subjected to reporters and tabloid journalists and photographers with long lenses. If you want to go shopping, you'd better do it online so someone doesn't ask you if you're going to wear that dress when you go out with me. This isn't about ego here, Jeannette. It's about being on display maybe ninety percent of the time. It's about a life that requires separation from people close to you, odd hours and maybe telephone sex instead of being together."

"Are you trying to scare me off?" she asked.

Even though the theater was dark, in the light flashing from the screen she could see the doubts in Zane's eyes. "I'm telling you what life dating me would be like, not only for you, but for Jonah."

In other words, if *she* wanted to try on being with Zane what harm could come of it? But if Jonah were with her, what would happen with him? Of course she didn't want him exposed to the publicity. What mother would?

"Up until now, I wondered if I was dazzled by you. You just took the dazzle away."

"And?" he asked, not moving a muscle.

"And without the dazzle, I still like who you are. I'm still very attracted to you. But I do have to think about the consequences for me and Jonah. Especially for Jonah."

"If I have to go through a trial, life is going to get even more hellish. I won't be able to stay away from public places—I'll be right in the center of them. Why would you even want to consider getting involved in all that?"

Why, indeed? She felt torn by the need to keep her and Jonah safe, but by other needs, too. She longed for a man to hold her at night. She longed to be in love. With Zane she felt sexy and more of a woman than she'd ever felt. He understood the way she mothered and her need to place Jonah first. In a situation like this, should she weigh the pros and the cons? Or should she go with her heart? In the past, going with her heart had brought her pain.

Jeannette watched the movie, but she didn't absorb very much of it. Whenever Jonah laughed, her gaze fell on him, but she was constantly and consistently aware of the tall man beside her, his muscled physique and heat evident even as he sat still.

"I can't tell you not to think this time," Zane said, leaning close again, his jaw almost brushing her cheek. "But when you do think about us, feel those kisses again, too. I'd kiss you now to remind you, but I'm afraid I'd get lost in you in the dark and Jonah would catch us."

"Would that be so bad?"

"Not if we knew what we were going to do."

But they didn't know…because they *both* had a lot to think about.

They watched the rest of the movie, sitting close but not *being* close.

When the movie was over and the credits rolled and the lights came up, Jonah ran to them, happy and excited. "That was great! I like the movies, better than TV."

Zane laughed, but there was a restrained quality to it. She knew this was hard for him, too. Should he get close to Jonah or should he not get close to Jonah? Did he even want to think about becoming a father?

He said, "I'm glad you liked it, but I think it's already past your bedtime."

"Are you coming home with us?"

Zane looked at Jeannette and then said soberly, "Not tonight, cowboy."

Did he expect her to protest? Did he think she might ask him to come over so they could make out after Jonah went to bed?

They wouldn't be any farther along then than they were now.

As she stood and helped Jonah with his jacket, Zane said, "I'll come out with you and help tuck him into his car seat. Then I'll follow you home."

"Aren't you afraid someone will see you in the parking lot?"

"The other movie hasn't let out yet. I'll check when we go out."

The side door of the theater exited onto the parking lot. Zane opened the door and then motioned to them. Jonah tucked one hand into Zane's and the other into Jeannette's as they walked to her car. She knew the picture they made to anyone who *was* watching, but it wasn't a true picture. That made her so sad.

Jonah scrambled into his car seat and then Zane adjusted the harness. Jeannette saw her son's eyelids already drooping. He'd had a lot of excitement and now all of it was wearing off. She had, too. The letdown as well as the decisions they both had to make were like a heavy weight on her chest.

After she closed Jonah's door, she gazed up at Zane. "I'd like to ask you to come over, but—"

He gently but firmly held his index finger to her lips. "Let's take some time," he said. Then he gave her that crooked grin. "That's all I have these days, plenty of time."

She wanted to throw her arms around his neck and kiss him until the world vanished. But she couldn't be that free with him. She couldn't be that vulnerable.

He went to his SUV which was parked two rows behind her. She slid into her car, started the engine and headed out of the parking lot. When he followed her, she knew he would do that the whole way home. She just really wished he was coming in with her, that he was staying in Thunder Canyon.

But it was an impossible wish. He was Zane Gunther, the country singer, and he belonged to someplace bigger than here. He'd leave and she'd have to cope with the heartache all over again.

Those would make great lyrics for a country song.

* * *

"See ya, Mom," Jonah shouted and waved as Jeannette drove away from Mel and Edna's front porch in the drizzling rain on Saturday afternoon. They'd asked if he could stay overnight and she'd given her permission knowing they loved having him there.

Jonah seemed so grown-up sometimes—too grown-up. Like when he told Mel and Edna, "I took a walk with Zane to see elk. But I ran and fell and had to go to a doctor. He was nice. He fixed me."

Of course Edna and Mel had been upset and worried about Jonah's stitches. There had been questions about who Zane was and exactly where he lived. Jeannette had known she needed to be very careful about what she said. "He's a nice man. He likes Jonah and is teaching him about the outdoors."

Edna and her husband had exchanged a look before Mel asked, "Where does he work?"

After thoughtful consideration Jeannette had answered, "He took a leave of absence from his job and is in Thunder Canyon on vacation."

They hadn't liked that answer very much. Before they could ask another question, she'd hugged her son, told him to have a good time and she'd see him after church tomorrow morning. Edna had wanted her to come for brunch before she took Jonah home. It would be a short brunch if they asked too many more questions.

She had to keep Zane's secret. If somehow his association with her got out and added more bad publicity on to what he was already experiencing, she'd feel it was her fault. He'd probably never forgive her. She wasn't sure why she always felt so guilty. She supposed it had started after her father left. She'd felt his abandonment was her fault. That was the major reason why she was so determined that Jonah would always feel wanted, never feel like a burden or a responsibility she didn't want to handle.

At night when she couldn't sleep, she had to admit she wondered how her marriage to Ed would have turned out. Would he have felt the same way as her dad? That he never wanted kids? Would the fact that she'd gotten pregnant and that's why they'd married always come between them? Would he have left, too?

Loving someone was so complicated. Or was it that loving the *wrong* someone was complicated? Falling in love with Zane seemed so easy.

Falling in love with Zane.

She felt so stunned by thinking it, even more stunned by admitting it. She hadn't intended to fall in love. She hadn't intended to put herself and Jonah at risk of hoping and dreaming, and then having those hopes and dreams smashed. Who Zane was and the circumstances surrounding his life could be lethal to a relationship…could be lethal to her heart.

Forcing herself to concentrate on her day's tasks, she realized she had time to stock up on groceries before her shift started at LipSmackin' Ribs. The new grocery store near the movie theater was having good sales she didn't want to miss.

The movie theater. An evening with Zane she wouldn't soon forget, for many reasons. Jonah hadn't stopped talking about it, and that had made it even more bittersweet. Every time she and Zane parted she didn't know if she'd see him again.

In spite of the rainy day, the grocery store was busy and she didn't waste any time. Checking out her list, she crossed off items as she dropped them in her cart. She didn't stray from the list very often, but she did splurge on a pack of Jonah's favorite cookies. Someday soon she'd make him home-baked ones. She suspected Edna was probably doing that right now.

She'd taken coupons from her wallet and was heading into the checkout line when she caught sight of the tabloid magazine. The woman at the checkout noticed her interest and told her, "It's a special edition. Just came in."

Jeannette read the cover: ZANE GUNTHER'S TRIAL DATE SET FOR DECEMBER. The smaller print underneath stated the trial would begin December 7 in Austin.

Why hadn't Zane told her? Was the tabloid right? How had the setting of the date affected Zane? Was he upset?

Did he want to talk to someone about it? Was that someone her?

She didn't buy the tabloid. After paying for her groceries, she headed for the parking lot, avoiding puddles, quickly packed the bags in her car and drove back to her apartment. After she'd stowed the frozen food in the freezer and the perishables in the fridge, she picked up the phone, took the piece of paper Zane had given her with the SAT phone number on from her purse and dialed.

He picked up on the second ring. "Jeannette? What's wrong?" he asked, his voice worried.

"Nothing's wrong here. We're fine. But I saw the tabloid in the grocery store. It said your trial date had been set. Is that true?"

There was a long pause. "It's true."

"When did you find out about it?" she asked, curious. Had he been keeping the information to himself?

"The night I got home from the movie theater. Dillon had called with a message from my lawyer."

"Are you all right?"

"I knew this was coming."

There was distance in his voice. Distance because he didn't want to think about it, or distance because it was none of her concern? She didn't know what to offer, or even what to say. She suspected a lot more was going on under the surface than he was letting on. But if he didn't want her to see it, there wasn't much she could do.

"I just wanted to make sure you're okay," she said lamely.

"I'm fine."

He was *so* fine he sounded remote.

Zane was not normally a remote man. But she had her pride, and if he didn't want to talk, she wouldn't hold him on the line. "I've got to get to work," she said.

"Have a good shift. And tell Jonah hi for me."

She thought he might want to make plans to see her again, but he was silent. All she could say was, "Goodbye."

After the call she was distracted as she dressed for work, as she served ribs and swiped clean red vinyl seats on booth benches. She mixed up a few orders and even forgot to pick up her tips. All she could think about was what Zane must be feeling, knowing the trial was coming up. She could imagine he was playing out the scenarios in his head—returning to Texas, warding off the paparazzi, holing up someplace, reliving everything that had happened. She was sure he was doing that over and over again.

What could she do to help?

By the end of her shift she knew what she was going to do, whether it was foolish or not. She was going to go to Zane and hope that he talked to her. He couldn't keep everything bottled up inside and that's what he was doing. He said he didn't have music in his head...that it was locked up inside his heart. He had to let his emotions out somehow. Maybe if they were alone at his place, he would.

When she exited the back entrance of LipSmackin' Ribs into the parking lot, she realized the rain had started again. The night was soggy and damp, with a chill that could mean ice on the top of the mountain. Still, she knew she had to try to get to Zane. She could call him again, but she didn't want him to tell her not to come. She didn't want him to tell her they were better off not getting involved.

She was already involved, whether she wanted to be or not. She'd fallen in love with him and she couldn't just walk away when she suspected he had feelings for her, too. If he didn't? Then she'd not only walk but run in the opposite direction.

Her windshield wipers swiped up and down as she followed the road out of Thunder Canyon a bit anxiously. Yet as she turned onto the lane that led up to Zane's house, she felt herself becoming more peaceful. Whether she was being foolish or not, she had to do this.

Her car skidded only once. Her tires spun in the slick mud, but finally took hold. A few minutes later she'd pulled in front of his garage and turned off the engine. She knew the house well after having cleaned it so many times. One small light glowed over the sink in the kitchen. The rest of the downstairs was dark. But through the front windows, she could see the light in the loft burned. Maybe he'd picked up his guitar out of desperation. Maybe he was writing music again.

She ran from the driveway to the porch and got wet in that short distance. She'd worn only a long sweater to work today, thinking the fall showers were over. Feeling damp and disheveled, and not the way she wanted to look at all, she still didn't hesitate to knock on the door.

Her first knock must have not had enough power behind it because no one came to open it. So the next time she knocked harder and almost pounded. Maybe Zane was in town at some bar…at a back table where nobody would notice him. Maybe he was at Dillon's. She'd thought about calling his friend to see if he'd spoken to him, but that didn't seem right somehow.

The door opened, and Zane stood there dressed in boots, jeans and snap-button shirt, looking sexy and surprised. "Jeannette, what are you doing here? You shouldn't have come out here, especially in this weather."

"I'm not afraid of the dark or a little rain. Can I come in?" She hoped from the bottom of her heart he wouldn't say no.

Chapter Ten

When Zane didn't answer her question immediately, Jeannette felt even more foolish and explained, "You didn't sound good when I called. You didn't sound like yourself at all. You didn't even sound like the guy I first met who was so grumpy. So I got worried and here I am." She'd run out of explanations and now everything was up to him.

"You shouldn't have come," he muttered again as the rain dripped off the overhang of the roof onto the porch.

"But I did." She stood her ground, knowing this tough-guy act of his was just that and it covered the frustration, dismay and worry he must be feeling with the trial date going public.

Stepping back, he didn't say anything, but just expected her to follow him inside. She took the open door as an invitation and stepped over his threshold.

The living room was dark, but he didn't seem to think anything of that as he crossed to the sofa.

She went to him and sat down beside him. "Were you up in the loft?"

He stared ahead into the dark shadows broken only by the glow of the loft light drifting down, the slight illumination in the kitchen. "I was up there staring at my guitar."

"You didn't hold it?" she asked, as if it could have been a baby finding a home in his arms.

"No. I don't know what I expected. Maybe I thought it would speak to me in some way. Or maybe I thought I couldn't resist picking it up. But that wasn't the case at all. I'd laid it on the desk that day Jonah had plucked it, and that's where it stayed."

She wished she could snap him out of this mood he was in. It was so melancholy, so filled with regret. Maybe if she kept him talking—

"Where's Jonah?" he asked, as if he suddenly realized someone was missing.

"He's with Edna and Mel, having a sleepover. They let him watch his favorite movies and tuck him in after reading as many books as he wants."

"That's what grandparents do."

"They let Jonah know he's loved. That's what matters. If Ed and I had married—" She stopped. She shouldn't be talking about this now.

But Zane seemed to need the distraction. "Go ahead and finish."

She let her thought find voice. "If we had married, we would have been over there a lot."

Zane's gaze dropped down to her hands and he studied them thoughtfully. "How long ago did you take off his ring?"

She went still, embarrassed and feeling awkward. "I never *had* a ring."

"But you said he proposed."

"It wasn't a big romantic offer of marriage. When I told him I was pregnant, he just suggested we marry and that was that." As her words landed in the quiet living room, she realized what she'd said sounded terrible. She'd made it sound as if Ed hadn't wanted to get married. And it hadn't been like that, had it?

More silence drifted into the room like a wispy invader.

Finally Zane rose to his feet. "I'm going to light a fire."

She *was* cold, chilled and would be glad for any warmth from a fire...*or* from Zane. His moves were efficient, his strength obvious, his purpose determined. Once he had the fire stoked, he stood with one arm on the mantel, looking down into the blaze. He looked so lonely standing there that Jeannette couldn't stay on the sofa.

She went to him and gently touched his arm. "What's next for you? With the trial coming up, what will you have to do?"

"You didn't read the whole tabloid story?" he asked sarcastically.

"If I would have read the article, I wouldn't have known if I was getting the truth. I'd rather have that from you."

He angled toward her but he still didn't touch her.

She dropped her hand from his arm.

His expression was unreadable as he stated, "I'm going to have to fly to Texas for depositions and paperwork and meetings in a few weeks. This trial is just going to make everything worse for all of us."

The firelight cast changing shadows across his face. "You're talking about the press hounding you and the family?"

"I'm talking about all of it—swearing to tell the truth, giving lawyers our version of the truth, publicists spinning all of it. I just want it over. And yet when it's over, I know the grief will never be over for the Tuller family."

This wasn't the first time that Zane had reluctantly revealed he was a man of deep feelings and deep convictions. Ashley's death had made him feel as if his life and his career had crumbled around him. But even that seemed to take second place to what her family was going through.

There was only one way that Jeannette knew how to help him deal with all of it. On impulse, she wrapped her arms around him and held on tight.

His muscles went absolutely taut. For a few moments she believed he was going to push her away.

Then instead, he ran his hand down over her hair. "Jeannette, do you know what you're doing?"

She lifted her head to gaze into his eyes. "I think so."

With a groan that came from the deepest center of him, his lips crushed down on hers. In his kiss she felt sexual hunger, but she also felt desperation and so much need that she didn't know if she could satisfy it. The fire was giving off heat to warm the room, but their kiss generated a different kind of heat that made the shedding of clothes almost necessary. While he attempted to remove her sweater, she worked on the snaps of his shirt. But neither could get very far with them both trying.

Zane took each of her hands in his, kissed her fingertips, then made quick work of ridding her of her sweater and then her T-shirt. She was restless and tired of waiting until he let her work on his snaps again while he unhooked her bra. Appreciatively, she ran her hands up his chest, letting her fingers sift through his hair. When his breath caught, she smiled, because she so wanted to please him. Her bra straps fell down her arms and he looked at her as if he'd never stop. He pulled her into another kiss, and worked his fingers into the waistband of her shorts, ridding her of her clothes so she was standing naked before him. The dancing light from the flames played over their skin, and she wondered if she could let this picture burn an indelible print on her mind. There was something so intimate about standing there, gazing at each other with anticipation and fervent desire.

"You still have your jeans on," she whispered.

"If I take them off, we might be done as fast as we started. And there's a problem. The condoms are in the bedroom."

There was no turning back now, even though Zane was giving her the chance to think...to change her mind. She loved him and she wanted to show him even if she couldn't tell him yet. "I can either wait here or you can take me with you."

Without another moment's hesitation, he scooped her up into his arms and quickly carried her down the hall to the master suite. Then he stood her by the edge of the bed. She fumbled with his belt while he pulled open the nightstand drawer and plucked out the box of condoms.

"I bought these last week," he said. "I didn't know if this might happen."

In other words, he was telling her he hadn't come to Thunder Canyon with any intention of taking a woman to bed.

She threw back the patchwork comforter and slid between the sheets while he yanked off his boots and then shucked off his jeans and briefs. As he faced her, she reached out and stroked his face.

Covering her hand with his, he said roughly, "Dammit, Jeannette, I need you."

"I need you, too."

His body was telling her all about his need and she

wanted to satisfy it. She wanted to give him an outlet and a release from all the emotion building inside of him. She wanted to give him love. She touched him, curled her fingers around him.

He almost sat bolt upright. "If you do that, I won't be able to satisfy you."

"Make love to me, Zane. Now." Her fingers caressed him in the most intimate way again. He let out a combination of a groan and a growl and rose above her.

After a steady look into her eyes to make sure this was what she wanted, too, he reached for the condom, hurriedly tore open the packet and slid it on. Then he placed a hand on either side of her shoulders, settled himself on top of her and pushed inside.

She was more than ready for him. It seemed as if she'd been ready for him since she'd met him. When he closed his eyes, she wondered if he was just feeling pleasure, or thinking, too. Then her own thoughts fragmented as he withdrew, then thrust inside again and again.

She felt as if he were teasing her. She just wanted him to stay buried inside of her so she could wrap her legs around him and pretend he was hers and she was his. He kept up the rocking motion, there and then not there, until she was crazy with need.

Finally, she gasped, "Deeper!" and he seemed to plunge to her soul. She wrapped her legs around his hips and in doing so was thrust into the oblivion of pleasure. Her whole body trembled as she sucked in a breath, called Zane's name and gripped his shoulders. The erotic sensations were so sublime that she was afraid if she didn't hold on she'd never find her way back.

Zane's release came shortly after hers. She felt the shudder and completion of his orgasm and wished this moment could last. She'd never felt this whole before.

She'd never felt this connected to a man. She felt as if she belonged right here for the rest of her life.

Zane didn't move and she didn't care because she just wanted to hold on to him like this forever. Yet when he looked down at her, asked, "Are you okay?" and then rolled off her, she felt forever slipping away.

"I'm good," she said, wanting to say a whole lot more.

"How *can* you be when we didn't have any foreplay? I hardly touched you. I never let wanting a woman make me so crass before."

She ran her hand over his shoulder. "I wanted you as much as you wanted me."

He studied her hard to see if she was telling the truth.

She couldn't know what he was thinking, but he seemed to be withdrawing more and more each second. "Don't push me away."

He ran his hand down over his face. "Can you honestly tell me you want to be part of depositions and press conferences and microphones and cameras being thrust in your face?"

"I want to support you."

"This secret life of mine in Thunder Canyon is going to end sometime. Someone is going to recognize me somewhere. I can't stay holed up in this house much longer. If we're seen together, what's going to happen to your life and Jonah's? Have you thought about *that*?"

"You told me to think about it while we were watching the movie."

"And *did* you?"

Actually, she hadn't. But she did now. "My life is like a treadmill. Since you came into it, I stopped the machine. Now I stop running and enjoy Jonah. I see all the things I have to be grateful for. You've done that for me. Maybe I don't want to think about tomorrow or next week. Maybe

I just want to enjoy being with you now. You're the one who said we could have a really good time while you're here."

What *was* she saying? She certainly wanted more than a few nights...a few weeks. She was in love with Zane Gunther. However, she imagined hundreds of other women had been in love with him, too. Long-term relationships hadn't existed for him since Beth Ann.

"I don't want you to have regrets," he said.

"Do *you*?" She could see that he did, and that hurt her deeply. "Don't say it," she requested.

"Don't say what?" he asked.

"That this was a mistake."

Then instead of looking at her as if he wanted to push her away, he tightened his arms around her. "If it was a mistake, it was a damn pleasurable one."

She let him hold her for a long time. She didn't want to move. She wanted to stay there all night. However, she leaned away and said, "I have to go back to my place. Edna and Mel don't know where I am. If they need me, they won't be able to reach me."

"You could call them with my SAT phone number, but it's an odd number and they'd wonder about it. You'll get a lot of questions."

They were both silent for a few minutes. She took that to mean that she'd have to leave. But as she started to slide away, he caught her shoulder. "I could come home with you and we could try out *your* bed."

She grinned at him. "Really?"

"Really. But I'll have to leave early. I don't think you'd want anyone to see me going in and out of your place in the morning. There'd be talk. I know how small towns are. Dillon's filled me in about the gossip brigade in Thunder Canyon."

She wanted to tell him that she didn't care, that talk was the last thing she was worried about. That was somewhat true. But she did have to live here, and Jonah went to school here.

Leaning forward, she kissed him on the lips. His arms encircled her and tightened, and he deepened the kiss. But then he broke away and said huskily, "Let's get dressed."

A half hour later, they were standing outside Jeannette's apartment. She unlocked the door and let them in, thinking about how safe she'd felt with Zane following her on the water-puddled road with the rain still pouring down. Ed had never made her feel that safe.

She took a deep breath and knew she had to stop making comparisons. Ed had been everyday life. Zane was a fantasy, and she'd better not forget that.

The fantasy seemed to take hold all over again as she shut the door and he took her into his arms and kissed her. It was a no-holds-barred kiss, a continuation of where they'd left off in his bed. She dug her fingers into the hair at his nape.

With a chuckle, he tossed his hat onto the table. "This time I'm going to make sure you're every bit as riled up as I am."

"What makes you think I wasn't riled up the last time?"

"Too quick. Women like it slow and we went way too fast."

She tried to get hold of her breathing and she held his head still. "Zane, I'm not *all* women."

Her words seemed to slam into him like a blow. His brow furrowed as he studied her for a few moments and then responded, "No, you're not. I would never mistake you for anybody but you."

As she took off her sweater, he was behind her, kissing her neck.

She shivered and he said, "Your clothes are still damp from the rain."

"I don't have a fireplace," she teased.

"Body heat works just as well." The smoldering desire in his eyes convinced her it was true.

A few minutes later her clothes were on the floor in a pile and his weren't far away. They were in each other's arms, too eager to kiss and touch to even get as far as the living room.

"I didn't think I'd want it to happen this fast again." He held her breasts and flicked his thumb across her nipples. His mouth and tongue kissed her stomach and then her navel.

She felt as if she were going to fly apart into a million pieces. She couldn't wait for him to fill her again. Fast was good. Yet everything he was doing was so delightfully intoxicating that she couldn't stop him...didn't want to stop him. His long fingers brushed their way between her thighs. Then he was kneeling in front of her, his tongue touching her, and she felt as if she were going to come apart. She held on to his shoulders, needing the balance, needing his support. Her orgasm came swiftly and she was so entranced by it that she almost didn't realize he was picking her up, setting her on the table. Her pulse racing, her eyes closed, she heard him tear open a condom. Then he was inside of her, filling her, satisfying her, taking her on a journey they'd begun at his house. She wound her legs around him and she had that feeling of oneness again as she trembled through another orgasm and he reached his. If the bottom dropped out of the world, it simply wouldn't matter...because she was holding on to Zane and he was holding on to her. And that's the way it was supposed to be.

They were still holding on to each other, trying to catch

their breath, their faces close together, not an inch between their bodies, when her phone rang. She started and so did he.

"I have to get that," she said anxiously. "It could be Edna."

Zane separated from her, reached for the cordless phone and handed it to her. She checked the caller ID. "It *is* Edna. I have to take it."

"Go ahead. I'll be right back." Stooping, he picked up his clothes from the floor and headed down the hall to the bathroom.

Nakedness, a few minutes ago, had been a natural thing. Now it didn't feel right somehow.

Jeannette hopped down off the table, reached for her sweater and slung it around her shoulders. "Hello," she said breathlessly, afraid Edna would hang up before she answered.

"Jeannette?"

"Yes. Is something wrong?"

"I couldn't reach you. I tried about a half hour ago."

"I was out. You didn't leave a message on the machine."

There was silence, as if Edna wanted to ask, *Out where?* But she didn't. "Jonah had a bad dream. He wanted to talk to you. When I couldn't get hold of you, he was worried."

"I'm here now. Let me talk to him."

Jonah came on the line. "Mommy?"

"Hi, honey. What's going on?"

"I had a dream."

"What was it about?" She pulled the sweater tighter, glad that video phones weren't a staple in every household yet.

"I walked on the mountain," he said in a small voice.

"You did? Were you all by yourself?"

"Yeah. I didn't wanna be."

"Can you tell me what happened?"

"I fell off!"

"You fell off the mountain?"

"Yeah."

"Then what happened?"

"Zane caught me."

She swallowed hard. "I see. Was *I* there?"

"Nope. Just Zane."

"So this wasn't really a bad dream, was it? Not if Zane caught you."

He thought about it. "No, just scary."

"Because you didn't want to be on the mountain all by yourself."

"Uh-huh."

"Do you think you can go back to sleep now? Or do you want me to come get you?"

Just as she said the words, Zane entered the kitchen. He was tall and brooding and a bit distant now. He had his jeans on, but his shirt was unsnapped, hanging open. How she wanted to touch him again. How she wanted to lie in his arms all night. But Jonah's well-being had to come before what she wanted.

"I'm gonna stay here," Jonah said.

"I'm sure Edna will like that."

"Can you sing me a song?"

She glanced at Zane. "Sure. Which one?"

"The one about the boy and the dog," her son requested.

So, self-consciously, in front of a man who had sung to millions of people, she sang a little song that was a track on one of Jonah's children's CDs.

When she was finished, he said, "Good night, Mommy."

"Good night, Jonah. I'll see you in the morning."

When Edna came on the phone, she asked, "Are you going to be there if he wakes up again?"

"Yes, I'll be here." After confirming what time she'd arrive at Mel and Edna's in the morning, she ended the call.

Zane took the phone from her and settled it on the counter. "I guess she'd prefer it if you had a cell phone."

"It's never been a problem. She's always known exactly where I'd be."

"Until now."

"I'm sorry we were interrupted." She watched as he fastened the snaps on his shirt.

"Don't be. You're Jonah's mom. You have to be there for him."

She wasn't sure what to say or do next. The mood had definitely been broken. "Would you like a beer? Some coffee?"

"No. I'd better go."

"Zane, you came back here with me so we could—"

She wasn't sure where to go with that one.

Stepping closer to her, he stroked his fingers through her mussed hair. "Thank you for coming up to the house tonight. Having you there meant a lot."

"I know you think you're on an island, Zane, and no one can share it with you, but that's *not* true."

"I have to figure out the best way to handle the trial and the publicity. You can't help with that."

"You're afraid I'll make it all worse." She could see *those* headlines. GUNTHER STARTS AFFAIR WHILE FAMILY SUFFERS.

He didn't answer her, and she suddenly knew she wasn't going to be sleeping in his arms tonight. "When you leave for Texas, for the depositions, will you be coming back to Thunder Canyon afterward?"

"I don't know yet. I don't know what my lawyer's going to advise. I don't know how long the preparations for the trial will take."

She wanted to say she could stand beside him, no matter what…that she could roll with the punches…that she and Jonah could adapt to whatever lifestyle he chose. But it was too soon to say any of that.

Since the phone call, something in Zane's eyes had changed. Tonight, when they'd made love, he'd been unguarded. Now he wasn't. He was patiently waiting until this conversation ended, and then he was going to leave. She wouldn't be a woman who clung to hope when there wasn't any. She wouldn't be a woman who would do anything to keep Zane Gunther in her bed. She only wanted him there if he wanted to be there. She only wanted him there if he could one day feel as deeply about her as she felt about him. She was glad her sweater covered her, grateful it was longer than her shorts she wore for work.

Something hot flared in Zane's eyes and she couldn't even guess why. He bent down to her, gave her a scaldingly short kiss, then picked up his hat from the other side of the table from where they'd made love.

"I'll call you," he said and left her apartment.

Still weak-kneed from the lovemaking and the emotional upheaval of the day, she sank down to the floor where the remainder of her clothes still lay, raised her knees and dropped her head into her hands.

The following day the rain stopped. In the afternoon Zane went to the shed out back to fetch another load of firewood. He'd felt like a bear with a thorn in his paw all day. He knew the reasons well enough…he just didn't want to think about them.

As he carried the firewood back to the house, he heard a vehicle coming up his drive. His heart leaped. Jeannette?

No. Whatever the vehicle was, it was more powerful than hers. Besides, why would she want to drive up here again after the way he'd left things last night? The truth was, having sex with her had shown him a side of himself he didn't like. He'd hardly been able to control his desire for her. The first time around he'd felt like a caveman. The second time—

Well, that hadn't been much better. He'd never, ever felt that vulnerable with a woman before. He'd never, ever felt so rattled, turned inside out, shaken upside down. So what had he done? He'd closed down. Hearing her sing that song to Jonah had tightened his throat until he could hardly get a word out.

He was mucking up Jeannette's life without even trying. What happened when the real circus started? What happened when vans with satellite dishes descended like a swarm of bees?

Would he return after his depositions in Texas?

If he was smart, he wouldn't.

Yet every time he closed his eyes, and even when he didn't, last night was a raw, vivid memory that wouldn't let up.

He'd taken the load of wood into the living room by the time his doorbell rang. When he opened the front door he couldn't believe his eyes. "Jeff! What are you doing here?"

His manager was stocky, a few inches shorter than Zane. His brown eyes penetrating, he lifted a shoulder in a shrug. "Because you don't seem to want to stay in touch, I decided to check up on you."

Jeff Nolan wasn't just his manager. He was a friend. They'd been together for years. They'd seen the worst and the best together in professional terms, and usually had an easy camaraderie.

His manager pushed his designer glasses onto the bridge of his nose. "Dillon gave me directions," he explained. "It's a good thing he and I get along. It's a good thing he knows you need me if you want to hold on to your career."

The silence of Zane's remote location weighed heavily on them both. Finally Jeff asked, "Well, are you going to ask me in for a beer?"

Zane showed his manager into the kitchen.

"Nice place," Jeff decided, removing his sport coat and hanging it over one of the chairs. He studied the country kitchen, even the Sub-Zero refrigerator where Jonah's drawing was taped and Jeannette's phone numbers were positioned under the magnet. With a smile, he accepted a bottle of beer Zane handed him, took out the chair from the table and flipped it around.

Then he sat on it, took a long swig and stared at his client. "We might be friends, Zane, but we hooked up in a professional relationship first, and that's why I'm here. Have you written any music while you've been up here?"

Zane knew his stubborn, don't-mess-with-me expression probably wouldn't keep Nolan at bay, but he tried it anyway.

It didn't stop his manager. "You *have* picked up your guitar and strummed a few notes, right?"

Zane stood there, his arms crossed over his chest, silent.

"Just who do you think you're punishing?" Jeff suddenly demanded.

Zane's stubbornness fell away. "You don't get it. I can pick up that guitar, but my fingers won't move. I can think about writing music, but the words and the music don't come."

That wasn't explicitly true anymore, he realized. Last night, after he'd gotten home, a phrase had played over and over in his head. But he'd shoved it inside and ignored it, knowing nothing would come of it.

"You've had four months to act like a hermit," his manager reminded him. "You've had four months to beat yourself up. How many months are going to be enough? Your band needs to play. Even though they've been with you for years, they can't wait forever."

Jeff wasn't the insensitive SOB he was playacting today. Zane knew his manager was trying to get his dander up, trying to make Zane yell or scream or vent in some way that would get the whole process going again. But this wasn't music block or lyric block. This was so much more than that.

"I can't forget what happened that night, Jeff. I keep seeing it in my mind, over and over again. I was powerless to help and I still think there's something I should have been able to do. Ashley Tuller was a sweet girl who didn't deserve to die because she came to one of my concerts."

"It was an accident," Jeff said slowly, enunciating each word. "Should security have been better? Yes. Should we have anticipated what happened at your bus? Yes. But you are *not* to blame for a girl falling and hitting her head."

"She was there because of me."

"Get over yourself. Get over the idea that you can control the world."

After a lengthy pause, Zane asked, "What do you want from me?"

"For one thing I want you to come out of hiding. If you

think inspiration is going to hit while you're holed up like this, I believe you're wrong."

Zane didn't think location had anything to do with it, but he kept quiet.

Jeff took another swig of his beer as if he had all the time in the world. Then he gestured to Zane's refrigerator door. "Nice picture. A kid draw that?"

Zane scowled.

Nolan motioned to the numbers where Jeannette's name was printed. "Jeannette. That has a nice ring. Maybe even an old-fashioned ring. Are you seeing somebody? Is that why you're still here?"

"What if I am?"

His admission seemed to slow Jeff down. "If you *are* seeing someone, someone with a kid, just how long do you think it's going to last? Until your bus rolls up here to drive you away?"

"You're exaggerating. Yes, I have to go to Texas to prepare for the trial. Yes, there's going to be a trial. But afterward, what if I come back here and forget about music altogether?"

Zane was as surprised as Jeff when that came out of his mouth. Was it the solution that would give him peace and bring balance to his life again?

Chapter Eleven

On Monday morning Jeannette felt Erika's gaze on her as she handed her the list of judges for the pageant.

"Is everything okay? You seem distracted today," Erika remarked.

Jeannette hadn't known Erika long, but in the time they'd been working together they'd become friends. Still, she didn't know how much to say. "You know Zane and I have been seeing each other?"

"Dillon told me Zane bought out the movie theater. That must have been an unusual date."

"Especially with Jonah along," Jeannette agreed with a smile.

"I know about child chaperones. Dillon and I worked together when we met. But whenever he came here, Emilia was center stage."

"I'm worried Jonah will get attached to Zane and then—" Jeannette broke off abruptly not wanting to put her fear into words.

"And then things won't work out?" Erika finished for her.

"How can they?" Jeannette asked, hoping Erika would see a solution more clearly than *she* could. "I've warned myself over and over again that there's nothing but disaster ahead. This isn't Zane's home. He's a star and famous. When he *is* performing, he could be gone three-quarters of the year. I saw the schedule he keeps."

"Isn't Google wonderful?" Erika asked. Then she looked Jeannette squarely in the eye. "Tell me something, are you attracted to Zane the mega-star or Zane the man?"

Jeannette remembered their first kiss and what Zane had said: *That was Zane the man who kissed you, not Zane Gunther the country singer.* "I've just fallen for *him*. It has nothing to do with what he has, but who he is. But what do *I* have to offer *him?* I'm small-town all the way. I have a son who has to come first. You know how that is. How did *you* handle it?"

Erika got a faraway look for a little while, then returned to the present. "Dillon and I had a rocky road. He had scars from his first marriage that still weren't healed."

"His son," Jeannette said.

"Yes, Toby. I can't imagine the pain of losing a child. Whenever Dillon interacted with Emilia, he thought of the son he'd lost, until…she won his heart all on her own. Dillon finally opened his heart to both of us. Actually, Zane played a part in that. He wrote his hit—'Movin' On'—with Dillon in mind and sang it for the first time when he performed here last year. We were in that audience and it made Dillon take a hard look at his life."

Jeannette could imagine Zane doing that for his friend. She wished she could hear him sing in person. Because Erika had been so open with her, she confided, "I'm afraid

Jonah and I are just a substitute for Zane's real life while he's here. Once he leaves, he'll forget us."

"You and I are more alike than you know," Erika assured her. "Dillon was only here temporarily, but he decided to stay. By the time I'd fallen in love with him, even though my roots were here, I think I would have followed him anywhere."

"Zane and I haven't known each other very long and I'm not sure he's even thinking beyond—" She stopped, knowing some things had to remain private.

"That's always a woman's fear," Erika empathized. "But as far as not knowing each other long, how long does it take to fall in love?"

Wasn't *that* the million-dollar question?

An hour later Jeannette wrapped up her work with Erika, then delivered flyers to the businesses on her list. Frontier Days was ten days away. The storefronts had posters in their front windows and an electronic billboard near the mall flashed the schedule of events. Jeannette liked being part of this community endeavor, feeling as if she were doing her part, bringing tourists into town and customers into businesses, giving residents of Thunder Canyon a chance to come together for this celebration. And Frontier Days *was* a celebration of where the town had started and where it was now.

Jeannette thought about all that as she let herself into her apartment. She had about an hour to do laundry, pay bills, then get ready for her shift at LipSmackin' Ribs.

She sighed. Bob Collins had sat at her station again yesterday, making remarks that made her uncomfortable. When he'd left, she'd breathed a sigh of relief. If only she could quit her job and find something better. But she couldn't quit until she knew she *had* something better.

Jeannette's washer and dryer were hidden in a closet in her kitchen. She was stuffing Jonah's play clothes into the dryer when her doorbell rang.

Could it be Zane? He'd said he'd phone her—

She slammed the dryer door shut, closed the closet and went to the door. But when she peeked through the glass beside the curtain panel, she didn't see Zane. Rather, she saw a shorter man dressed in a tweed sports jacket, white oxford shirt and black slacks. She had no idea who he was.

He must have seen her shadow at the glass because he called, "Ms. Williams. My name is Jeff Nolan. We have a mutual acquaintance. I'm his manager."

Obviously the man didn't want to announce Zane's name to anyone who might be passing or within earshot. What was Zane's manager doing on her doorstep?

There was only one way to find out.

Cautiously she opened the door a few inches. "Do you have any identification?" she asked.

The man raised his brows, took out his wallet and showed her his driver's license. His address was Nashville. He slipped a photo from his wallet and handed it to her. Zane and Jeff Nolan were standing on a stage at what looked like a county fair. They were both smiling at whoever had taken the picture.

Jeannette opened the door the rest of the way, inviting the man into her kitchen. "I don't have much time," she said. "I'm due at work in about forty-five minutes."

Mr. Nolan glanced around and seemed to sum up what he saw. "Zane didn't send me here if that's what you're thinking. Yesterday I saw your number on his refrigerator and I used the reverse directory to find your address. He'll probably be mad as hell if he finds out that I showed up here."

Well, at least the man was straightforward. She could be, too. "Why did you feel the need to come see me?"

"Zane's private life is his private life. I'm not here to assess whether you're a gold digger or whether you want to sell your story to the nearest tabloid."

"I would never—"

"It doesn't matter to me. What matters to me is Zane, his music and his career."

She wasn't sure what to say, so she waited for more.

"When I saw your child's drawing also hanging on Zane's refrigerator, I took notice. I don't think that's something Zane has ever done before—hung a crayon drawing in his kitchen. So from that, I figured out you and your kid must be pretty special to him."

She could only hope that was true. She still kept silent.

"If that's the case, Ms. Williams, then you should care about Zane's career."

"I want him to be happy, but that's hard for him right now."

Mr. Nolan nodded. "Yes, I know it is, but *hard* doesn't mean *impossible*. I came here because I'd like you to try to influence Zane to try to write, to get back to his music, to pick up that guitar and play."

"Don't you think Zane *wants* to perform again?"

"I don't know if he does. I think he's punishing himself by not picking up that guitar. You might be able to encourage him…to force the issue a bit. That's all I ask."

Leveling a glance at him, she asked, "Do you want Zane to sing and write songs again because of the revenue he brings in for you?"

Nolan emphatically shook his head. "No. I want Zane to sing and write again to save his heart and soul."

"Mr. Nolan—"

"I'm not being overly dramatic. Zane *is* his music. Without it, it's like he's half a man. Making the next CD and planning his concert tour used to give him purpose. Now he doesn't have a purpose. He can sit on top of a mountain and contemplate his navel all he wants. But at some point, that navel is going to get boring. Sitting on the mountaintop isn't going to be the peaceful experience it was when he first came here. He can't find peace in a place. He has to find that peace in his soul."

"Maybe Zane is trying to find a different life than the one he had," she suggested, hoping that might be true.

"Maybe. But walking away cold turkey never works, at least not for long. He left everything surrounding his life, but he's going to get pulled back into it in a few weeks. He's going to remember what he misses, and he needs to be prepared for that."

Jeannette saw the common sense behind everything Mr. Nolan was saying and she confided, "He shuts down whenever I mention his music. When my son accidentally plucked his guitar, Zane just set it aside as if it was an old coat he was hanging in the closet. I'm not sure my encouragement will make a difference."

"Will you try?"

"On one condition. I'm going to tell him you were here and what you asked me to do."

Nolan scowled at her. "That might defeat the whole purpose."

"I won't keep secrets from Zane. Not about something as personal as this." She thought about the secret she *was* keeping, the fact that LipSmackin' Ribs might be stealing recipes from DJ Traub. She'd handle that in time...when she figured out how to do it. But for now, she would tell

Zane his manager had visited her. It was the right thing to do.

"All right," Nolan agreed. "If that's the way it has to be. Maybe you can plant a seed."

It would be wonderful if she could because she understood that music was a part of who Zane was…a very important part.

"A date?" Jeannette asked, as if she hadn't heard of such a thing. She'd almost been asleep Wednesday night when Zane called, but now was coming fully awake.

He chuckled. "Yes, Ms. Williams, I'm asking you for a formal date. You and me, and whatever we choose to do. Do you think Mel and Edna would babysit?"

"I don't know. I can ask. Should I get dressed up?"

"You can wear whatever you'd like."

"It's been so long since I wore a dress, it'll be a treat." She'd love to pretty up for Zane and watch his eyes go to that deep-desire green… "I might even add perfume," she added a little coyly.

"Do you want me to imagine where you're going to dab that perfume?" His voice was husky, as if he was already doing that.

"You can guess. Then we'll see if you're right." Was she actually flirting with him? Is that the tone she wanted to set for their first official date? Or was it their second? "We did have a movie date," she reminded him.

"Jonah was there, so I decided that didn't count."

"So your definition of a date is no children around?" she asked with a laugh.

"My definition of a date is the two of us together, preferably *alone*."

She wondered what he had in mind. Certainly they

wouldn't be going to a public place. A little pang hit her hard at that. She understood his reasons, but on the other side of it, she wondered if he'd be embarrassed being seen with her. After all, she wasn't anyone special.

"When's your next night not to work?" he asked.

"Sunday night."

Sunday was four days away. He must have been thinking the same thing because he said, "I want that date with *you,* but I'd like to see Jonah, too."

"Matching up schedules is tough," she agreed, "but since I work Friday night, Jonah is getting his stitches out and then we'll be spending the afternoon together. Would you like to join us?"

"How about the two of you join *me* and we'll look for that elk again? I have my digital camera buried somewhere in my suitcase. He might get a kick out of seeing the pictures on my laptop."

"That's a great idea. Do you want me to just drive him up to your place after we finish at the clinic?"

"No, I'll pick you up. I don't like the idea of the two of you driving down that mountain road alone."

He was being protective and in this case, she liked that. "I'll let you know tomorrow about Mel and Edna for Sunday."

"That sounds good. Seeing you and Jonah again sounds good, too. When I'm not with you, Jeannette…" He stopped, then it seemed he reluctantly admitted, "I miss you."

He wasn't telling her he had deep feelings for her, but missing her was *something.* She wanted to tell him about Jeff Nolan visiting her, but she didn't want to do it over the phone. And they probably wouldn't be able to talk Friday with Jonah with them. She might have to save that serious discussion for Sunday night.

Sunday night. What *did* Zane have planned for them?

Saturday morning Zane paced restlessly back and forth across Erika's living room, although he had to be careful not to trip over Emilia's toys. The almost-three-year-old seemed to be involved in several projects at once—building a house with blocks, feeding her favorite doll and pulling around a duck toy that quacked. Suddenly she wanted to tug a three-foot plush horse into the mix.

"Dillon gave her that, didn't he?" Dillon thought big and it looked like a present he'd buy for his daughter.

"He bought it for her last year for her birthday. This year it's a t-r-i-c-y-c-l-e," Erika spelled out so her daughter wouldn't guess. "We're having a small party for her Wednesday evening, my mom and some friends. You're welcome to come."

But as soon as Erika said it she saw he'd refuse. "Right. No public appearances right now. I forgot. So, what brought you here this morning? I know I make a good cup of coffee, but—"

"I've got a problem I thought you might be able to help with. Jeannette needs a babysitter for Jonah tomorrow night. She asked Edna and Mel Lambert, but they refused…said something about going bowling. She thinks they're upset she's seeing someone."

"But they don't know who, do they?"

"No. And if they knew, their attitude could go either way."

"But you don't want them to know."

"Not yet. So I was wondering—is there anyone that you and Dillon use regularly? Other than your mom, I mean. I don't want to impose."

Erika thought about it, then she pushed her long curly brown hair behind her ear. "You know what? *I'll* babysit for Jeannette."

"You're kidding!"

"No. I have some work to finish up for Frontier Days next week. And after Jonah goes to bed, it will be quieter at Jeannette's apartment than here, I'm sure. Dillon can sometimes be a distraction."

"You're still newlyweds," Zane said with a grin.

Erika blushed a little. "And I love being a newlywed. But next Friday is going to come whether I'm ready or not, and I want to be ready. Where will you be taking Jeannette?"

"I'll be taking her to Chez Zane. I'll light candles and bring in a gourmet meal." As he said it, he saw Erika's smile slip away. "What are you thinking?"

"Do you really want to know?"

"Yes, I do." He realized now he'd come to Erika's in person instead of calling because he wanted her take on his relationship with Jeannette.

"Most women don't appreciate hidden affairs. I was involved in one before Dillon. My circumstances were entirely different because the guy I was seeing was seeing someone else. But Jeannette might feel you're embarrassed to be with her."

"I'm hiding *myself*, not the relationship."

"Are you sure? Are you sure you just don't want to see another tabloid headline like, COUNTRY STAR DATES WAITRESS?"

"Do you think I'm that shallow?"

"I think you're a man with a lot on your plate. I know you bought out the movie theater. I also know the two of you just want to be alone. But…" she trailed off.

"But maybe something different than my log house is in order?"

"That's up to *you,*" Erika said with a shrug.

Suddenly Zane had an idea he thought would be a good one. He'd just have to enlist DJ Traub's help and hope Dillon's cousin agreed.

It had been fairly easy, really, Zane thought as he parked his SUV near the back entrance at DJ's Rib Shack, glanced around to make sure no one was watching, then escorted Jeannette inside the back door of the restaurant. DJ's busy time on Sunday was after church, through lunch and into the afternoon. Sunday evenings were slower. Tourists who were going to attend Frontier Days hadn't started arriving at Thunder Canyon Resort yet, so Zane had offered to donate whatever DJ would have brought in tonight to charity and DJ had agreed. He didn't need money any more than Zane did, so they both felt good about it.

DJ had posted the "Closed After 7PM Sunday" sign yesterday and had the closing announced on the local radio station. Zane knew with the shades down and the lights dimmed, he and Jeannette would have privacy, yet an atmosphere different from his log house. He was beginning to think of that log house as his and that was crazy. But especially when Jeannette and Jonah were in it, it felt like home. On Friday they'd had a ton of fun, hiking and shooting pictures of elk. But after he'd taken them home and Jonah had gone to bed and Jeannette asked him if he wanted to stay, he'd declined. Not because he wanted to but because he felt he should. He remembered vividly what had happened in her kitchen last time he was there. Before Jonah found them in bed together or asked too many questions, Zane needed to straighten out some things in his own life. Tonight, however, he'd take Jeannette back to his place and they'd be totally alone.

As they entered DJ's restaurant, Jeannette looked a little…unsettled. "What's wrong?" he asked.

"Oh, nothing's wrong," she said quickly. "I just didn't expect to come…here. I thought we might go to your place."

"My place comes afterward," he said with a wink.

Jeannette gazed around the restaurant as if she hadn't seen it before.

"Do you come here to eat?" he asked her.

"Actually, no. Jonah and I don't go out much. That painting is beautiful."

"DJ's wife, Allaire, did that. She's an art teacher at the high school."

Just then, a pretty blonde came from the kitchen into the restaurant. "Zane. Hi! Everything's all ready."

"Allaire," he said with some surprise. "I didn't expect to see you here."

"I hope you don't mind, but we're trying out a new menu item on you. Baked chicken potpie. You can give it a try and then give DJ your verdict."

Zane introduced Allaire to Jeannette.

"I'm sure everything will be wonderful," Jeannette said.

"DJ thought you should have something simple for dessert, but I opted for a chocolate cheesecake recipe," she confided to Zane. "You can take the rest of it along home with you." And she added, "Right inside the kitchen door there's a control panel on the wall. Hit the green button and you'll have some music. It's not country tonight."

Zane was grateful for that, and at the twinkle in Allaire's eye he suspected it was romantic music made for slow dancing. That sounded like a wonderful idea. "Thank you for going to all this trouble."

"No problem." She motioned toward a table that was covered with a white linen tablecloth and laid with silver, crystal, a bottle of wine in an ice bucket and a few flowers in a vase.

"I just thought DJ's could use a little remodeling for one night. Enjoy yourselves." Then Allaire was gone, letting the back door lock behind her.

"DJ and Allaire seem like pretty great people," Jeannette murmured.

"They are. The town had a field day with gossip about them, but that's Allaire and DJ's story to tell. Maybe sometime they'll fill you in."

He realized he was talking as if this date were only the beginning. From her expression, he could see she had caught the meaning behind his words, too.

Jeannette was wearing a long, taupe all-weather coat tonight. As her fingers went to the buttons, he automatically stepped behind her to take it from her shoulders. On the drive here her perfume had teased him, along with their conversation about it. When he took the coat from her shoulders, he noticed she was wearing what women called a little black dress. It was deceptively simple, with a long zipper up the back. While he hung the coat over his arm, she turned to face him and he noticed the V-neckline was sedate, yet the point dipped, oh so slightly into her cleavage. The long sleeves somehow made that neckline even more noticeable, and he found himself swallowing hard. The dress didn't have a waist, but it molded to her hips and stopped just above her knees.

This dress topped her outfit for LipSmackin' Ribs in spades. With high-heeled black shoes that sported sexy straps, he could hardly think straight as he looked at her.

Even her hair was different tonight. She'd piled it on top of her head and arranged it in a loose bun. Shorter strands wisping along her cheeks vied with her dangling gold ball earrings for notice. Her eyes seemed huge under her bangs and he realized she knew how to use makeup effectively for one of the most natural looks he'd ever seen. Her plum-colored lipstick matched her nail polish. She was one put-together woman.

"You're staring," she murmured. "Did I smudge something?"

"Lordy, no, you didn't smudge a thing. In fact, you should be a makeup artist for some of the models I know."

She suddenly grinned. "You like a more subtle look?"

"I like *your* look. Come here. I've been waiting to do this since I picked you up." He laid her coat over a chair and wrapped his arms around her.

She leaned back, studying him. "Don't think I didn't notice the lack of beard stubble. You look different, too."

"More recognizable?" he joked.

"With your white shirt and bolo tie, you're pretty impressive. Now I know why the ladies swoon."

His green eyes twinkled with both amusement and heat. "Are *you* swooning?"

"Not yet," she responded breathlessly.

He couldn't suppress an obvious smile. "You really are one tough cookie. You won't just drop at my feet. Do you know what that does to my ego?"

"Helps it diminish in size?" she asked tauntingly.

"Come here," he said again, this time pulling her so close that neither of them could breathe.

Then his lips took hers in a sensual kiss that told her this was only the beginning of tonight and there was a lot more to come. When he broke away, he took off his hat and walked it to one of the hat pegs on the wall. Then he came back to her, feeling an attraction that practically hogtied him. Did she feel it, too?

The thing was, when he caught Jeannette looking around DJ's, she seemed terribly uncomfortable. He didn't know if that had to do with him or the restaurant.

"Allaire said the food was ready, so we better eat first. Baked chicken potpie sound good to you?" he asked.

Jeannette focused her attention on him again, all smiles now. "It sounds wonderful. My mom used to make chicken potpie. She'd add carrots and potatoes, the largest pieces of chicken, celery and onion and whatever herbs she could find. Then she topped the whole thing with a piecrust. It was a lot of work and she didn't make it much, but I loved it whenever she did."

Zane looked at the side dishes Allaire had prepared. "We've got corn bread, hush puppies, sweet-and-sour cucumbers, along with cranberry relish and chocolate cheesecake. This is more than dinner, it's a feast. Are you ready to dig in?"

Before they dug in, though, Zane picked up the bottle of white wine and showed her the label. "Are you interested?"

"Can I have a taste first?"

"The lady's a wine connoisseur!"

"No, the lady's not. I just know what I like and what I don't." He poured the wine and offered it to her for her inspection. She swirled it in her glass, smelled it, then took a few sips. "It's very nice. I think it will go well with the chicken."

"My thoughts exactly," he said, tasting his. "Isn't it great to know we agree on something?"

"I think we agree on a lot of things."

Zane poured more into her glass, but not much into his. At her raised brows, he said, "I'm driving."

She seemed to like the idea that he was responsible. Already he'd decided she was a woman who liked fun, but within certain parameters. And she always figured out the consequences.

Knowing he had to get something off his chest, he said, "I want you to understand that tonight is a date, Jeannette. If you want to have dinner and go home, that's what we'll do."

She laid her fork by the dinner she'd hardly touched. "What do *you* want to do?"

He shifted on his chair, one-hundred-percent sure of exactly what he wanted. The sizzle between them never stopped. The racing of his heart whenever he was around her, or even when he just thought about her, was unusual and unsettling.

A vulnerability about Jeannette always required complete honesty on his part. "I've come on strong with you. I feel a little out of control when I'm around you," he admitted. "I just want to be sure you're on the same page as I am."

"I think you've controlled yourself admirably," she returned with a little smile.

"You're not going to run to the tabloid and spill the fact I acted like a caveman?" he asked, half in jest.

But she picked up the part that *wasn't* half in jest and she looked hurt. "Do you still not trust me?"

Why had he asked that? Why had he even brought it up? Because that was his life whether he liked it or not? "Can you forget I asked that?"

She hesitated, and the silence in the empty restaurant seemed more foreboding than intimate. "Without trust we don't have much of a relationship."

Instinctively, he reached across the table and took her hand. "I trust you."

An odd expression crossed her face. It looked something like guilt. But a second later it was gone, and he guessed his imagination was working overtime. His adrenaline was rushing faster through him with each thought about later. Was that why every word and expression seemed to matter?

Her smile was back now as she squeezed his fingers and his whole body went on alert. "I'm on the same page as you, Zane. I want to go back to your house with you after dinner."

They gazed into each other's eyes for what seemed like forever. Then Zane cleared his throat and picked up his fork, not caring one whit what they ate, just wanting to go back to his house and get naked in his bed with her.

But then Jeannette said the words that fill every man's heart with dread. "There *is* something I want to talk to you about. But that can wait until later."

Talking and having sex didn't always go together. Talking could kill the moment and the passion. Yet, gazing into Jeannette's eyes, he was almost as curious about what she wanted to talk about as he was where her perfume dabs were located.

Almost.

Chapter Twelve

Jeannette watched Zane poke a log until the fire in his living room burned brightly. The fire between them had been burning brightly all evening—from the moment he'd picked her up until their slow dance after dinner at DJ's. He'd kissed her while they were dancing as if there was no tomorrow. She'd clung to him as if she'd expected the night to last.

However, she had more than one thing to discuss with him. From the moment they'd stepped into DJ's Rib Shack she'd felt guilty about keeping Woody's secret. After she'd met Allaire, she'd felt even worse.

But first, they had to talk about Zane's music.

He'd discarded his Western-cut sport coat with his Stetson. His white shirt made his broad shoulders seem even broader. The black string tie clasped by a horseshoe, along with his black jeans and boots, fulfilled the sexy image he portrayed on stage. But she knew the man *behind* the image, and that's why she was here, wanting an intimate end to the evening, yet knowing she had to touch him emotionally first. To do that, she might douse his desire.

After he slid the poker into the stand alongside the fireplace, he came to sit beside her, a good foot away. Because they'd be in each other's arms if they didn't keep some distance?

He seemed nonchalant as he said, "You had something you wanted to talk about?"

"Jeff Nolan came to see me last week."

Zane's brows furrowed and his hands balled into fists. "You're not serious!"

"I am. He's concerned about you."

"Oh, I heard his concerns. He was here, too. How did he even know where to find you?"

Zane looked angry, and she wasn't exactly sure why… yet. "Something about he saw my number on your refrigerator and used a reverse directory."

Zane swore, looked away, then back at her again. "I'm sorry. He had no business bothering you."

"It wasn't a bother, Zane. At first—"

"What? Did he insult you? He can come on too strong at times."

"No, he didn't insult me. But at first, I wasn't sure why he was there, if it was for his own sake or for yours."

Consternation took the place of anger on Zane's face. Although the crinkle lines around his eyes were still deep, his brow was less furrowed. "I don't understand."

She took a deep breath. "He wanted me to convince you to play again."

Wind whistled against the side of the house. The popping of the fire seemed overly loud. That was because the room was so silent.

Finally Zane said, "Okay, so you told me why he came. I'll call him tomorrow and rip him from here to next year."

After a pause, Zane pulled his bolo tie loose and set it on the arm of the sofa. After opening the top two buttons of his shirt, he moved closer to her. "So that's finished and now we can get on to the best part of the evening."

Bracing a hand on his chest, she shook her head. "I think we need to talk about this."

A guarded look came into his eyes. "About how Jeff should leave you alone?"

Knowing he wanted her to drop this, she still couldn't. "About how you need an outlet for your emotion. You said yourself, country music is about heart and soul and pouring all that out into lyrics. You did that for years. Now, suddenly, you're bottling everything up. Maybe if you strummed your guitar until—"

"Do you think I haven't tried?" he asked angrily. "After Jeff's visit, I picked up my guitar. I strummed it. I got a couple of chords out, but there was nothing behind them."

"I think there's *too* much behind them," she amended softly.

"And what do you want me to do about that?" His gaze was almost cold. "Switch instruments? Write in a journal? Burn every tabloid that comes out? Maybe take up golf so I have a new hobby?"

His frustration tore at her heart and she knew she couldn't take his anger personally. "I'm not the enemy, Zane. Neither is your manager. He thought if I encouraged you, *that* could make a difference. I know you don't want me to interfere, but I just think if you could find your music again, you'd be happier."

The seriously defensive expression on his face dissolved. Coldness dissipated into the warm tenderness she was beginning to know so well. When he moved even closer, he encircled her with his arms. "*You* make me happy. You say I need an outlet for everything I've bottled up. Well, I think I've found one."

Heaven was in Zane's kiss. He might have kept his desire in check most of the evening, but now it was flagrant, ready to be acted on. Maybe the only way to help Zane was to lie naked with him and become vulnerable. Maybe if he witnessed *her* vulnerability, he'd become vulnerable, too. She realized he had to let go of the control he wanted so desperately to keep in place. He had to give up responsibility for things he couldn't change. He had to stop building walls and go back to building bridges and bonds and connections. Maybe he wasn't ready to talk about his feelings, but maybe he could give feeling in his touch, in his murmured words, in his need of her.

His hand went to the zipper at the back of her neck and started to slowly pull it down. The sound carried with it intent and promise.

"I guess we're done talking." She was already breathless from anticipation.

"Talking is highly overrated," he assured her as he kissed the corner of her lip, then her neck, then lower.

"Are you finding any of those spots where I dabbed perfume?" she teased, her words wobbling a bit.

"I'm headed there." His voice was already rough with desire.

He slipped her dress from her shoulders and helped her out of the sleeves. "What do you think about making love in front of the fire? This time I have a condom in my pocket."

She laughed. "Only one?"

He leaned back and studied her. "We're going to need only one. This time we're going slow, and you're going to be screaming for me to take you until I'm done."

She was trembling already, just at the thought.

Zane undressed her slowly with exquisite kisses and arousing touches. She matched kiss for kiss and touch for touch, but somehow he always seemed to give more. On the floor, in front of the fire, she found joy and passion in his arms. As he'd promised, by the time he rolled on the condom, she was begging him to come to her.

But Zane didn't hurry that, either. When finally he let their desire consume them, she did scream his name. Sated beyond her imagination, loving him with all her heart, she tried not to think about tomorrow. Zane still hadn't mentioned tomorrow, or commitment or a future.

What was she supposed to think or feel about that?

He missed her, dammit!

Zane entered LipSmackin' Ribs from the back entrance instead of through the mall, the shadow of beard stubble darkening his jaw again, sunglasses perched on his nose, his Stetson drawn low. He'd driven Jeannette to her apartment last night before midnight because Erika needed to get home and because Jeannette had to go to work today. She was working a long shift from mid-morning until at least 7:00 p.m. He knew he shouldn't be here. Maybe tourists were starting to arrive for Frontier Days. He could tell by the Monday lunch crowd. It was usually a slower day, but today the restaurant was hopping.

But the lunch-goers weren't really on his mind. Last night was. It had been incredible! Yet when he'd taken Jeannette home, he'd gotten the feeling something was bothering her.

Today he wanted to find out what that was. He wanted

a repeat of last night. Stopping in here served two pur-
poses. He got to see her pretty smile again and maybe
they could make plans for tonight. He'd bring in dinner
for her and Jonah, they'd spend some family time with
her son and then maybe he could stay over. He could slip
out before Jonah woke up.

Something about that plan bothered Zane, but he didn't
analyze it too much. He was just hell-bent on seeing Jeannette and feeling that crazy rush of adrenaline again.

Crazy Rush. Wouldn't that be a great song title?

But songs weren't on his mind, either.

After another glance around the restaurant, he finally
spotted Jeannette at a table close to the bar. Even though
her back was to him, he recognized her ponytail, the curve
of her neck, her long, delicious legs that had been wrapped
around him—

His body responded to the pictures in his mind as he
angled around a group of customers to see if he wanted
to approach her right here. There didn't seem to be any
place in this restaurant that was quiet.

Stepping around a man who was as tall as he was with a
fringed suede jacket, Zane stopped short. Jeannette wasn't
happy. In fact, she looked incredibly upset! A big, burly
man at the booth she was waiting on was gripping her
forearm and eyeing her lasciviously.

What the hell was going on?

Zane didn't hesitate to stride to the table for a closer
look. When he got within three feet he heard the man
say, "Come on, Jeannette. I've been tippin' you good for
weeks. I'm sure you can serve up more than lip smackin'
ribs. When your shift's over, you can come to my place.
Or I can go to yours."

When Jeannette responded politely, "I don't date customers," and tried to pull away from him, the man's expression turned ugly.

"You've been swingin' that tush around here like you're askin'—"

Zane saw red, blue, green, yellow and every other color in the spectrum. No man had a right to touch a woman without her permission. But he guessed this man didn't follow any chivalrous rules.

In a beat of the country song, Zane was there at the table, his voice as cold as steel as he ordered, "Let her go."

The beefy man ignored Zane, still staring at Jeannette's face, still holding on to her, so Zane tapped the man's shoulder. "I said *let her go.*"

He heard a murmured "Zane" from Jeannette. He sensed that the diners had stopped eating and were watching. But he was too far into this to back down now.

The man released Jeannette's arm, stood and faced Zane. "Who says so?" he demanded in a threatening tone.

Without any hesitation at all, Zane responded, "Zane Gunther says so," pushed back his Stetson, ripped off his sunglasses and was ready for anything he had to do to protect Jeannette.

The sleazy customer took a step back and looked flabbergasted. His jaw dropped as he merely stared at Zane. Other customers watched now, too. A few had stood. A couple held out cell phones as if they were taking pictures. In that moment, Zane knew he had just restarted everything he had been trying to stop.

So be it.

Spotting Woody Paulson, the manager of LipSmackin' Ribs, Zane grabbed Jeannette's hand and led her toward the man. "She quits." Then, his arm around her waist, he hurried her outside through the back entrance and straight to his SUV.

She looked shell-shocked as he told her to fasten her seat belt, then slammed her door. He rushed to the driver's side, climbed in and took off as fast as he could. He knew a few customers had come out of the restaurant after them. He had only a few seconds to zoom out of the parking lot and lose any cars that might follow.

But he was hardly out of the parking lot exit when Jeannette demanded, "Pull over."

He glanced at her. "I can't. We'll have people all over us with cameras in a Montana minute."

"Pull over!" she repeated with even more energy.

This time, the trembling agitation in her voice got to him, and he did what she asked. He could still see the outside marquee of the restaurant from where they were parked.

"Do you know what you just did?" she asked, her voice shaking.

"Yeah. I blew my cover to protect your honor."

When she turned to face him, he realized he'd never seen Jeannette look so upset. Not even the day Jonah had gotten hurt.

Her chin quivered, her words came out in a rush, but they were clear and precise. "I could have protected my own honor just fine if given the chance. You didn't have to blow your cover for me. You didn't even have to be in that restaurant. You have no right to make decisions for me."

"After last night I thought I'd have some say in your life," he returned quickly.

"*Say* in my life? You didn't even tell me what last night

meant to you. Yes, the sex was good. But is that all it was? Just sex?"

The turmoil of the past few months rolled over Zane as he gazed into Jeannette's eyes. "This isn't the place to have this discussion. In a few minutes, a reporter's going to be on our tail."

"Is that a problem because you still don't want to be seen in public? Or is it a problem because you don't want to explain *me?*"

In more turmoil than he wanted to admit and not even certain why, he stated, "You don't realize what reporters can do!"

"You haven't given me the chance to realize what reporters can do. I'm pretty resilient, Zane. I've had to be. But that's not the issue. You have enough money that you can take a break from life and go live in an ideal world on top of a mountain. I have to deal with real life. I have to go back to LipSmackin' Ribs and beg for my job back, so I can take care of Jonah and keep my insurance." With a flick of her wrist she unfastened her seat belt and then opened the door.

There were two cars exiting the parking lot now, zooming up behind them. Someone was hanging out the window on the passenger side, a camera aimed at them.

"Go, Zane. Go back to your mountain. I have to get my job back." Jeannette slammed the door so hard his SUV shook.

He wanted to stop her. He wanted to go after her. But even if he did, what would he say? His life was a disaster. As it was, the public might just think she was a waitress and he was a customer in the restaurant rescuing her. Not much of a story there, thank goodness.

As he watched Jeannette practically run back to the restaurant before he could take another deep breath, he now clearly understood she didn't *need* to be rescued. What would she say to reporters if they did bombard her? The simple spin he'd come up with?

With a pickup truck and a van coming up behind him now, he knew the first thing he had to do was lose his tail. The second thing he had to do was fortify his mountain-top retreat. The most important thing he had to do was to make sure Jeannette and Jonah were protected from the press. It all depended on her first comments to them. Should he call her and tell her that?

Go back to your mountain. I have to get my job back.

She probably wouldn't even take his call.

Jeannette was shaking, upset and near tears when she reached the restaurant. A group of young adults there gaped at her in awe. "Do you know Zane Gunther?" one of the girls asked.

A news van pulled up in the parking lot and slid into the slot Zane had vacated. Jeannette knew this was just the beginning. If she didn't handle this carefully, both she and Jonah would be besieged. She didn't know what had gotten into her. Really intense feelings from last night that had simmered in the sleepless dark had boiled up to bite her when Zane had rescued her at the restaurant. And he *had* rescued her. The only reason she was fighting his in-terference so hard was because she didn't know how he felt. Was he willing to let her walk away? Would he come after her? Would he tell the legitimate press about her?

She felt blindsided by everything that had happened. Thinking mostly of Jonah, she responded, "He was in the restaurant and rescued me from a bad situation. He must be a very nice man."

But the young woman was more perceptive than she thought. "Why did you run back here?"

Why had she run back here into a situation she was beginning to hate? She'd complained about Bob Collins before, but Woody had still let him into the restaurant, hadn't said a word to him. The question now was, What was her self-respect worth? What was her integrity worth? She had to go to DJ Traub and tell him what Woody was doing. And she had to look for another job. She could apply at the Tottering Teapot, a café downtown. Or on the administrative side? She'd apply at Ethan Traub's office and at Thunder Canyon Resort. She'd find *something*. She'd work three jobs if she had to. But she wouldn't stay here.

Turning to the young woman who had asked her the question, Jeannette said, "I came back to make my resignation official. I can't work here anymore."

Then she turned away from the group and went inside. If reporters descended on her, she'd give them the same answers and soon they'd go away. Especially if Zane didn't have any contact with her.

And why would he? She'd run away from him...and the most special night of her life.

Mel answered the door when Jeannette arrived at his house to pick up Jonah. She was wrung-out and probably looked it. After she'd left LipSmackin' Ribs without looking back, she'd felt heartsick and worried. Heartsick because she loved Zane and feared he didn't love her... and worried because he'd revealed his identity because of her. Guilty, too? Why not? She'd driven around for a while, not wanting to go home with Jonah, fearing reporters might be camped out there. But she'd have to go home sometime.

This morning when she'd dropped Jonah off, Mel had told her Edna was still in bed. That was highly unusual. Had Edna's refusal to babysit caused her to think Jeannette would be mad at her? Jeannette didn't know. She just hoped maybe they could talk it out. Maybe she should warn them her photo could appear in some tabloid. Cell phones took great pictures these days.

Mel was his same cheery self and Jonah hugged her with all of his four-and-a-half-year-old boyhood enthusiasm. She hugged him back, concerned about finding another job, yet confident she could do whatever she had to in order to take care of the two of them.

Mel capped Jonah's shoulder. "Why don't you go out to the kitchen table and we'll finish putting that puzzle together. Gran wants to talk to your mom for a little bit." His brown eyes met Jeannette's. "We'd both like to talk to you, but I need to keep Jonah occupied."

His words surprised Jeannette. She straightened from her hug with her son to see Edna entering the living room. She looked a little wan and Jeannette hoped she wasn't sick. She hoped Edna wasn't going to give her some kind of bad news she didn't want to hear.

After Jonah left with Mel, Edna motioned to the two recliners. "Why don't we sit?"

Sitting meant this wasn't going to be a short conversation. Jeannette kept her long sweater on, knowing Edna hated her outfit as much as she did. "Are you all right?" Jeannette asked. "You look a little pale. I was worried this morning because you're always up when Jonah arrives."

"I had some things to think over," the woman said, focusing on her hands in her lap, rather than Jeannette.

"First of all, I'm sorry we said we wouldn't babysit for you last night."

Jeannette leaned toward this woman who had become dear to her. "I understand. Really, I do. You take care of Jonah so much and I'm grateful for that."

"It had nothing to do with going bowling," Edna admitted. "We didn't even have any plans when you called. I just—"

"You just didn't want to think about me dating someone else."

"We've known this day would come. We've been afraid if you find someone else, we'll lose contact with you and Jonah."

"That *won't* happen," Jeannette assured her. "Jonah knows you're his grandparents. Even if I meet someone, we'll still be close."

"*Have* you met someone?" Edna asked, her gaze finding Jeannette's.

"Today I honestly don't know what to say about that."

"We don't have any right to poke into your business," Edna said, as if Mel was sitting there beside her.

"You care. And I do want to tell you."

"First, I have something to tell you." Edna's determined voice told Jeannette she was going to say her piece.

Jeannette tried to bolster herself, waiting for whatever came next.

Edna's eyes filled with tears and a few spilled out. "I should have told you long before now. I don't want you to blame Mel because *I'm* the one who thought we should keep quiet."

"Quiet?" Jeannette was really lost, not understanding at all.

"It's time you know the truth about Ed's accident."

Jeannette suddenly went cold, not knowing where this conversation was headed.

"Ed had been drinking that night. We knew the coroner and asked him not to tell you about Ed's blood alcohol level."

Jeannette couldn't quite absorb it. "He'd been drinking?"

"I doubt if it was the first time," Edna confessed. "One night he stopped by, I could smell liquor on him. But I didn't say anything and I should have. I think he was drinking because he was scared about you having a baby. I'm not sure he wanted to get married and have responsibility for anybody but himself. I didn't think there was any reason you should know. After Ed died, I thought knowing would just make you feel worse. But now that you've met someone, I realized you should have the truth. I'm so sorry we kept this from you. Can you forgive us?"

Absorbing what Edna told her, Jeannette felt the weight of guilt slip from her shoulders. It was time to let it. Her pregnancy *had* been an accident. She didn't purposely forget to change that patch. She had just forgotten. But when she'd learned she was pregnant, she had *wanted* her baby. She had wanted to be a mother and embraced the idea wholeheartedly. Ed hadn't. He should have told her he didn't want to get married. He should have told her about his fears. He hadn't. He'd chosen to drink instead of confiding in her. He'd chosen to drink and then climb behind the wheel.

Looking at Edna's expression and her tear-filled eyes, Jeannette really understood that Ed's mother had just wanted to spare her more heartache. That's what you tried to do for the people you loved.

Slipping off the chair, she knelt at Edna's feet and took

the older woman's hands in hers. "Of course, I forgive you. You were trying to protect me and Jonah."

The two women were quiet for a few minutes until they both got control of their emotions. Finally Edna squeezed Jeannette's hand. "So…tell me about this man you went out with last night."

Jeannette felt her throat tighten, but then she revealed, "His name is Zane Gunther."

At the shock on Edna's face, Jeannette knew she was going to confide in her. She needed some maternal wisdom to help her figure out what to do next.

Chapter Thirteen

On Thursday afternoon Zane opened the door for Dillon, then shut it against the prying eyes of reporters, against the possibility of long lenses on cameras, against the almost constant presence of the news vans parked outside. Well, not right outside. They were all gathered down at the bottom of the lane where the property began.

Dillon looked as if he'd been through a war. "Do you know how hard it was to convince your security team I'm a *friend* of yours? Haven't you convinced Roscoe to come back?"

"Not yet. I'm working on it."

"I've been waiting for you to call. Are you going to tell me what happened with Jeannette?" Dillon demanded, obviously offended by Zane's silence.

"Don't you believe the papers?" Zane returned with his Texas drawl. "I rescued her from a bad situation and was found out."

"Like I believe *that* was the whole story. In her comments she didn't even admit she *knew* you."

"She's smart. That was the best thing for both of us."

Zane sank down onto one of the kitchen chairs, expressionless and stoic. His thoughts and feelings were in a jumble. He was more upset about what had happened with Jeannette than the chaos outside and that baffled him.

"You're saying the words, but I don't think you're believing them." Dillon pulled out another chair and squarely faced his friend. "Jeannette was over at the house this morning and she wouldn't talk about what happened, not even with Erika. They're working like crazy to get everything finished up for Frontier Days tomorrow. She looked like she hadn't slept. She said she and Jonah stayed at Edna and Mel Lambert's the past two nights."

So that's where she'd gone. He hadn't been able to get hold of her. The bodyguard brigade he'd sent to her apartment said no one had gone in or out. Zane had assumed she just didn't want to talk to him, so he hadn't left a message on her machine. When he talked to her again, it had to be in person. Still, he wasn't sure what he was going to say.

"You don't look any better than she does," Dillon informed him with a bit of satisfaction.

"Something must be going around," Zane jibed.

"Knock off the I-don't-care attitude, Zane. I know you too well. What happened to cause this storm?"

A storm certainly was a good name for it. He felt as if he was being torn in two, by his feelings for Jeannette and the life he had to deal with. So, after considerable deliberation he spilled to Dillon the entire story of what had happened.

Dillon's expression changed as Zane ran through the

events—an arched brow, a frown, a why-didn't-you-know-better look. But to his credit, he kept quiet.

"I tried to give the guys tailing me a run for their money and finally lost them. But by then someone had texted a picture to so-and-so who knew so-and-so who got in touch with so-and-so. They eventually found out I rented this place. I should have used a fake name."

"And Jeannette?"

Zane threw his hands up in the air. "She hasn't called. She hasn't tried to reach me."

That's when Dillon gave his assessment of the situation. "And why *would* she? Zane, what possessed you to think you could control anything she did? You had no right to tell her boss she was quitting, let alone drag her out of the restaurant. I'll bet she's never been so furious with anyone. What were you thinking?"

"I *wasn't* thinking! Okay? I was seeing everything we'd done the night before. All I had to do was shut my eyes and picture her. I could feel her hands on me again." He swore vociferously. "Dammit, Dillon, I can't get her out of my head. I haven't been able to since I met her. And after having sex with her—"

This time both of Dillon's brows arched. "Are you sure those are the words you want to use? Because that could be the whole problem here."

"I don't know what you mean." Yet the niggling inroads Jeannette had made into Zane's heart told him that wasn't true.

"Did you simply have sex with Jeannette Williams? Was she a one-week stand, a one-month stand? If that's true, I can't quite get why you were so upset when you saw another man's hand on her arm."

"He was threatening her."

"*Was* he? Or was he just trying to get close to her? Was it any of your business?"

"He wasn't fit to wipe her feet."

"In *your* mind, which is my point exactly."

Zane stood and paced the room, raked his hand through his hair, turned his thoughts every which way until he had to admit the obvious. "I felt she was *my* woman."

"And you were jealous."

"Hell, yes, I was jealous! And I was angry. He had no right to touch her. She needed somebody to protect her. She needed someone to tell this scumbag that what he was doing was wrong."

"And you would have done this for *any* woman?"

Again he thought about it. "I might have done it for any woman, but I probably wouldn't have felt what I felt with any woman."

Dillon didn't have to make a point again.

"What am I supposed to do?" Zane practically yelled in frustration. "What woman wants to put up with this? Beth Ann didn't. And Jeannette has a son. How could we ever protect him?"

"There are lots of celebrities who have children. If you have the right security and you live in the right place, you can enjoy an almost-normal life. You know that, Zane. So why are you fighting this so hard?"

"She's special, Dillon. She doesn't deserve what the press would do to her."

"They might love her. They might see this as a Cinderella story...*if* that's what we're talking about here. What *do* you feel for Jeannette Williams?"

Zane was silent. He couldn't put into words what he felt for Jeannette. Not to Dillon anyway.

"Tell me something, Zane. You've made this decision

on your own, that Jeannette can't or won't want to handle your lifestyle. Have you ever asked *her?*"

"It's never gotten that far. It's not as if we were serious."

"Weren't you?" Dillon shot back quickly. "Weren't you serious from the beginning? You knew she had a son. You bonded with her little boy. You went after her as if she was too special to let go. What wasn't serious about it?"

"I've been through this before, Dillon."

"Years ago. And Beth Ann was young."

"Jeannette's not much older."

"There's a world of difference between the two of them and you know that." The two men stared at each other.

Finally Dillon relented with the questions. "Zane, I know what happens when you're not in a relationship. You're alone, and you get used to being alone. Suddenly someone comes along, and you have to be a little flexible, you have to change the way you do this or the way you think that. You wonder if it's worth it. But then you see her smile, and you know it is. I never imagined *I'd* find happiness again because for so long I felt unworthy of love. You're the one who helped me realize I couldn't continually punish myself and live in the past. You're the one who gave me the kick in the butt that I needed. And now I'm here to return the favor. What kind of tribute is it to Ashley Tuller's young life if you continue to live a hermitlike existence?"

At that last question Zane felt his face go pale. That was one question he'd never asked himself. Now might be the right time to do it.

Without waiting for Zane to get his footing again, Dillon stood.

"You're leaving?" Zane asked.

"I don't think *I'm* the one you want to see. I think you

have some heart-and-soul wrestling to do with yourself and I'll only get in the way. But I do think you need to listen to the lyrics of your song, the one that will probably win an accolade at the Country Music Awards in November, whether or not you're there. Get out your iPod and listen to 'Movin' On,' Zane. *Movin' on from the heart-ache into the sunshine.* That's what you need to do. You have my number if you need me...or Erika. She'd love to see you back at Frontier Days."

"Don't push," Zane growled.

"Someone has to." And on those last words, Dillon left the house.

Dillon had left a legacy of words, and Zane thought about each and every one of them. He paced the kitchen and then went to the living room and paced there, too. He deliberated on Jeannette's comments to the newspaper. Had she been trying to protect him? Did he believe she didn't really know him? A little over three weeks. He'd met her three and a half weeks ago. Yet in some ways he felt as if he'd known her for a lifetime. In others, he wanted each day to be a new exploration of her and the life they could have together.

The life they could have together.

Had he just had sex with her? No, he had *made love* to her. Their joining Sunday night had been mind-boggling. Something gnawed at his memory, something Jeannette had said. Right before she'd left his SUV she'd tossed at him—"You didn't even tell me what last night meant to you."

No, he hadn't because he'd felt too much and he hadn't wanted her to know it. But now, he knew exactly how he felt about her. If he ever *could* sing again, he'd want to sing only to her. That's the phrase that had been going through his head ever since they'd made love the first time. *Singin' only to you. Just to you.*

He walked from the kitchen to the foot of the stairs and peered up into the gathering darkness of the loft. He didn't know what he was going to do about Ashley Tuller's family and the trial. But he did know he had to do something to get him on solid footing with Jeannette again, at least long enough for him to ask her one very important question. Did she want to stand by him?

Because he wanted to stand by her.

He loved her.

With that confession ringing in his heart, he mounted the stairs. In the loft he picked up his guitar and held it, hoping something would come.

The big blue-and-white-striped tent was emptying of the people who had come to the fairgrounds to watch the Miss Frontier Days pageant on Saturday. Jeannette had overseen most of it and was gathering up errant score sheets for the contestants when she spotted Erika approaching her.

"How did it go?" Erika asked.

"It went off without a hitch. With the talent competition in the early afternoon and the evening gown competition finishing up before dinner, we had an even bigger crowd to announce the winner. Laila Gates won Miss Frontier Days hands-down. I heard she received three marriage proposals!" Jeannette felt a gnawing ache in her heart when she said it with more enthusiasm than she felt. Marriage proposals weren't anything to joke about. Then she wondered if *any* of Laila's suitors had been serious.

Relationships were serious. But now she just had to concentrate on being a good mother to Jonah. Today Erika had suggested he play with Emilia while her mom watched them both. Jeannette had liked that idea and so had Jonah. Her affair with Zane might have tanked, but she'd made a great friend in Erika.

Suddenly Jeannette spotted a couple gathered in a group near the back of the tent. DJ Traub and his wife, Allaire.

Erika said, "I can take the score sheets. I'm going to have to drive back into town in a while to tie up loose ends with some business owners."

A little anxious about what she was going to do, but knowing she had to do it, Jeannette asked Erika, "Do you have a few minutes to wait? I need to talk to DJ Traub."

"Sure, go ahead. Then I'll tell you what I've lined up next for you. By the way, I was speaking to Bo Clifton earlier today and he said he's looking for an administrative assistant. You might want to give him a call."

"Just call the mayor?" Jeannette asked, a bit surprised.

"Bo's a great guy. I gave him your name, so if you call he'll know who you are."

"You're a real friend, Erika. Thank you."

"I know what a hard worker you are, and a detail-oriented person. You'd be great in Bo's office."

"I'll call him as soon as I get a chance."

Erika handed Jeannette Bo's business card. "He said you can call his cell phone. Now go talk to DJ, then I'll give you your schedule for this evening."

During Frontier Days, Jeannette was Erika's Girl Friday, going where she was needed. Thank goodness Erika had kept her busy this week. Even so, Zane was constantly on her mind and in her heart. Her heart hurt every time she thought about the way she'd reacted to what he'd done. Still, she really hadn't had a chance with him. That's what hurt her most, especially when she thought about giving her body and heart to him when they'd made love.

She should have known better, she really should have.

DJ and his wife were an attractive couple. Allaire recognized her immediately and smiled broadly. "Hi. It's good to see you again."

Jeannette felt the same warmth from Allaire that she'd felt at the restaurant the other night. Allaire introduced her to DJ and Jeannette took the plunge. "Can I talk to you a minute? There's something you need to know about your competition."

DJ's face filled with curiosity. "Sure. Let's move over here." He and Allaire went with her to a quiet corner of the tent.

Without hesitation Jeannette told him what Woody had wanted her to do and why she hadn't come to him sooner.

"I understand," DJ assured her. "You needed the job and the insurance. I'm grateful for you telling me now. I'll look at anyone we've hired lately carefully. At least I know to watch out for moles. Did you find another job yet?"

"Not yet, though I do have another prospect."

"Well, if it doesn't pan out, you can come work for me."

"How do you know you can trust me?" Jeannette asked honestly.

"Because Allaire told me about your dinner with Zane. He wouldn't go to all that trouble for someone who wasn't trustworthy."

Jeannette felt as if her heart were going to break in two. Her throat tightened and for a moment she was close to tears. Then she quickly composed herself. "Thank you for the offer. I really appreciate it. I'd better get back to Erika and the rest of my duties for Frontier Days."

Erika had been talking to someone, but finished her conversation when Jeannette approached. "Is everything okay?"

"Everything's great. If the job offer with the mayor doesn't work out, DJ will hire me. Now, what would you like me to do next?"

"I think you'll enjoy this assignment. I'd like you to check in on the local talent performing at the arena. Kayla Johnston who organized the day with the singers and the band is doing a great job. But I just want you to make sure the end of it goes smoothly."

"This sounds like an easy assignment," Jeannette said, although listening to music, especially if it was country, would remind her of Zane.

"This is the last thing I want you to do today, so you're free afterward. You've done a great job, Jeannette. You really have."

Ten minutes later Erika's words warmed Jeannette as she walked to the concert theater in the cool evening air. Frontier Days attendees milled about and she waved to a couple of people she knew. She'd dressed in her black leggings and a turquoise sweater for her chores today, but had left her coat in her car. She could hardly believe it was the first day of October and winter was just around the corner.

Jeannette made her way through the front parking lot of the fairgrounds arena, ran up the steps and saw one of the front doors was propped open. Several people were flowing out and she waited, then went inside. The arena was cavernous for a town the size of Thunder Canyon. But the resort drew in its share of tourists and when the town attracted a headliner, they needed the seats here. The band on the stage was strumming and a brunette was singing her heart out. That's what singers did. They sang what was in their heart. That's what Zane couldn't do anymore.

She had to forget about Zane for the time being, although she didn't know how she was going to do that. Just listening to the bands and singers would bring back everything she knew about him, everything she'd found when she'd searched his name on the internet.

To her surprise, she saw Dillon standing at the last row. He was on his cell phone. That seemed odd because most people would go outside to take calls with the music loud in the background. However, when he saw her, he hooked his phone back into the holster on his belt and beckoned to her.

The downstairs at the arena was about half-filled, listeners sporadically dotting the seats. He smiled at her and when she reached his side, he said, "I was just talking to Erika. She said if I saw you, we should go up and sit in the front row."

Puzzled, Jeannette walked beside Dillon. He glanced at her every once in a while to make sure she was following. The front row was filled except for two seats at the very center, as if someone had saved them just for her and Dillon.

Jeannette settled herself in one of the seats with Dillon beside her just as the band finished their number. After a few minutes to set up, she knew the next group would be coming out. The curtain closed…and she waited.

Zane had never been more nervous in his entire life. Not even when he performed in front of thousands of people. He was going to be taking the biggest risk he'd ever taken. But it was time to open up his life again. It was time to confront whatever came his way and deal with it the best he could. It was time to tell Jeannette exactly how he felt.

This was about Jeannette, and him, and Jonah and the family they could form. He couldn't be concerned about the audience and how they might react to him. If they booed, they booed. The tabloids had stirred things up, so had the interview shows, and he really didn't know if his fans would stand behind him. But this was for Jeannette, not only to tell her how he felt, but to make a public statement that they were together.

At least he hoped they'd be together.

Stepping from behind the wings where he'd been keeping a low profile, he knew the days of doing that were over. He settled his guitar strap over his shoulder, went to the center of the curtain, then waited for it to go up.

When the crowd recognized him, there was startled silence. Then someone shouted, "That's Zane Gunther!"

What happened next filled Zane's heart with the promise that his music mattered. Someone in the audience stood and clapped, and then others followed. Soon the whole audience was on their feet applauding.

But he didn't care about the whole audience. He only cared about the woman directly in front of him. She was standing now, too, and clapping hard.

Zane held up his hands for the audience to stop, but they only clapped harder. Taking the microphone from its stand, he walked out to the very edge of the stage.

He held up his hand again, then said, "Thank you. You don't know how much this means to me."

The clapping stopped and the audience went quiet. They took their seats, not knowing what to expect.

"You might all start booing because I'm not here for a concert."

There were murmurs and someone called, "Sing 'Movin' On.'"

Zane gazed down at Jeannette and she gazed back. She didn't look away.

He said into the mic, "For now, I'm here to sing to only

one person, and she's sitting in the middle of the front row. I'm not going to do this with a mic because this song is just for her. I'm hoping it will mean as much for her to hear it as it did for me to write it."

He left the microphone in its stand and hurried down the side steps to where Jeannette was seated. Standing in front of her, his throat tightened up and his mouth went dry. But then he took a deep breath, thought about what this meant and began strumming. The chords came easily. The words he'd written and worried over the past few days leaped from his heart into the air. He began:

I'm singin' to you, only you.
I'm missin' you, only you.
I'm regretting everything I couldn't say and what
I did wrong.
I'm sorry for being blind and thinking I was strong.
You were afraid to give your heart because I didn't
understand.
You needed the safety of my love and an outstretched
hand.
I'm reaching out to you, hoping you'll hear love in
my song.
Because I mean to be yours through my whole life
long.
So now I'm singing just to you for the rest of my life.
I'm singin' only to you, if you'll just be my wife.
If you'll just be my wife.

There were tears in Jeannette's eyes and one rolled down her cheek.

Zane had to make sure she understood exactly what he was doing. His fingers left the strings. "The name of the song," he explained, "is 'Singin' Only to You.' That's what I'm doing today. And in that song, if you didn't quite hear it, was something I don't usually put in my songs. So just to make sure you understood—"

He swung off his guitar and handed it to Dillon. At the same time he spotted Erika in the side aisle holding Jonah's hand. Jeannette's son was wearing the cowboy hat Zane had given him.

Then Zane knelt down on one knee in front of Jeannette, took her hands in his and asked, "Will you marry me, Jeannette Williams? In the past month I've learned what it means *not* to be lonely. In the past month I've learned what it means to let somebody into my heart. I want you to stay there always. Will you marry me and make a life with me no matter where that takes us?"

Her tears were really flowing now and he could feel wetness gathering in his own eyes because she was smiling at him, and looking at him with as much love as he felt for her.

"Yes, I'll marry you," she answered surely. "Wherever you go, Jonah and I will go. And we'll make a life together."

Out of his shirt pocket, Zane pulled a heart-shaped diamond ring and slipped it on her finger. The stage lights created rainbows in it as she wrapped her arms around his neck.

The whole audience was on its feet now, trying to see and hear. But Zane was oblivious to them because he was kissing Jeannette and the applause all around them was simply a backdrop to his murmured "I love you" when he broke away.

"I love you, too, Zane Gunther," Jeannette assured him. Then she added, "Both the country singer *and* the man."

He kissed her again, not knowing what was going to come next, but looking forward to having Jeannette beside him whatever it was.

* * *

Late that night Zane's arm circled Jeannette's waist as he peered over her head into one of his guest bedrooms where Jonah was sound asleep. "I think he likes it here," Zane joked, hoping that was true.

"He does. I can tell. And he's happy we're getting married."

"So am I," Zane easily agreed. "I want to be a real dad to him. You know that, don't you?"

She caressed his face. "I do."

He felt such a rush of love in her simple touch that he wanted to gather her close. But there would be time for that in a little while. "What did Edna say when you called her?"

"She said she can't wait to meet you. Thank you for inviting them to lunch tomorrow. She's *so* excited. I had to confide in someone after I ran out on you. She told me to wait a week to see if you contacted me. If you didn't, then I was supposed to pick up the phone and call you. And if I really loved you, I was supposed to apologize until you believed me."

"I would have believed you right away."

They drifted into the living room together. Zane walked her to the picture window where he peered out between the slats of the blind. "I don't know how good security's going to be up here. Even with my team at the bottom of the mountain preventing anybody from driving up, persistent reporters could camp out there with a long lens and we'd never know it."

He swung around to look at her. "I'm worried about you and Jonah. Are you sure you're ready to accept all of this as part of your life?"

Her gaze steady and true, Jeannette didn't hesitate to say, "I love you, Zane. I think you're underestimating the residents of Thunder Canyon. I think they'll help ensure your privacy. Small towns can be protective."

After he considered that and how the audience at the concert hall had been so supportive, he admitted, "I'm thinking about selling my place in Utah and buying this. Thunder Canyon might be a good town to settle down in for most of the year."

"After the trial, will you tour again?"

"I don't know. I'm not sure about anything career-wise right now except for the fact that I'm going to be writing songs for you and Jonah. How do you think Jonah would like Nashville? My studio's at my place there."

"I think he's going to like being wherever you and I are."

Suddenly unable to control his desire to hold her, he scooped her up into his arms. "What do you think about a Valentine's Day wedding? The trial will be over, and you and Jonah will have had the time to get used to the idea of marrying me."

She laughed and gave him one of those tender looks he loved so much. "I think Valentine's Day would be perfect."

As Zane carried Jeannette to his bedroom, he suspected he was going to have a lot to sing about in the days ahead…with Jeannette and Jonah as his inspiration.

* * * * *

There was a definite appeal to him, too, as he sat across from her with that crooked grin, all playful cowboy.

What would be the harm in just one date?

But then something went swirly in her belly, melty and hot, trickling downward until it settled in the core of her.

She shoved the sensation aside.

"Come on, Laila," Jackson said, his brown eyes glinting with that flirtatiousness she'd seen before. "I'm just talking about a date, not a marriage proposal."

Wasn't he a card.

Or, more to the point, a wild card.

Dear Reader,

Here we are, back in Thunder Canyon! This time, I've got a real bad boy—Jackson Traub, oil man, Texas rancher and all-around scoundrel. In the first book of the series, Jackson earned quite the reputation for himself while becoming the town's most notorious, ultimate bachelor.

So who would be the perfect foil for him? Maybe…the biggest *bachelorette* in Big Sky Country?

These two have some major fireworks going, and I hope you like their flirting, dating…and of course, falling in lov-ing.

When you're done reading, I would love it if you would come on over and check out my website, www.crystal-green.com. You'll find contests, a link to my blog for updates and information about all the continuities and other books I'm lucky enough to write!

All the best,

Crystal Green

THE HARD-TO-
GET COWBOY

BY
CRYSTAL GREEN

First published in Great Britain 2013
by Mills & Boon, an imprint of Harlequin (UK) Limited,
Eton House, 18-24 Paradise Road, Richmond, Surrey TW9 1SR

© Harlequin Books S.A. 2011

Special thanks and acknowledgement are given to Crystal Green for her contribution to the Montana Mavericks: The Texans Are Coming! series.

ISBN: 978 0 263 90101 6
ebook ISBN: 978 1 472 00468 0

23-0413

Harlequin (UK) policy is to use papers that are natural, renewable and recyclable products and made from wood grown in sustainable forests. The logging and manufacturing processes conform to the legal environmental regulations of the country of origin.

Printed and bound in Spain
by Blackprint CPI, Barcelona

Crystal Green lives near Las Vegas, where she writes for the Mills & Boon® Cherish™ and Blaze® lines. She loves to read, overanalyze movies and TV programs, practice yoga and travel when she can. You can read more about her at www.crystal-green.com, where she has a blog and contests. Also, you can follow her on Facebook at www.facebook.com/ChrisMarie.Green/1051327765 and Twitter @ChrisMarieGreen.

To my beautiful, caring, hardworking mom—
you are the treasure of the family and
we value you beyond measure. Love you so much.

Prologue

Laila Cates stood on the stage in front of the cheering crowd, dressed in a white evening gown and a blue sash while holding a fresh bouquet of celebratory flowers.

"A five-time winner!" said the master of ceremonies, whose voice rang through the tent where the pageant was being held. "Give it up for Laila Cates for taking yet *another* Miss Frontier Days title!"

She touched the crown on her head. It'd been a long time since she'd been up here. Seven years since she'd stopped entering the pageant, seven years since she'd wanted to be known for more than what was on the outside.

But this year she'd come back to prove a point to Thunder Canyon.

Scanning the crowd, she saw the happy faces of the neighbors and friends she'd grown up with. People she worked with at the Thunder Canyon First Fidelity Bank, day in and day out. Her best friend, Dana, who'd entered Laila into the pageant without Laila even knowing it, clapped harder than anyone else.

She'd been the one who'd dared her to prove a point to the town, and Laila had taken her up on it, singing a song during the talent competition that emphasized a woman's hard work in this world and the accomplishments all of them could celebrate as they grew older.

And the judges had clearly appreciated it, recognizing that every year that passed by for a woman could be a plus rather than a negative.

After the noise subsided, Laila went to the microphone, shaking her head. "So I'm twenty-nine going on thirty. The jump to a new decade seems to be a big deal in most women's lives. We're supposed to be leaving behind our best, most youthful years, and truthfully, I've been a little nervous about that. I mean, this is when we get wrinkles, right? This is when our looks begin to fade." She smiled again. "Well, that's why I decided to compete in the pageant this year, to see if any of that mattered when it comes right down to it."

A few hoots, hollers.

She went on. "You all have shown tonight that age and life experience are important—that they add to who we are and how others see us. And, even though this is definitely my last time competing for the title, I'm looking forward to a new win each year, except not on a stage. In life. In *everything*."

Another round of applause, and Laila gave a jaunty little salute to the crowd, ready to give up the stage to all the other women who wanted to show Thunder Canyon what they had to offer—no matter what their age—in the future.

That was when the audience parted to let through a strapping, broad-shouldered man with blond hair.

At first, Laila thought he was merely there to offer congratulations. It was Hollis Cade Pritchett, the man she'd been seeing on and off for years on a casual basis. Cade, as he was known to just about everyone but his sister and her husband, accepted what Laila had professed all along—that she never wanted to get married—and that had apparently suited him just fine.

Until now, it seemed.

"Marry me, Laila," he said loudly.

As his deep voice carried, Laila blinked, then put her hand over the mic. The device whimpered with feedback as a wave of silence traveled over the audience.

This wasn't like Cade, to be joking around. And she suspected that it *was* a joke, because he was acting... different. Heck, she could even say that the normally levelheaded woodworker might've even tipped back a few beers, judging by the high flush on his cheeks. But Cade wasn't a big drinker.

So what explained the intensity in his gaze?

His brother, Dean, broke out of the crowd and stood by Cade, wearing a tight grin and slapping him on the back, buddy-style.

"Don't listen to him, Laila," the youngest Pritchett boy said. "*I'm* the one you should marry!"

Okay—now it was pretty obvious from the way Dean slightly slurred that they *had* been indulging for some odd reason. Like his brother, Dean was the strong, silent type, hardly prone to tomfoolery like this.

By now, the crowd had broken into a chorus of laughter, urging the Pritchetts on.

Laila kept her composure, as well as her sense of humor. This was starting to feel like a circus act, but maybe she'd only encouraged that by competing in the pageant at this age when it was supposed to be a young girls' competition.

She would take her knocks, because using a pageant title to make a statement about inner beauty was loaded with irony, and not everyone was going to get it.

It was just another idea some of the townsfolk probably wouldn't take seriously from her.

Just then, another man came to the front of the stage—a guy who wasn't as familiar to Laila, even though she knew darn well who he was.

Who didn't?

Tall, lean and roguish in his jeans, boots and black Western shirt, Jackson Traub was new in town—one of the Texans who'd come to Thunder Canyon to develop his family's oil shale business.

And he was also known to be a troublemaker who'd caused a wild ruckus at his own brother's wedding reception several months ago.

Was he about to stir things up here, too, just for the heck of it?

Just because rumor had it that he enjoyed raising Cain?

Laila should've been sending him a "Don't you dare do it" glare, but…

But just look at him.

She was too busy taking in a deep breath, feeling a burst of tingles as they rolled through every single inch of her while he grinned up at her on the stage.

Lord help her, but a bad-boy reputation did something to a girl who'd spent her life doing everything right.

He swept off his hat and held it over his heart while raising his own voice over the crowd's. "Neither of these boys is worthy. *I'm* going to marry the lovely Laila!"

Something primal hit her in the belly, and hard.

But it had nothing to do with the ridiculous proposal. Nothing at all.

It was only that his brown hair had been tousled so carelessly by the removal of his hat, and even from the stage, Laila could see the glint in his dust-devil brown gaze as he looked up at her and grinned even wider.

In spite of everything, she grinned right back, though hers was of the sweet/sarcastic variety. No one was going to make a complete mockery out of this night.

And no one—not even a slick Texan—was going to make it all better with a naughty smile and a joke, either.

Jackson Traub lifted an eyebrow, as if appreciating her feisty look.

As if challenged by it.

It took some effort to drag her gaze away from him—my, did it ever—but she turned her attention back to the audience while their laughter died down.

"See?" she said. "Here's proof that life really doesn't end after your twenties, girls. Everything improves with age, including the amount of attention."

As cheers erupted, she waited for silence before continuing.

"But you all know that my heart belongs to Thunder Canyon. And, for all you fellas out there who'd planned to offer more proposals, you know I adore every last one of you, but I must tell you once and for all that I. Am. Never. Getting. Married. Life's too short!"

As the place went nuts, she winked at the crowd, then smiled at the Pritchett brothers, telling them that there were no hard feelings about their ill-timed shenanigans.

Dean was glancing at his brother, as if to gauge Cade's reaction.

And what Laila saw in Cade almost chipped away at her heart.

It seemed as if he'd just been kicked in the gut, his face ruddy, his hands fisted at his sides.

Oh, God. *Had* he been serious about proposing?

No way—not when she'd been very clear over the years how she felt about settling down. Not Cade Pritchett—a man who never impulsively shouted out things like proposals in front of a hundred other people.

Without a word, he turned to leave, his shoulders stiff, and Dean followed him, leaving the third suitor behind.

As Laila met the amused gaze of Jackson Traub, the last man standing, he put his hat back on, then touched the brim. The gesture might've been a touché from someone who clearly appreciated her firm stance on singlehood. Word had it that he'd even caused that scene at his brother's reception because he was the ultimate bachelor, and he was intent on swearing off matrimony himself. It was just that he hadn't exactly been speaking to a sympathetic audience at a *wedding,* for heaven's sake.

Before he turned around and disappeared into the crowd, he sent Laila one last wicked grin.

Then he was gone, leaving her with a burning yen to see him again, for better…

Or for worse.

Chapter One

Nearly a week later, Laila sat at a corner table in the bar section at the Hitching Post, keeping her eye on the entrance as she traced the sweat off the mug of a lemonade she hadn't touched.

She'd been playing phone tag with Cade, and they'd finally agreed to meet here tonight, among the after-work crowd enjoying Happy Hour in this rumored former house of ill repute that'd been turned into a bar and grill.

She tried to ignore the line of ranch hands at the bar—the men who kept glancing over and peering at her from beneath the shade of their hats. One in particular, Duncan Brooks, who worked on Mayor Bo Clifton's spread, was trying to catch Laila's attention.

Then again, he always was, and she wished he wouldn't do that. The mustached, stocky cowboy was forever looking at her with that moony gaze men some-times got when they were around Laila—that struck-by-a-beauty-queen gander that made her wish she had set out to clear up everyone's perceptions of her from the very first time she'd been old enough to date.

With a polite nod to Duncan—nothing more, noth-ing to encourage him—she took a sip of her lemonade and shifted her attention to the painting over the bar. It featured the Shady Lady herself, Lily Divine, draped in diaphanous material, wearing a mysterious smile. Long before Thunder Canyon had experienced its re-cent gold rush and the place had moved from a sleepy spot on the map to a boomtown with a resort that at-tracted the rich and adventurous alike, and long before the town had undergone an economic fall that they were still recovering from, Lily had been a woman of ques-tionable morals. A supposed heartbreaker.

Was that what Cade thought about Laila now, after she'd shot him down at the pageant?

Was that why he hadn't been returning her calls?

She would soon see, because he was just now walk-ing through the entrance, pausing to glance around for Laila.

She waved a tentative hello, and his hands fisted by his sides, just as they had the night of the pageant. He walked toward her in his sheepskin jacket—a neces-sity now that the weather had finally turned from In-dian summer to October cool.

Laila held back a frown. It was tough to see Cade Pritchett in such a state. He was a hardy man, a local hero who'd played down his part in rescuing a young girl from drowning in Silver Stallion Lake about a year ago. Naturally, he'd refused any accolades.

He was the best of guys. The best of friends—until recently.

She'd already ordered a soda for him, and as he doffed his jacket, tossed it over the back of a chair, then sat, she pushed the beverage toward him as if it were a peace offering.

"I wasn't so sure you'd come here tonight," she said.

Cade didn't utter a word. After years of dating him—never serious enough to have gotten totally intimate with him, though—Laila nevertheless knew enough about Cade to realize that he was weighing whatever he was thinking carefully before saying it.

She also knew that when he spoke, it would be in a low voice that would give most any girl delicious shivers and, not for the first time, Laila wondered just why it didn't affect *her* like that.

What was wrong with her that she didn't feel *that* way about him...or about anybody, much, except for a couple of men who'd seemed like Mr. Rights until they'd proven to be Mr. Maybe-Not-After-Alls?

A flash of roguish brown eyes and an equally devastating grin flew across her mind's eye, but she quashed all thoughts of Jackson Traub.

He certainly wasn't her type, and she'd been reminding herself of that all week.

Cade met her gaze head-on. "I've been doing a lot of thinking lately, and what I have to say to you now isn't impulsive or ill-considered. I've even been thinking about what I came here to tell you long *before* the pageant."

She didn't like how this was starting. "I'm not sure I know what you're talking about."

"The future, Laila."

His direct manner made her wary.

"You're not the only one who's entered a new phase of life," he said. "When a person gets older, he starts to reassess where he's been. Where he's going."

His blue gaze was so intense that Laila prayed he wasn't about to say what she thought he was going to say…

But he went and said it, anyway.

"I wasn't fooling around when I asked you to marry me."

She tried not to react, even though it felt as if a shadow had steamrolled her. "Cade, I didn't mean to embarrass you by turning you down so publicly, but you know how I feel about marriage."

"I know how you always *said* you feel."

Now Laila was really confused. Had she been sending Cade mixed signals or something? But that couldn't be the case. She'd always been *very* clear on her feelings about staying single.

"Cade…" she said softly just before he interrupted her.

"Just listen… I know full well that you're not in love with me. But we have a lot to offer each other in spite of that."

He paused, and she searched his gaze, seeing that there was something deep going on in this man. Sadly, she even wondered if this had anything to do with how Cade had lost the woman he'd wanted to marry to an early death years ago.

Maybe that was why Laila had been drawn to him, as a companion more than anything else. He had shut down emotionally after his lover's passing, and he'd probably seen in Laila a person who didn't get involved much with heavy emotions herself.

Did he think that she would never expect more out of him than he was capable of giving after having his heart broken?

The realization left her a bit hollow. It wasn't that she couldn't love anyone, it was just that she'd always thought of herself as a career woman—one who'd worked her tail off to become branch manager of the bank. One who, admittedly, loved to flirt and play the field to a certain point.

At her silence, he had straightened up in his chair, as if thinking that she was actually considering his point. He seemed so confident now that a scratch of pain scored her.

"Right before the pageant," he said, "I had a good long talk with my brothers."

"And with your other friend, Jack Daniels?"

Cade's skin went ruddy. "All right. A little whiskey was involved, and the more I had, the more I decided I wanted to get an answer from you once and for all about where we were headed. And I don't regret bringing this up, Laila, not even in such a spectacular fashion. Not even if I made a donkey of myself at the pageant and my own brother took enough pity on me to propose, too, turning my folly into a joke everyone could laugh off."

What she needed was for a hole to open up in the ceiling that would suck her right into it and out of this discussion. "I—"

"I need to finish what I came here to say."

He'd raised his voice and, from the corner of her gaze, she saw Duncan Brooks stand away from the bar, obviously hearing Cade and not liking his tone one bit. Laila sent a reassuring smile at the ranch hand, letting him know everything was okay.

Appeased, Duncan went back to drinking his beer, hunched over it as he leaned on the bar.

"I'm tired of being alone," Cade said. "Aren't you?"

She sighed, hating that she would have to be terribly blunt. "No."

He frowned.

"Why does that surprise you?" she asked. "You know I love my life. I love going home to my apartment every night and eating what I want to eat, when I want to eat it. I love watching what I want to watch on T.V.…"

"You don't ever get lonely? You never wake up at night in your empty bed and wonder if it's always going to be that way?"

She didn't know what to say, because there *were* times when that exact thing happened—shadows on the pale walls, the inexplicable sense that she was genuinely alone.

But then she would go right back to sleep, waking up to a new day, loving her life all over again, even as an itch of loneliness remained in the back of her mind.…

Still, there were good reasons she was never going to get married, and the biggest one was because of what she'd seen in her mom. Laila's mother had tried her best not to show how life had let her down. Even though Mom loved all six of her children, Laila had seen how she had ordered college catalogues and paged through them with a slight, sad smile at the kitchen table after she thought all the kids were in bed. She'd heard Mom say on more than one occasion that she should've taken her studies more seriously and that Laila shouldn't ever rely on her looks when she had such a brain.

And she also knew that Mom had settled down young.

Too young?

Always wondering, never having the courage to ask, Laila had promised herself that *she* would give life a chance before getting serious with anyone, and she was damn happy with her decision as it stood.

Right?

She pushed aside her drink and rested her elbows on the table. "Loneliness is no reason to get married, Cade."

His jaw hardened as he surveyed her. Then, hardly swayed, he said, "We can learn to love each other... I can even give you children before it's too late."

Oof.

That really got her. But she wasn't sure why Cade's words smarted the way they did.

Had she been thinking about her future lately, even beyond wrinkles, in a more profound way than she even admitted to herself? And, heck...

She even wondered if she'd actually entered the Miss Frontier Days pageant for the final time because she'd needed some kind of reassurance that she *was* still young enough to be desirable, that she didn't need to change her life and get validation from marriage or kids...

Her throat felt tender as she tried to swallow. She didn't like what she was thinking, and she wouldn't let Cade's words bother her. But how could she tell him that she didn't feel more for him than companionship?

Just as she was wishing again for that hole to open

up in the ceiling, there was a stir in the Hitching Post as someone sauntered inside.

As soon as she saw Jackson Traub bellying up to the bar in a dark brushed-twill coat with his Stetson pulled low over his brow, her body flared with heat.

Star-spangly, popping, sizzling heat.

Something she *definitely* didn't feel for Cade.

She must've been staring, and Jackson Traub must've felt it, because as he ordered a drink from the bartender, he pushed back his hat so she could see his brown gaze locking onto hers.

Her heart seemed to shoot down to her belly, where it revolved, sending the rest of her topsy-turvy, too.

She expected him to give her one of those grins he was so good at, expected him to maybe even wink as a reminder of the night he'd lightheartedly proposed like a scoundrel come out of nowhere.

But he only turned back to the bartender as the man slid a glass of what looked to be straight-up whiskey to him.

Jackson Traub scooped it right up, then downed it before ordering another, ignoring Laila as if nothing had ever passed between them.

Baffled, she stared down at the table.

Was he ignoring her?

Or could it be that he really didn't remember their "moment" at the pageant?

Or maybe there just hadn't been a "moment" for him...

Rascal. He was truly making her wonder. But let him play his games. She'd been dating since sixteen, when her parents had finally allowed it after she'd blossomed early. She had a pretty good sense of when a man was interested or not.

Still, she peered over at Jackson Traub again, just to see if he was looking.

He wasn't.

"Laila?" Cade asked.

He sounded offended that she'd mentally wandered from the conversation. In fact, he was looking more intense than ever—so much so that Laila sank into her chair, wishing fervently, once again, for that hole in the ceiling to appear, suck her up and take her away from all the truths Cade was making her face tonight.

Jackson was a patient man.

He was also mildly perceptive, if he did say so himself, and he knew when a woman—even a cool beauty queen like Laila Cates—was aware of his presence.

As he nursed his second whiskey, he nodded to the man at the end of the bar, an acquaintance Jackson had met during his short time here. Woody Paulson, the manager of LipSmackin' Ribs, a joint that didn't so much compete with the rib restaurant of Jackson's cousin, DJ, as stay in its shadow.

Woody nodded back to Jackson, but the interaction didn't take his mind off Laila. He wondered if she was still watching him, yet he refrained from taking a peek. Instead, he imagined her in that white evening gown, the first time he'd seen the infamous Thunder Canyon beauty in person, on the stage, her long, wavy blond hair silky under the crown she wore, her blue eyes bright, her skin smooth and pale as cream.

A challenge if he ever met one.

A woman he wanted with every beat of his pulse.

He hadn't initially come to Thunder Canyon for a good time, though. Months ago, it'd been his brother Corey's wedding that had brought him here, and Jackson had stayed just long enough to throw a few punches during the reception before returning to his gentleman's ranch in Midland, Texas, then back to work for the family oil business, where he spent the weekdays in his city penthouse.

During the past few months, he'd been thinking hard about the mess he'd created up here in Montana during Corey's nuptials. At first, Jackson had chalked it all up to just being a bad day, and he'd had a few too many champagnes as well as a few too many thoughts about how his brothers seemed to be falling prey to marriage, an institution that Jackson had never cottoned to.

So he'd spoken his mind at the reception, saying that matrimony was a great way to ruin a relationship. And, as if *that* wasn't awful enough, he'd gone on to pretty much call his two married brothers wusses.

He'd said that *he* would never change his life for a woman, and he'd damn well meant it.

Needless to say, the brothers Traub hadn't taken kindly to his opinions, and Jackson had left Thunder Canyon with his fists and face bruised, knowing that he'd gone too far. But he'd tried his best during his time away to think on how he was going to make it up to his family.

Not only that—he'd really taken a good look at what he had or hadn't accomplished during his thirty-four years here on earth, and he didn't like the view much at all.

That's why, when his older brother Ethan stepped up his attempts to explore oil shale extraction opportunities, Jackson saw an opportunity not only to get into his family's good graces again, but...

Hell. In spite of his shortcomings, he loved his family more than anything, and he just wanted to make them see that he wasn't a loser who would always start fistfights at weddings. The superficial guy who could be so much more than the company "schmoozer" who closed deals and wooed clients.

So here he was, back in Thunder Canyon, convinced that he could finally put what brains he had to some use in getting this new branch of Traub Oil Industries started. He'd actually persuaded his brother, Ethan, that he could head up community outreach and education, since Traub Oil Montana was exploring new, more environmentally friendly ways of extraction at the Bakken Shale; he would also be working with the ranchers and landowners from whom the company had bought or leased rights.

Even though Jackson wasn't here for the long run, he was going to make his time in Thunder Canyon matter, but that didn't mean he couldn't use a little entertainment while he was around....

He finally took a sidelong glance at Laila Cates, but she'd gone back to her conversation with Cade Pritchett, whom Jackson only knew because of his outburst at the pageant. Honestly, Jackson had felt for the man after he'd shouted out that proposal. In fact, after Cade's brother had come to his rescue with another marriage offer to Laila, Jackson had impulsively broken in with his own. It wasn't so much for Cade's sake as Laila's because, even under her unruffled façade, Jackson had sensed how vexed Laila had seemed on that stage, and if there was one thing Jackson was, it was a sucker for a woman, especially one who seemed embarrassed that her big night had been shot to hell by an unexpected profession of devotion.

He was pretty sure that someone like Laila was used to men falling all over her, although not in such a mortifyingly public way.

And he wasn't about to be like the other guys.

At present, as Laila sat there looking as uncomfortable as all get out once again, Jackson could tell she was in another tight spot, that here was a woman who was just about telepathically asking anyone in the room to interrupt the conversation she was having.

Now it wasn't as if Jackson would've done what he did next if Laila hadn't been providing a clear opening for him. If she was having a grand old time with her date, he would've stayed a mile away from her.

But being the woman-loving sucker he was, he turned from the bar, getting an even better look at her. His heartbeat picked up.

She was dressed as if she'd just come from work, in a stylish dark gray pinstriped suit, and her wavy mass of blond hair—shiny and silky enough to make his fingers itch to touch it—was swept up in a style that left some strands framing her face.

And...that face.

It belonged to a beauty queen, all right. High cheekbones, full red lips, long black lashes, delicate eyebrows and all.

Now it was more than his heart that was thudding.

To rescue her again or not to rescue her?

There wasn't much of a choice, and he left his whiskey glass at the bar as he crossed the floor.

She seemed to know he was coming before he even

got there, and that did something to him—riled him up inside, stretched a string of lit firecrackers through him.

"Well," he said as she parted her lips, as if to utter something before he beat her to it. "If it isn't my bride-to-be."

Okay, there it was. If she gave any indication that he was intruding, he would go.

He even gave her another chance to shoo him off. "I didn't mean to interrupt anything—"

Cade and Laila spoke at the same time.

"You are," the man said.

"You're not," she said.

Jackson had sure called it correctly. And when Laila nudged a chair away from the table with her foot, she only emphasized the point.

Had Cade proposed again to this woman who'd announced to the whole town that she *Never. Wanted. To. Get. Married?*

Was that why she looked like a deer caught in the headlights?

Cade had seen her pushing out the chair, too, but Jackson only tipped his hat to them both, then took a seat, signaling to a waitress who came right over, all smiles.

"What can I do you for?" she asked.

"A round of beers," Jackson said. "On my tab."

When she scuttled off, she left a view of the bar, and Jackson couldn't help but notice that many a male gaze was turned his way, obviously envious that he was sitting at Laila's table. One man in particular—a cowboy with a chunky silver belt buckle and a mustache—watched Jackson for a moment too long before looking away.

Cade's voice rumbled. "Not tonight, Traub."

Jackson was checking in with Laila, whose smile was forced, even though it seemed to be asking him to stay, no matter what.

Sure enough.

When Jackson faced Cade, the man seemed likely to wring his neck, if the sight of his bunched fists on the tabletop meant anything.

Time for some peace talk. "Just introducing myself around town." He stuck out his hand for a shake. "You can call me Jackson."

"I know who you are." Cade shot Laila a glance, and if it could speak, it would've said, *You gonna do anything to get him out of here or should I?*

But when Laila only took a sip of the lemonade that had been waiting in front of her all this time, Cade stood, got out his wallet, then tossed some bills on the table.

When he spoke, it was to Laila, and it was far quieter than Jackson expected.

"Just think about what I said."

Then he was gone, leaving only the background murmur of bar discussion over the strains of Merle Haggard on the jukebox.

The waitress came with the beers, and Jackson decided that if Cade wouldn't be around to drink his, he would gladly do the honors.

He didn't make anything out of the sassy smile that the waitress gave him, instead taking a swig of his drink, then leaning back in his chair and grinning at Laila.

There was a little beauty mark near the tip of her mouth, and he wished she would smile, just as prettily as she had on that stage last week. But he was out of luck. She only traced a pattern on the table from the condensation that had dropped down from the lemonade mug.

"Was I in the wrong when I sat down here?" Jackson asked.

"No, you weren't. Thank you. It was one of those discussions. You know—the kind that you don't want to have in the middle of a bar?"

"Glad to have been of assistance."

She sighed, still tracing pictures on the table. Jackson couldn't make hide nor hair of what she was drawing.

"If he puts the moves on you again," he said, meaning to cheer her up, "you just give a holler. He's big, but I can take him."

There it was—a wisp of a smile now.

"Truly," he added. "I know how to dodge and weave. Also, I've got a twin back home who's always willing to stand up for a lady, too."

"Good heavens—there's more than one of you?"

He chuckled. "I'm afraid so." Getting even more comfortable, he propped his booted ankle just above his knee. "But Jason's far less reckless. That's what everyone says, anyway."

"I'd heard you're a rebel, even before you showed up at the pageant to cause mischief."

He took that in stride. "Heard from who?"

She had a flush on her cheeks, and it looked so sweet that Jackson's veins tangled.

"I'd heard," she said, "just in general. Thunder Canyon's a small town, so gossip travels."

"I know. That's why I proposed to you, Miss Laila—because *I'd* heard you were the perfect woman for me."

Her gaze widened.

He laughed. "You don't have to say it again—the part about your never getting married. The message came through loud and clear at the pageant."

She blew out a breath, as if she'd been dreading having to repeat it to yet another suitor. It made him think that Cade's pageant proposal had been much more than just an impetuous moment, that it bothered her far more than she'd let on in public.

That she was just as determinedly single as he was?

"I happen to agree 100 percent with you about the holy state of matrimony," he said. "I'm not sure what the appeal is."

"Ask your brothers, Corey and Dillon. I'm sure they can wax on about it."

"No, thanks. It's bad enough that Ethan just got engaged, too. I never thought I'd see him strapping himself to a ball and chain. All I can do now is hope that Jason and my sister, Rose, stick with me."

"You talk as if the rest of your family has abandoned you or something."

He paused. He'd never thought of it that way before, but that's what he'd been feeling during Corey's wedding—abandonment. Being left behind while everyone else traveled ahead to what were supposed to be bigger and better things in life.

She seemed to realize that she'd hit some kind of target on him, whether he'd meant to show it or not.

"Or maybe you're just a born rebel," she said. "I could tell the minute you jumped into the fray at the pageant that your skills were instinctive."

"Hey, I was only trying to ease a tense situation." He shrugged. "And maybe have a little fun."

"I rest my case."

He picked up his mug, toasted her with it, then drank.

When he was done, she was watching him, her blue-bonnet eyes narrowed just the slightest bit, as if she was turning over a million questions about him in her head.

If she was sitting there wondering what went into the creation of a rebel like him, he wasn't about to give her answers.

He wanted to get back to the flirtation. He hadn't met anyone in Thunder Canyon who'd made him forget all the tough questions that had been echoing in his brain ever since the wedding brawl, and he wasn't about to lead her into thinking that he was the kind of guy who was even comfortable having that type of conversation.

Leaning his elbows on the table, he sent Laila his most lethal grin.

"If you're thinking of asking me questions, don't."

"Questions about what?"

"Serious stuff. The kind of questions that come after a first date."

She laughed, as if he'd stepped over a line she'd already drawn with him. "Are you saying this is a date?"

"Nope." He lowered his voice. "But when we do go on our first one, I'm just laying out some ground rules. I don't want to hear any of the kind of questions that make you narrow your eyes like that."

She was flustered, and he hadn't expected that from a graceful, composed woman like Laila Cates.

"When we…?"

"When we go on our first date," he said, completing her sentence, enjoying the hell out of the chase.

Because he always got what he wanted when it came to women, and Laila Cates wouldn't be an exception.

"I never said I would—"

"You didn't have to, Miss Laila. But you know damn well that we're going to go out." He lifted an eyebrow. "It's just a matter of when."

Chapter Two

He sure was cocky, Laila thought, her pulse racing so fast that it felt as if she was running.

Jackson Traub—arrogant and altogether too confident.

And they were talking about a date.

Her. *Him*.

She could just imagine what her parents—no, the whole town—might say if they caught wind of this conversation. Laila Cates, the proper bank manager, the woman who did everything according to the letter, hanging around with a rabble-rousing Texas stranger.

But then a different type of thought altogether started to take shape in her mind....

What if going on a date with a fly-by-night man like Jackson Traub could convince Cade Pritchett that she really *wasn't* longing for stability and marriage?

Suddenly, she liked the whole idea. Especially since, even if she *wasn't* looking to settle down, there would be no future with Jackson, anyway. Because the talk around Thunder Canyon was that he was merely here to work on that oil shale project.

Here and gone.

There was an appeal to that. And there was a definite appeal to *him,* too, as he sat across from her with that crooked grin, all playful cowboy, the complete opposite of a man like Cade.

What would be the harm in just one date?

But then something went swirly in her belly, melty and hot, trickling downward until it settled in the core of her.

She shoved the sensation aside.

"Come on, Laila," Jackson said, his brown eyes glinting with that flirtiness she'd seen before. "I'm just talking about a date, not a marriage proposal."

Wasn't he a card.

Or, more to the point, a wild card.

"Very funny," she said.

"Don't tell me a man doesn't have a chance with you." He sent a glance over his shoulder, toward the door where Cade had disappeared only moments ago. "Or maybe there's something else to it."

She had the feeling he was going to go somewhere she didn't want to go.

"Maybe," he said, "there really is something between you and Pritchett, even if you were desperate to get away from him less than five minutes ago."

Jackson said it in a teasing way, as if he didn't believe it for a second.

Was there anything this Texan didn't see? It was as if he could read her through and through.

Yet she refused to dignify his question with an answer. She knew when a troublemaker was stirring it up.

He chuckled, just as the jukebox went silent, leaving only the laughter from the bar patrons.

She crossed her arms over her chest.

"We both know that there's no way you'll end up with a nice guy like Pritchett." He put the glass to his lips, drinking.

His throat worked with every swallow.

She couldn't take her eyes off him, couldn't stop herself from thinking what it would feel like to have her lips against that throat, the warm skin roughened by stubble from a five o'clock shadow.

But she managed to pull her gaze away before she offered evidence that he was right about her being attracted to a bad boy over a good one.

"I may not end up with Cade," she said, "but that doesn't mean I'd put myself in the position of ending up anywhere with you."

He put down the drained mug. "Shot through the heart, Miss Laila. You've got some excellent aim."

"And *you* don't know enough about me to go around predicting who's my type and who's not."

"I can sure guess." He sat back in his chair, long-limbed and laconic.

A wise girl would have gotten up from the table by now, heading through the door for home, where it would be safe. But here she was flirting with him.

And she didn't want to stop.

He said, "I surmise that, all your life, you've dated men who are steady. Men who drive just five miles above the speed limit—and that's their idea of living dangerously. And yours, too."

He didn't even seem to be expecting a response—not judging by the long, cocky stare he was fixing on her, one that suggested he knew how madly her blood was flying through her veins, just from being near him.

When had she ever felt like this before?

Was it curiosity that was keeping her here? Or was it because the big 3-0 was looming above her like a net, ready to drop and wrap her up in the great unknown?

Whatever it was, she finally, quietly dared to say, "And just what would a man like you have to offer on a…date?"

Jackson lowered his ankle from where it'd been resting on his knee. "I drive a whole lot faster than the speed limit, for one thing."

"And you'll be driving just as fast out of town, once you're done with your business here."

"So I will. But a woman who doesn't aim to settle down wouldn't care so much about my leaving. We understand each other's philosophies on that."

Was he saying that they had something in common? That because she didn't have any plans to get married, she was just like him?

The notion should've disturbed her, but instead, it sent a shot of adrenaline racing through her body.

"Come on, Laila," he said, leaning toward her even closer. Charmingly. Devastatingly. "One date. That's all I'm asking for."

She swallowed. "That's all?"

What was she doing?

"One date is all…for now." He stood to his full height, towering above her, then leaned down until his words brushed her ear with warmth. "But I'm pretty sure you'll find that one date won't be enough."

And, with that, he ambled away, not even bothering to get her phone number or arrange a time to pick her up.

Just as cocky—and tempting—as he'd been when he'd entered the bar.

"Seriously?" said Laila's best friend, Dana Hanson, while sitting in a chair by Laila's office desk the next day. "You're actually going out with that pugilist?"

Laila closed the glass door that separated her working space from the rest of the bank, which bustled with people during lunch hour. Dana, who was wearing her sandy hair in a conservative upswept style that artfully hid the purple streak she'd decided to add last weekend, had pushed her decorative Clark Kent glasses to the crown of her head in her awe of Laila's situation.

"I *think* I have a date with the pugilist," Laila said, staying near the door where she could keep an eye on things.

"How is it that you're not sure?"

"Well, he asked me out then just sort of…left me hanging."

"A proficient tease. He sounds like an all-around bad seed." Dana waggled her eyebrows. "*I* would go out with him, just for the adventure."

"I'm not sure I should, even though I kind of said I would." Laila shook her head. "He has me all confused."

"Then that's why you're into him. He's different. He's the guy who makes our straight-arrow golden girl feel like she could get a little tarnished. And he throws you for a loop when you don't normally get riled up by men." Dana pointed at her. "That's why you like him."

"Technically, I didn't say yes to a date."

"But you didn't refuse."

"I should've."

"Why?"

Laila gave up trying to make sense out of any of it, then motioned to the suit she was wearing—a black and white advertisement for dedicated businesswomen everywhere. "Because of this, Dane. Because maybe I'm a little…"

"Bored with it all?"

Nodding, Laila leaned her head against a wooden reinforcement by the door. All around, her office seemed so bland, with its chrome touches, the fake potted flowers in strategic places. Real ones would've been prettier, but it took commitment to maintain them.

"I know, life's rough," Dana said. "Every man wants the beauty queen. It must be a slog, fending them all off."

"You know what I mean by bored."

"Yeah. And I'd have some compassion if you weren't you."

She knew her friend didn't mean anything cruel by that; Laila had tried all her life not to be smug about her looks, appreciating what God had given her while always working for more.

"I have to say, though," Dana said, "that when the Pritchett boys and then this Traub fellow proposed at Miss Frontier Days, I did feel for you. I actually regretted entering you into the pageant…for about two minutes."

"No major harm done."

"So if he does take you out, where do you think it'll be?" Dana asked, not even remotely off the subject of Jackson. "Bowling? Cow-tipping in the fields?"

"Hilarious."

"You've totally been thinking about your choices."

Lying was futile, and Dana was smirking now.

"What?" Laila asked.

"You're fidgety about this. Laila Cates, I've never seen you so nervous, not even back in our junior year, when you had your very first date, with Gary Scott."

Nervous? Her?

Couldn't be.

Laila opened the door, smiling caustically at her friend. "Isn't it time for you to get back to the loan desk?"

Dana smoothed down her red skirt and headed for the exit. "You're affected, Laila. A-F-F-E-C-T-E-D."

And she left, still smirking.

Laila tried to get back to the paperwork on her desk, plus the million-and-one to-do items on her list, but she just couldn't focus on work. So it was almost a relief when she saw the bank's elderly owner, Mike Trudeau, walking by the windows of her office.

She'd been waiting for her boss to come in for hours and, even before she went to him, she marked him off her to-do list, then rose from her seat. With a smooth gait, she went outside, following him to his own office, which was decorated with a huntsman's touch, featuring kitschy, homey things like a mallard clock and a painting of buffalo roaming a prairie.

He was standing behind his desk, accessing his computer when she walked in.

"Morning, Laila."

Casual, friendly, with the silver hair of a grandpa… He shouldn't have intimidated Laila in the least, especially since he'd shown up to check in on his business dressed in jeans and a bulky sweater, just as laid-back as usual.

And, as usual, Laila put on the same façade that made everyone think that nothing ever got to her.

"Morning, Mike. Do you have a moment?"

"For our reigning Miss Frontier Days? Always."

He motioned toward the chair in front of his large oak desk, and she sat, crossing her legs, slipping a folder toward him.

"Ah," he said. "Do we have another idea today?"

She was used to this bit of harmless condescension in his tone, and she kept smiling, even if every idea she brought to him seemed to end up in the garbage heap. Or, more likely, she suspected that there was a vortex that could only be accessed through a drawer in his desk, and that was where her ideas went.

But that didn't stop her from trying again, especially since this particular idea was closer to her heart than usual.

"Yes, sir, I've got another one," she said, folding her hands in her lap.

He didn't make a move to open the folder, so she started her pitch, determined that he would at least hear it.

"It's no secret that most people in Thunder Canyon have been hit hard by the economy," she said, leaving out the fact that Mike Trudeau himself was flush right now, along with his bank.

"True enough." He was still fussing with his computer.

"And I know you've expressed an interest in getting this town back on its feet. You've been meeting with the mayor, along with other leading members of the community. I don't know how many ideas you've come up with, but if you'll take a look at some figures I've put together to support what I have in mind…"

Mr. Trudeau finally opened the folder, but his expression didn't change.

Laila cleared her throat. "I think the bank is in a position to make more loans to struggling local homeowners and small businesses in Thunder Canyon and, as you'll see, I've proposed some avenues to do that, while benefiting our business in the long run."

"Interesting," he said, paging through the folder.

Laila couldn't stop looking at the top of his silver head, and when she realized that her fingers were clutching her skirt, she loosened her hold.

Mr. Trudeau closed the folder. "Looks like that college business degree did you some good, Laila."

"Thank you, sir."

"Beats getting an MRS degree, like the girls in my day used to do."

Laila kept her mouth shut. Even though she'd decided to major in business because she thought she should, rather than out of a love for the subject, she was proud of her accomplishments. So were her parents, who'd always emphasized a firm work ethic in their household.

Her boss sat in his chair with a sense of finality. "I'll go over it, Laila. Thanks for your work."

She almost said, "But…"

Yet she didn't, even if, so many times before, she'd heard Mike Trudeau use the same brush-off.

Sometimes, when she talked to him, she felt as if

there was no substance in her at all. But maybe this time he would believe that there was more to her than what he saw—something she'd tried, and failed, to prove all too recently at Miss Frontier Days.

Holding back that frustration, she got up, thanking her boss again, then headed for the door.

She shut it behind her, adapting a pleasant expression for the customers who greeted her on their way to the tellers' windows.

In spite of what had just happened, as long as Laila could use her brain, she was going to *keep* putting proposals on her boss's desk. She would keep on fighting the good fight....

On her way across the tiled lobby, a woman's voice stopped her.

"Laila!"

She turned to find Jacey Weidemeyer, one of her friends from high school who patronized the bank. She was dressed in jeans and a thick sweater that almost hid the reminder of a recently pregnant belly.

And she was holding a baby.

For some reason, Laila's heart twisted at the sight of the newborn in Jacey's arms, an infant swaddled in a pink blanket with a tiny knit hat covering her head, her eyes closed in sleep, her skin smooth and rosy.

"Oh," Laila whispered. "She's beautiful."

Jacey stroked her daughter's cheek. "Meet Hannah. This is the first time we've gotten out of the house since I gave birth."

Laila touched the baby's little hand. Tiny nails. Tiny fingers.

Her heart seemed to sink inside her for some reason.

Jacey said, "We're going to have a reception in a few weeks. I'll email you an invitation."

"I'd…" What, love to go? It was the last thing Laila thought she would ever have said. She amended herself appropriately. "I'll be there."

After they finished chatting and Jacey left for the teller's window, Laila looked after her and Hannah, pangs invading her deep and low.

Was it because of what Cade had said last night about how he could give her children before it was too late?

Having no idea, Laila went back to her office, leaving the door slightly ajar behind her.

By the time a chilly, star-pinned night hushed over Thunder Canyon, Jackson had left the brick office building that his brother, Ethan, had established for Traub Oil Montana in Old Town and arrived at the Thunder Canyon Resort to meet some of his family for dinner at DJ's Rib Shack.

He shed his coat and hat in the hostess area and walked into the restaurant, with its family-style benches and booths filled with customers, pictures of sepia-toned cowboys and a visual history of Thunder Canyon revealed in a mural painting.

It wasn't two seconds before Ethan came over to him.

"So I hear you've already gotten busy here in town," his older brother said.

Jackson was tall, but Ethan had a couple of inches on him, and he was dressed for the field in boots and jeans since he'd returned from the Bakken Shale today.

It would seem that Big Bro was talking to Jackson about work, yet that wasn't *quite* the case.

Ignoring Ethan's jibe, Jackson headed for a private

back dining room where special events were often held, including tonight's family gathering that DJ had called, though no one knew the reason yet.

Ethan followed. "Weren't you the one who said that you'd probably be in Thunder Canyon only long enough to work on this project and then you'd be going back to Midland?"

"That's what I said."

"Well, it sure looks as if you're settling into this place fine enough to me. You're dating a local girl."

Jackson sat at a dining bench. The aroma of DJ's famous rib sauce was already making his stomach grumble.

"It's just a date," he said lightly. "And Laila Cates is fully aware that it's not going to turn into anything more. And just so you know, my social activities won't affect my work here."

Ethan sat across from him. "If you had the kind of track record that didn't include a string of heartbreaks for your dates, I *wouldn't* be worried. From what I know, Laila Cates is the town sweetheart. You mess with her, you mess with every man who's had his eye on her. Traub Oil Montana doesn't need that kind of PR. It's your job to see that this town wants to work with us."

It was obvious that Jackson still had a lot of work to do when it came to earning his family's trust, but he was going to accomplish it. His real dad would've wanted that. Even Pete, his stepfather, would be proud of that sort of determination, and Lord knows that after what Jackson and the rest of his brothers had put Pete through, the man deserved some consideration.

Good thing that the rest of the Traub kids were coming around to seeing that these days, too, after Pete's heart attack and recovery.

"I don't aim to make trouble," Jackson said, meeting his brother's dark gaze.

Ethan seemed to realize that Jackson meant it—at least for the moment—so he let it go.

That didn't sit right with Jackson, though. He wanted his brother—all his siblings—to know that he was going to come through for them, that he wouldn't screw up again.

He wanted them to have some faith in him.

More of his relatives arrived—Dillon, Corey, their cousins DJ and Dax. A waitress took their orders, then left to place them while everyone made small talk, chatting about their work and lives as well as the latest gossip about ex-town councilman Arthur Swinton and his heart attack and death in jail. He'd been incarcerated for embezzling funds from Thunder Canyon, and his mere name left a sour note in the room.

Drinks were served. Jackson had ordered a soda, showing his brothers that he wasn't such a wild man that he needed a drink in hand at all times. The champagne at Corey's wedding had done enough damage.

Whether or not his siblings noticed the gesture, they ate in peace when the food came.

That was, until DJ brought up some unsettling news.

"Get your fill while you can," he said. He was a quiet man most of the time. Didn't dress flashy, preferring flannel shirts and jeans to a cowboy hat, boasting the same dark eyes and brown hair that seemed to be the hallmark of the Traub family.

Ethan said, "What do you mean?"

DJ put down his fork, then wiped his mouth with

a napkin. "I mean that LipSmackin' Ribs is making a play for all the business in town."

And that was obviously the reason he'd brought them together tonight.

A chorus of support for DJ filled the room. Everyone knew that his ribs had a stronghold in Thunder Canyon, as well as other joints sprinkled throughout the country. An upstart rib outfit in the new part of town didn't have anything on DJ's.

Jackson was still taking in the announcement. Strange, but when he'd met Woody Paulson, the manager of LipSmackin' Ribs, a time or two at the Hitching Post bar, the man had never let on that there was an underhanded takeover afoot. He knew that Jackson was a Traub, too.

Had Woody been laughing to himself the whole time, thinking about how he was working over the family right under Jackson's nose?

DJ tried to seem as if he wasn't too worried, but something about his gaze belied that. "LipSmackin' somehow got in tight with the Hitching Post, and they're providing the ribs for them now."

Jackson just shook his head. DJ was decent. Real decent. Never one to screw over a competitor. And Jackson felt protective of that sort of nobility in his cousin.

In his family.

"Let me get this straight," Dax, DJ's brother, said. He was the true rebel of the group and had always reminded Jackson of James Dean in a brooding way. "A tavern that's been in Thunder Canyon for generations has turned its back on one of its own in favor of a bunch of strangers?"

Jackson knew that by *strangers,* Dax wasn't including the Texas Traubs, who had strong family ties to Thunder Canyon. And he could tell that Dax's blood was boiling for the sake of his brother, too.

"This is what they're telling me," DJ said. "I had an exclusive contract with the Hitching Post, but *had* is the operative word." He carefully set down his napkin now. "I'm not going to lie to you all. This is hitting the Thunder Canyon branch of the Rib Shack hard, and it hurts the bottom line of my entire business."

Jackson could see how this affected DJ personally as well. His cousin's skin was a shade of red, as if he was angry, maybe even embarrassed at being treated so shabbily by a neighbor.

And if their neighbors were treating DJ like this, then that left the Traubs to back each other up.

Jackson's jaw had gone just as tight as Dax's appeared to be.

"I can't believe the Hitching Post did this," Dax said.

Dillon, the levelheaded doctor, stepped in. "Maybe there's a good explanation."

"Sure," DJ said. "LipSmackin' Ribs undercut me on cost in a way that the Hitching Post couldn't say no to—not in these economic times. I can't really blame them for accepting the offer, either. It's just good business."

Corey interrupted. "And bad loyalty."

DJ shrugged. "Either way, LipSmackin' Ribs can't possibly be making a profit, from what I can gather. There's just no way."

"Then why the hell are they doing this?" Dax asked.

No one at the table knew.

But all Jackson could gather was that his cousin was hurting, and that was an affront to *him*.

It was something worth fixing.

When he left that night, he didn't go straight home. He drove through Old Town, intending to drop by the Hitching Post since Woody Paulson often stopped there around this time for a drink.

The way Jackson had it figured, brokering a better understanding of the situation would be simple: He was acquainted with the manager of LipSmackin' Ribs in a friendly manner. Why not ask him what was going on?

And who better to do this than the community relations guy for Traub Oil Montana?

Jackson felt good about this constructive method of going about it. He was turning over a new leaf—a diplomatic one.

A helpful one.

He tried to mellow the memory of DJ's wounded expression that kept niggling at him as he walked into the Hitching Post, spying Woody at the bar nursing a brew as the silent jukebox sat sentry in the corner.

Jackson approached the man, a fortyish refugee from Vegas. He still carried some of that old-school air about him in his creased brown trousers and a tan long-sleeved silk shirt that had seen better days.

When he saw Jackson, he raised his mug.

"Evening, Traub," he said.

Jackson kept on his coat and declined to order a drink when the bartender approached. Then he greeted Woody right back.

The other man went back to his beer, and that struck Jackson as just being wrong. Here the manager was, part of a scheme to undermine DJ, and he didn't seem to mind at all. It even occurred to Jackson that perhaps Woody had only made a habit of grabbing a drink at the

Hitching Post because he'd been making LipSmackin' deliveries all this time.

"I heard about your new contract with the Hitching Post," Jackson said in a civil enough manner. "I suppose congratulations are in order."

Woody froze for the briefest second, then muttered a thanks, but didn't meet Jackson's gaze.

That didn't sit well, either. Jackson didn't like weasels. Didn't like dishonesty on any level.

"It's only unfortunate," he said, doing a fine job of keeping himself in check in spite of his rising dander, "that your business has to be at the expense of my family's."

"It's a cutthroat world out there, Traub. You're a professional man. You know how things are."

"Sure, but as far as memory serves, I never did draw blood from anyone. No one in my family has."

Woody surveyed Jackson, his gaze bleary. "Aren't you the honorable bunch."

Drunk. And just this side of ornery.

Had someone had a bad day?

If Woody hadn't sounded so mocking—as if he'd pulled one over on DJ—and if Jackson hadn't been so swayed by his cousin's genuine sense of concern about his business, he might've let Woody's attitude slide.

Woody stood away from the bar and walked off, and Jackson was about to let him go for the time being.

That is, until Woody looked over his shoulder and bellowed, "Tell DJ that he shouldn't be afraid of a little healthy competition. Tell him to just man up, for God's sake."

Everyone in the bar had gone still, turning to Jackson to see if he was going to stand up for DJ.

Still thinking he could settle this constructively, Jackson followed Woody outside to the boardwalk, near the hitching post that had given the tavern its name.

"Listen, here, Woody," he said. "There's no need to—"

"You're just itching for a fight, aren't you?" the man said, slurring even more.

"No, thank you. But—"

The punch came out of nowhere—a slam of numb pain that blasted into Jackson's jaw.

Instinctively, he punched back, connecting with Woody's eye, sending the man to his rear.

Jackson's knuckles throbbed and he shook them out, sighing. Goddamn it. And he wasn't cursing from the emerging pain in his jaw or hand, either.

"Hellfire," Jackson said. If his dad had been around to see this, he'd be shamed, all right. Awfully shamed. "Now why'd you have to make me go and do that, Woody?"

Woody put a hand over his eye, groaning as Jackson left him, knowing that there would be hell to pay, not only with his conscience, but with his family, too.

Chapter Three

"So how does it feel to be the scourge of Thunder Canyon?" asked Jason Traub on the other end of the cell phone line.

Jackson moved the phone to his other ear while grabbing a coffee from the Town Square cart. The late-morning air nipped his skin as he put a tip in the server's jar, nodded at the man's thank-you, then strolled away, working his sore jaw before answering.

"Being a scourge here doesn't feel any different than being one anywhere else," he said to his twin, who'd called him from Texas after hearing about last night's little scuffle with Woody Paulson.

"You're just damn lucky the man didn't go to the cops. That's all Traub Oil Industries would need, Jackson."

"I know." He'd been beating *himself* up about it, and

he was willing to take his own punches. He'd already gotten a few verbal ones from Ethan when he'd shown up in the office early this morning as well. When his older brother had inspected Jackson's jaw, not even finding a bruise, he'd said that Jackson could've used some black and blue to remind him of his misstep.

"Needless to say," Jackson told Jason, "last night wasn't my finest moment. But, believe me, it's *not* gonna happen again."

"Isn't that what you said after Corey's wedding?"

Duly chastised, Jackson wandered to the edge of Town Square, to where a wrought-iron bench waited under an autumn-leafed oak. Around him stood Old West storefronts, comfortable and weathered.

Maybe it was the sight of those old buildings that made Jackson say, "I swear, Jason—I'm making a new start here."

"Beginning when?"

"Now." It was a vow, and he'd never meant anything more in his life.

He really had been fortunate that Woody Paulson hadn't made a bigger deal out of last night. Then again, the other man had thrown the first punch, so it wasn't as if he was innocent in all of it.

But that was no excuse.

Jason wished Jackson the best of luck and signed off, back to his own duties in the Midland offices. Back to his own better-brother-than-Jackson life.

After stuffing his phone into his coat pocket, Jackson took a drink of the black, bracing coffee. He peered farther down the street, knowing just what he would find.

Solace of a sort.

The bank where Laila was working right at this moment.

He smiled, picturing her—blond, blue-eyed, beautiful Laila—and the world seemed right for a moment.

Then again, that was how it always was with him. Women made him feel better, that's all there was to it. And Laila wasn't any different than the rest.

On a whim, he accessed his phone again, dialing what he knew to be her cell number. He'd charmed it out of a friend of a friend of hers after neglecting to have asked her outright for it the other night.

What fun would that have been? The chase was always the best part.

Her phone rang, and when she answered with a curious "Hello?" his heart gave a surprising flip.

Then he reminded himself, *No different than the rest,* and went on.

"Morning, sunshine," he said, taking the chance that she would recognize his voice, even though his number wouldn't have been identified on her phone screen.

When she didn't answer right away, he wondered if he'd been wrong about her remembering him. Laila Cates probably had a hundred men ringing her every morning and calling her "Sunshine."

"Jackson?" she finally asked, and he could've sworn that there was a sparkle in her voice.

But, just as his heart was turning another one of those odd flips, her tone cooled again.

"What can I do for you?"

He laughed. Yup—hadn't he pegged Laila for a challenge right off the bat? "I believe we've got a date to plan."

"Oh?"

"Did you think I forgot?"

"I imagined it wasn't high on your list of priorities. It sounds as if you've been busy with other matters around town."

"Ah." He propped one booted foot on the bench, touching his jaw. "So you heard about last night."

"I told you—news travels fast around here."

Shooting another look down the street, to the stately bank, he pictured Laila at her desk, all polish and prettiness in a business suit. His heart gave a tug.

All he wanted was to see her again.

"Did you ever stop to think," he said, "that if I were to be kept busier, I wouldn't get into so much trouble?"

"Sure. And I can suggest a few things for you to do around Thunder Canyon. You can hike, ride ATVs in the mountains, shop at the resort…"

"I didn't mean to imply that I'd like to do any of those things alone."

He thought he heard her shuffling some papers, and his gut tightened at the image of her being businesslike. He had a thing for serious women, because it was a lot of fun to make them less serious.

"Which one of those would *you* prefer doing?" he asked.

"With you?" She paused just long enough to set him up. "None of the above."

"You're sore at me because I didn't call sooner."

"No, I'm not."

"You don't have to say it. A woman like you is probably used to guys falling all over themselves to set up dates and I neglected to follow protocol."

She huffed out an exasperated sigh, and he grinned.

"Know what sounds good to me?" he asked before

he pushed her too far. "A picnic. A good old-fashioned afternoon at the lake. I'll get it all together and pick you up at your place tomorrow at noon."

"But—"

"It's a Saturday, Laila. The best date day of the week."

"I was going to say that there's a chance of rain in the forecast."

He glanced up at the wide, fairly clear Montana sky. He wasn't sure that, besides Texas, he would ever get such a fill of gorgeousness anywhere else.

"I'm willing to take a chance on it," he said. "How about you?"

Of course, he wasn't talking about the weather, exactly, and she seemed to know it, as several seconds meandered by.

For a moment, Jackson actually thought she was going to turn him down, and the mere possibility shot him straight through with a disappointment he'd never felt before.

But that's why he'd chosen Laila Cates—because she wasn't easy. And because…

Hell, because she did something to his libido.

She finally came back on the line. "Okay. Noon."

Excellent. "See you then, Miss Laila."

As Jackson hung up, he smiled. He'd told his brother, Jason, that he was going to be on his best behavior from now on.

But that didn't necessarily include being a good boy with the woman who'd said yes to spending tomorrow with him.…

Silver Stallion Lake sat in a secluded spot in the mountains. Surrounded by pine trees, it was in October limbo—between the time when winter would bring out the ice skaters and when summer filled the water with swimmers.

Laila cast a glance at the overcast sky just before she laid a blue picnic blanket over the ground. As she sat, spreading out her wool skirt over her boots, pine needles crunched beneath her.

"Not to worry," Jackson said, bringing over a thermal bag, plus a tote of more food, from his rented pickup. "The sky's not going to open up anytime soon."

She ran a subtle gaze over him. Brushed-twill jacket, those jeans that hugged long legs, and scuffed boots. He'd taken off his hat, leaving his hair a dark, heart-poking mess that the slight wind played with.

A trill sang through her, but she told herself that, after this afternoon, there would be absolutely no more dates. She was hoping that Cade would hear about this one, and it would serve its purpose, letting him know that she had—without a doubt—no interest in the marriage he'd suggested.

"You really think you're that persuasive?" she asked Jackson as he returned to his truck and brought back a cooler. "Commanding the weather to do whatever you want it to?"

He offered a cat's-gonna-eat-the-canary smile, and she glanced away before her body did something silly, like flushing so red that she would sigh, just to cool it off.

"I can be persuasive enough," he said, sitting down next to her.

Close.

So close that she could smell the scent of pines—and

she knew it wasn't from the trees. It was mixed with the musk of man. Of him.

She reached into the food tote, just for something to do, and started to pull out a loaf of French bread that he'd obviously picked up at the market, along with the bottle of Beaujolais wine he was taking out of the cooler.

As he began to uncork it, she finished unloading the tote—the cheeses, the apples—and got out a plastic plate or two, along with a knife for cutting.

"You certainly know how to stock a picnic," she said, motioning to the wine.

"You know what they say. Somewhere in the world, it's Happy Hour."

"Just not in this part."

He sent her an amused glance, his dark eyes alive with that glint that so often sent her belly spinning.

"Why, Laila," he said, "you're rather prim, aren't you?"

She concentrated on opening a packet of Havarti cheese. "Today? Yes."

"Because you think you need to raise your defenses with me. Well, I guess I understand why that'd be. You don't know me from Adam. Why shouldn't you be on your guard, especially after everything you've heard about me?"

"Is everything I've heard wrong?"

"Probably not."

She sliced the cheese, careful not to look at him, lest her heart start thudding and she began to think something could happen here. Something fun and...

She put an end to those thoughts. "It's just interesting. You're…different from the rest of your family. Your brothers, at least."

"There're a lot of us. Six, altogether. Standing out ain't such a bad thing."

She finally peered up to find that he'd drawn one leg up so he could lean his arm on his knee. He was looking at the mountains, almost as if he was somewhere else.

Intrigued, she paused in her work, just in time to see him shrug, then pick up an apple and a knife, cutting into the fruit.

"My mom has told me a few times that I remind her of my dad," he said. "My real one. Not my stepfather, Pete Wexler."

The way he said it made her think that he'd loved his real dad a lot. More than he cared to let on to her.

"Did they get divorced?" she asked. "Your mom and your real dad?"

"No, he died when Jason and I were six. Oil rig accident."

"I'm sorry to hear that."

He didn't say anything for a moment, but she noticed that the cuts he was making to that apple were turning it into a ragged thing.

"Two years down the line," he said in a casual voice, "Mom married Pete. Most of us thought it was too soon, and we weren't what you'd call dream children for him." A smile swiped his mouth. "I might have very well been the worst of anyone."

"And that's how you became a rebel." She thought about the pieces of their conversation from the Hitching Post, tying them into the fragments he was giving her now.

"I guess I did test the new man of the house to his limits," Jackson said, "until I figured out that Pete had a high threshold for tolerance, and he was going to take whatever I, or the others, dished out to him. That's when he earned my respect, even if I wasn't always so good at showing it. I still looked to my older brothers as the leaders of the family, but there was something about Pete's outsider status that I appreciated. And, let me tell you, my mom appreciated that *I* appreciated. Believe it or not, I was the first Traub boy to come around to Pete."

And just when Laila thought they might be having an actual revealing conversation, he peeked from under his lowered gaze, and she knew that he'd just been giving her enough to lead her into another hour of this date. Then another.

He really was an expert tease, doling out information like bread crumbs.

"Your turn," he said, as if daring her.

All right then. "My story is that I know when a man has parsed out just the right amount of information to lure in his date."

He seemed caught off guard by being called out like that, but then he put down the knife and apple, taking out wineglasses from the cooler and pouring the light red liquid into them.

"Well played, Miss Laila," he said. "Well played."

He handed her a glass, and they clinked. A tiny spark of happiness bubbled inside her. She liked trying to keep up with a guy like Jackson Traub.

They drank, and the wine slid down her throat. It seemed to go to her head right away, but that couldn't be right.

Could it be that she was already feeling lightheaded, thanks to him?

It wasn't long before he was back to drawing her out again.

"I hear you've got six kids in your family, too," he said.

"Five girls, one boy. My parents kept trying for a son until Brody, the youngest, came along." Actually, it'd been her dad who'd yearned for a son so badly that Mom had agreed to keep going.

Again, Laila thought of Mom sitting alone at the kitchen table, along with all those college catalogues and a wistful expression.

"A house of girls," Jackson said.

"Don't you go near any of them."

He chuckled.

"I'm serious," she said.

"I wouldn't do any such thing."

"Don't you have a reputation to uphold?"

That's when he got serious, too. "I've got one beautiful Cates woman right here. That's enough for me."

She blushed furiously, and she wasn't sure if it was because he seemed to mean the compliment with every beat of his heart or if it was because he'd used the word *beautiful*.

Couldn't he have said *smart*? Or *engaging*? Or...

She stopped right there. She'd never complained about her looks. It was just that she wished he knew that she brought something more to the table.

* * *

For some reason, Jackson had brought the conversation to a standstill.

Was it something he'd said, when all he'd been doing was being genuine?

Whatever it was, a shadow had rolled over Laila's gaze, and it wasn't from the clouds above.

She took a slice of cheese, nibbling on it. He tried not to watch her mouth, the sensuality of each movement, the fullness of those lips he was dying to kiss.

Instead, he got things back on track—if he didn't, there would certainly be no kisses at all.

"See, I need to follow my own advice," he said, lightening his tone. "I told you at the Hitching Post that this kind of talk isn't suited for first dates." And he'd meant it, too, at the time—before he'd gotten way too comfortable here with Laila and found himself telling more than he usually would have.

At his comment, the corners of her mouth turned up, as if she was fighting a smile.

Encouraged, he went on. "So how about those... Hey, what sports teams do you all have here in Montana?"

"College and high school ball. Most don't generally talk about professional sports much around here, unless you're in my house on a Sunday during the fall. That's Football Day—a real big deal. I even forgo sleeping in, and I get up by seven in the morning to take a jog to the Stop 'N' Shop market for chips and dip to bring. It's my big contribution to the festivities."

He didn't want to go back to the family talk. It was too personal, and he'd given up as much as was safe.

"Okay," he said. "Since sports talk isn't the conver-

sational subject of choice here in Thunder Canyon...
How was work yesterday, honey?"

The mischievous endearment made her quirk her
brow. "Just like any other day, darling."

There. Back on track.

"Rumor has it that you're a real mover and shaker at
that bank," he said.

"Sometimes I wonder how much moving and shak-
ing I'm doing, to tell you the truth." She tilted her head.
"Listen to me—I sound like I'm not content with my
job."

"Aren't you?"

"Yes. For the most part. It's just that..."

He felt another serious moment coming on, but he
didn't stop it. This was where it always seemed to end
up with Laila. There was much more to her than he'd
expected, and she turned him upside down in more than
just the lust department.

Jackson tossed a bit of apple into his mouth. Yup,
Laila Cates would've made a good woman for settling
down with, if that was in his nature. Or hers.

She still hadn't finished her sentence, so he urged
her on.

"It's just that what?"

She gave him a look, as if asking if he was truly interested in this.

She must've read in him that he was.

"It's just that I'm frustrated with my boss," she said.
"I've got a proposal sitting on his desk—and not the
first one, either—but I can guarantee that he hasn't
given it the time of day. You know, he was supportive
in promoting me to the manager position, but sometimes I think that he doesn't want me to go beyond that.

He's got… I guess you could say old-fashioned ideas of where a woman belongs…and that's below a man."

The shadows Jackson had seen in her gaze earlier had come back now—the same ones that had arrived when he'd pointed out that she was beautiful.

Was this the same woman who'd entered a beauty pageant not a week ago and won with flying colors?

But why had she entered if not for a crown?

He recalled her speech. *Y'all have shown tonight that age and life experience are important—that they add to who we are and how others see us.*

Age and life experience.

Laila wanted to be more than just a beauty queen.

Realizing just now how far out of his depth he was—he was the last man on earth she should've been sitting here with, even on just a lone date—Jackson steered the discussion to where he was more comfortable.

"You ought to turn up the heat inside that bank," he said, teasing again, reaching over to the thermal bag to take out the hot food he'd purchased from the market. "You should march right up to that boss of yours, ask him if he's read your proposal and take names while you're kicking butt. Forget the sweet approach."

"You'd know about kicking butt, wouldn't you?" she asked, but there was a smile there.

It drew his gaze to the beauty spot at the tip of her lips.

Play it slow, Jackson, he thought, as his desire revved right up again.

He spooned some Swedish meatballs—comfort food—onto the plates. "Yes, Laila. I'd know about kicking butt, but I only did it with Woody Paulson because he started up something he shouldn't have."

And Jackson hadn't been smart enough to end it in a better way.

"You know what *you* ought to do?" she asked.

"I'm afraid I'm about to hear."

Undeterred, she gestured to him with her wineglass. "You ought to try the sweet approach instead of kicking butt."

"The sweet approach." What did she think he was—a pansy who liked to tiptoe through the tulips?

His Texas-sized ego cringed at the thought.

But it also let him know that Laila was right, even if he didn't have to be *sweet,* for God's sake.

He would just have to…mellow.

He watched as she leaned back her head, enjoying the day, smiling to herself. The gesture made something glow inside him, too.

Maybe one date wouldn't be enough with her. He had the feeling that he could use more of Laila Cates during his temporary stay here in Thunder Canyon. He needed her kind of balance if he was going to keep his temper as well as his promise to his family.

But could he do that without having this become an actual relationship?

They dug into the meatballs, mashed potatoes and broccoli with Hollandaise sauce that he'd laid out, small-talking about nothing much more than Thunder Canyon. She told him about the gold rush a few years ago, the rise of the resort, the struggles the town had endured.

All the while, he couldn't help but watch her more, wanting her.

Determined that he would have that kiss by the end of the date.

While they cleaned up, stowing the bags and cooler in the tarp-covered back of the pickup, he glanced at the sky once more.

Still cloudy.

But when had clouds ever kept him from anything?

"What do you say we take a walk?" he asked. "Work off some of this food?"

Laila slid a hand to the back of her neck, holding up her blond fall of wavy hair. She flushed, no doubt from the Beaujolais.

"Working off some of those brownies you got for dessert might not be a bad idea," she said.

He took that as a yes and walked away from the truck, waiting for her to catch up.

They didn't talk much as they strolled, just taking in the ruffle of water on the lake from a slight wind, the sound of silence up here in the mountains. A deer darted across their path, coming out from behind a boathouse attached to a dock.

Its hooves thudded on the wood, and as the animal ran toward the pines, its footsteps were cushioned by the dirt. Right afterward, a rabbit sprinted behind the spindly-legged creature, as if scrambling to catch up with it.

Laila laughed. "Bambi and Thumper."

He laughed, too, and their gazes fused.

And, damn if her blue eyes weren't just as big and wary as Bambi's.

His gaze rested on her mouth. Those lips—lush and red and set off to perfection by that beauty spot.

Before he knew it, he was bending closer to her, hearing her soft intake of breath, feeling the heat rumbling through him.

But maybe it wasn't him at all, because her lips formed words.

"Thunder."

Another roll of it shook the sky, just before rain started to patter down.

Just before she took his hand and ran toward the boathouse.

They clattered inside, leaving the door open, laughing just as the sky opened up to let loose a spill of rain.

"What were you saying about clear weather?" she asked, her face damp, her hair just the slightest bit wet—enough for him to reach out and touch it, just to tame a rain-kissed wave.

Then he did what he'd been dying to do before: leaned down to press his mouth to hers.

Chapter Four

Laila had been thinking about what his lips would feel like for the last hour, so she wasn't sure if this kiss was really happening…or if it was just a fantasy.

Because fantasies were a lot *like* this: the pressure of his mouth on hers, wet and warm, at first soft but then growing more insistent with every thud of her pulse. The scent of him—masculine, clean, filling her senses until her head swam and her knees went weak.

This was a kiss.

This was more real than real could have ever been for Laila, and it had taken nearly thirty years for her to get here, to a place where she was feeling a need so deep inside that it actually ached.

But why him—the wrong kind of man for her?

Or maybe the very right one.

She grabbed onto the lapels of Jackson's coat, just

as he pulled back ever so slightly—just far enough so that she could still feel his breath on her lips.

"Glad we got that out of the way," he whispered.

She could tell that he was smiling while he said it, even though her eyes were still closed, as if she didn't want to come out of the wonderful haze of this desire.

"Glad?" She finally asked, and she sounded like a dolt. But her brain was in too much of a muddle for it to be functioning properly.

All she wanted was for his lips to be back on hers as the rain tapped away on the roof of the boathouse, imitating the rhythm of her heartbeat.

"I never," he said softly, "leave the first kiss until the end of the date. There's too much jumpiness beforehand. Better to get it out of the way so that you can enjoy that second kiss—the one that comes when a man drops off a woman at her doorstep."

"Just before she invites him inside?" She didn't want to ask how many women had done just that to Jackson Traub. Didn't want to know anything but that he was going to keep on going right here, right now with *her*.

He laughed, and it rumbled through his chest. She could feel the vibration in her fingers, where she was still holding on to his coat.

And that was his only answer.

Then...

Then it wasn't Jackson who continued the kiss.

It was Laila who stood on her tiptoes, putting her hand on the back of his head, winding her fingers through his thick hair and bringing him down to her lips again.

She thought she heard him make a sound—almost a groan—and he wrapped his arms around her, crushing her mouth against his as she lost her balance and stumbled backward until she was against the wall. Something fell from a hook next to them, but she didn't bother to see what it was, although it felt like a length of canvas had come to rest against her leg.

No, she was too lost in him, responding like a wild woman, a perfect match for the notorious Jackson Traub as he brought her against his hard body. His belt buckle dug into her belly when he lifted her and, from the feel of what was beneath that buckle, she realized just how excited he was.

He entered her with his tongue, exploring, making her breathing come so fast that it burned in her lungs. Every inch of her skin was on fire for him and, as they came up for oxygen, she just had time to realize that she was a little bit afraid of what he was doing to her.

Afraid of how close she was to losing *all* control with him.

Sanity was just within her reach, and as he ran his lips over her neck, she had enough time to tell herself to put a halt to this before it was too late.

She had never been "that kind of girl"…

…But when he found the erogenous zone behind her ear with his mouth, she sure wanted to be.

Just a little bit more, she thought to herself while she turned to liquid. *Just a few more minutes….*

But her common sense dissipated in the steam of her craving for him, the chugging of her pulse.

She tugged his shirt out of his jeans, slipping her hands to his waist.

Warm. So warm. And hard with muscle, too.

Her thumbs whisked over the lines of his stomach, and he leaned his forehead against hers.

"What're you asking for, Laila?"

He was warning her, but she didn't care. She just went on and on, smoothing her palms upward, over his ribs, then to his muscle-corded back.

She probably should have heeded his caution, because it was as if she had switched on something inside him.

With another groan, he insinuated his hands under Laila's sweater, mapping her waist with his fingers, with tickling strokes that made her bite her bottom lip. And when he cupped her breasts, she arched away from the wall, urging him on.

He didn't hesitate, unfastening her bra as if he was an expert in hooks and lace. While using his thumbs to circle her nipples, he whispered roughly into her ear.

"Is this what you want?"

She could barely say yes, but she heard the whispering echo of that particular answer inside her, and it came out of her mouth like a gasp. He heard *that,* because he lifted her higher, so that her legs were around his hips now, her sweater bunched so that she could feel the cool air on her skin, her breasts.

When he lowered his head to her, the heat of his mouth took over.

He laved one breast while palming the other. A kiss, a suck, a nip, every motion stabbing her with heat until she felt as if she was being punctured by a feeling so strong, so good that she wanted more lovely pain, more adrenalized hurt.

The ache came to settle between her legs, beating, pulsing, as he took more of her breast into his mouth.

And, still, she wanted him to go on.

He lifted his mouth from her, panting.

Like a wanton thing, she grasped her skirt, pulling on it, inching it up. Asking him without any words.

He laughed softly, understanding what she needed.

He let her slide down the wall a bit, just until she was standing again, held up only by one of his hands while he eased the other under her skirt, between her legs.

With a touch, she nearly exploded.

She gasped as he pressed his fingers against her, then whispered to her again.

"Laila…"

He sounded just as far gone as she was, and that gave her another jolt. A stimulated one.

His passion was the most powerful aphrodisiac of all—better than succeeding in her job. Better than winning the affections of any other man.

Jackson was all that existed for Laila right now.

But then it ended just as quickly as it had begun.

With a long exhalation, Jackson removed his hand, pulling down her skirt without a word, making sure her bra and her sweater were in place.

Confused, Laila stayed against the wall, still pounding with lust.

Had she done something wrong?

He had to have noticed the question in her expression, because he leaned forward, bracing his hand against the wall just over her shoulder.

"The rain stopped," he said.

"What does that mean?" she asked, and she hated that her voice sounded shaky.

Had he merely wanted to prove a point to her?

Dammit, how dumb was she? Falling into the trap set by this well-known scoundrel? He'd probably just wanted to get a piece of the town golden girl.

And he'd sure done it.

"Well, Laila," he said, backing away, tucking his shirt into his jeans. "The rain stopped, and it's a good time to go back outside."

What?

"Jerk," she said, pushing past him toward the boat-house door.

"Laila," he said, sounding truly sorry. "Wait…"

"Stuff it."

"Hey." Then his tone changed back to a scalawag's tease, just as it always did whenever things got a little too serious with him. "I don't want you to think I'm easy, is all."

Now she wasn't just confused, she was mortified as she exited the boathouse, rushing onto the dock, back toward the place where he had parked the truck.

She barely noticed the wet ground, the rain-fresh air and its added chill that slapped her cheeks. She was still too heated-up, too…

Turned on.

Damn him, she thought, walking ever faster, as if she could outpace him…

…as well as what had emerged inside her during their time in that boathouse.

As Jackson followed the path that Laila was blazing back to the pickup, he gave her all the room she needed.

Things had gotten *way* out of hand back there. He hadn't meant to do much more than kiss her, but…

Well, then the woman he had thought was so prim and proper had just up and disappeared, bringing out a Laila who wasn't an ice princess as much as a fire-brand.

But what was even more shocking to Jackson was what *she* had brought out in *him*—a protective side, of all things.

A gentleman who hadn't wanted to take advantage of her?

He was still trying to figure that out. With any other woman, he would have taken full grasp of the situation, but there was just something about Laila that made him want to slow everything down.

To savor every moment he would have with her before he left town.

And thank God he would be leaving, because he didn't know how long this side of him would last.

In the near distance, he saw Laila quickly approaching his pickup truck only to come to a full stop, shaking her head, putting her hands on her hips.

She must have just realized that the only ride home she had was with him.

Thinking they could both use a few extra minutes to cool off, Jackson took his time getting to the truck. Chances were that he came off as being just as arrogant and teasing as usual, but that wasn't the case this time.

He didn't dare poke fun at the situation, so he went straight to the passenger's door and opened it for her, then walked over to his side.

Without a word, they settled into their seats. From the way she was staring straight ahead through the rain-dotted windshield, he had no doubt that he should be glad that he was out of her line of vision. She could've probably cut him in two with just a look right now.

He started the engine, then activated the windshield wipers. They whined across the glass, filling the fraught silence.

Dammit, he couldn't stand this anymore.

"Believe it or not," he said, "you're probably going to thank me later for calling a halt to things."

He should have phrased it differently.

"I *doubt* I'll be thanking you for putting the ultimate whammy on me, Jackson."

"I wasn't putting a whammy on you."

He wanted to tell her that he had gotten just as carried away as she had, but she had already crossed her arms over her chest and, in Woman Language, that meant she wasn't open to a damn word he might have to say from there on out.

Still, as Jackson drove away from their picnic spot, he didn't let this setback faze him.

To get her this riled up…it meant she actually liked him, right? Laila Cates definitely wasn't one of those women who accepted a date with a man just because she had a carnal itch to scratch. She also wasn't the kind who had dollar signs in her eyes and wanted to get a piece of the action from someone like an oil man with money to burn.

She was genuine.

And he actually liked that about her.

It was a real quiet ride home as all those notions swirled around in Jackson's head; the silence was made even more obvious as the shroud of evening fell around them.

By the time he pulled up to her Old Town apartment building—a quaint redbrick structure with window boxes and garden paths—she had obviously had enough time to stew. And from the way she was clutching the handle of the door, he could tell that she was ready to explode out of the cab the second he pulled into a parking space.

When he parked and cut the engine it didn't take her but a second to bust out of the truck door, slam it, then make a beeline for her apartment.

Suddenly, Jackson realized how empty the cab felt without her in it.

Rashly, he got out and followed her down the flower-lined path. He got to her door just in time for her to shut it in his face.

All right. Just a little obstacle.

"Laila," he said through the wood. He would take the chance that she might be right on the other side, just waiting for him to leave.

Hell, he could almost feel her there, and he leaned against the doorframe, as if that may bring him closer to her. "You might think that this is the end of it, but it's not."

Next door, a light went on, filtering through the window and onto the damp sidewalk.

Neighbors. Nosy ones at that.

"I aim to change your mind about today, Laila," he said softly. "You're gonna see sure enough that I meant no disrespect to you. That..."

What else could he say?

That I'm smitten with you...?

As if she would believe that. He hardly even believed it himself, knowing it would just be something tempo-rary.

But those were hardly sentiments with which to woo a lady.

He eased nearer to the door, lowering his voice. "If you're there on the other side, listening, hear this—I'm going to win you over before I leave town, Laila. You can bet on that."

Thinking no more was necessary, Jackson sauntered back to his truck, nodding to Laila's elderly neighbor, who was watching through her window.

She pulled back from sight just as Jackson got to his truck, hoping that Laila *had* heard him.

And that she had taken his promise to heart.

Laila had certainly heard every word, and when she went to bed that night, it was with the certainty that she wouldn't be getting much sleep.

She didn't, because she couldn't stop thinking about why Jackson had put on the brakes and, minutes later, told her that he was going to win her over....

Worse yet, when she woke up near the crack of dawn the next morning, it wasn't because her mind was still racing with all the contrary thoughts Jackson had put there. It was because her body was being run through with restless, electric sensations—physical memories of what Jackson had done to her yesterday.

Throwing off her covers, she went to wash up, put on some sweats and read the Sunday morning paper, which she found on her stoop wrapped in plastic, protected from more rain during the night.

"Good morning, Laila," said a voice from the stoop next door.

Laila looked up to find Mrs. Haverly in her quilted yellow housecoat, her gray hair tousled.

"Morning," Laila said.

"Had a bit of excitement last night?"

Oh, man. Her neighbor had apparently been watching the big drama.

"Just a date," Laila said. "That's about it."

"He's cute. I remember back when I could've had a stud like him come courting."

Laila merely laughed, even though Mrs. Haverly had just offered way too much information. Then she held up her paper and wished Mrs. Haverly a good day.

As she closed the door behind her, she thought that it was good to have neighbors—they kept watch when you were gone; they could be like an extended family.

But, darn, they could put their noses where they didn't belong.

The central heating kicked on, and Laila plopped onto her beige faux-leather couch. It matched the rest of the room, which she'd decorated with the restrained hand of someone who liked paintings by Renoir, fake green plants and a sleek home-theater unit.

Next to her, on an end table, was the only thing in life that Laila needed to take care of—Lord Vader, whose goldfish colors weren't exactly reminiscent of a dark villain. But when Laila had purchased a tiny Death Star model to go inside the fishbowl, she couldn't resist the name.

She laid her head on the back of the couch, watching Vader swim around.

"What do *you* think?" she asked. Of course, her fish wouldn't answer, but talking to her pet was better than talking to herself. "Should I give Jackson Traub a chance to explain himself?"

Vader went on swimming, hardly giving a hoot.

"I know—why should I be fretting about this when he's going to be gone soon enough, anyway? And why should I even care about *that* when I'm not even looking for someone to keep on dating?"

Laila sighed because she already had her answer, even without talking to Vader. She *enjoyed* being with Jackson. More than enjoyed, actually, based on how she had reacted to him in the boathouse.

Vader disappeared behind the Death Star, and Laila raised her head from the couch, thinking that this flagrant lack of concern from her pet was not a good sign. Or maybe she was just listening to her better instincts now.

Would she do well to cut her losses with Jackson immediately, avoiding any more entanglements?

Yeah, that was probably the safest way to go about this. She'd had her one date with the cowboy and wasn't beholden to him to go on another.

Ignoring the knot that had formed in her stomach, she finished reading the paper. After that, when she was just leaving her apartment to take her usual jog to the market for Football Day bean dip and chips, she told herself that she was already feeling better without Jackson. It could even be that Cade would soon hear about her date with the Texan, since Mrs. Haverly was known to be a gossip, and Laila's purpose for going out with Jackson in the first place would have come to fruition.

She put on a pair of sneakers, grabbed a tote bag, then went outside to brave the cloudy morning. She never listened to music while she jogged on the way to the market then walked back—the distraction seemed sacrilegious here in Thunder Canyon, where there was so much to appreciate: the song of birds, the stillness of the air, the trees all around her.

It was a quick trip to the market, and as she started her walk back to her apartment, she hardly even minded that she looked a tad disheveled in her sweats with her hair in a messy ponytail and wearing very little makeup.

At least, she didn't mind until she walked out of the parking lot and onto the road, where, after a few minutes, she heard the purr of an engine behind her.

Glancing over her shoulder, she recognized the blue pickup immediately.

Her heart just about rammed out of her chest.

Jackson?

She resisted the temptation to sprint. Good heavens, she had almost forgotten how she had told him about her normal Football Day morning run yesterday during their picnic.

But she still remembered what he had said just before he had left her alone last night.

I'm going to win you over before I leave town, Laila. You can bet on that.

As her pulse jigged, his truck pulled up alongside her, but she kept from looking over at him.

Her body hummed, remembering.

Wanting.

"Need a ride?" he asked through the open passenger-side window. He was as friendly as could be, as if there had never been any hard feelings between them.

"I'm fine." She started to walk faster, but realized it wouldn't do any good.

Then she became ultra-aware that she was in sweats—and that she hardly looked like a beauty queen.

But wasn't that a good thing? Maybe she would scare him off.

As usual, he was persistent. "Are you sure you don't need a lift? It's not out of my way."

Laila couldn't stand another half hour of him dogging her.

She halted, hands on her hips, and he stopped the truck. Behind him, the road was empty.

"Jackson, what're you doing?"

He seemed bewildered at so simple a question. "I'm offering you a ride."

She blew out a breath. "Why are you on this road, first thing in the morning, on my side of town?"

She knew that he was staying in a condo up at the resort. Renting, naturally.

He offered her a maddening, charming grin. "I know this is your Sunday routine, so I took the chance that I might catch you here."

"Were you waiting in the market parking lot for me?"

"Yeah, but I stayed occupied. Brought the paper with me." Another grin, telling her that he was aware that he had skirted her main point.

She would have liked to smack that grin right off his face if it wasn't so...

Endearing?

Great.

Then his grin mellowed. "I just want to talk to you, Laila, clear the air. I don't like the way we left things last night."

A flutter of excitement in her belly made her put a hand there, yet she took it away before he could notice.

But she might have been too late on that, based on the way his gaze had followed her gesture.

In spite of what her body was doing to her, she was damn sure going to keep to what she had vowed this morning—that she wouldn't have anything more to do with trouble.

"We don't suit each other, Jackson," she said, hoping *that* would put him off once and for all. "And I'm sorry you had to hang around the market all morning to hear that."

He seemed to fight a smile. Was he remembering just how well they suited in the boathouse?

"What I mean," she said, "is that you're a playboy. Your lifestyle doesn't mesh with mine in general."

"This, from a woman who's had suitors since she first learned to bat her lashes."

She was just about to offer her next retort when he delivered the capper.

"Aren't *you* something of a playgirl?"

His reasoning tied up her tongue.

Was she just that—a playgirl? She had never thought of herself that way before, but if she was applying a certain definition of the term to *him*, why wasn't it good enough for *her*, too?

She was a playgirl who had never wanted to settle down, who had broken hearts without meaning to.

And she was probably just like Jackson.

"We really are two of a kind," he said, his arm curved over the steering wheel, careless, casual.

That was when yet another truth hit her, right along with the first one. She realized that Jackson was looking at her just as he always did—with appreciation. This entire time, he hadn't even seemed to notice that she wasn't all dolled up.

Whether she liked it or not, that scored a few points with her.

"Laila," Jackson said, and the sound of her name coming from him was what finally did her in. He had a way of saying it that gave her pleasant shivers.

"Give me another chance," he said.

She wanted to tell him to get lost, but she was sure that her expression said something else entirely.

Jackson smiled, encouraged. "One more chance. That's all I'm asking for. Tomorrow night, after you get off work. I'd like to take you to the Gallatin Room up at the resort."

He was pulling out all the stops, offering to bring her to the fanciest restaurant in Thunder Canyon. Still stubborn as hell, though, she was going to make him work even harder than that.

"I don't know," she said.

"Come on, Laila."

The way he said her name…

Dang it, she couldn't resist. Why not just *one* more date?

"Okay," she said.

"Great." He sat back in his seat. "I'll pick you up at your place. Seven o'clock?"

"Seven's fine." Boy, how did she manage to sound as if he wasn't rocking her world?

Now that they had everything straight, he was back to the first order of business. "Are you sure you don't want that ride?"

"No, thank you." She wasn't about to give him a close-up view of Workout Laila Cates, no matter how much he seemed not to notice her dishabille. "I'll just see you tomorrow."

"Good enough." He put the truck in gear. "And Laila?"

She lifted an eyebrow in query.

He jerked his chin at her. "I like how you wear that saucy ponytail."

With that, he drove away, leaving her to think that even though she had refused his ride today, she was bound to get a wild one tomorrow night.

Chapter Five

"The Gallatin Room," said Laila's younger sister, Jasmine, with a sigh as she, Laila and the other three Cates girls gathered in the kitchen at the family ranch just before the first football game of the day. "He's taking you to the *Gallatin Room*."

Holding back a dizzy grin, Laila nodded while putting her tortilla chips into a plastic bowl. The reality of her next date with Jackson had set in, making her a little nervous now.

Nervous, but almost embarrassingly excited.

Her youngest sister, Abby, said, "Fancy times, Laila."

She sent a smile to Abby, who, in her early twenties, had always grown up in the shadows of all the Cates sisters. But with her long brown hair and big brown eyes, she had just as much going for her as the rest of her family.

Not that she seemed to know it, though.

Laila wished she could tell Abby as much while her youngest sister put together a salad, and Jasmine arranged other snacks on the kitchen table. Annabel and Jordyn helped her.

Jasmine said, "Jackson Traub's a real looker. Does he have any brothers just like him?"

Jordyn and Annabel laughed at Jazzy's usual enthusiasm for the opposite sex.

"He's got a twin in Texas," Laila said. "But I can't speak for his status."

Her sister flipped her long blond ponytail off her shoulder. "Oh? When's *he* coming to Montana?"

"Don't know."

Jordyn interrupted, still terribly interested in Laila's business. "So is Jackson as crazy as everyone is saying he is?"

Crazier, Laila thought.

"He's got his moments," she said.

As Laila brought her snack bowls to the table, Annabel snagged a tortilla chip.

"He punched out Woody Paulson," she said. "He sounds kind of dangerous."

"Dangerous?" Laila laughed. Not for an instant had she ever felt in danger being around Jackson. In fact, he made her feel...

She wanted to say "right at home," but was that really the case? Because oftentimes, she wasn't sure that the propulsion of the blood through her veins was very comfortable at all, even if she liked it.

She felt herself blushing and hoped none of her sisters noticed. "He's not that bad. Jackson's just...a good-time guy."

"Mr. Right Now," Jazzy added.

"Not quite." Laila leaned against the table. "He's more like Mr. Defies Definition."

"That's just a short-term thing," Jordyn added, stealing a chip before Annabel could snag another one from the bowl. "Laila, once you get to know him better, he could be a catch, and you'd be a fool to discount him this early on."

"Yeah," Annabel said, smacking away Jordyn's hand from the chip bowl. "Why are you just going on one more date with him and putting the kibosh on any more than that? You should give him more of a chance."

Behind the kitchen counter, where Abby was gathering silverware, Laila thought she heard a chuff, as if her youngest sister was thinking that Laila didn't give many men a chance.

Little did Abby know that Jackson had gotten *quite* the opportunity just yesterday at the lake.

Laila's skin burned every time she thought about him pressed against her, his body hard and ready...

She cleared her throat, thinking that it was almost time for the blessed game kickoff, and she would be able to escape this sisterly grilling and get to the family room.

"Jackson," she said, attempting to end the topic, "isn't going to be around Thunder Canyon long enough for there to be much of any chance, girls."

"Okay, then," Annabel said. "So he'll be out of here soon. But, in the meantime, if Jackson's a good-looking guy with plenty of money and, as usual, you're not seeking a permanent commitment, why limit yourself?"

Jordyn wagged her finger in Laila's direction kiddingly. "That's all you do is limit yourself, Laila. Just ask poor Cade Pritchett."

Abby dropped a piece of silverware in the kitchen, and everyone jumped.

"Sorry," Abby said.

Jazzy didn't pay any attention to that. "Laila, if you ask me, you're just plain crazy. Jackson Traub's a hunk. I'd totally get as much out of him as *I* could."

Abby said from the kitchen, "No one is good enough for perfect Laila."

It sounded as if she was ribbing Laila just as lightly as her other sisters were, but there was a slight prickle to Abby's tone. Laila had always had the feeling that her youngest sister thought she didn't deserve all this attention from guys.

She only wished she knew what was going on with Abby today. She wasn't usually like this, except when it came to talking about men.

Just as Laila was about to ask, the sliding glass porch door opened, and Dad ducked his salt and pepper-haired head inside.

"Ready for the beef?" he asked.

Jazzy laughed, no doubt thinking about the meat market they had just been talking about.

Dad stepped inside, and the aroma of barbecue slipped in, too, right along with Laila's twenty-year-old brother, Brody, who was carrying a plate of grilled steak strips for soft tacos.

Laila couldn't help but poke fun at Dad. "Looks like it's time for your team to lose, Pop."

He glanced pointedly at the Montana State Bobcats sweatshirt she was wearing with her jeans. "Little girl, your team doesn't even have any skin in today's NFL game. You rooting for the Chiefs?"

"If you're rooting for the Broncos...then yup."

It had always been this way—Laila getting Dad's and Brody's goats by cheering for the opposite football team on game day. Dad had gone to college in Colorado, taking up the fever for the state's professional team, too, and he'd passed along his Bronco enthusiasm to his only son. Laila had no allegiances, though—even if, on occasion, she would give in and root for the Broncos, just to make the men in the family happy.

Her sisters, who cared more about the food and the company on their Sundays together than the games themselves, had already lost interest and were beginning to load up their plates.

But Brody was a different story. He pointed at Laila in challenge. "You gonna put your money where your mouth is? How much you have?"

"The usual twenty," Laila said. "And I'll use my winnings wisely after the Broncos lose."

Mom entered the room at that point and, even though Evelyn Cates came off as being at least ten years younger than her fifty-one years, it was like looking into a mirror of the future for Laila. She only hoped that there wouldn't be a slightly regretful shade of blue in her own eyes.

"I hear you throwing down the gauntlets in here," Mom said.

Without comment, Abby passed her on the way out of the room, and Mom shot an "Is she okay?" look to Laila.

She merely shook her head, unable to explain. Whatever the case was, though, soon she was going to have a good sit-down with Abby, getting to the bottom of whatever was bugging her sister.

"Is all forgiven?" Jackson asked DJ that afternoon in the Rock Creek Diner, a newer place in Old Town where Jackson had requested they touch base, just so he could make sure he hadn't caused his cousin more grief after the Woody Paulson incident.

DJ, dressed in a flannel shirt and jeans, stretched an arm over the back of a red-upholstered booth near the front of the establishment. Nearby, at the lunch counter, a few ranch hands were watching the Chiefs/Broncos game, drinking beer and eating burgers.

"Don't worry about a thing, Jackson," DJ said. "I might've laid into Woody the way you did. I just wasn't there to do it."

"Thanks for saying so."

"Hey, you didn't make matters any worse with Lip-Smackin' Ribs than they already were."

A waitress in braids delivered their food—a Reuben for DJ and a big bowl of chili plus thick sourdough bread for Jackson. They thanked her, and for the first time in Jackson's life, he didn't watch a waitress walk away.

It was just that he didn't have the urge, and that gave him pause.

Did it have anything to do with Laila?

His pulse did a few jumping jacks, and he thought it better to stop thinking about her, even though it had been a near impossibility since seeing her this morning and managing to wheedle another date out of her.

He must have been wearing a goofy kind of smile, because DJ said, "What's got you so giddy?"

Jackson just shrugged, trying not to offer any more of a tell on his face.

His cousin chuckled. "Heck, I already know about your date with Laila Cates. No reason to explain."

Jackson had just been about to dig into his chili, but his spoon remained poised above the bowl.

Was it that obvious?

He didn't like being so transparent. It made him feel stripped bare for a second, and he scrambled to cover up.

"What makes you think I'm getting giddy about Laila Cates?" he asked.

At the lunch counter, he thought he sensed a shifting, so he decided to keep his voice down.

"Whoa," DJ said, hands up. "Didn't mean to ruffle your feathers."

"I'm not ruffled."

Again, he thought he heard something at the lunch counter. A laugh?

When he glanced over, he saw a couple of cowboys looking at each other, as if they knew what it meant to be ruffled by Laila Cates. Maybe they had even had their hearts broken by her. Who knew?

Jackson's bachelor pride burned. Worse yet, he even felt as if something was slipping inside him—out and away.

Before he could think twice, he said, "It's not as if I'm shedding my ways for anyone."

Not even Laila?

The stray thought bashed into him, but it had no place in his head.

"I see," DJ said, even though it appeared as though

he didn't—not with that grin he had going as he bit into his sandwich.

"Laila's about the most beautiful woman I've ever seen, and who could resist that? But when I leave Thunder Canyon, I'll leave. No looking back."

Out of his peripheral vision, he saw one of the ranch hands at the counter glance over his shoulder, and when Jackson looked over, he recognized him as a guy who'd been at the Hitching Post the other night—the mustached, silver-buckled cowboy who'd seemed more interested than anyone else when Jackson had sat down at Laila's table.

Now the man's gaze seemed flinty, as if there was a trace of hard jealousy there, and instead of feeling like the cock of the walk, Jackson just felt as if he had done a wrong to Laila by being so flippant about her.

Before he could say something else to DJ—something that could explain the careless remark he had made—the door to the diner dinged open, and a man and a woman walked through.

At first, the sight of the female's blond hair and blue eyes threw Jackson for what was definitely a giddy loop. But it was only because he was still thinking of Laila, as if she owned some part of him already.

Then he realized that *this* woman wasn't Laila at all, and the brown-haired, green-eyed man in jeans and cowboy boots with her wasn't just any old guy.

It was Zane Gunther, the country music star.

Everyone in the diner turned in their seats to see him, not only because of his fame, but because he had become a true part of Thunder Canyon lately, after going through a passel of trouble. A young girl had died after one of his concerts, and her parents had brought a civil suit against Zane and his promoter.

He was holding the blond woman's hand, and Jackson remembered her name now. Jeannette Williams.

There was something special between them. Something that gave a tweak in Jackson's chest.

The hostess went over to the couple. Other people in the diner did the same, including DJ, who shook their hands.

Putting down his napkin, Jackson followed, thinking the singer could use all the support he could get right now, with his trial coming up in December.

"So good to see the two of you," said the hostess, a matronly woman with fluffy brown hair.

Zane smiled. "We thought we'd grab a meal before heading down to Austin."

"What's in Austin?" asked an old man who leaned against the back of a booth.

"We've got some preparation and depositions to take care of for the trial," Zane said.

DJ spoke up. "You let us know if you can use any character references or anything."

The group reinforced DJ's comment, and the hostess said, "We're behind you all the way."

Zane and Jeannette seemed touched, and he gripped her hand all the tighter.

"Thank you for that," he said. "You don't know how much it means to hear it."

Just as it seemed the greetings were over, the hostess squealed, then grabbed Jeannette's hand.

"And what's *this*?" she asked.

Now that Jackson looked closely, he could see what

the hostess was talking about. On Jeannette's finger, a heart-shaped diamond ring glittered.

As everyone oohed and ahhed, Jackson faded back into the crowd. The sight of an engagement ring made him...itchy.

But the loving looks that Zane and Jeannette were exchanging got to him just as much. It was obvious that with this woman, Zane was going to come through whatever challenges he had to face.

What would it be like to have someone like that by his side, too?

Jackson dismissed the thought. It just felt a little empty to know that some men were built to be with a significant other, and some weren't. There were no doubts where *he* stood.

After Zane and Jeannette told everyone that they were hoping to get married on Valentine's Day, they thanked the crowd again and were ushered to their booth. DJ and Jackson returned to sit at their own table.

"Nice couple," Jackson said, just to make conversation, hoping that DJ wouldn't talk about Laila again.

"Things are going well for them." DJ wrapped his fingers around his soda glass. "Zane's going to come out of that legal mess just fine, and as for Jeannette, her job helping with Frontier Days led to her getting a position as an administrative assistant in the mayor's office. They've had a hard run of it recently, but life has turned around for them. Good things couldn't happen to better people."

Jackson agreed, and that was why he didn't ever expect there to be any "good things" like diamond rings or Valentine's Day marriages in his future.

* * *

The next night, Laila had gotten ready for her second date with Jackson *way* too early, and she was fairly bubbling with anxiety as she sat on her sofa—something she had been doing for about a half hour now.

She ran her hands down the dark blue dress she had chosen. It was straight, silky and maybe a little too sexy with the strappy pumps she had paired with it. And her hair… Was it better to leave it up in this French starlet style or take it down?

She glanced over at her fishbowl, where Lord Vader was happily swimming about.

"Am I overdoing it?" she asked her pet. "Is he going to think I care way more about this date than I actually do?"

Her fish could've given a flying fig.

Some confidant.

But watching Lord Vader swim did calm Laila a bit—not enough to still her heart, though. It was just that she kept thinking about the advice her sisters had given her yesterday, how they had encouraged her to keep seeing Jackson, even if there wasn't a future with him.

So why be nervous if this was such a casual, fun fling?

When she saw a flash of headlights through her curtains, she stood up, adrenaline racing.

But she didn't go to the door. Not yet. It would be catastrophic if Jackson thought that she had been just waiting here for him like some old maid who didn't have anything better to do.

He knocked, and she counted to five, grabbed her

coat from the sofa, blew a kiss to Lord Vader, then answered.

She opened the door to find Jackson standing there just as long and lean and cocky as usual. But then...

Something happened.

She couldn't explain it, other than that it was a change in the cool air, a shift of feeling and perception.

He looked her up and down, took off his cowboy hat and held it over his chest.

"Laila," he said.

And she couldn't even say his reaction was caused by how gussied up she was. He had worn the same look yesterday morning, when he had caught her walking back to her apartment in her sweats.

It was almost as if she took his breath away just by standing near him....

Normally, she would've handled the situation with aplomb. She was used to compliments, although she appreciated the sentiments that went behind every single one of them.

But this?

This was something else.

She didn't know what to do but say, "I decided against the sweatsuit tonight."

His gaze seemed hazy, and she even thought she saw him swallow with more difficulty than usual.

Without saying anything more, he reached out his free hand.

His gesture seemed to mean much more than just helping her out the door. Taking his hand seemed to signal that she was going someplace new, different.

Impulsively, she nestled her hand in his and, right away, a kick of desire jarred her.

All he had to do was touch her and she got shaky.

Good heavens.

After closing her door, they walked the short distance to his pickup. During the ride up to the resort, he turned on the radio, covering their lack of conversation.

By the time they got there, Laila had composed herself, silently repeating again and again that she had dated *plenty* of good-looking guys before, that she had always been in control of romantic situations and she should have no problem doing that now.

The Gallatin Room, which had a muted ambiance, featured a spectacular view of the mountains. The maître d' sat them at the best table in the house, in front of the window, candlelight flickering from a frosted-glass sconce.

Laila opened the menu, having no idea what she would order, even though she had been here a couple of times before—neither of which had made her freak out like *this*.

"I don't know if I'm excessively spoiled," Jackson said, pulling her out of her jitters, "but I've been to so many fancy restaurants that I always know what I want straight off."

His voice, low and mellow, went a long way toward smoothing out her anxiety, and she lowered the menu. "This is what you do for Traub Oil? Take people out to nice places?"

"It's what I *did* do at Traub Oil in Texas. As you can imagine, I'm pretty good at courting clients."

Um, yeah. She imagined he had cornered the market on courting a long time ago.

"And what exactly do you do now, here in Montana?" she asked.

"They call it community outreach. See, one of your local boys, Austin Anderson, has got an engineering background, and he's working on more environmentally beneficial ways to extract oil from the Bakken Shale. I'm in charge of educating people about the developments on that front. And I'm here to be a liaison between Traub Oil Montana and the people we leased or bought land from in the Shale."

It was a more mature position than he'd had before, she realized. "How do you like the switch?"

"From party boy to responsible citizen?" He grinned. "It's working so far, as long as I don't meet up with Woody Paulson again."

"And as long as you don't have any more brothers who get married?"

"A point to the lady."

His gaze glittered in the candlelight, and she had to glance back at her menu before she slid down in her chair like wax going hot and slippery under the heat of fire.

She still couldn't make up her mind about the food, but being unable to make decisions wasn't exactly a new thing when she was around Jackson.

"The *coq au vin* is always good," he said.

"Sounds perfect to me." She wasn't exactly sure what it was since the description didn't offer many details, but she trusted him.

She shut her menu, just in time for the waiter to arrive and introduce himself, plus the specials of the night. When the sommelier came, she recommended a Pinot Noir from Oregon to be paired with the *coq au vin,* which Jackson was also having.

Soon, they were breaking artisan bread from a basket, dipping it in olive oil. All the while, Laila couldn't keep her mind straight, since it kept wandering to places it shouldn't stray: places like the boathouse, where she had let him—and herself—go way too far. Like the front seat of his pickup, where she wondered if he was going to try to kiss her again tonight.

Like the bedroom, where, if she wasn't careful, they might end up.

But they wouldn't. God help her, they *couldn't,* because even if he wasn't in Thunder Canyon long term, that didn't mean she would suddenly forget her pride and become someone who slept with anyone.

Still, she couldn't stop thinking of Jackson's fingertips on her skin, stroking over her until the hair raised on her arms and until she went tight in her belly, warm and curdled…

"What's going through that head of yours?" Jackson asked, and it seemed to come out of the blue of her fantasies.

She sat up in her chair, dabbing the napkin over her mouth to buy herself some time. If she said anything right now, she just might stammer.

"Nothing much," she finally managed.

"Aw, don't tell me that, Laila. You're a complex woman."

Slowly, she looked up at him. Complex?

She remembered how he hadn't seemed to care that she had been wearing a sweatsuit yesterday, how he had looked at her as if she was, for all the world, perfect in his eyes.

As if she didn't have to dress in anything but herself for him.

"I'm thinking," she said, turning her gaze to the window and the view, "that this is a really good night, Jackson, and that I'm glad I came."

When she turned to him again, she saw that he had gotten that roguish grin on his face, and she knew that he was just as happy to get away from serious subjects as she was.

"The night's hardly over," he said softly, making her stomach whirl.

Making her wonder, once more, what would come at the end of this date.

Chapter Six

The night was like a stretch of never-ending torture for Jackson as he sat across from Laila in the Gallatin Room, yearning for her with such ferocity that he thought he might be pulled apart long before he drove her home.

He managed to last through the main course, dessert, the slow walk they took through the boutique hall of the resort, then to his truck.

It was yet another quiet ride home, but unlike the last time, on the way back to town from Silver Stallion Lake, the silence was weighted with something other than hard feelings.

He could feel the air just about vibrating between them, humming with possibility, and he knew she was wondering what kind of moves he planned to make.

Part of Jackson wanted to go for it—seduce her as

he would seduce any other woman. But, with Laila, he didn't want this anticipation to end. It was too enjoyable, like a fine bourbon you would nurse, reveling in the taste, the warmth slipping down from throat to belly.

When they reached her apartment building, he pulled into a different parking space than he normally used; around the corner, away from the windows, near a maple tree that somewhat blocked them from view.

He allowed the engine to idle, leaving on the radio, which was playing an old Charlie Rich tune. The singer was mulling about what happens behind closed doors, after two people find themselves alone for the night.

Just like now.

Laila hadn't opened her door yet, and Jackson wondered how long he could keep her here, her citrus-breeze scent filling the truck's cab.

She finally glanced at him from under those lush eyelashes, smiling a little. "Thanks for tonight. It was nice."

Lord knew how she did it, but she made his heart buck.

"Nice," he said, repeating her description. "That's all it was?"

"You know what I mean."

She tucked a long blond strand that had escaped from her upswept style behind her ear just as Charlie Rich sang the part about how his woman lets her hair hang down…and how she makes him feel glad that he's a man.

And Jackson felt all man right about now, too, with his heartbeat traveling downward, lower and lower until it pained him.

Take it slow, he reminded himself. *No reason to rush when the buildup is so good.*

Laila gave him another long look, and she must have seen what she was doing to him, because she got a glint in her eyes—the kind of glint *Jackson* was known for. At least, that was what they told him.

It was confident.

Bold.

Jackson's pulse double-timed.

"So," she said, her voice low and throaty. "I guess we've fulfilled our date quota."

"A quota."

"You asked for just one more, and here it was."

He wanted to say that it wasn't enough—that he couldn't even think of being in Thunder Canyon, knowing she was there, too, yet never seeing her again.

"Laila," he said softly, resting his arm on the back of the seat, his hand so close to her shoulder that his fingertips tingled. "There can be a lot more to come."

She swallowed, and he noticed that the windows around them were paling from the bottom up with the beginnings of steam.

Before she could give him a sassy rejoinder, he eased closer to her, subtly yet surely.

He was so near that he could hear her intake of breath as if it was his own.

"We're going to see each other again," he said. "Don't you doubt it."

"You assume quite a bit," she whispered.

He drew even closer, to where he knew she would feel his breath on her mouth.

"I assume enough to know what you're dying for me to do right now."

And he leaned in the rest of the way, fitting his mouth over hers.

In a roaring burst, he was enveloped in passion and heat, her lips parting, responding. Her hands gripping his coat and pulling him closer.

Without thinking, he wrapped her in his arms, dipping her back against the door as she bent her leg, nestling even nearer to him.

A flash of desire split him in two, and he felt as if they were in that boathouse again, with him losing all mental faculties, with him needing her so damn much that it scared the wits out of him.

He pulled back a little from her, looking down at this woman who captivated him and made him want to say things he shouldn't ever say to anyone. He looked at that beauty-queen face, but it wasn't her prettiness that got to him—there was something in her gaze that pulled him in with even more inexplicable force.

It was deep inside her, down in the blue of her eyes. There, he thought he might even be able to see a quality that she had never shown anyone else before, though he couldn't be sure.

The sight of it shook Jackson to the core, causing him to stop altogether.

Too far, he thought. One more step, one more kiss, and he was going to cross a line he might never be able to go back over.

And what would he do with her then?

What would *she* do with him, once he started to disappoint her with his inability to commit?

Gently, he tweaked her cheek with a finger, then let her go, moving to his side of the truck with a grin that covered his disappointment at having to pull back.

Some men were born to be good for others. He wasn't one of those. Never had been, never would be.

The furrow of Laila's brow made him all the more rankled until she gathered herself, smoothing out her dress and buttoning her coat.

"Well, Jackson," she said, "if I didn't know any better, I'd say that you're a pro at playing hard to get."

She didn't sound angry this time, maybe because she had already known what she was in for with him. And, oddly enough, that made Jackson feel the slightest bit better. If they both knew what to expect from each other, there would be no more disappointment.

"You've got me," he said, holding out his hands, as if in surrender.

"Do I?"

She said it with a bubbled laugh, and if he didn't know any better, he would've thought that there was a pop of frustration beneath it.

For a moment, he got more serious than he had ever intended.

"Yeah, Laila. You've definitely got me."

The air seemed to go still, probably because he meant it—at least in the heat of this moment.

He didn't trust himself to mean it tomorrow...or anywhere down the road.

She opened the door, snapping the tension apart. "Thanks again. I really am glad we went out."

He watched her get out of the truck, then stroll away. Common sense told him to stay put, to leave her be, but then he found himself climbing out of the cab, too, walking toward her door, where he'd just say a last goodnight then leave.

She was unlocking her front door when he approached

her bottom step, and he remained there, all too certain that he wouldn't be able to stop himself from going inside if she gave him even the slightest indication that this was where she wanted to take the date.

It was as if she knew better than to ask him in, too, and she gave him a little grin.

"Drive home safe," she said, taking her time in closing the door while the light from behind her made her hair golden.

"Just promise me you're going to kick some butt at that bank tomorrow," he said, as if he couldn't stand for the night to end.

She paused, apparently remembering their conversation a couple days ago during their picnic.

Then she shrugged. "I'll kick butt only if *you* refrain from it. How's that for a deal?"

"Sounds reasonable."

She laughed, shut the door all the way, and when the lock clicked into place, it was as if something inside Jackson had been closed, too, just begging to be opened again.

Jackson had gone home and taken a good cold shower. It had done its part in getting his head—and the rest of him—back together, but the next day during work, he found himself at his desk, staring out the window in the direction of Laila's bank.

Of course, he couldn't see it from here, but just knowing that she was merely five minutes away was killing him.

He got through a day of setting up meetings with some of the families that Traub Oil Montana was leasing land from, but he called off work when his brother, Ethan, stuck his head inside the door.

"Got a minute?" he asked.

"Today I have more minutes than I know what to do with," Jackson said, thinking of all the time he would have to fill when he went back to his condo tonight. Every one of those minutes would be punctuated by his longing to see Laila again.

"We've got an impromptu family meeting going on in the conference room," Ethan said.

Without any more information, his sibling disappeared. Jackson got up from his desk, thankful for the interruption until he walked into the conference room to see his brothers, Dillon and Corey, plus Dax, at one end of the long table. His younger sister, Rose, who had been in PR and communications for Traub Oil until she'd begun working in Mayor Bo Clifton's office, was standing just under a mounted TV screen, her arms crossed. Their expressions were stoic enough, but the look on DJ's face was the worst.

Jackson took a seat next to his cousin. "What's going on?"

Corey said, "We're here to hammer out what we're going to do about this brewing rib war once and for all."

DJ said, "After our last meeting, Dillon reminded me that this shady business maneuver from LipSmackin' Ribs wasn't the first—just the most blatant. You all know Zane Gunther's fiancée, Jeannette, used to work at the other joint for a time."

Everyone nodded.

Dillon, who was good friends with Zane, took over. "Jeannette had told me that, before she left her job with

LipSmackin' Ribs, she was asked to spy on DJ's Rib Shack."

"I didn't take it seriously at the time," DJ said.

Corey jumped in. "But then their ribs started tasting like DJ's. They must have found *someone* who agreed to spy on the Rib Shack."

Ethan rested a shoulder against the wall, near a window. "In hindsight, now we know that Jeannette's news should've been taken more seriously."

"How seriously are we going to take it now?" Jackson's blood was beginning to simmer again, just as it had the night when he had gone to talk to Woody at the Hitching Post. And seeing DJ with his expression so solemn only made Jackson's temper rise all the more, even though he had promised to control it.

But that felt nearly impossible.

"I'm with Jackson," Dax said, his leather jacket creaking as he leaned forward. Then he addressed the whole family. "I've been telling DJ since our last meeting that LipSmackin' Ribs is going beyond traditional competitive marketplace tactics. And we're here now because I, for one, think that Woody Paulson made this whole thing very personal when he threw a punch at Jackson. I don't know what's going on, but it's not just business."

"Hey, now," Dillon said. "I'm sure that both Woody and Jackson would admit that things just got out of hand between them."

In other words, the fight hadn't been entirely Woody's fault, Jackson thought. Half of him wanted to sink down in his seat at that, anticipating the looks he might get from his family. But the other half?

It wanted to fight, not only for DJ, but for the entire family's honor.

"So what are we going to do about LipSmackin' Ribs then?" Jackson asked.

No one spoke.

He stopped short of hitting the table to shake them all into action. "They've declared war on us. Are we just going to wait until they fire another shot?"

Dax nodded. "It's no surprise that I second Jackson."

One down, five more Traubs to go, and Jackson could see by the stubborn expressions on his relatives' faces that they needed some more persuading.

He pulled out the most powerful weapon he could think of—one that wouldn't necessarily affect DJ, but one that would strike true at the hearts of his brothers and sister.

"Dad would've wanted us to stand up for family," he said, believing it with all his soul. Although he had been just a kid when his real father had died, Jackson had always lived under the impression that his dad had been noble—that he had been perfect in a lot of ways.

He would have held his children to a high, all-for-one, one-for-all standard, and Jackson had spent a lot of time trying to live up to that. And oftentimes failing.

The rest of the Traubs merely stared at Jackson, as if they couldn't believe their brother had dared bring up their father's name in this.

Dillon blew out a breath, as if it would calm down the rest of the room, too. Then he said, "None of us were really old enough to know what Dad would've wanted, Jackson. Furthermore, I doubt he would've wanted any kind of war, under almost any circumstances."

Jackson held his tongue. It could be that Dillon was

right, but Jackson didn't want to admit that—it would have meant that he didn't know much about his father at all.

Rose finally said, "Why don't we ask the person who's most affected by this?" she said. "DJ? What do you think?"

Slowly, DJ rose from his chair, his body so tense that Jackson thought he might break apart any second.

"I think," he said, "that when a man is being attacked, he doesn't go forward unarmed. But—" he added "—he doesn't provoke the other side, either. There have got to be ways to counter LipSmackin' Ribs that don't include extreme measures."

Jackson realized that he had fisted his hands on the table, and he loosened them, suddenly remembering his deal with Laila.

No more kicking butt. More...sweetness...instead.

Or not so much *that* as subtlety.

As the idea permeated him, he realized that this was probably what his real dad would have truly wanted— that honor wasn't necessarily brought about by the use of fists.

Jackson just wished he knew for certain.

That same day, Laila couldn't seem to sit at her desk for more than a few minutes at a time.

She just couldn't get her mind off last night's date.

And Jackson.

She could really strangle him. One minute, he was wooing her by candlelight in the Gallatin Room, and the next they were in his truck cab, with that soft country song playing and him smelling so good and inching closer to her...

Close enough that she couldn't have said no to him about anything.

But she had lucked out in that area, she guessed. Again, he had been the one to back off what would surely have been a compromising situation in her parking lot, had any of her neighbors passed by and seen beyond the steamed-up windows. Once again, Laila had been ready for a whole lot more from Jackson than she had gotten.

How weird was it that he was actually somewhat of a gentleman when she—the supposed lady—was hardly acting genteel? Of course, she was sure that this whole act of his was designed to string her along and drive her so crazy that she would hop all over him when he finally decided to stop toying with her, but she rather liked being reeled in like this.

Or was this actually his way of *chasing* her?

For the next fifteen minutes, she did her best to work, and when she saw Mike Trudeau in the lobby, chatting with some of the tellers who didn't have customers at the moment, she finally recognized a chance to be productive.

If there was one thing that Jackson *had* given her, it was that piece of advice about kicking butt.

She smoothed down her forties-style pantsuit and tried not to think about yet another instance when her boss would shoot her ideas down or give her that look that said she was nothing more than someone who should have pursued an MRS degree in college.

Mike Trudeau had wandered over to Dana's desk, and as Laila's best friend adjusted her glasses and smiled at her boss, Laila sucked it up, stood from her chair and went out her door.

Kick butt, she kept hearing Jackson say.

She approached Dana's desk just in time for her friend to push a recalcitrant strand of taboo purple hair back into her conservative 'do before the boss noticed.

"Morning, Miss Cates," Dana said, tongue in cheek.

Mike Trudeau turned around, all grandpalike in his cable-knit sweater. "Hello, there, Laila. Happy Wednesday."

It was actually Tuesday, but Laila didn't correct him. "Morning."

"I was just telling Dana that I'm off on a trip."

Dana picked up a pencil, absently winding it through her fingers. "A hunting jaunt for Papa Banker," she said to Laila.

"I should've guessed." Laila put on her best, most persuasive professional smile and aimed it at her boss.

Kick butt!

"Mike," she said, "is now a good time to touch base with you before you leave?"

"Well…"

Again, it was Jackson's Texas round-'em-up voice she heard saying, *Don't let him off the hook….*

Unwilling to accept no for an answer, she began walking to her boss's office. When she glanced behind her, just to see if this was working, she saw that he was surprised.

And the look Dana had on her face?

Happy as all get-out. She might as well have been pumping her fist in the air because if Laila had told Dana once about her frustrations at the bank, she had told her a million times.

She made herself right at home in his office, taking

a seat, crossing one leg over the other, as polite as possible while he walked inside and waited by his desk.

Not giving him a chance to lead the conversation, she started in. "Did you have a chance to read my latest proposal?"

"I…"

She would take that as a negative.

Then she did something she never thought she would do in her life—she launched right into the nitty-gritty of her idea, selling it as she had never sold anything before.

In fact, she might have even been channeling Jackson Traub and his silver tongue.

When she was done talking about the benefits of loaning more money to the community's small businesses and homeowners, Mike Trudeau was watching her, a tiny smile pulling up the corners of his mouth.

"Why, Laila," he said, "I didn't know you had it in you."

"These ideas? I've laid them out for you more than once, Mike."

He chuckled, and she could tell he was recognizing that he had been called out.

"I like this," he said. "Go-gettedness. Now I saw enough in you to recognize that you could run a bank, but you've got a lot more going on, don't you?"

A lot more. More than a face. More than the surface.

She couldn't help but glow at that.

As her boss finally sat down and started to run some numbers with her, she didn't stop glowing. It didn't even diminish when she got back to her office, where, for the first time in her career, she leaned back in her chair, kicked up her heels and rested her fashionable boots on the desk.

What now, though?

Even though it was a quarter to five, she didn't want to call it a day and go home. Lord Vader, swimming around in his fishbowl, wouldn't care much about her big victory today.

She thought about asking Dana to go out and celebrate, but then she remembered that her friend was going out tonight with her on-again-off-again boyfriend, a traveling salesman who was in town for a couple of days.

What about her other friends, though?

Laila went through her mental address book, only to realize that just about everyone she used to have girls'-nights-out with were married with children.

That twang of yearning blasted through Laila again as she thought of babies...and Cade telling her that maybe they could get married before it was too late.

Here she was, sitting around, not knowing who she could share her good news with. Wishing she knew Jackson well enough to just call him up and say, *"Hey— want to hang out? Want to be my friend?"*

Friend, indeed. He was nothing of the sort. He wasn't the kind of guy who would genuinely care about all her long-range plans and successes.

Puzzled that she would even want this from him, she put her feet on the floor. She knew who she could depend on, always and forever. Her family.

Wasn't it time to finally sit down and talk to Abby?

Laila opened up a desk drawer, took her cell phone out of her purse and called her youngest sister.

Abby answered on the fourth ring. "Hello?"

"Hey."

Her sister detected Laila's upbeat mood right away. "What's going on? Did you win some kind of lottery?"

Laila sighed, wanting so badly to get to the bottom of Abby's remarks. "No jackpots, just a good day at work."

"Glad to hear it."

"And I want to have some fun, too. Celebrate a minor victory with my boss. You want to go to the Hitching Post with me? My treat."

Abby's hesitation made Laila think that her sister knew there was an ulterior motive here.

"Abby," Laila said. "Come on. It'll be fun. When's the last time I got to spend quality time with my sis?"

"It's been awhile, hasn't it?"

"Yeah." Laila was smiling. "So what do you say?"

It didn't take long for Abby to respond, and that had to be a positive sign.

"Sounds good."

"All right. I'm going to head there straight from work."

"Great. And Laila?"

"Yes?"

Abby seemed to rethink whatever she had been about to say. Or maybe she just wanted to say it when they were together.

"Nothing. I'll see you soon, okay?"

They signed off, and Laila closed her phone, more confused than ever about what she had done to her little sister to merit the standoffish treatment.

And what she could do to make whatever it was better.

Chapter Seven

"Jackson," said Rose as they left Traub Oil's office building, "you'd better not be following me."

"Aw, Rose…" He was always one to take the opportunity to razz his little sis. "You know I live for dogging you during one of your dates. The minute I heard you'd be going out, I knew I'd have to sit across the room from you at the Hitching Post and make threatening faces to whoever it is you're meeting in such secrecy."

Not true. He just had a mighty yen for those burgers the Hitching Post sold and wanted to take one home. After the last meeting with the family, he had assured them that he was building up to talking to the manager at the Post one of these nights when he was in, making the case for DJ's ribs. Jackson was sure that, as a good customer and persuader in general, he might hold some sway.

Rose rolled her blue eyes just before Jackson fell behind her. With her red hair and fresh complexion, she looked much younger than thirty. For some reason, the girl had a real tough time finding the right man, and since coming to Thunder Canyon, she had become determined to discover her Mr. Perfect.

Jackson knew her mission had something to do with how the rest of his siblings seemed to be falling, one by one, to the big bad force known as love, but what was the point?

He pulled on his coat, although this evening wasn't quite as chilly as last night. "Don't worry, Rose, I'll be out of the Hitching Post before *you* have your date eating from your delicate hand."

"Oh, I'm sure he won't be that simple to win over. Besides, we only agreed to meet for drinks, so this isn't a full-blown date. I'm not sure he's ready for that yet."

"Who?"

"Cade Pritchett."

As Rose went on her merry way ahead of him, Jackson stopped in his tracks.

Pritchett?

Not only was it a surprise that Rose was meeting with the man, but what would happen when Jackson saw him at the Hitching Post? This would be the first time he would be encountering his rival for Laila's affections since he had "saved" her that one night when Cade had been having that intense conversation with her.

But since Pritchett was going out with another woman—Jackson's sister, to boot—did that mean he was over Laila?

Now Jackson wasn't just wondering if there would

be any hard feelings between him and Cade—he was also wondering whether the man was going to end up breaking his little sister's heart if he was still interested in Laila.

Those were definitely good enough reasons in and of themselves to still go to the bar and grill. Yet there was also something else pushing Jackson to continue on his way there.

If his real father was looking down on him at this very moment, he might be proud not only of how Jackson was coming to terms with handling the rib war, but that he wanted to smooth things over with Cade—and he would do it while looking out for Rose as well.

Shoving his hands into his pockets, he let his sister walk alone, trailing far enough behind her so that she would have time to settle into her date at the tavern.

When he walked into the bar area, the place was bustling with activity—waitresses fulfilling Happy Hour orders, townsfolk huddled over the bar tables, the sound of utensils and the low murmur of the jukebox.

Rose and Cade were already at a small table. When she spied Jackson, she narrowed her eyes in a "You never listen, anyway" manner, then gave an accepting wave.

Cade turned around to see who she was greeting, stiffening his spine once he saw it was Jackson.

A decent man would go right on over to say hi, to let Cade know that there was no reason to nurse any hard feelings because of the situation with Laila. More importantly, though, a decent man would let Pritchett know that he was being watched, just in case he was merely stringing Rose along.

This one's for you, Dad, Jackson thought, sauntering over to their table.

Rose greeted him first. "This is why I love small towns—no privacy whatsoever."

Jackson extended his hand to her date. "Cade."

He accepted the handshake. "Traub."

Although Pritchett offered nothing more than that, he nodded at Jackson, and Jackson got the feeling that Cade just wanted this awkwardness between them to be over and done with.

Did that mean Pritchett didn't mind that Jackson had gone out with Laila a time or two? *Had* he decided to move on?

Jackson sent a gauging look to Rose, who was clearly ready to resume the date.

"Have fun, you two," Jackson said, tipping his hat. "Not too much fun, though."

"Scram," Rose said, grinning.

Jackson chuckled, glad to see that Cade was wearing something of a grin, too.

He retreated to the bar, where there was only one space open, between an elderly cowpoke and a middle-aged man who had his back to Jackson while he drank wine with a woman Jackson guessed to be his wife.

Unfortunately, the seat was within earshot of Rose and Cade's table.

But neither of them seemed to notice Jackson with their backs to the bar, a distance between them that was roomy enough to scream *FIRST DATE* while being intimate enough to let everyone know that they were together.

After asking the bartender if the manager was in tonight—he wasn't—Jackson gave his burger order and, while he waited, he caught Rose's voice.

Maybe his attention was even snagged because of one word she uttered in particular.

"You know he's been seeing Laila," Rose said in her usual straightforward manner. "Don't you?"

Laila. Her name echoed in Jackson, reverberating, chiseling away at him in ways he had never suspected could happen.

Pritchett hesitated, as if he'd been caught off balance. But if he had hoped Rose wouldn't address the elephant in the room, he was dating the wrong girl.

"I'm aware that they've been going out with each other," Pritchett said, somewhat carefully.

"Are you still aiming to marry her?"

Jackson was riveted.

"Now, Rose…" Pritchett said.

"It doesn't mean you can't have a drink with a girl, as you're doing now. I'm only getting a sense of what's what, Cade. You can't blame me for not wanting to waste my time." She paused. "I'm not naive enough to think that you wouldn't still have some feelings for Laila, even if she turned you down."

Jackson almost felt what Pritchett must be feeling in his gut—a well-aimed punch from a well-meaning woman.

"I'm here to have fun," Pritchett finally said. "That's what you want, too, right?"

"I'm all for it. But I'm not about to embark on a date with a man whose gaze is always on the nearest doorway."

Pritchett must have had that quiet, thoughtful look on his face that Jackson had seen before, because Rose added, "*Do* you still have your sights set on Laila, even if you're here with me?"

When Cade didn't answer directly, Jackson's hackles went up—not only for his sister, but because he had earlier misjudged Pritchett. Clearly, he still carried a torch for Laila.

"Rose," he said, "the truth is that I'm a realist. And I know Laila doesn't love me, but I want to marry and have a family. I figure a good case of 'like' may be better than a passionate relationship that's doomed to burn out."

"So you're just marking time until she comes around?"

"I wish you hadn't started this conversation."

"Better now than later."

Pritchett sighed. "The bottom line is that Laila's got a lot of common sense, and she'll get back in touch with it. No one wants to get old by themselves."

Jackson could almost picture Rose's stunned expression as Pritchett continued.

"Everyone gets tired of being alone."

Another beat passed before Rose answered. "Not *that* tired."

"Well, I'm to that point, and I've been dating Laila a good long time. If I didn't have to start over with someone else, I'd be satisfied. I don't want to wait the amount of time it takes to see if I'm compatible with a woman when I already know that's how it already is with Laila."

It was all Jackson could do not to turn around and ask if Pritchett was hoping to make Laila jealous by being seen in public with another woman. But, then again, there had been rumors Jackson had heard lately about Pritchett—something about a girlfriend who had died pretty suddenly and how he had emotionally shut down afterward.

How much did that have to do with his philosophy?

Even more confusing, why had Rose decided to go out with Cade Pritchett in the first place? Because she really *was* tired of sitting home alone?

Even though the fine hairs were raised on his arms, Jackson told himself just to sit there and not say a word. Rose was no shrinking violet, and she would have everything under control. And as far as Laila went?

Hell, he was damn sure Cade Pritchett didn't have a chance.

Pritchett offered one last comment. "I don't want to risk a life without companionship and children, Rose, and if I have to settle to get it, that's what I'll do."

"Wow," she said. "To me, a loveless marriage would be a fate worse than death."

And, with that, it seemed as if their date was over before it had even started.

Jackson peered over his shoulder to find Rose and Pritchett drinking their sodas, silent as could be. It reminded him of some of those long rides home that he had endured with Laila.

Jackson found himself smiling like a fool, just at the thought of her, and he cleared his throat.

The sound made Pritchett look back at Jackson, and from the expression on the other man's face, it seemed as if he had known that Jackson was nearby the whole time and had merely been warning off his rival by being honest about his unchanged intentions when it came to Laila.

Jackson didn't break gazes with him until the man

turned back around to his drink. And when Jackson checked in with Rose, just to see if *she* was the one who needed rescuing from Cade Pritchett this time around, he noticed that his sister was watching the doorway, none the worse for wear.

A cute female whom Jackson knew to be one of Laila's sisters had walked into the Hitching Post, but in spite of the family relationship, she didn't resemble Laila all that much, with her long brown hair.

Was her name Abby?

Thing was, Abby had come to a standstill, her gaze smack-dab on a distracted Pritchett. She seemed to be realizing that he was on a date with Rose, and the look on *her* face...

Good God, was the girl head over heels for Cade Pritchett?

Jackson glanced at his sister, who had looked over at him, too, raising her eyebrow in a what-the-hell-is-going-on? gesture. She had recognized Abby's lovelorn expression right off the bat as well.

It was also obvious that Rose had already cut loose from her date with Cade.

Jackson smiled at her, and she shrugged.

Across from the bar area, Abby had found a table and slipped into a chair. And not a few seconds later...

It was as if Jackson sensed Laila before she even entered. But when she did, the room seemed to go quiet, everything blocked out but Laila as she started to unbutton her long felt coat. She smiled at Abby and gave a little wave, tucked a wayward strand of blond hair that had escaped her barrette behind an ear and went to her sister's table.

Jackson was a whirl of conflicting emotions—a

foreign, enveloping warmth creeping through him, primal heat in the places that were always affected by Laila.

A war that was forcing him to choose a side.

When he glanced away from her, telling himself that he wasn't going to cross the room to say hi—that he should stay away until he could make sense of what was happening to him—he saw that Rose had spied the look on his face, too, just as she had done with Abby.

She was wearing a wondering, surprised smile, and Jackson turned back to the bar before she could react to anything more on him.

Abby was the first person Laila had seen in the Hitching Post, and she didn't even look around before embracing her little sister.

She must have hugged her too enthusiastically because Abby laughed, then patted Laila's back as they both sat down.

"You'd think we haven't seen each other in forever," Abby said.

"I feel like we didn't get to spend much time together on Sunday." There—that was a good enough hint as to the main reason she had asked Abby here.

But as soon as Abby was in her chair again, Laila could tell that her sister was more unfocused than ever. She picked at her napkin, and there was a distance in her gaze.

"Is everything okay?" Laila asked.

"Sure."

Their waitress arrived to take their order—breaded cheese sticks, buffalo wings and pink lemonade. As the ponytailed woman left, Laila took off her coat and rested it on the back of her chair.

That was when something curious happened.

Abby snuck a peek across the room, and it was such a furtive gesture that Laila just had to take a gander in the same direction.

Cade Pritchett was sitting at a table with a redhead whom Laila knew to be one of the Texas Traubs. Rose, Jackson's sister.

Abby turned right back around, her face flushed.

Before Laila could think too much about it, her attention was snagged by a familiar sight behind Cade and Rose: broad shoulders under a brushed-twill coat she knew all too well, brown hair curling out from under a cowboy hat and over the coat's collar…

Her heart gave a painful yet enticing leap.

Jackson.

As excitement swirled through her, Laila vowed to sit in her chair and not move a muscle. Dammit, after everything he had put her through, teasing her until she could barely see straight, *she* wasn't about to go up to *him*.

The waitress brought their drinks and appetizers, but Abby only played with her straw.

"Abby…" Laila said.

Her sister interrupted. "Doesn't it bother you to see him on a date?"

At first, Laila thought Abby was talking about Jackson, but when she took a second look over to where he was standing at the bar, it became obvious that he was there alone.

Alone and open for the taking, if Laila crept up behind him, slid her hands under his coat, over the muscles of his back, hearing him suck in a surprised breath as he recognized her...

Laila shook off the fantasy, determined to really listen to Abby. "Who are you talking about?"

"Cade." Even though Abby didn't say it with a lot of attitude, it somehow seemed as if Laila had offended her in some way.

"No, it doesn't bother me to see him here with another woman." Laila smiled, reaching out to touch her sister's hand, which was balled next to her drinking glass. "I'm glad Cade is getting out there again."

"It must've taken a lot for him to do it, after the way you treated him."

Gobsmacked, Laila sat back in her chair. "I never expected him to propose to me, Abby, especially the way he did."

"I'm not saying it isn't a good thing that you turned him down." She sighed, her brown eyes softening. "It's just that I feel for his hurt pride."

She said it in such a way that Laila blinked.

Did Abby...?

Was she...?

Abby had to know what was going through Laila's head, because she made an "Oh, please, don't even think it" gesture. "I've been like a little sister to him for years," she said. "Of course I'm going to be concerned about him."

Okay, that made sense. Abby and Cade did have a close relationship, so why *wouldn't* she have looked at the proposal fiasco from his side?

Just as Laila took another glance at Cade's table, Rose had finished her soda and stood up. She had put on her coat, and Cade had followed suit. They were now heading toward the door, but not before Rose squeezed Jackson's shoulder in farewell.

He touched the brim of his hat, then watched them leave. And when he glanced over his shoulder, at Laila, she knew that he had been aware of her presence in the room for a while.

With a grin, he turned back to the bar.

It was a replay of that other night, when he had been pretending not to notice her while she had sat at a table with Cade.

Laila let out a frustrated sound—something close to a "grr."

Abby was rubbing her temple with one hand. "Would you throttle me if I asked for a rain check tonight?"

"Do you have a headache?" Something was most certainly going on with Abby—maybe even more than her concern about Cade—but this didn't seem to be the night to investigate it.

Yet when would the right time come with her sister?

"My head's killing me," Abby said. "Big time."

"I don't mind a rain check at all. But Abby?"

Her sister had risen out of her seat and had her coat in hand. "Yeah?"

Laila wished they didn't have a seven-year canyon between them, wished they had been closer while growing up.

Abby seemed to be feeling the same thing, and she offered a tentative smile. "I know we need to get some things cleared up between us. I'm serious about having a good talk another time."

Just before Abby left, the sisters hugged, then Laila watched Abby go.

She was just about to sit again—only to finish her

drink and snack on the appetizers, she told herself—
when a deep voice sounded from just over her shoulder.

"You've got to stop following me around."

As shivers tumbled down her skin, she glanced at
the bar, realizing Jackson wasn't there anymore.

Nope, he was right in back of her now, so downright
handsome and appealing that her entire body was aflut-
ter.

"I think you've got that backwards," she said. "You're
hounding *me*."

"Think again." He held up a food container. "I've
got an alibi—I came here to pick up some dinner."

She gestured toward the abandoned appetizers and
drinks on her table. "And I don't have a good excuse to
be here?"

"Box that food up and we'll find somewhere to eat
together, away from here," he said, and it was with such
casual demand that her chest folded in on itself.

Who was he to order her around?

Who was she to *like* it?

With a rebellious stare, she sat down in her chair.
Nope—she wasn't going anywhere with him. Not that
easily.

Laughing, he joined her, then just as careless as you
please, propped up his boots in the chair beside her and
dug into her food.

While he was making quick work of the buffalo
wings, he said, "I'm sure it didn't escape your notice
that Cade was here with my sister."

"I saw." She took up a cheese stick, nibbling on it,
liking it when she saw that Jackson was paying quite a
bit of attention to how she ate.

He seemed to realize what he was doing, grinned to

himself, and took a swallow of Abby's untouched lemonade. Then he said, "They left early, Cade and Rose. I suspect he was walking her to her car, and that was the end of it."

"It wasn't meant to be."

"He's still got his hopes pinned on you, Laila."

Suddenly, the playful mood let up a little.

Jackson finished off a wing. "I overheard him talking to Rose about you."

Great. "What should I do to make him see that it's not going to happen?"

"Keep dating me." He wiped his hands on the napkin just before he went for the cheese sticks.

"And that should solve everything." Laila crossed her arms over her chest.

"Hey, you've done what you can to discourage Cade. Now you just have to live life."

She supposed he was right. "All I can hope is that he'll find someone someday."

Jackson got a mysterious gleam in his eyes. "Maybe sooner than you think."

Before she could ask him what he meant by that, he just up and left the table, throwing down way more money than the check would require and heading for the rear of the establishment, back to where she knew there were pool tables.

Did he want her to follow or something?

Well, it would be a long autumn in hell before she gave in to his wants.

Just as she was finding her spine when it came to Jackson, he paused near the back wall, leaned against it for a moment, acknowledging that she was making a big stand against him.

And when he shot that grin at her, then jerked his chin toward the back room, her veins pulled within her so violently that she felt like his puppet.

Let's call a truce, his gesture seemed to say, and Lord help her, but she was all for it.

At least she *sort of* was. She did enjoy the flirtation, the maddening frustration of butting heads with him. It made her blood race, made her feel more alive than she had in...

Well, ever.

He continued toward the back, and like the marionette she was, she grabbed her coat and purse from the back of her chair and followed.

For now.

By the time she got to the back room, he was already racking up the pool balls, and his grin told her that he had known she couldn't resist him. Jerk.

"Name the stakes," he said, hanging the racking tray back on the wall and chalking his cue stick.

"Oh, a gambler, are we?"

"I know when to hold them and when to fold them, all right."

"That's poker."

"The same basic rules apply here." He nodded toward the table, setting the chalk on the corner. "So... what are we going to bet, Miss Laila?"

Her pulse was jumping, urged on by his soft, I-dare-you tone.

"I'll bet that you're much better than I am," she said, the words barely getting out as she carefully folded her coat and purse over a nearby chair.

"You don't play?"

She offered an innocent lift of her shoulders, a liar

through and through. Little did Jackson Traub know that her parents had a pool table in their rec room.

He smiled, dangerous and hardly worthy of trust. "Then I'll go easy on you."

"Oh, please do."

He spread his arm, indicating that she should shoot first. She went to the wall, grabbed the stick of her choice, then chalked the tip, acting like she barely knew what to do.

"I guess," she said, "that I should bet something small."

"Since you're gonna lose?"

"Who knows?" She sent him a saccharine smile. "You just might have an off night."

"How about this—if you lose, I get…" He seemed to think about it.

"A kiss," she said.

"I've already gotten a kiss."

And from the expression he was wearing, he had enjoyed taking it, too.

Taking every single one of them.

"Then," she said, "you'll just have to make do with another kiss. But, again, you might not win."

"And if *you* do?"

"You'll have to leave town pronto, mister."

He laughed. "Not before I throw you over my shoulder and take you with me."

The primal image dug deep into her belly, warming her—no, *heating* her. Was it just because of the sexual thrill?

Or was it because he had said he would take her with him, even in jest?

She shut the very possibility out of her mind. She

would never leave Thunder Canyon, her family, her friends.

And he definitely wouldn't be staying.

The very thought gave her more courage than usual, gave her a shot of freedom to do what she wanted to do with a man who wasn't asking for a commitment.

She bent down to the table, ready to strike—and when she did, the balls scattered, two striped ones going into the pockets.

"Is it too late," she said, "to amend my bet? It already looks like you'll be leaving town with your tail between your legs after everyone hears about how you were whooped by a girl."

She felt him in back of her, one of his arms bracing her left side as he caged her by positioning the other on the right.

His voice was warm in her ear. "What kind of stakes are you thinking about now?"

Something much higher than I ever thought it would be, she thought as her heart seemed to get squeezed by an invisible fist.

"If I win," she said, turning her face so that his lips barely touched her cheek, "I—"

Before she got the next word out, he had scooped her up, bringing her to him, his mouth crushing down on hers.

Chapter Eight

It all happened in such a passionate blur that Jackson barely remembered dropping his cue stick, grabbing Laila's coat and purse from their chair, then sweeping her out the back door and to the Dodge Aspen coupe she had parked nearby.

He set her down on the ground, snatched the keys from her coat pocket, unlocked the door, picked her up again, slid her over the long front seat and to the passenger's side, then took his place behind the wheel.

Then he drove until he found a tree-darkened cove on the side of some road.

There he cut the engine and she stared at him in the breath-heavy quiet, her eyes wide, just before he — dragged her onto his lap, resuming their kiss, as if they were two teenagers necking at a drive-in movie.

As she responded with just as much enthusiasm as

any hormone-addled kid, he ran his mouth over her neck, her soft skin carrying the scent of a summer afternoon.

She panted. "You never did let me finish what I was going to say back at the Hitching Post."

"You aim to finish now?" he asked against her throat.

She grabbed onto his arms as he nipped at her. "Of course I want to fin—"

He raised his head. "Laila?"

"What?" A whisper. Needful.

He wanted to tell her to stop talking, to forget about the bets they had been talking about at the pool table, forget all the games they had been playing.

But instead of saying anything, he looked into her eyes, the blue of them lit by the moon shining through the car windows. He reached up, carefully unpinning her hair from the barrette that was holding it back from her face.

When her blond waves tumbled down, he sucked in a breath.

Beautiful. Damn she was so beautiful, and it wasn't just because of her hair or her face or the graceful curves of her figure.

What was it then?

And why couldn't he seem to get enough?

He shed his coat while she watched from her spot on his lap, then pushed the material into the corner of the long front seat. As if in acquiescence, she took off his cowboy hat, banishing it to the back.

Their breaths were coming in ragged rhythm now, and a flaring hunger was tearing him up from the inside out.

"Do you still want to talk about what you were going to say at the Hitching Post?" he asked.

But that wasn't what he wanted to know at all, and she seemed to realize that he was asking if they should stop now because, this time, he wouldn't be the one who would pull away, giving her some flip excuse about her thinking he was easy to get or something.

She answered by leaning down to him, pressing her mouth to his with such tenderness that he groaned a little, low in his throat.

Her lips were soft, warm, and his head got fuzzy again. At this instant, she owned him, and it should have sent him running.

Yet he stayed right here, skimming his hands down her arms, feeling the smooth fabric of her suit as it whispered beneath his fingers. He reached her hands, then her thighs, resting his palms on the sides of her legs, where her long suit jacket covered her fashionable, fitted pants.

His stylish lady.

His darling for the night.

Right now, he wanted a hell of a lot more than that, though. He wanted…

How long with her? A week?

A month?

Or…?

His mind blanked as they kissed once more, a lazy whirl of passing moments and heartbeats. He entered her mouth with his tongue, and she rocked against him, a move that could only be instinctive.

But she was obviously waiting for his cue, probably because he had teased her too much in the past, leading her on, then backing off.

Not now, though—he was at his limit.

He undid one button on her jacket, then another.

As her chest rose and fell, he gave her one more opportunity. "What were the stakes of the game going to be, Laila?"

She obviously understood his coded words, yet before she could answer, he slid his fingers into her opened jacket, feeling warm flesh, the toned lines of her waist.

"I was just going to ask for a kiss, too," she finally said.

And he gave it to her, whether she had won the pool match or not. She had already won *him* over, and that was all that counted.

Afterward, he still kept his mouth on hers, even as he sketched his hands up her waist.

"Are we square now?" he asked, coming to her breasts.

He cupped them, feeling lace, rounded softness, hearing her gasp yet again, sharper this time as she leaned back her head. The sound bolted into him, lancing and tearing, and he wanted to hear what she would do if he touched her in all the right, hidden places.

He ran his thumbs over her nipples, bringing them to pebbled nubs.

She didn't ever answer his question but, then again, he hadn't meant for her to. She only bit her lip, shifted on his lap, drove him that much more to a brink he wasn't going to come back from tonight—not if the throb of his nethers told him anything.

With deft movement, he unhooked the front of her bra, peeling back the lace so he could see her in the moonlight.

And…dammit all. She was beautiful here, too, her breasts full, just slightly tipped up, as if begging for him to sip at them.

But he just wanted to look first. Wanted to memorize her so that, when he was gone, he could remember.

He trailed his knuckles under her breasts, shaping, his groin getting harder by the second.

"You're killing me," she said.

And she was doing the same to him.

He leaned forward, touching the tip of his tongue to a nipple. Then he did it to the other one, taking his time, making her hips wiggle as she grew even more restless.

When he thought he had tortured her enough, he took her all the way into his mouth, sucking, pressing his hands against her back to bring her even closer.

She ground her hips into him, giving as good as she was getting, finally making him draw away because all he wanted now was to have her fully against him, laid out on the seat, every inch his.

Pulling one of her legs so that she wrapped it around him, he eased her down to the cushions. He brought her hips up so that they were flush against each other, and they strained, just like those teenage kids at the drive-in, steaming up the windows again.

The steam gathered inside him as well, pulsing and pushing, tapping like a time bomb.

He couldn't take any more of this, and he reached for his coat, propping it under her head.

Her light hair spread over the brushed twill, the seat, a fall of waves that struck him hard.

His Laila.

Slowly, he reached for one of her legs, stroked his

hand down the length of it until he came to the slick leather boot she was wearing. He pushed up her pant leg, pulled down the boot's zipper, the sound buzzing through the air, imitating the blood that was swarming him with heat.

After taking off her silky sock, he gave the same attention to her other leg.

Then he swept his palms to the back of her, traveling up her calves, her thighs, to her rear, bringing her up against him again as she arched and exhaled.

He found her pants zipper on the side, and he undid that, too, tossing the material to the floorboard.

Feverishly, she unbuttoned his shirt, stripping that off, fumbling with the fly of his jeans, then pushing down the denim. Pushing down her panties and getting rid of those.

As she took him in her palm, he just about exploded.

"Hold on…" He didn't even know if she understood what he had said, because it had come out so garbled. He reached into his jeans pocket, pulled out a condom, managed to unwrap it and sheathe himself.

"Oh, Jackson…"

He lifted her hips, pushing into her on a moan and, suddenly, he couldn't think any more.

All he could see were a million lights in his head, blinding him, needling him with their piercing heat. They flowed with his body as he drove into her, out again, then in, and she moved with every one of his thrusts, little sounds of delight urging him onward until those lights in his head throbbed, painful, impaling him, lifting him—

He did explode then, and he fell just as hard, his sight and mind coming back to him moment by moment, making him realize that he was holding tight to Laila, as if never wanting to let her go.

And she was holding just as tightly to him.

Jackson buried his face in her thick hair, breathing her in, thinking that he could stay this way for the rest of his life.

Afterward, they had pieced themselves back together, not saying much to each other, because what *was* there to say?

I usually don't move this fast with a man, even if I date a lot of them....

It just sounded like an excuse she didn't want to make—not while her body was still vibrating at a low, sensual hum, craving another round of him.

She never wanted this night to end.

Something inside her wondered why she should let it.

Kick butt, she thought to herself. *Why not get exactly what you want?*

Holding to those thoughts, she buttoned up her suit jacket. Jackson, who had already gotten dressed, too, turned on the car motor and it growled. Outside, tree branches left jagged silhouettes against the moon-bathed sky.

Ratcheting up her courage, she went for it. "I don't know about you, but I'm not ready to go home."

He glanced at her, coasted his fingertips over her cheek. It could have been a trick of the moonlight, but she thought she saw exposed emotion in his gaze, although she couldn't say just what that emotion was.

"Me, either," he said.

Her heart twisted, as if it was intent on going somewhere she had never been willing to venture.

But that couldn't be. Laila never fell for anyone.

Yet what if...?

No, she told herself. This was only the afterglow. She wanted more adrenaline, more excitement singing through her, that was all.

He was tracing his thumb over her cheekbone. "How about you call in sick tomorrow?"

She laughed. "I haven't called in sick for years."

"Okay." He stopped touching her. "You're right. Don't let me be a bad influence on you."

"You weren't influencing me so badly ten minutes ago."

At first, she couldn't believe she had been the one to say that, but why not? She had played it safe for so much of her life—why not invite a little game changer now? It wouldn't be a long-term thing since Jackson wasn't here to stay, anyway.

It would be a no-loss situation with so much to gain.

He was smiling at her comment. "Don't mind my saying so, Laila, but I'd like to keep influencing you."

"Then what do you say we get out of here?"

He gave her a long, serious glance. He paused like that for such a time that Laila even began to wonder if he was fighting something in himself—the same thing she was facing about getting involved with him.

But they had already gotten involved in a manner of speaking.

Way involved.

As if making up his mind the best that he could for the time being, he backed the car onto the deserted road, switching on the headlights. They lit the way ahead of them in a soft, warm glow as the bushes and trees and fences passed by.

It didn't take long for her to come to the conclusion that he was taking her to his rented condo up at the Thunder Canyon Resort.

Once they were inside his place, she surveyed the surroundings: leather furniture, glass tables, framed nature pictures on the walls. Modest for an oil man, but that was Jackson, in spite of how much flash his smile held.

He seemed to guess that she was thinking this wasn't a reflection of him—not a true one. "You can get anything at the resort. The concierge arranged for a decorator to rustle up a few items to make me feel at home."

"Ansel Adams?" she asked, stopping in front of a famous black-and-white photo of the mountains in Yosemite.

"If I've got to decorate, why not?"

She gave him a curiosity-filled glance.

"Okay," he said, hanging his coat and hat on a rack near the doorway. "So I like his stuff. He's got a way of making me calm down when I need to. My ranch house has recently benefited from his pictures."

So she *was* seeing a side of him that she hadn't anticipated.

She liked imagining Jackson at home, relaxing in his house, then going outside each dawn to ride a horse, work in the stables while the sweat glistened on his skin. She liked thinking of how he would shower off all that work-earned perspiration.

A zing flew through her. She had felt the sweat on his arms and chest and everything else not so long ago, and she was dying to feel it again.

"It's a gentleman's ranch," he said, breaking into her wicked musing. "That only means it's basically a hobby. I go there on weekends, live in the city closer to the Traub Oil Texas offices the rest of the time."

"So it's like a sanctuary?"

He had been sauntering over to her, and now he eased her coat off with breath-suspending deliberation. Her skin came alive under the slip and slide of material, under the sensation of his fingers trailing down her arms.

"I guess it's just like that," he said, his voice low and scratchy. "Maybe someday you can see it."

As soon as he uttered it, she thought that he might have regretted doing so, because he turned away from her, taking her coat and hanging it next to his on the rack.

Had he been overcome by what had happened tonight? Had he spoken before he had thought twice about inviting her to what he thought of as his private retreat?

Joy raced inside her, just at the notion that he might be feeling the same way she was—scarily head over heels, willing to test what might be between them.

He laughed, and all of a sudden, she doubted that she was on the same page as he was.

"Now that I think about it," he said, "I've never brought a woman to the ranch."

"I get it, Jackson." It might be time to lighten this up. "It's your man cave."

"Doesn't every guy have one?"

"My dad does. He needs a break every so often, too. Sometimes he'll go to a cabin near his favorite fishing hole. He keeps telling us kids that, when we retire, he'll take us with him, but not a minute before."

"My own father had a retreat. My real dad." Jackson's brown gaze grew darker. "Mom said he liked to go hunting every so often. I think he might've had a cabin in the woods, just like your father, but I'm not sure if that's something I made up about him or if it's real."

Sensing that the vulnerable part of Jackson was just below the surface, she walked closer to him. It was probably a safe guess that he didn't show this side to many people, and she wanted to be a part of this while she could, while she was still feeling close to him.

She rested her hand on his arm. "You miss him, even though you didn't really know him."

He nodded. "There are times when I imagine he's still watching me and my brothers and sister from the Great Beyond, and he might be a little disappointed in what he's seeing. In me, at least."

"Every son wants to make his dad proud."

Jackson didn't say any more, as if he could cover up what he had already shared. But so much about him had already come together for her: how his commitment-shyness might just stem from his never wanting to have his heart broken again, just as it had been when his dad had died. How he might even be running for his life with *her,* even if he had shown her much differently earlier tonight.

She brushed her fingers over his cheek, then turned his gaze back to hers. "You have so much going for you, Jackson. I hope, even when you're back in Texas, you remember that."

Something expanded in his pupils, the black of them opening up.

Another release of emotion?

It could very well have been, because he cupped her

jaw with his hands, leaned down to her, kissed her with such passion and force that she wondered if he was trying to forget that he was going to go back to that gentleman's ranch in Texas all too soon.

Hours later, predawn slipped through the curtains in Jackson's bedroom, casting a slice of murky light over the woman in bed next to him.

Laila was still sleeping, his covers pulled up to her chest, one of her arms flung over her head, her hair fanned over his pillow.

A stray emotion cuddled up to Jackson, and it felt as if it had been lost for years, just coming home now.

But it couldn't be...*that*. The L-word. It made no sense, because love didn't fit into his world, wouldn't ever fit in. He just didn't have room for it.

Then again, he had sure acted as if love was in the cards last night, when he had told Laila entirely too much about himself. That seemed to happen a lot with her, though.

As he watched her in the dim light, a memory tried to push the comforting feeling away from him: a vague recollection of his mom just after Dad had died—a flash of her sobbing at his funeral. Then another piece of the past: an image of Mom sitting in her car in the driveway while Jackson looked out the window with his twin, Jason, waiting for her to come in. It had taken her what seemed like hours, even though it had to have only been a fraction of that before Dillon and Ethan had gone out to bring her inside.

Even now, Jackson's heart hurt for her. It hurt for him, too, as well as for his siblings. They had all been roughed up by their dad's death.

So why was he thinking of that now?

Needing something to make him feel better, he concentrated on what he always seemed to concentrate on when he needed it the most—the beautiful, temporarily-his woman next to him.

He traced a finger down Laila's nose, her chin, to her jaw, where he lightly tickled her.

Sleepily, she shrugged, batting his hand away.

He laughed, and she opened her eyes.

"Obviously," she said, her voice kittenish, "I'm not used to being woken up by someone—especially if he's a self-appointed alarm clock."

Nestling an arm over her, he lay back down. "Just how many someones have there been?"

There—that would inject some much-needed reality into this morning after.

She blushed.

"Oh, come on," he said, pulling her closer to him. "I, of all people, won't judge."

"It's different for men. You can sleep with as many women as you want and nobody will think twice about it. I've always held my cards close to my chest, especially in Thunder Canyon." She pushed back a hank of disheveled hair. "It'll be bad enough if anyone sees your truck still parked in town and wonders why you never made it home."

"They won't know I'm with you."

"They'd have to be blind to avoid that conclusion."

"Then I'll tell you what—you can get your car out of my garage and back home before dawn fully breaks and I'll call a ride to take me to the office today."

She lifted an eyebrow. "My—you're good at arranging these things."

"What can I say?" He snuck a hand under the covers, over her belly, and she gasped. "I know what I'm doing."

He tickled her again, and she squealed softly.

"I'm going to torture any information that I want out of you," he said.

"Okay, okay!" Then she smacked his hand. "Two. There have been just two men I've…"

"Loved?"

As she hesitated, his chest seemed to split open. He didn't like knowing that she'd had feelings for other guys.

"I wouldn't say love, really," she said. "I might have thought I was close to it at the time, but it turned out that it was just a couple of false alarms. Still, those instances were the nearest I've ever gotten."

She flushed again, glancing at him, then away.

He didn't want to wonder what she was really talking about, if she was thinking about what she felt for *him*.

"Anyway," she continued, "by most standards, I haven't been around the block much. The last time I was with a man, he was a consultant at the resort— an architect. I thought we were going places until we weren't."

"You realized that what you felt for him wasn't love." He had enjoyed saying that a little too much.

"Yeah, and afterward I was sure I'd never be capable of it." Her gaze went wistful. "And before that, my very first time was in college, senior year. He was a football player. Quarterback."

"Doesn't that figure?" He could have guessed that the beauty queen and the homecoming king would have gravitated toward each other, just as they did in most high schools or colleges.

"It's true—we were such a walking cliché." She pulled the covers up to her collarbone, turning toward him. "But the same thing happened with Quarterback Jeffrey—I cooled off in our relationship before…"

"…You could commit."

She nodded, touched his chin with her fingertips, as if to feel the scratch of his five o'clock shadow. "You would know that story well enough."

"What have I been telling you? We're two of a kind."

He smiled at her, and when she did the same, his pulse quickened.

"Know what?" she asked.

"What?"

"I just thought you asked me out because you'd set your cap for the local beauty queen. You were adding to your collection of conquests."

Shame nicked him, and his first instinct was to skirt the truth. Why hurt her unnecessarily? They would have had enough of each other by the time he left Montana, so why rush a breakup along?

Besides, he didn't feel that way now, and he didn't want her to know how much of an ogre he had been.

"Don't say that, Laila. The first time I saw you, there was…" Something. He rushed on, refusing to think about it too much. "I saw a spark in you, a flame… there are probably a hundred different names for what attracts one person to another."

"Right." She said it as if she hadn't expected him to get deep on her, and that tore at him a bit. "Maybe we were intimate in another life, and you saw the reflection of my reincarnated soul in my limpid gaze…."

"Cute."

Her eyes got that look that told him things were about to go back to square one, with her running and him chasing.

But he had already left all that behind.

"Laila, I just want to see you again. No more cat-and-mouse games, no more silliness. I want to be with you every day and every night while I can."

She absorbed his candid statements, then whispered, "A fling. That's what they call it, right? Something discreet?" Her voice broke a little. "Temporary?"

He didn't want to hear the rest, didn't want to face the decisions he would have to make someday—not while she was so soft and warm next to him now. Not while he could believe, just for the moment, that there was something here with Laila that he couldn't live without.

He put an end to the conversation by kissing her, and as she melted in his arms, he forgot the definition of *temporary* altogether.

Chapter Nine

Days passed, forcing Laila to always look forward to the nights, when she could leave work and be with Jackson.

He was her addiction of choice right now, and she kept taking him in large doses.

The fact hadn't been lost on Dana, either, and when Laila got home from work tonight, her best friend called her on it over the phone.

"Where did you go so fast today?" Dana asked.

Laila was getting ready for Jackson, who usually dropped in near seven o'clock with take-out dinner—a habit that had formed all too quickly, with Laila barely even realizing it had happened.

The ritual might have given her second, third and fourth thoughts about seeing him if she hadn't known that their relationship was just a fleeting thing.

A fling.

Wrestling away a dull ache in her chest, she tucked her cell phone between her shoulder and ear while buttoning the roomy red sweater she had cuddled into. "I only came straight home, Dana."

"You've been taking off like a shot from work a lot lately." Her friend sounded a bit pouty.

"I've just been…busy."

A knowing chuff. "I'm going to assume it's not because you're putting in extra hours at your kitchen table on your proposal that Mr. Trudeau is developing now. Jackson's the reason."

Caught.

And it wasn't as if Laila and Jackson had made a spectacle of themselves in public. They had been lying low, basically because neither of them wanted their families to start believing they had some big deal going on.

Nonetheless, Laila couldn't fib to her best friend about her undercover liaison. "You're right," she said, going downstairs. "It's Jackson. But keep it quiet, okay?"

"Oh."

Laila didn't like the sound of that "Oh."

"I mean," Dana said, "I'm just kind of surprised you're seeing him exclusively."

She halted at the bottom of the stairs. "Why?"

"When Laila Cates goes out with a guy… Let's just say you've never been as busy as you are right now."

Busy.

What the heck did that mean?

"If you're saying that I'm so into Jackson that I'm ignoring everyone else in my life, that's not true." Laila wasn't *That Girl*.

Dana just laughed, as if she knew much better.

Laila rolled her eyes. *This* was exactly why she and Jackson weren't shouting out their fling—because everyone would assume there was much more going on than there was in reality.

"Just have fun tonight, Laila," Dana said. "I'll see you when I see you."

"Wait…" The *busy* comment was bothering her because she had always disliked it when her own friends seemed to disappear into RomanceLand when things got hot and heavy with a man. "Let's do lunch over the weekend. Saturday, noon, at the Tottering Teapot?"

"All right." And Dana was appeased. "Say hi to Jackie Boy."

"I will."

After hanging up, it wasn't long before Jackson arrived, pizza box in hand when she met him at the door.

"I had a yen for some pepperoni," he said, strolling on in as if he was already comfortable in her apartment.

Somehow, she didn't mind that. And she would have if any other man had done that.

Busy, she thought. *Am I?*

He kissed her hello, sending her blood pumping.

"You're quiet tonight," Jackson said.

She shook her head, afraid to answer, because if she began to talk about what was gnawing at her, it would become an issue. And that was why she liked seeing Jackson—because, with him, there were no issues, just good times.

He looked down at her for a moment longer, then kissed her again, slower and sultrier this time, as if he could chase away whatever was troubling her.

As always, she was putty in his hands, leaning into

him, feeling as if she would be content never to come out of a kiss with Jackson Traub.

He smoothed back her hair, leaned his forehead against hers. "All better now?"

"Life is wonderful."

She smiled, and off he went to the kitchen, again, just as if it was his. But she was actually grateful for his casualness—it reminded her of what they were to each other...and it wasn't anything serious.

Once more, Dana's voice came back to Laila.

Busy...

Laila joined him in the kitchen, getting plates and napkins while he doled out the pizza slices. Soon everything was back to the way it should be with them, with her and Jackson flopping onto the couch, getting ready for some relaxing in front of the TV.

Companions—two people who just delighted in being with each other, no strings attached.

He cast a look to Lord Vader's bowl, where the fish was puttering around.

"Wouldn't you rather have a dog?" Jackson asked.

"I'd love one, but Lord Vader is more my speed."

"Because he or she ignores you?" He cocked an eyebrow. "That trick always does seem to work with you."

She smacked his arm because he had the gall to refer to all the times he had played it cool in the Hitching Post, only to stoke her interest.

He laughed. "It's just that dogs are the best pets of all. I've got a few on my ranch."

She had been about to bite into her pizza but didn't. "Are they pet dogs? Or do they help on the ranch?"

"I've got both kinds, and I'm the one who likes to

take care of them when I'm there. You know what they say about dogs being man's best friend. It's true."

Laila still couldn't wrap her mind around this. "*You* have actual pets."

"Yeah, why wouldn't I?"

Um, because he was the last person on earth who seemed interested in being any kind of caregiver?

"It's just…" She laughed. "So very paternal of you, Jackson. I never would've guessed."

"Now you don't have to."

He took his bite of pizza, having no idea that he had just tilted her world off its axis. He had been wrong about one thing when he had described himself to her early on—he *could* commit.

She tried not to let it matter, but damn, it did. Because, as it turned out, it wasn't that he couldn't bring himself to care for someone—it was that he had already made a choice not to care for her.

But when had he ever promised anything more?

When had she come to expect it?

Not liking where her thoughts were going, she turned on the TV with the remote. Courtroom drama filled the screen, the volume low.

"Good old *Judge Judy*," Jackson said.

Laila, whose stomach had tied itself into knots, put her pizza aside. At least the TV would keep him from asking her if she was okay again.

"I watch her every weeknight," Laila said. "I was raised on this program—it's my mom's favorite." She even remembered how Mom had always made a point of getting dinner on the table and done with before *Judge Judy* came on. "Mom always loved how Judge Judy wields her brainpower."

Had her tone of voice given Jackson some kind of hint about her present, wistful mood? Had he done the math and multiplied that with the quiet way she had greeted him at the door?

He had put aside his pizza as well, so she thought that maybe he had seen past all her joking tonight.

Dang, his ability to sense her moods got to her.

But wouldn't it be nice to have a man around who balanced a little sensitivity with testosterone?

Just thinking about it sent a pointed longing through Laila—a yearning she couldn't afford.

As he rested his hand over hers, she thought it might be a good time to ease his mind and let him know that she wouldn't complicate their time together with deep emotions.

"Mom always did tell me," she said, "that brains come before beauty. I took that to heart. I made my successes in life top priority because I knew that what I built for myself would always be more solid than what someone else could give me."

"Are you explaining why you're not going to fall in love with me, Laila?"

He had said it kiddingly, but it was obvious that he got the gist of what she was trying to do.

For a second, it seemed as if he was just as baffled about what was happening with them as she was, that he was about to get all serious on her again.

Then he pulled out that patented charm-touched grin of his and lightly tugged on her hair.

"Darlin'," he said, "if there were two more unlikely people to fall in love in this universe, I'd be hard-pressed to discover them."

It should have made her breathe easier, but instead, it felt as if all the oxygen in her lungs had been punched out.

Nonetheless, she grinned right back at him, showing him that she was fine with what they had…even if she was starting to suspect that she wasn't.

What the hell am I doing?

Jackson asked himself that for about the hundredth time as the Saturday afternoon sun struggled through a bank of clouds. The light barely touched on the Halloween-painted windows of the Tottering Teapot, where Laila had told him the other night that she would be meeting Dana for lunch.

He was sitting in his truck outside, thinking that he would surprise her by picking her up and spiriting her off to a day of driving through the country before the autumn leaves deserted the tree branches for their winter bareness. When he had made up his mind to do this, he hadn't realized that he was doing a very boyfriend-type thing.

Hell, they had woken up together in his bed this morning. Shouldn't he have had his fill of her just from that?

Nope—not from the way his body was going through withdrawal, as if she somehow nourished him in a way that nothing or no one else could.

He recalled what he had said the other night to her about how they were the two least likely people ever to fall in love. And dammit all: As soon as he had uttered it, the comment had struck him as a downright lie.

Across the street, Laila came out of the Tottering Teapot with Dana, whose long, sandy hair sported a vivid purple streak near the back and whose off-the-wall clothing resembled something a Brit might have worn back in the days when Madonna had first hit the scene. But all Jackson really saw was Laila, with her blond hair in a low side braid. She was dressed in a striking gold cashmere sweater and a pencil-straight plaid skirt with knee-high boots.

Just that easily, Jackson's heart was dust.

She hugged Dana goodbye and spotted Jackson in his truck, waving to him with a beaming smile, then crossing the street.

With every step, his heartbeat got that much louder, overtaking him.

He got out, going around to open her door. Aware that many pairs of curious eyes were on them, he ushered her inside without making a big lovey-dovey production of it. If she noticed, she didn't seem to mind.

Two of a kind, he thought again—except maybe Laila had a foolproof heart, something he had also thought he possessed.

Girding himself, he climbed back inside, where the scent of her had already infused the air.

"I didn't know you would be here," she said.

"I was in the neighborhood." Total bullcrap. "How was lunch?"

"Chatty, fun. Very girly."

"Do I want to hear just how girly?"

"For the most part, no." Laila folded one leg over the other as she faced him. "We talked about Dana's dating life. Then, while we were still on the subject of men, she asked if Cade had pushed his wedding agenda on me lately and I told her no."

"Maybe he's come to the realization that you weren't

just putting him off about getting hitched. You were giving him the straight truth."

"I hope so. Dana thought that he's finally getting the hint because I'm still hanging out with you."

Was that what they were doing—hanging out?

Jackson shifted in his seat. She hadn't exactly invited him over to meet the parents or anything. He supposed that when that happened, it would be a red flag, and that was when he would start to worry.

"What else did you two talk about?" he asked.

"Oh, just you. Dana's as curious as anyone about *the* Jackson Traub."

"And what did you tell her?"

Laila hesitated just long enough to make him think that she wasn't going to let him know.

"I told her that I'm having the time of my life." She ran a finger over the back of his hand, which was resting on the seat.

Pricks of yearning invaded him, and he tried to hold them off.

It was as if she was the one who was playing hard to get today, and she put her hand in her lap, seeming so far away from him.

"We also talked about work," she said. "How my proposal is coming along, all that."

"Kicking butt at that bank now," he said with a sly grin that let her know he had something else to add to the discussion besides.

"What're you grinning about?"

"I don't know, but it might have something to do with being inspired by that 'kick butt versus sweetness' deal we made."

"Do tell."

Shrugging, he said, "I think I've come up with a way to do my job and help DJ with the Rib Shack at the same time."

"Yeah?"

"Yeah." His smile grew. "Since my job is to do community outreach, I've been intending to have an open meeting or two to help educate everyone about the oil shale project. But with the way business is going for DJ, we also need to get the community behind *him*. So why not combine the two goals? Why not host some town halls where the locals can be informed *and* be treated to DJ's ribs? It'll be good promotion for both of us."

Laila crept her hand back across the neutral zone to where his was still resting on the seat, and she clasped hers over his. Warmth suffused him from fingers to toes.

"That's a really great idea, Jackson," she said.

She didn't voice it, but from the look on her face, she was also thinking about how his family would be proud that he had found a way around brute force with Lip-Smackin' Ribs. About how, if his father were around, he would be busting his buttons, too.

He turned his hand over, holding hers, and they stayed like that.

Just the two of them.

They were only interrupted by a soft ding from Laila's cell phone.

She ignored it, but he nodded to her purse, somewhat relieved. Saved by the bell from having something like hand-holding mean a lot more than it should.

"Go ahead," he said, reaching for the ignition and starting the truck.

"It's just a text message," she said, looking at the

phone screen. "From Dana. She says that she just drove by and we're still sitting here in the truck. Then there's some cheeky speculation that I'm not even going to repeat."

"Leave it to Dana." As the engine idled, he glanced out the window, his gaze latching onto a man strolling down the walk, his hands stuffed into his blue jeans pockets, his large silver buckle catching what was there of the sunlight.

Jackson also took in the ranch hand's mustache, recognizing him yet again from the Hitching Post and the Rock Creek Diner.

"Who's that?" he asked, gesturing toward the cowboy.

She looked, then said, "Duncan Brooks."

The cowboy had spotted Jackson and Laila in the truck, and he slowed his steps, paying too much attention, setting Jackson on edge.

"And just who is Duncan Brooks?"

"Drive and I'll tell you."

Jackson gunned the accelerator, and when he glanced in the rearview mirror, he saw that the ranch hand was still watching them.

"You were saying?" Jackson asked.

Laila held up her hands while shrugging. "He's had a thing for me for a while. Shy, soft-spoken guy, works on Bo Clifton's ranch. I've never encouraged him."

"Just one of your army of admirers, huh?"

"What—are you afraid of a little competition?"

She laughed, and he did, too. But he was remembering how Duncan Brooks had been at that lunch counter the day Jackson had stupidly told DJ that he had been attracted to Laila because of her looks and that, once he left Thunder Canyon, she would be out of sight, out of mind.

The first town hall meeting for Traub Oil Montana's Bakken Shale project came a week later.

Laila wandered around one of the large tents that had been erected outside of DJ's Rib Shack, which was connected to the Thunder Canyon Resort. The meeting had already adjourned, and it had featured a presentation by Austin Anderson about his ideas for environmentally sound oil extraction and how Traub Oil's business could benefit the community. Now the citizens who hadn't gone next door to the food tent for DJ's ribs were milling around, talking to Austin, Ethan Traub and Jackson near the front.

She took a moment to watch Jackson, who was wearing a sharp suit today. And, yow. He wore it well, even with his cowboy hat.

But what impressed her even more was how he listened so attentively, how he seemed to know the way to ease the fears about change among those who had come to the meeting with questions.

Had he gone from a rebel to a more solid man during his time in Thunder Canyon?

She noticed how Ethan stood by his brother's side, a subtle grin on his face. Even a proud one, if Laila said so.

It warmed her that Jackson could stand tall with his successful siblings now. Oddly, his success meant as much to her as her own…

A man's voice broke into her thoughts.

"He did real well."

Laila turned to find Corey Traub standing nearby, watching Jackson, too.

Tall, with light brown hair and brown eyes, Corey seemed just as satisfied with Jackson as Ethan was. "You've been a good influence on him, Laila."

She should have been used to blushing by now—Lord knows she had been doing it enough since Jackson had come to town—but here she was again, fighting the heat on her face.

"He did this all by himself," she said. "I've got nothing to do with it."

Corey gave her an amused glance. "So you say."

When Laila caught sight of her neighbor, Mrs. Haverly, approaching from the left, Corey squeezed her arm and wandered off.

Mrs. Haverly wasn't alone—she was accompanied by a towering plate of free ribs as well as Joelle Vanderhorst, a silver-haired, hoity-toity woman who was known far and wide in Thunder Canyon as a cutting gossip.

Wonderful.

Mrs. Haverly was as sweet as pie when she greeted Laila. "Your boyfriend sure puts on a good meeting."

Her boyfriend?

Had Mrs. Haverly been keeping track of Jackson going in and out of Laila's apartment?

Double wonderful.

Laila didn't bother to tell Mrs. Haverly that *boyfriend* didn't describe what Jackson was to her. "I'll tell my friend you said so. He'll be pleased."

The older woman didn't react to the innocuous description; she merely chowed down on the ribs as Joelle stood there with her arms crossed.

"Your 'friendship' with him is very surprising," she said to Laila.

Before Laila could think better of engaging in conversation with the biggest town busybody, the woman added, "Who thought you would take up with a stranger as opposed to one of the local boys who spent so much effort courting you over the years?"

"I'm sorry, Mrs. Vanderhorst," Laila said. "I didn't realize my life was up for analysis."

The woman put a hand to her chest, obviously affronted. Mrs. Haverly chuckled, her mouth ringed with rib sauce.

"I'd take up with that Jackson Traub," she said.

At least Laila's horny neighbor was on her side, and Laila sent her a grateful smile just before excusing herself.

Who cared what any of the others thought?

It bothered her more that *she* cared so much that there was a stinging ache inside that wouldn't go away, no matter how hard she tried to chase it off.

As Jackson shook hands with Theo Cushing, a small business owner who had asked a few questions about the Bakken Shale that had been answered today, he kept an eye on Laila across the tent.

She had retreated to a corner of it, near the beverage table, where she was pouring herself a cup of water. For some reason, after she had left Mrs. Haverly and the stately older woman who had joined them, her shoulders had gone stiff and she seemed…

Bothered?

He was about to go to her when Mike Trudeau, Laila's boss at the bank, approached Jackson. Ethan shifted his position so he could check in on the conversation that Austin was having with a science teacher from the high school.

Trudeau shook Jackson's hand with hearty enthusiasm. "Fascinating stuff you've brought to us today. Thank you for it."

"Just be sure to go next door for some of those ribs," Jackson said. "DJ's are the best."

"I can't disagree with you there. The wife won't let me within a mile of that other place." He was obviously talking about LipSmackin' Ribs. "She says it's terribly lacking in class."

Good to know that they had an ally in this prominent businessman.

Then Trudeau glanced across the room, to where Jackson's gaze had strayed again.

To Laila. Always Laila.

"She's really quite a woman," the older man said.

"Yes." Jackson felt the same pull toward her that he always did. "She is."

"Yup, those pretty ones are sure great to have around. Laila's the jewel in our bank's crown, if you ask me. I suspect we have a good many customers who come in just to look at her."

Jackson bristled. Was this man insinuating that he took Laila for granted? Or even that he had given her promotions and entertained her proposals for all the wrong reasons?

"I hope I'm wrong," Jackson said, doing everything he could not to let his dander rise and take over. "But it sounds as if you don't take her all that seriously, even if she brought you a hell of an idea recently."

Trudeau seemed to realize he had misspoken. "No,

no—she did bring a damn good idea to me this time. I was just saying—"

"That she's pretty." This man had pushed a button in Jackson because he knew how much it hurt when people took Laila only at face value. Jackson also knew how much her boss's comments would bruise her if she were privy to them.

It probably even mattered that Jackson was trying to make up for having said something just as stupid himself, to DJ, at that diner.

As Trudeau started looking as if he wished he could take everything back, Jackson told himself to calm down.

To keep following Laila's advice about mellowing the kick-butt attitude.

"Just so you know," he said to her boss, keeping his voice friendly, "Laila's more than a jewel in a crown. She might glitter real nicely, but her value comes from what's beneath that sparkle."

He had said it with such emotion that Trudeau's gaze had gone soft, as if he was seeing something about Jackson that even *he* wouldn't acknowledge.

But it was clear now—clear for all the world to see. Jackson Traub was…in love.

Trudeau patted Jackson on the upper arm, and it seemed at first to be because he was apologizing. Yet there was also an admission there, man-to-man, one guy who had recognized that the other had spoken in defense of his woman.

Trudeau left, but Ethan, who was standing next to Jackson again, had apparently heard everything.

He leaned over to whisper in Jackson's ear. "Another

Traub bites the dust, huh? Weren't you the one preaching against matrimony at Corey's wedding?"

Jackson cursed under his breath, then said, "It's strictly casual between me and Laila."

"And *that's* strictly BS," Ethan said.

Unfortunately, Jackson didn't have much of an argument, especially when he saw Laila across the tent looking at him, then glancing away as if she didn't want to be caught in the same impossible place he had found himself in.

Chapter Ten

After the town hall meeting, Laila had taken a seat inside the open, three-story-high lobby of the resort's main lodge. It seemed that business had picked up today, thanks to the event, and people milled around the free-standing fireplace as well as the life-sized elk statue.

She had come in here, where warmth from the fireplace toasted the area, to wait for Jackson, and her nerves were wavery as she waited for him to arrive. She had seen her boss, Mike Trudeau, talking to him, and it looked as if Jackson had gotten upset for some reason. Also, he had kept glancing over at Laila, which only added to her suspicions that they had been chatting about her.

Had Jackson even been *defending* her because of something her misogynistic boss had said?

Her heart beat like delicate wings at the thought of Jackson being her knight in white armor. Yet his behavior didn't sound like it belonged in any "fling." It almost felt as if the rules were changing on Laila, and she didn't know what would be coming next.

Heck, she didn't even want to know what the conversation had been about, and she didn't want to ask.

Her phone dinged, and she checked it to find a text from her sister, Jazzy.

Mom and Dad are requesting the presence of you and Mr. Jackson Traub at Football Day tomorrow. Be there or you're on your own for birthday cake, missy!

Laila kept staring at the screen. She had nearly forgotten that, the day after tomorrow, she would be turning the big 3-0. All this running around with Jackson had kept her mind off it and, for that at least, she was grateful.

But…an invitation from her family to bring Jackson to Football Day? No matter how much he and Laila had been trying to keep everything on the down low, their efforts clearly hadn't paid off if her family thought it was time for him to meet them.

The ultimate sign of commitment, she thought. *Meeting the parents….*

"What does that text say that's so interesting?" It was Jackson, sitting down beside her on one of the leather sofas that decorated the lobby.

Laila angled her cell away from him so he wouldn't see the invitation on the screen, but as she ran her gaze over him, she felt a sighing thaw—the realization that she actually *wanted* Jackson to come with her to her family's. That, in spite of her grand public announcement at the Miss Frontier Days pageant, she *Might. Like. To. Be. Married.*

To him.

Someday.

How hopeless was that, though?

A sense of sorrow welled up in her. Leave it to Laila Cates, single girl extraordinaire, to fall hard—and for the most entrenched bachelor on earth at that.

As Jackson tipped back his hat and gave her a smile—not a charming grin but a *real* smile that dug way down into her heart—she fell for him that much more.

What if she was wrong about him wanting to be a bachelor for the rest of his days? Was it too much to hope that, like her, he had undergone a profound change in such a short time?

Now she *wanted* to know, so she sucked up her courage and showed him the screen of her phone.

He read it, his expression impartial as he leaned back against the sofa, carelessly stretching his arm along the top of it.

When he spoke, he had reverted back to that amused tone that made her wonder what she had been thinking when she had questioned whether or not he was capable of change.

"It seems," he said, "that I'm being summoned."

"That's fair to say." She eased back against the cushions as well, training her gaze on the comers and goers walking from one end of the lobby to the other, feeling Jackson's arm against her upper back, loving the sturdy sensation of him against her, even though she knew it was fleeting. He had reminded her of their temporary situation with the way he had reacted to that text.

So she protected herself, falling into the same flirty groove that had always defined them. The safe way.

"You should consider yourself lucky," she said. "My parents' house is something of a sanctuary for me. You'd be the first 'companion' of mine to breach Football Day."

"Are you telling me that your parents' house is like my ranch…or a cabin in the woods?"

"Just like either of them."

As he toyed with the hair at her nape, she nearly fizzed into a pool of contentment. She almost wished tomorrow and Football Day—or any other part of real life—would never arrive, just allowing them to sit here, never minding what would eventually come down the road for them.

A few people glanced over at them, but who cared if she and Jackson looked like a couple right now? They had been fooling themselves for a while, thinking they could hide what was going on between them—to avoid all the expectations being "together" would bring.

Why not live for the moment while they could?

Her heart felt heavy as he asked, "Why haven't you ever invited a date to your family's house, Laila?"

"Because the ranch is off limits on Football Day. It's a time I've only shared with my sisters, Mom, and my dad and brother. It's a separate little world."

"And you've never wanted all your worlds to collide."

"There was no reason for them to. I'm pretty good at compartmentalizing."

"I have been, too."

She noted the use of past tense, felt them both getting in deeper.

He said, "What happens when your brother and sisters bring people over?"

"*Nobody* has ever shattered the walls of Football Day. My sisters have invited guys for dinner on Saturday night so they could meet my parents, but the entire family hasn't been there."

So why was *Jackson* being summoned in front of the whole family? Laila reached for a reason. "I'll bet they invited you tomorrow because of the birthday thing. See, I made them promise that they wouldn't make a big deal of my thirtieth, so we agreed we would just eat some cake tomorrow and that would be it. Everybody's even going to give me presents on their own. I'm sure they want to include you because they think…"

She trailed off.

But he knew what she had been about to say.

"They think that, no matter what you've told them, we're serious about each other."

Laila exhaled, and he stopped playing with her hair.

"It'd be a lot of fun if you came over," she said, "but please don't feel that you have to."

She hadn't meant to say it dismissively. Had she done so because she was getting ready for him to bug out of the invitation, anyway?

He cupped her head, pressed it toward him, spoke into her ear, stirring her hair. "But they're serving birthday cake, Laila. Is there a human being in existence who'd say no to that?"

Leave it to Jackson to inject some levity.

"My big, bad birthday," she said. "I guess you should be there to see it run me over like a semi."

He kept his mouth against her head, just above her

ear, and it felt so natural, so right, that she went on talking.

"I used to laugh about the whole idea of being nervous about aging. Why care? *Who* cares? That's what I used to think, anyway."

His steady embrace told her it *was* okay. "I heard your Miss Frontier Days speech, so I have an inkling of what your thirtieth birthday means to you. Everyone else in town might think that Laila Cates has the big, bad birthday under control, but most women wouldn't go out of their way to compete in a pageant to prove a point about how being older means being better."

"It was a real silly thing to do." Then she went a step further, telling him more than she had ever told anyone else. "It was even vain."

"It was human." He took her chin between his fingers, turned her face toward him, so that she was looking into his dust-devil-colored eyes. Now, though, it seemed there was calm there, a settling.

"It's just like you said at the pageant," he murmured. "You're getting better with every day. And I imagine that'll extend to every year, as you learn new things, gain new experiences."

Like this one with him?

Would she be older but wiser after *they* parted ways?

"How would you know that I've improved when you just met me a short time ago?" she asked.

He lifted his eyebrows. "You've grown on *me* every day."

She was a mess by now—in a good way. A whipped-up, stirred-up storm of affection.

Not wanting to torture herself any more, she conjured a smile, moving on.

"Really," she said. "You don't have to suffer through pink cake and a truly terrible rendition of the birthday song at Football Day. I grant you a reprieve, Jackson Traub."

He laughed softly, kissed her on the temple.

She pulled back from him, scanning his expression. Today might have been the first time they had acted like this in public, but from the intensity in his brown eyes, she was certain that he had done it without regret.

Did he care for her more than she knew?

"Listen," he said. "I suspect that your family is real curious about the guy you've been spending so much time with, and I have no reservations about going over there with you and showing them that I hold no threat in taking away your title."

"Title?" Somehow, she doubted that he was talking about Miss Frontier Days.

Jackson laughed. "You know that one you wear so proudly? Miss Fiery Independence?"

Oh, yeah. That one.

She kept the smile on her face. He had just outright told her not to think that, just because he would undergo a day with the family, this was the next step in a developing relationship.

She had been an idiot to think anything like that could ever happen.

"Good," she said, acting as if none of it was chomping away at her heart. "We'll show them that there's no chance you're going to steal me away."

He agreed. "Yup, serves them right for being nosy enough to invite me over."

She laid her head on his shoulder, almost believing the fibs, too.

* * *

Sometime before Jackson awakened from sleep, he dreamed of red flags.

They had flown like warning banners that snapped in a brutal wind, surrounding him, whipping out at him, leaving welts on his arms.

Meet the family, he had heard in the wind. *Slip a ring on her finger, march up the aisle...*

Then, in his nightmare, those flags suddenly disappeared, leaving him standing in a void. But when he peered down at himself, he saw that he had been returned to normal—he was even back on his ranch now, in front of his cabin, wearing jeans and spurs on his boots while he carried a saddle.

He saw himself walking up the stairs to his door, and in a surreal haze, he knocked on it, as if he didn't even live there anymore.

The door opened, and all that emerged was a hand, palm up, as if some kind of phantom was asking for something.

Inexplicably, Jackson knew just what it was, too, and he bent down, put his saddle on the porch and stripped off his spurs.

Somewhere, he heard the resurgent moan of the wind, as if it was saying, "Noooo."

He heard the snap of those red flags.

But he handed those spurs over, anyway, and, in return, those ghostly hands gave him a bunch of sharpened pencils.

At first, Jackson didn't know what was what—not until he looked down again to see that his jeans and boots had turned into a business suit and polished designer shoes.

A pencil-pushing geek…?

With a start, Jackson opened his eyes. Sweat cooled on his skin as his gaze found Laila sitting up next to him in bed, the covers bunched down around her waist, revealing the eyelet-flowered nightgown she was wearing. Her blond hair fell loose and wavy past her shoulders.

"Jackson?" she asked, touching his arm.

He glanced around, seeing that he was in Laila's cream-and-peach wallpapered bedroom, where nothing had changed.

And nothing would ever change.

Relieved, he ran a hand through his hair, then sat up to give her a kiss good morning. But, just for good measure, he checked Laila's ring finger.

Nothing there.

"What're you doing?" she asked. "Are you okay?"

"Not really." He gave her another kiss, then pulled her onto his lap. "Just had a bad dream is all."

"Must've been a doozy."

"It was. But it's over."

She bit her lip, as if wondering if she should ask about the details. Or maybe she was even about to tell him that she'd had a bad dream, too.

Apparently, she decided against pursuing whatever it was, then ruffled his hair, scooting out of bed. His heart seemed to follow wherever she went.

He leaned back against his pillow, feeling as if this was the flip side of a dream—the good part.

But then he thought about those red flags again. Was he afraid that committing to Laila was going to make him into someone who would have to give up his thrilling playboy life for a much more sedate one?

Yeah. That was a pretty logical conclusion.

As they got ready for the morning—with her taking her usual jog to the market and him reading the paper as Lord Vader dillydallied in his fishbowl—Jackson wondered if he should still go to the Cates' ranch for Football Day.

After all, that dream had been his subconscious warning him off after yesterday, when her family had asked her to bring him over.

But Jackson thought of how Laila might feel if he stayed away. Strangely, he couldn't stand the notion of making her sad or embarrassing her, and that far outweighed any discomfort he might undergo.

Hell, he could handle the Cates family and come out of the experience unscathed.

When Laila came back from her jog/walk with chips and dip in her grocery bag, he was already showered and dressed. It didn't take her all that long to ready herself, too, and that shocked the sugar out of Jackson since he had always surmised that a beauty queen would take much longer than anyone else to primp.

Then again, if Laila had taught him anything, it was that she wasn't any normal Miss Fiery Independence.

They arrived at the Cates Ranch about a half hour before kickoff and, just before climbing out of the truck, Laila smoothed out her Bobcats sweatshirt and adjusted Jackson's shirt collar under his coat.

"When they inevitably grill you," she said, "I predict it'll be with finesse. You won't have to worry about my brother or dad—they'll no doubt be talking about the football. Besides, I'm sure they'll respect that Man Code you all have going. But my mom and sisters…?"

"Wait—Man Code?" he asked.

"Yeah. Where it's pretty much agreed that the women of the house will take care of all the jawdroppingly intrusive questions."

"How do you know this if you've never invited a guy over before?"

Laila smiled, and his eyes were drawn to that beauty spot near one upper corner of her lips. His stomach tumbled, the rest of him wishing he could get her out of here and alone for the rest of the day.

"Believe me," she said. "I know my family well enough to make guesses about their behavior. But don't worry—I'll run interference and deal with all the overexcited woman queries. And I'm sure they'll see early on that there's nothing serious happening, and they'll back away from the grilling and leave us alone within the first hour."

"Boy—you've got this all planned out, don't you?"

She kissed him on the cheek, then exited the truck, leaving him wondering why he felt a little empty because of this plan of hers.

Was it because it felt…unreal?

He recalled that awful dream he'd had this morning and decided that he would go along with her scheme, unreal or not.

Mr. Cates met them at the front door, and from the first second, Jackson could tell by the way he looked at Laila that her prediction had been very wrong.

She was clearly the apple of his eye—even if he *had* wanted a son so desperately that he and his wife had birthed five daughters to get there.

If she had said that the men of the family would be a piece of cake to deal with, Jackson dreaded what was in store with the women.

"Dad!" Laila said as she hugged him.

Meanwhile, Zeke Cates kept eyeing Jackson over her shoulder.

Jackson merely put on the charm, hoping it would work with the big man.

Laila broke away from the embrace, gesturing to Jackson, but before she could introduce him, Zeke stuck out his hand for a shake.

"I know who Jackson Traub is," he said.

Jackson tried not to think that Zeke, like everyone else, had heard a thing or two about him around Thunder Canyon and was putting out a stern warning in the guise of a polite handshake.

When they gripped hands, Zeke's shake was enough to crush bones.

Yup, Father Bear had kept his ears open in town.

"Glad to meet you," Jackson said.

Laila laughed, then casually forced the two men's hands apart.

"Dad," she said.

Zeke took the hint from his daughter, then spread out his arm to welcome them into his home.

As Jackson and Laila entered, he could feel the older man's eyes still lasering into him.

"Sorry," Laila whispered.

They walked into a family room where Brody, the youngest of the Cates brood, greeted Jackson. He looked to be in his early twenties, and his welcome was hearty and easy enough to make Jackson semi-comfortable.

Then he heard a woman's voice from behind him.

"This must be Jackson."

Turning around, he found himself face-to-face with

a beautiful woman who couldn't be anyone but Laila's mother.

She didn't settle for a handshake, going in for a hug straight off.

As Jackson responded in kind, he glanced at Laila, who was shooting him an impressed yet confused look. She apparently had misread both her mom and her dad. Hell, Zeke was even behind his wife, trying to seem as if he wasn't about to just take Jackson by the ear and drag him into the nearest private room for that grilling that was supposed to come from the Cates females.

Maybe the ladies in this family would be far stealthier in their social ways, Jackson thought. Laila had said there would be some female finesse involved.

Laila introduced him to her mom. "Evelyn Cates, Jackson Traub."

"Great to have you here." Evelyn was wearing a high ponytail, plus a frilly gingham apron swiped by flour over a pair of faded jeans.

"Thank you, ma'am."

"Oh, for heaven's sake—no ma'ams, please." Evelyn was undoing her apron and, judging by the heavy aroma of baked cake in the air, cooking time was done.

Jackson acknowledged her with a nod. He had taken off his hat, but now he shed his coat. Laila grabbed them, yet she didn't leave the room.

And that was probably because of what came next— a whole fleet of lovely women, every one of them smiling at Jackson as if they had a list of questions for him.

For the first time in his life, he didn't want to be in a room full of females.

With a stern expression—one that Jackson thought might serve to caution her sisters about getting fresh—

Laila introduced him all around. He already knew some of their names, but, nevertheless, he could barely keep up with who was who. Maybe that was only because his mind was spinning, filled with the remnants of his psychotic dream from this morning. Any second, he expected one of the sisters to raise a red flag and another to hand him a bunch of pencils.

"Mom," Laila said, standing in front of her sisters as if she could keep them at bay, then handing Evelyn her bag of chips and dip. Her mom took his coat and hat, too. "Can we help you in the kitchen?"

The other woman got a sly smile on her face. "Yes—I think we do need some help."

As she urged Laila forward, she winked at Jackson. He hadn't realized it, but Brody had disappeared during all the fuss.

"Come along," Jazzy said, pushing at her siblings and laughing all the while.

The only Cates woman who remained a little behind was Abby, her long brown hair contrasting with all the blond in the room. She sent Jackson a long, considered glance, then turned around without comment.

All right then.

As they all entered the dining area, Jackson saw the reason that Brody had disappeared.

"Happy early birthday!" said Laila's brother as he held a pink-frosted cake with a bunch of lit candles.

Everyone else yelled it out, right before launching into a lively version of the birthday song, clapping along. The Cates family had a crazy way of singing it, though, just as Laila had indicated, with some kind of harmonizing that came off as goofy and endearing.

When they were done, they hugged Laila, kissing her, making her laugh.

But as Jackson took his turn in embracing her—and he made sure it was merely a friendly hug—he saw something in her eyes that he doubted anyone else had caught in all the gaiety.

Sadness? The reflection of thirty plus one-to-grow-on candles burning in her gaze…the specter of a future that she wasn't so certain about.

As her family celebrated around her, Jackson also realized that none of them really understood what this birthday meant to Laila.

His heart cracked a bit at that, and he rested a hand on her shoulder, letting her know that he, of all people, got it.

But it didn't seem to be enough. Not to him, anyway.

Sending a smile to him, Laila turned toward the cake, closed her eyes, made a silent wish. What it was, he had no idea.

He wasn't even sure he wanted to know.

She blew out the candles with the help of her sisters, and they all applauded as her mom took the cake to the table.

"Let's dig in," Brody said, rubbing his hands together and grabbing a plate just before he began to load it with food. "The game's gonna start soon."

As the family buzzed around Laila, she kept looking at that cake with its guttered candles, and in that moment, Jackson vowed to make this as painless a birthday as possible for her.

Monday, after work, Laila went straight home.

Jackson had asked if it was okay for him to come by

before Dana and a few of her other friends arrived to pick her up for a low-key dinner that they had planned a while ago, long before Jackson had come to Thunder Canyon.

Funny how things changed, Laila thought as she locked up her car. Funny how, now, she only wanted to spend this night—the first one of her new decade—with *him,* even if they weren't a true "couple."

She could tell that, after yesterday, her family wasn't as sure as they had been that Laila had finally found a man to settle with. She and Jackson had persuaded them during the day that he was merely one of her casual suitors by being friendly yet a bit distant with each other.

Had he decided that she would want him to act that way?

Maybe it was for the best, though. Yes, her sisters—and even her dad—had tried their darnedest to juice information about Laila and Jackson's dating status out of them. But by the end of the first game, after she and Jackson had sat in separate chairs and kept their hands off each other, it was obvious that the brood had run out of questions for them, thinking that Laila was just being Laila and would lose interest in Jackson within a few weeks.

It was a relief, because that was what she and Jackson had been aiming for, right? And, even though Dad had eventually warmed up to Jackson during the day and her sisters, Brody and Mom had clearly liked him, Laila had kept reminding them about how he wasn't intending to live in Thunder Canyon, for the long term.

That was the part that had put the lid on any more speculation from Laila's sisters—the part that had re-emphasized that the relationship would go no further than a fling.

And that was the part that weighed on Laila every time she thought about it.

She got to her door, opened it, stepping inside to a semidark room, lit only by the hint of light from her kitchen.

"Jackson?"

Without a word, he walked into the family room and when she saw what he was holding, her chest constricted.

It was a lopsided cake with one burning candle on it.

The lone flicker lit the smile on his face. "Happy birthday, Laila."

She didn't trust herself to speak through the sudden, sharp tightness in her throat.

He set the cake on the end table by the sofa, near Lord Vader's bowl, then dug into his jeans pocket, producing a little wrapped box.

He seemed almost shy, the smile on his face uncertain, as if, maybe, he had overstepped the boundaries they had set with each other.

After handing that box to her, he said, "It's nothing big."

"You shouldn't have gotten me anything."

Still, she tore off the wrapping to find a black velvet box. Inside, there was a silver bracelet with intricate whirling designs. Tiny rubies were embedded within it.

She recognized the work from a custom boutique in Old Town, and their items weren't cheap.

"Jackson..."

"It was pretty. It'll look great on you."

He didn't say any more than that and, after she slipped on the bracelet, she glanced back at the cake. A bittersweet pain pierced her. So sweet, so *thoughtful*. He had gone to some effort, and that was what mattered the most.

"One candle," he said. "That's all I put on the cake because this is the start of something new for you. The first year of the rest of your life. We should all be able to start over every so often."

His words had a hopeful ring to them. It wasn't that he merely understood all the reasons that she had gotten quiet when she had seen all those candles on the cake yesterday—Jackson knew what it was like to want to start over, too.

She wished she didn't have to blow out the candle. Yesterday, when she had done it, it had been as if she had been extinguishing the birthday wish she had made—the fervent hope that he *would* stick around, and that she could be enough to make him want that.

"You made this for me?" she asked, the words catching in her throat.

"I tried." He chuckled. "Can't say my future lies in the direction of baking, though."

"It's…beautiful." She bit her lip, afraid that she might start to cry, because it *was* beautiful. More than she dared to let him know.

"I realize," he said, "that Dana and the girls are going to pick you up soon and you're probably going to be having more cake tonight, but I just wanted…"

She went to him, enveloping him in a grateful hug. He had known just what she needed on this birthday.

He wrapped his arms around her, too—so tight, so comfortably.

"I wish I could just stay here with you tonight," she said into his chest.

She thought she felt his arms tense, and she remembered the bad dream he'd had yesterday morning. She had been watching him sleep, and he had never known that she had seen the emotions crossing his face—the wary lines, then the panic.

A bad dream. She had been having them, too, with her literally strolling around Thunder Canyon, barefoot and pregnant.

But it had dawned on her that it wasn't such a nightmare.

He leaned down, his mouth against the top of her head. "Is that the wish you're going to make when you blow out the candle—that you want to stay here with me tonight?"

"No." She rested her cheek against his broad chest. "I won't be gone all that long, anyway, so why waste a wish?"

He pressed her to him, and they remained that way, until the candle started to burn lower, wax coming to roll down the side like little tears.

"Make your wish, Laila," he said.

When she did, it had nothing to do with staying with him tonight.

I wish I could find a way to ask him to stay forever, she thought, blowing out the candle.

Chapter Eleven

Should she ask Jackson to stay?

Or would it be better to ask him to go before everything got way more involved and so much worse?

There was only one person Laila could think to turn to after the night of her birthday: the one person who had comforted her after her first and only bad mark on a book report in grammar school. The one person who had stroked her hair and told her everything would be all right when she had been turned down by her first choice of college.

The next morning, before going into work, Laila sat across from Mom at the kitchen table in the Cates ranch house, her hands cupping a mug of hot jasmine tea. Dad was taking a ride around the spread, so he wouldn't be back for a while.

"Are you sure you're feeling all right?" Mom asked, stirring sugar into her own mug.

"Yes, I'm fine."

Mom had already commented on Laila's flushed cheeks and put her hand over her daughter's forehead, thinking that she was here because she was under the weather. Laila wanted to say she was only heartsick. And that she had never moaned and groaned to anyone about a man before as she was about to do.

How should she start?

Mom made it easy on her, blue eyes brimming with compassion. "Your being here today has nothing to do with having the flu or a cold. Am I right?"

Laila nodded, taking the first step. And, already, it felt a little better.

"I never thought this would happen to me," she said, her voice on the verge of breaking.

Mom scooted her wooden chair closer to Laila's, leaning over to catch her eye. "Oh, honey, none of us can control what happens to our hearts. If we could, we'd all be drones." She clasped Laila's hand. "When you allowed Jackson to come over on Sunday, I knew something big was up, even if you were fighting to hide it tooth and nail."

"I didn't do such a good job of hiding, did I?"

"Neither did he."

Her mom wouldn't tease her like this, and at the observation, her spirits lifted.

Mom squeezed Laila's hand. "Why don't you tell me about it?"

There was something about talking to your mom that you couldn't get from chatting with a best friend, Laila thought. Wisdom, experience, a ruthless sense of protection, and she held to Mom's hand for all those qualities.

"I have no idea when I started feeling this way about him," she said.

"Jackson?"

"Of course, Mom."

"Then just say his name. Come out with it."

"Jackson." There, she had finally put his name out there for all the world to hear, starting with her mother.

Laila risked a glance at her, finding Mom smiling, looking so young, as if she had been transported back years and years into her own memories.

"Even though you and Jackson were trying to seem casual with each other when he came over," she said, "there was no fooling anyone. I would see him slip you a look, and you slip him one right back. Your dad and I would do the same, way back when."

"You still do that now. Except…"

"Except what?"

Laila forged ahead, broaching the deep-seated reasons she was here.

"Except," she said, "when there were times I thought you wished life had gone a little differently."

Mom frowned.

"Surely you know what I mean," Laila said. "You've always told me to develop my life outside of men. 'Don't rely on anyone else to make you feel valued'—that's what you've always said to *all* of us. And I took that to heart because…"

Mom pushed back a strand of hair that had slipped down to block Laila's face. "Because why?"

All those times Laila had seen the longing on her mom's face while she looked at those college catalogues, all those veiled comments about traveling to places she had never gotten to visit came back to Laila.

"Sometimes I think that you got married before you were ready," she said.

"Oh, honey. Yes, I did get married in my flush of youth, but I think you've misinterpreted some of the lessons I've tried to teach you."

"Am I wrong in thinking that you regret not being able to pursue your studies? And that you never got to sow your wild oats and live all by yourself before raising a family?"

Mom's smile was patient. "I wouldn't trade my life with Zeke for anything. Same with you kids. Maybe I enjoy indulging in the whole 'road not taken' fantasy about what my life could've been, but if I had never married or had children when I did, I would be so incomplete, Laila." She gave her a lowered glance, emphasizing her next point. "I encouraged you to develop a career and an independent spirit because I saw in you, even from a very young age, that you had a real fire. I wanted you to think about all your options because you had so many, but I never meant to scare you off marriage. I feel terrible that I did."

"Don't, Mom."

As her mother sighed and then sipped her tea, Laila allowed everything to soak in. Her mom was right. Somewhere along the way—in high school? college?—she might have taken all Mom's advice too far. She had become comfortable with being single, with being in control of life by controlling the men in it. And whenever that control threatened to break, as with her quarterback or architect, she had called it off.

Then there was Jackson, who had thrown her for

more of a loop than any of them, and ceding some of the control that she had treasured made her feel as if she was allowing herself to become weak—to give up everything she had worked so hard to earn in life, like her job, her individuality.

"When you got married," Laila asked, "did you ever feel as if you were becoming… Well, something other than yourself?"

"You mean, did I feel as if Zeke was infringing on my personality and I would never have that part of myself back? Maybe. But I would've never become the person I am today—a person I love—if it wasn't for Zeke. I wouldn't give back who I am now for the world."

Laila drank some of her tea, realized it had gone a bit cold.

"There's more to it all than that, isn't there?" Mom asked.

"Yes." She put down her mug. "It's just that, for the longest time, I thought I could have it all—a career, a social life, freedom—while having men in my life. But with Jackson, I'm so afraid that I'll have to give up some of that."

"And you still want it all."

"Yes, Mom, I do."

But could she have it?

Mom said, "Truthfully, I'm not sure you can have it all—not at the same time. But I think you can find a balance as well as a lot of happiness in the effort."

Laila turned that over in her mind, but in her heart…

Her heart had already decided, and that was the reason she felt ripped apart between two warring factions. She had spent too much time being stridently single to give up everything she thought was at stake this easily.

Mom said, "Are you in love with Jackson?"

Even after all this, she was still too afraid to say it out loud.

Was she waiting until he said it first?

"Ah, well," Mom said, crossing one leg over the other as she got ready to sip from her mug again. "You don't have to tell me. A mother can always see into her child's heart."

"Like a crystal ball," Laila said, trying to smile.

"Just like that."

As Mom drank, Laila wondered if her mother was right—if she could see a future in which her daughter lived happily ever after with Jackson, with no regrets.

And no heartbreak from the Texas bad boy.

Even a couple of days later, Laila and Jackson were still doing their lying low routine, visiting each other's homes, spending the nights in each other's arms, going about their business as if nothing was threatening to break under the growing weight between them.

Laila would watch him when she believed he wasn't looking. Over dinner, on the sofa, she would silently will him to give her a sign that she could pour her soul out to him. There had been so many times when she had almost started up *the* conversation, but she had always chickened out.

Her need to tell him everything was pushing at her, though, and she didn't know how much longer she could last by staying silent.

There were even times when she told herself that maybe this was never meant to be, and she should just let it go. Getting over him would be easy once he was gone.

Today, she was with Dana during their lunch hour,

shopping in a crafts boutique in Old Town for spangles that her friend wanted to use on her "Liberty Belle" Halloween costume. Laila was just as distracted as she had been the past couple of days, if not more.

They were on the boardwalk, where other lunchtimers passed them.

"Earth to Laila," Dana said, bopping her with the craft store shopping bag.

Laila sent a vague smile to her friend. Then she realized that Dana wasn't going to let the subject go this time.

"Ever since your birthday," Dana said, "you've been off in the clouds."

"I'm here."

Her friend chuffed. "I see your body, but the inner Laila is AWOL."

Laila had spent so much time trying to sort this out herself that it was obvious she had gone into some kind of shell. It wasn't fair to any of her friends.

She glanced around, grabbed the sleeve of Dana's conservative bank jacket, then pulled her off the boardwalk. Others strolled by, watching, then moving on.

"I've been trying to do it," Laila said.

"Do...what?"

Her heart popped in her chest. "Tell Jackson that I'm ready."

No other explanation was required for Dana.

"You?" her friend asked, taking the Clark Kent glasses from their resting place on top of her head and putting them over her eyes, as if she couldn't see straight without them.

But Laila knew better. Those glasses were just for show in the bank.

"Yes, me," she said.

Dana enfolded Laila in a big hug, squeezing her hard. When she pulled back, she cuffed at a little wet streak that had leaked from her eye.

"Don't mind me," Dana said.

Laila held her hand. "I'm not going to leave you behind. And there isn't even a guarantee that Jackson—"

"Oh, of course he adores you." Dana fluttered a dramatic hand in front of her face. "It's obvious to everyone in town that the man would swim an ocean for you, but you're both such stubborn mules about admitting it." She sucked in a wobbly breath. "I'm so happy for you."

Laila hugged her again, and from the way Dana held to her, she knew this was about more than Laila deserting her. Dana and she had gone to their first school dance together, as fluttery as new butterflies as they had waited for a boy to cross the room and talk to them. She and Dana had kept scrapbooks of their dreams and hopes.

She *was* happy for Laila.

They separated, both laughing, recovering, drawing more attention from everyone around them, but Laila didn't care. She was a new woman after admitting this to Dana—she felt as if she could go tell Jackson right now.

But she kept thinking that even a little pause from him, a hint that he wasn't going to commit right back to her, would shatter her.

So when would be the perfect time to let him know?

Dana linked arms with Laila as they stepped back onto the boardwalk. The day had a slight chill to it, and each of them pulled her jacket and coat tighter around them.

"Promise me," Dana said, "that you're not going to go all Bridezilla now."

"I promise." And she meant it. After all, Mom said there could be a balance, and Laila was going to find it.

As they strolled in the direction of a town square lunch cart to pick up something to take back to the bank, they passed the brick building where Traub Oil had its offices. Feeling a magnetic draw to it, Laila slowed her steps.

Dana pinched her. "There's still time on lunch break to say hi to your boyfriend. Maybe even to tell him—"

Anxiety shook up Laila.

"Go!" Dana gave her a tiny push and then was on her way.

But Laila just stood there for a moment longer. Would Jackson see it on her face—that she had decided once and for all that he was the one for her?

A niggle haunted her. What if he had already seen it before and he had chosen not to do a damn thing about it?

She heard footsteps on the gravel behind her, and she turned to discover a mustached ranch hand in a low-riding cowboy hat, a thick flannel coat, a big silver belt buckle.

Duncan Brooks.

She sent him a polite smile as he awkwardly greeted her with a nod, his hands in his jeans pockets.

"Laila," he said.

He barely made eye contact with her, and she felt sorry for him in a way. He was a bit of a loner, and whenever she had talked with him before, it had been a stilted experience.

"Hello, Duncan," she said, spying his red-and-white pickup parked near the boardwalk. There were feedbags in the back of it, and she surmised that he must have made a store run here in town.

He didn't go anywhere, as if he was trying to figure out how to talk to her. Laila didn't want to be rude, so she waited him out.

Finally, he adjusted his hat, glancing up at the Traub Oil building.

"I don't want to presume, but I was just wonderin'... About that Halloween party your parents put on every year... You'll be attending that tomorrow night, won't you?"

She held up her bag from the crafts store. "I'm putting the finishing touches on my costume when I get home." She had been keeping her Snow Queen outfit a secret from Jackson, and he had, in return, teased her about the costume *he* was putting together. She doubted he would come as anything other than what he was.

A halo of warmth surrounded her heart.

And it all felt nice and wonderful until Duncan cleared his throat, then said, "I was only wondering... If you would... If you needed..."

Was he trying to ask her to the party?

"Duncan," she said gently, "I'm going with Jackson Traub. But we'll see you there, right?"

"Sure." He had gone tense, reminding her of Cade Pritchett after she had rejected him, too. She wished these situations didn't have to come up.

He started to tip his hat to her but hesitated.

Laila waited for him once more, hoping that he wasn't going to ask her out for a different time.

What he actually said startled her.

"Excuse my bluntness, Laila, but I can't believe you're with Jackson Traub. He doesn't respect you as you should be respected."

She shook her head, ready to argue. Duncan didn't know the real Jackson.

"He's going to use you and throw you away," Duncan said. "Mark my words."

"Why would you say that to me?"

Duncan shuffled in his boots, but when he spoke again, it was with some conviction. "He ain't keeping it a secret. I heard him not so long ago in the Rock Creek Diner, crowing to his cousin about how he only went after you because you're a pretty face. And when he goes away, he's going to do it without another thought."

Her legs felt brittle.

Just a pretty face...

Jackson couldn't have said that, much less in public, where someone like Duncan Brooks could overhear. Jackson knew how much it would wound her, because she had spilled out her soul to him about what it felt like to have people underestimate her. He had even told her to go out there and kick butt.

He had cared. He had changed from that bad boy who probably *would* have run around town being so callous.

Hadn't he?

Duncan saw her doubt, and he took off his hat and held it over his heart. "I'm so sorry, Laila. I just thought it was fair to let you know."

He gave her one last sympathetic glance before putting his hat back on and walking away toward his pickup.

Numb, Laila didn't move. The man who had charmed

her, snuck his way into her heart, where no one had ever been before…

According to Duncan, that man had said *that* about her.

She still couldn't believe it, because if he *had* said it, it would mean that, all this time, he had only taken what he wanted from her, setting her up for the big fall when, after he left, he wouldn't have to stick around to pick up the pieces. He had been every bad thing anyone had ever said about him.

Worse yet, had Jackson really *ever* seen anything in her but her looks?

As the numbness went from her chest all through her body, she had to wonder if she would ever be more to anyone than a Barbie doll.

A trophy that a bad boy would grab and leave behind when the shininess wore off.

Chest tight, hardly able to breathe, she looked at the brick Traub Oil building, but the stinging blur of her gaze made it hard to see much more than a big, slashed red heart.

Jackson had been standing by his tinted office window for about ten minutes now as he talked on the speakerphone with his twin, Jason, who had called him just to catch up.

But it was hard to concentrate on a phone call when he could see Laila down below, near the oak-laced town square. She and Dana were down there, and he wondered if Laila was going to come into the building.

In anticipation, his pulse twirled, imitating the swirly candle he had put on her birthday cake the other night.

Just remembering how it had felt to see her so happy

at a simple gesture—one he had made so easily—swept him away again.

If one smile from her could make his night, what could she do to the rest of his life?

God help him, but he wanted to know. He just had to find the right time to put his heart out there, to take the risk of telling her.

But would she decide that they had no future and turn him down, just as she had done to her former boyfriends who had come close, only to leave with their hearts on the floor?

Jackson almost forgot he was on the phone with Jason.

"Hey," said his brother from over the line. "Where did you go?"

Jackson turned away from the window. "I'm here."

Even though he couldn't see Laila any more, it was as if he still had her in his sights, vivid, everpresent.

"So what about Thanksgiving?" Jason asked. "Mom wants to know if you can make it down."

"I…" What was Laila doing for Thanksgiving?

His office door opened, and Ethan and Corey entered, both taking quiet seats in the leather chairs under the lasso clock on the wall.

"Damn, Jackson," Jason said. "Maybe I'll just call back."

Ethan spoke up. "He's only in La-La Land, Jace. Give him a break."

"His brain is mush," Corey said, "because he's got a real live *girlfriend*."

He drew that last word out, and Jackson leaned over to his desk, grabbed a piece of paper, wadded it up and then threw it at both his brothers. It hit Corey in the head and ricocheted over to Ethan, winging his shoulder.

Both brothers thought that was hilarious, and Jackson went for another piece of paper.

"What the hell is going on there?" Jason asked. "Are you running a madhouse?"

"Pretty much," Ethan said, ducking Jackson's follow-up.

"Next time," Jackson said to Ethan and Corey, "it'll be the pencil holder coming at you."

They pretended to be scared, then laughed, stretching out their legs, getting cozy.

Unable to help himself, Jackson wandered back to the window, just to catch a glimpse of Laila again.

When he saw she was now talking to that cowpoke, Duncan Brooks, he remained at the window, yet another unfamiliar emotion claiming him.

Jealousy.

Jason said, "Jackson, when you decide about Thanksgiving, give Mom a call. She's waiting, and you know she doesn't like to be kept on a hook."

"I'll do that."

His twin hung up, but Ethan and Corey didn't make a move to leave. Jackson wasn't even paying much attention to them because his full focus was on Laila, who had gone from a polite posture with Duncan Brooks to tilting her head, leaning forward a little, as if she was trying to understand something he was telling her. His hat was even over his heart.

What the hell?

Corey said, "Why don't you bring Laila to Thanksgiving, Jackson? Mom and Pete would love to meet her."

"I think it's time," Ethan said.

Yeah, Jackson thought. Time for him to walk downstairs and see what was going on.

He went for the door, still seeing Duncan with his cowboy hat in that heart-covering position, as if he was calling on Laila for a dance or something.

After going down the stairs, he came to the lobby, just as Laila entered the doors.

He didn't ask what she had been talking about with Duncan Brooks. Hell, no—she had a fire in her eyes that told Jackson something bad had happened out there.

"Tell me it's not true," she said, her voice sounding as if it had been shredded.

And…the hurt. It was all over her for some reason— from her tortured expression to her fisted hands.

"Laila?" he asked.

She headed for the side of the lobby as people looked after her. Jackson ignored them and followed her, straight to the women's restroom, where the door had just been shut.

Knocking, he repeated, "Laila?"

Without waiting for an answer, he eased open the door, hoping no one else besides Laila was in there.

And it was empty, but for her. She had her hands braced on the counter, her head down, leaving a long strand of hair that had escaped from her barrette covering her face.

"Did I do something?" he asked, shutting the door behind him.

When she glanced up at him, her gaze was reddened, as if she was about to cry.

"What did Duncan Brooks say to you?" Jackson asked, ready to go after him.

"He…"

When Jackson went over to her, she backed away toward the wall.

The breath bolted out of Jackson. He recovered just enough to say, "I don't understand…"

She merely shook her head, and it seemed as if she had to gather everything she had within her just so she could speak.

"Once, I asked you if you had set your cap for the local beauty queen when you came here."

The suspicion about what Duncan Brooks had told Laila crept over Jackson with the slow surety of coming devastation.

"I asked you," she continued, "if the only reason you invited me out was because you wanted to add me to your collection. You said no." Her expression crumbled. "Now that I think about it, you didn't even deny it. You went on to tell me that, when you first saw me, you noticed a spark, and that's why you wanted to get to know me."

"I did," he said, knowing now that it had been so much more than just a spark.

She shook her head, her eyes even mistier now. "Duncan Brooks heard you say something that puts you in a whole other category than who I thought you were."

His world started to wobble. Why hadn't he just told her earlier that he hadn't meant to say what he had said? That, at the time, he had wanted to take it back, even though he had desperately been trying to persuade himself that he wasn't falling for her?

"I should've told you all about that conversation I had with DJ in the diner," he said.

She went back to the counter, leaning against it as

if her faith in him had been the only thing holding her up until now.

He continued, hoping that he could redeem himself. "It was wrong of me, Laila. And I didn't mean a word of it. If I could take it back, I surely would, but—"

"Do you know how it makes me feel to know that you're just like the rest of them?" she whispered.

Like the rest of them—adoring her for her beauty, never bothering to look any deeper.

It was like a bladed thrust to everything he had started to believe about himself since he had met her. But she didn't give him the opportunity to tell her that he had changed, and it was because of her.

His love for her.

She wiped at her eyes, struggling like hell to overcome more tears, and her fight to do so ripped at him.

"You really are a playboy," she said. "I just bought into your act."

Now he was the one who needed the crutch of the counter, although he kept himself from reaching out for it.

Laila, the only one who had seemed to look past *his* reputation. He had pushed her too far.

"Laila," he said, "the only reason I said what I said to DJ is that I didn't know what else to do. I…"

The words—the big *I've-fallen-for-you* ones—almost escaped from his mouth, but then instinct took over, years and years of self-preservation.

Besides, she wasn't going to believe that he had changed. He had already done enough damage to her that she would remember this moment—this heart-killing crash—every time she saw him from now on.

As she rushed out of the room, the door slammed

behind her, just as she had shut the door on him before, on their first date when he had teased her to the point of frustration.

It seemed like a lifetime ago.

He turned, looked in the mirror at Jackson Traub, seeing the pain in his eyes.

Seeing a crushed man who was missing something vital without Laila.

Chapter Twelve

That night, Jackson sat at the dining table in his condo, a beer in hand, trying to drown his sorrows.

But he had no taste for it any more.

None of it.

He had left the office early, intent on going out, chasing a good time and forgetting about Laila altogether…

Unfortunately, even *that* had left a taste as bad as this beer.

Now, with every swallow, he realized that he didn't want to forget the feel of her silky blond hair tangled through his fingers, her smooth skin under his hands, her soft mouth—the softest and most desirable in the world—murmuring sweet nothings under his kisses…

Jackson thumped the bottle onto the table. This wasn't working at all. Hell, he hadn't even gotten through one beer yet and he already felt hung over.

How could he cure himself, though?

Not for the first time, he was tempted to grab his phone, call her, apologize. But he knew it wouldn't be enough. And he knew that if he showed up at her doorstep full of more excuses, it wouldn't do any good, either.

He tugged a hand through his hair just as a knock sounded on his door. When he didn't answer, his phone rang.

Checking the ID screen, he saw DJ's name.

Crap.

Instead of answering his cell, Jackson went to the door and pulled it open. DJ was on the other side, closing his own phone, making Jackson's generic ringtone come to a halt.

His cousin took one look at Jackson and said, "They told me you were a disaster when you left. They were being kind."

When Jackson had last seen his brothers, it had been post-Laila, after he had numbly climbed the stairs and gone to his office, sat in his chair for a while just staring straight ahead of him, then left. Corey and Ethan had tried to talk to him, asking him what had happened, but Jackson hadn't responded.

He hadn't had the heart.

Without being invited in, DJ brushed past Jackson, shedding his coat and hanging it on the rack.

"What're you doing?" Jackson asked.

DJ went to the living area and took a seat on a stuffed leather couch. "Babysitting you. Your brothers seem to think that you're going to get into some trouble tonight."

"Why aren't they here to stop me?"

Raising an eyebrow, DJ said, "Let's think back to a few months ago… Corey's wedding…? Fists flying, Traub brothers brawling, you leading the way…?"

Jackson just wiped a hand over his face, then sat on the opposite end of the couch from DJ. "And that's why they sent you—because you're the most diplomatic of the family."

"They know that something's really wrong, Jackson, and they're ready to swing over here at a moment's notice if you need them."

In spite of that assurance, Jackson felt more isolated than ever. He loved his brothers, but they weren't Laila.

He had allowed her glimpses that no one else had gotten—or he feared would *ever* get.

"Word is," DJ said, his brown eyes full of sympathy, "Laila ran crying out of the Traub Oil building just before you came upstairs. Why?"

No hiding it anymore.

But Jackson didn't even *want* to hide it. He just wanted her here again.

He broke down, telling DJ just about everything: the flirtation that he thought wouldn't ever get so serious, the part where they had *gotten* more serious, the seriousness of what he was feeling now.

"What I told you at the Rock Creek Diner… When I said that I had wooed Laila just because she was beautiful…?" Jackson shook his head. "I was wrong. Even then, I was attracted to her for a whole other reason, but I didn't have an inkling of what it was."

"Now you know it was love."

See—even DJ knew it.

Jackson leaned his forearms on his thighs. "Now I

don't even want to drive a mile out of Thunder Canyon because it'd be too far from her. I couldn't admit that back then or today, though. And when Laila confronted me with what I said, I should've…"

Revealed his heart to her.

Should've, could've, would've…

"Jeez, Jackson," DJ said. "It's obvious that you're a mess, and if you don't go to her and tell her everything, you're never going to forgive yourself. Believe me."

"Is that what you did with Allaire?"

DJ's face took on a glow, one that Jackson had also felt when he had been watching Laila from his office window today, moments before she had come into the building and dismantled his life.

"My wife," DJ said, "was the one who didn't know what she wanted. I always did, even when we were younger. Allaire just needed a big gesture from me—needed to see that I was never going to give up, no matter how tough the going got."

And, suddenly, every bleary thing around Jackson got a little clearer.

"If Laila's what you really want," DJ said, "then humbling yourself is a strong first step, Jackson. You've got to show her that this obstacle is nothing compared to how you feel about her. That is, if you're ready."

Jackson remembered that man in the mirror—the distraught "disaster" who had lost his heart when Laila had run out of the restroom.

And it was just a matter of getting up off this couch and getting his tail in gear to show Laila that he *had* become a better man because of her.

"I'm ready," Jackson said.

As DJ stood by, the first thing Jackson did was

suck up his courage, calling Mrs. Cates to explain, apologize…

…and hopefully to plan.

The next evening at the Cates ranch house, Zeke and Evelyn's annual Halloween bash was in full swing.

Every costume from that of a joker to a witch to a ghost was represented by the guests. The house was decorated with Halloween streamers and doodads: Crones on broomsticks hanging from the ceiling, huge sparkling spiderwebs in corners, paper skeletons dangling on the walls. The aromas of pumpkin cake and caramel-dipped apples filled the air while howling, haunted house sounds added to the festive atmosphere.

Laila was standing near her mom's upright piano, which was shrouded with cobwebs, in the family room with Dana. Her friend, outfitted as a red-white-and-blue-spangled Statue of Liberty, had decorated herself with a couple of flourishes to make her the belle of the ball: her hair was streaked with patriotic colors, her toga swirling with firecracker designs, her Victorian ankle boots decorated with ribbons.

Even though Laila had thought about not coming to the party altogether, much less wearing the long ethereal white dress with snowflake sparkles that made up much of her Snow Queen costume, Dana had dragged her out of the apartment. Laila had gone along with it only because she knew that her family would never let her live it down if she begged out of the party. Mom, in particular, had put the hard sell on Laila to attend last night. Even when Laila had countered that things weren't going so well with Jackson and she would rather stay home, her mom had told her that what she truly needed was to be here.

"Trust me," Mom had said.

So here Laila was, and the more she saw people having fun around her, the more she asked herself why she was allowing a relationship that was only supposed to be brief in the first place to get her down.

She would be darned if she let anyone see how much agony she was experiencing because of Jackson.

"Another glass of punch?" Dana asked, keeping her eye on some single men from town who had been invited by Laila's parents. They were trading jokes with Matt and Marlon, Laila's cousins, plus their fiancées, Haley Anderson and Elise Clifton.

"I'm punched out," Laila said.

She sure *felt* that way, too, as if she had been blindsided after a slam to the stomach. Last night, she had left work early and ghostwalked through the rest of the day. It had only been when she had lain down in her empty bed that she had figuratively hit the floor, knocked out.

Obviously, Jackson hadn't cared enough to call her after their fight. Maybe she had shamed him into believing that she thought he was dirt.

What man would come around after that?

But, damn her, with every beat of her heart, that was all she wanted him to do—reach out and explain.

Unless…

She tried not to think about it, but the mental specter was always there…

Unless he truly *had* been using her for a disposable good time. Unless she genuinely was just a crown that he could claim and brag about.

But, if that was the case, what about the way he had

kissed her? What about the way he had looked at her as he had held her in his arms?

Heart heavy, Laila toyed with a spiderweb on the piano until Dana cleared her throat.

"Just hang in there," her friend said way more optimistically than Laila could understand. "You'll be okay. Trust me."

Her mom had said the same thing.

Laila nodded, and Dana gave her a one-armed hug. A diamondlike snowflake sparkle floated out of Laila's unbound hair, where she had pinned a bunch of them.

Laila watched the glittering flake drift to the ground then sit on the carpet, as lifeless as she felt. And just as useless.

Someone was laughing nearby, and when Laila glanced up, she saw that Jazzy had brought Annabel and Jordyn over to Marlon and Matt, plus the pack of construction workers who had wandered over with water guns and green face paint slashed over their cheekbones. Army men, on the go. Nearby, Abby hung out with Brody, every once in a while casting a compassionate glance Laila's way.

Dammit, she felt like the poor loser among the bunch.

She smiled at Abby, showing that she could be just as good without Jackson.

Abby toasted her with her punch glass.

"Well," Dana said, glancing at her bicentennial watch as if she was expecting someone, though Laila couldn't imagine who. "I've got to powder my nose. You?"

Laila told herself that the pain in her chest would go away in a minute. "No, I'm fine."

"It's okay for girls to trek to the restroom together, you know. It's not a party foul."

"Really, you don't have to handle me with kid gloves." Now she felt like she was baggage.

Would she ever feel normal again?

She doubted it, because it seemed as if her ribs had been pried open and her heart excised. A macabre Halloween prank come early.

Maybe she should've dressed up as an unfeeling ghoul.

Dana touched Laila's arm, said she would be right back, then made her way through the crowd toward the hallway.

Laila was just about to force herself to join most of her sisters—who were dressed alike as Greek muses—when someone new walked into the room.

It was Dean Pritchett, and he was with his brother Nick, neither of whom had dressed up as more than Western outlaws with fake guns and holsters by their sides.

Was it Laila's imagination, or did Abby perk up a little on her side of the room?

Just as Laila thought she might have, her little sister seemed to lose interest in the Pritchett brothers.

Something told Laila that it was because Cade wasn't with them, but she shushed that thought away. Abby had explained about her friendship with Cade, and it was ridiculous to doubt her.

Dean spotted Laila and came over while Nick joined her other sisters, hugging Jazzy, Jordyn then Annabel hello.

Greeting Laila with a friendly embrace, Dean started up some small talk before he broke the *real* ice and said, "Cade is working overtime on a project, so he won't be around for a while tonight."

She knew how Cade got with his woodworking, but she also wondered if he had stayed away from the party because he thought she would be here with Jackson.

What a tangled web.

Dean spotted her parents and waved them over to say hi. Dad was dressed as Buffalo Bill Cody, fake beard and all, and Mom was Annie Oakley. And if all of them were attempting to entertain Laila and put Jackson out of her mind by being extra lively and talkative, it almost worked.

Almost, because in her chest, she could still feel that injury he had left—the soreness around her heart.

Why *couldn't* she give him one more chance to tell her who he might be now instead of who he had been a few weeks ago? Didn't she owe herself at least that? Some closure?

All Laila could hear were moaning creaks and cackles from the haunted house sound track.

She must have looked pretty pathetic standing there alone in the crowd, because Mike Trudeau even came over to talk to her. He was dressed as a huntsman and actually hadn't even been around the bank all week, due to another trip to the woods.

"Evening, Laila," her boss said.

"Hi, Mike."

He tapped his fingers against his punch glass, apparently trying to whip up the courage to say something to her.

He finally found it. "Being out of town this week, I'm afraid I didn't get around to apologizing for something that requires it. Maybe Jackson already told you, but..."

Jackson...

"I'm not sure what you're talking about," Laila said, although she suspected this had something to do with the chat Mike and Jackson had been having at the town hall, when it seemed as if Jackson wasn't too happy with her boss.

"He *didn't* tell you?" he said.

"No..."

Her words disappeared. She hadn't asked Jackson what he had been talking about with Mike Trudeau. Hadn't wanted to know because it went against all the "fling" and "temporary" markers that they had forced on themselves.

Her boss pursed his lips, then came out with it. "I haven't been entirely fair to you in work matters, Laila, and Jackson pointed that out to me. He about tore my head off, as a matter of fact." He nodded. "You deserve to have someone like him around, taking up your back as he does. Frankly, I'm surprised that he didn't crow to you about how he came to your rescue."

...taking up your back like he does...

Her boss motioned toward the entryway. "It's just that I thought I should get in my apologies to you before he came inside the house to make sure that I—"

She had already put her punch glass down on the piano, going toward the door.

"Laila?" called Dana from somewhere inside the party.

She smacked into a wall of man, gasped, looking up into the one face she had been aching to see.

An implosion rocked her. He hadn't dressed in costume—he was who he was in a long-sleeved Western shirt, jeans and boots. His hair was tousled from having taken off his hat, and, in one hand, he was holding a bunch of long-stemmed red roses.

They locked gazes for a moment that was battered by the anguish of yesterday. But there was something else in it, too.

As Laila stood away from him, her hand to her chest, her heart raced, as if it wanted to take off.

Or push her back into his arms.

"Evelyn," said Jackson. Her mom had come up behind them. "Thank you for extending the invitation."

Invitation?

As Mom stood beside Jackson, she gave Laila an innocent look, then grabbed onto Dad's hand as he arrived, too. He seemed on guard, although Laila knew he had taken a gruff shine to Jackson by the end of Football Day. It was clear, though, that Mom had explained to him what was going on right now, and he was behind whatever plans she had concocted.

Had Jackson gotten together with Mom to broker a truce and now everyone was in on this?

Laila thought of how Dana had made sure she had gotten here, no excuses tolerated, and how her siblings had welcomed her with overly open arms.

Her brother, sisters and Dana formed a circle around Jackson and Laila, as if waiting for something big to happen.

He said, "Don't be angry with your Mom, Laila. I told her what happened, and when she heard me out, she asked me to come over. I'm glad the whole family is here, too, because I have something real important to say, and it starts with a heartfelt apology about everything I've done in the past."

The Halloween special effect noises kept on, a whistling wind that added to the tension. Besides that, Laila heard someone mutter in the background.

"Here he goes, making another scene."

Jackson heard it, and he obviously knew what the peanut gallery was referring to.

"This isn't my brother Corey's wedding," he said in a level voice. "I haven't had any champagne tonight, and I'm not going to be making any speeches about how marriage stinks and how the entire state of matrimony is a big mistake. That's not why I'm here."

Someone else coughed, as if they doubted Jackson. Maybe they had been at the wedding and they couldn't imagine that there was any difference in him between then and now.

But he *had* grown up, becoming a man Laila could not only desire, but love. That was why yesterday had hurt so much, because of the suspicion that she had been wrong.

Yet, now, he waited before her, braving her family and friends, not knowing how she would react to him, standing tall with all those apology roses in hand.

A burn crept up her throat, her eyes stinging as Jackson stepped forward, handing her the flowers. Every petal seemed to tell her how much she was worth to him. If she couldn't read it in the bouquet, she sure could do it from the look in his eyes.

He was making a big gesture but, truly, all she had needed was him.

Jackson's pulse was racing a mile a minute as he stood there holding those roses. He felt every eye in the room on him, especially those of Laila's family.

Do her wrong again, they seemed to be saying, *and there'll be a high cost.*

But he was here to do right.

This time when he proposed, it was for real—not some joke at a beauty pageant.

"Laila, it wasn't so long ago that I didn't deserve to tread in the footsteps you made. But somewhere along the line, you brought a light to my head. And to my heart. You showed me decency, patience…even sweetness." He could barely breathe. "I can't see a future without you, and I ask with humility, hope and—Lord believe it—seriousness for you to spend the rest of your days with me."

The Halloween noises over the stereo abruptly stopped as a kind soul turned off the sound track. That left the high volume of Jackson's heartbeat in his ears as Laila broke into tears.

The flowers seemed to wilt in his arms.

Crying?

Was that how a woman said yes?

But then, just as he was at his lowest, she rushed to him, and he dropped the roses so he could pull her against him full force.

"I do," she whispered into his ear. "I will. *We* will. My boss just told me what you said to defend me at the town hall. I wanted so badly to believe in you, though, even before he—"

"It's okay, Laila. Just so you say yes tonight."

The entire room broke into cheers and applause, but they were only wisps of noise while Jackson cupped Laila's head with one hand, her back with the other, holding on for dear life.

Then she raised her tear-stained face to him, and he

realized that he still had so much to tell her, so much to straighten out.

But when she kissed him, he knew that everything would work. No doubts in his head, heart, soul.

They escaped out the door, but not before she grabbed their coats from the entry. She pulled him out front, where dusk was just lying down for the night and the lights from the ranch house windows breathed softly, like warm relief.

When she put on her coat, her flowing white dress whisked out from her hem. The last of the sunlight caught the diamond snowflake glitters in her long hair.

A queen, he thought. His queen for the rest of his life.

Then he remembered.

"Dammit," he said, stopping their progress. "I clean forgot."

As she faced him, he reached into his jeans pocket, coming out with a diamond ring that matched her sparkle. He had bought it today, mulling over the jewelry counter in Bozeman with care and consideration. With the hope that she wouldn't turn him down.

When she saw it, she sucked in a breath.

"I bought it," he said, "after giving a lot of thought to how I was going to go about winning you back. And I've been doing a lot of that during our relationship, haven't I? Always trying to woo, to win."

"That's because I demand effort," she said, nestling close to him, stroking his cheek with her fingertips. "Maybe too much at times."

"You were doing what I needed you to do, Laila. And, yesterday, when you came to me, all teared up…"

"No more apologies."

But he wanted there to be no trace of doubt, and he framed her face with his hands, looking down into those soul-deep blue eyes.

"I take a while to learn. And, for most of my life, I've been real comfortable not learning, just staying in a rut, marching to the same love-'em-and-leave-'em tune. I thought that I truly believed that a one-woman existence wasn't for me. I'd seen what love did to my mom after Dad's death, and *I* knew what it felt like to lose him, too. I never wanted to feel that way again."

"I know, Jackson."

He peered down at her. "You had me figured out long before I even did?"

"There was a lot to untangle, but I saw through you pretty early on, just as you did with me."

They were the only two people who could do that for each other, Jackson thought. Maybe that talent was a big part of love, and since he had never found it before, he'd had no idea when it had hit him so swiftly and thoroughly.

She laughed through her tears, and he dried them with the pad of his thumb, not liking to see her cry, wanting to do anything he could to stop it from this day forward.

"It was such a stupid fight," she said. "Wasn't it?"

"I was the cause of it. It was bound to come, anyway, with all we weren't saying to each other. I'm just glad we're on the same page now."

"The page that says we've also figured out our future plans?"

She was asking if he wanted to go back to Texas, abandoning Thunder Canyon.

But this town had caught his fancy, too, and he knew that staying here was important to Laila.

"Thunder Canyon is my home now," he said, "just as much as you are."

He took her hand in his, looking at her as if she were the diamond-studded heavens all wrapped into one woman.

Slipping the ring over her finger, he said, "My wife-to-be."

She looked at the ring for the longest time, and he realized that she was crying again.

But when they connected gazes, he saw that they were good tears, and that made him happier than he ever thought he could be.

"My husband," she said, and he liked the sound of that.

Liked it way more than a former scoundrel like Jackson Traub would have ever thought.

Lost and found in each other, they kissed under the setting sun, the two least likely people to ever find love finally discovering it with each other.

* * * * *